ZODIAC ACADEMY

LIVE AND LET LIONEL

CAROLINE
PECKHAM SUSANNE
VALENTI

BOOKS BY CAROLINE PECKHAM & SUSANNE VALENTI

Solaria

Ruthless Boys of the Zodiac
Dark Fae
Savage Fae
Vicious Fae
Broken Fae
Warrior Fae

Zodiac Academy
Origins (Novella)
The Awakening
Ruthless Fae
The Reckoning
Shadow Princess
Cursed Fates
The Big A.S.S. Party (Novella)
Fated Throne
Heartless Sky
Sorrow and Starlight
Beyond The Veil (Novella)
Restless Stars
Live and Let Lionel (Novella)

The Awakening: As Told by The Boys (Alternate POV)

Darkmore Penitentiary
Caged Wolf
Alpha Wolf
Feral Wolf

Caroline Peckham & Susanne Valenti

Interior Formatting & Design by Wild Elegance Formatting
Map Design by Fred Kroner
Artwork by Stella Colorado

ISBN: 978-1-916926-22-6

Live and Let Lionel/Caroline Peckham & Susanne Valenti – 1st ed.

I dedicate this book to none other than me, King Lionel Acrux.
For I am great beyond measure, handsome and humble, valiant and a visionary.
I have been tested by the stars; my enduring spirit celebrated by them through the crown laid upon my brow.
This is a glimpse into my story and that of the enemies who tried to thwart me. It is the first snippet of the ten-thousand-page memoir that I shall release upon the culmination of my victory in the war.

All hail your noble Dragon King.

King Lionel the First

WELCOME TO SOLARIA

Here is your campus map.

Note to all students: Vampire bites, loss of limbs or getting lost in The Wailing Wood will not count as a valid excuse for being late to class.

Asteroid Place
Terra House
Jupiter Hall
The Orb
Mars Laboratory
King's Hollow
The Howling Meadow
The Wailing Wood
Earth Observatory
Venus Library
Mercury Chambers
Aer House
Aer Cove
Fire Arena

LIONEL

FOREWORD BY LIONEL ACRUX

Herein lies a collection of tales which allude to the rise of my greatest enemies – those who seek to claim my rightful place and thwart me in my ascension. It is with utmost contempt that I present such works to you, the words which follow little more than a list of blights upon my life which have mounted up against me one by one.

Of course, you may be wondering why I warn you of this, or indeed why I have allowed such records of the tattered lives of my adversaries to remain legible at all, but I assume that if you are reading the following pages, then you will do so with the eye of one who sees the truth behind the words. There is desperation here, a jealousy so poisonous that indeed it has led to a threat against the greatest Dragon ever born. But worry not, for I am the Dragon King and my might is far greater than that of any whose tales lay awaiting you beyond this missive.

And so I trust in you, dear subject, to read the truth of this collection of emotional garbage and see the Fae depicted within it for what they are – devious, jealous and utterly inferior.

No doubt once you have devoured their words and excreted them like the sewage they are, you will see as clearly as I do that there is only one Fae worthy of your devotion in the coming war and align yourself to the army of the Dragon King. It is still not too late to proclaim your devotion to me before the stars and go down in history as one of those enlightened souls who truly saw the world for what it was and knew a worthy monarch when you were presented with one.

Forever your humble and gracious king,
Lionel Acrux the First.

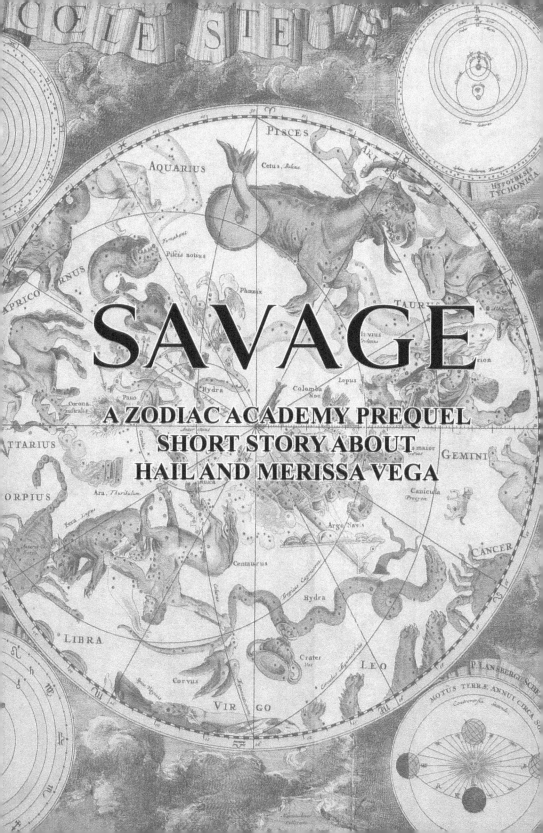

SAVAGE

**A ZODIAC ACADEMY PREQUEL
SHORT STORY ABOUT
HAIL AND MERISSA VEGA**

LIONEL

FROM THE LAIR OF LIONEL...

This first tale speaks of the woeful conception of the blight known formally as Gabriel Nox – son of the whore queen Merissa Vega who concealed his parentage, and in so doing, allowed his escape from my clutches as a boy. A mistake I have vowed not to make again. *(Please note that the escape of Gabriel Nox alongside Lance Orion and Gwendalina Vega from the custody of Lionel Acrux and his queen Lavinia Umbra while they maintained residence at the Palace of Souls is to be struck from historical records upon the victory King Lionel expects to claim in the ongoing war).*

Secondly, the following transcript tells of the unlikely and often cursed meeting which took place between Hail Vega (informally known as the Savage King) and his eventual wife Merissa Adhara. It is a sad reality that in hindsight I can now see that I never should have allowed the then king to travel to Voldrakia. At the time, of course, I had used his absence to tighten my foothold within Solaria, coiling more puppets under my control with the use of Dark Coercion like the cunningly brilliant creature I am known to be, but even I could never have foreseen the outcome of his voyage abroad.

No Seer then living was able to predict the changes which would occur when he brought his foreign bride home, merging his bloodline like he had no qualms whatsoever about producing Heirs of questionable value and Order.

So, it is with regret that I look back upon this time in my rise to power, yet as you will no doubt see, their union was nothing so very special, merely a chance meeting and a spell of bad luck for me. As the history books shall tell, I overcame the problems served by their union and rid myself of both of them before long anyway, so this slight blip in my plans was nothing more than an inconvenience in the end.

I only wish I had disposed of them before they managed to breed...

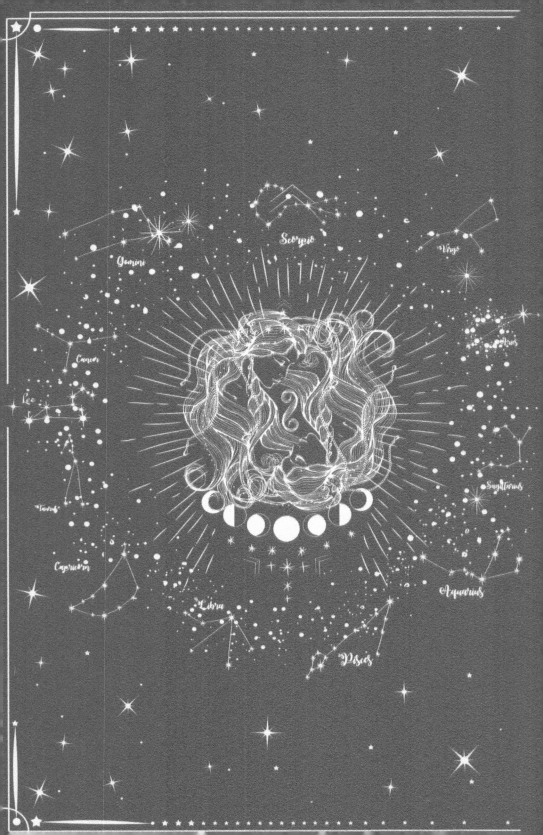

MERISSA

CHAPTER ONE

The clock ticks ever on. Light shifting into dark. Each beginning leading to an end. And try as we might, none can escape the last breath eternally. All must face that final call. The question is; what mark will you have left in your wake, princess of the burning empire?

The clash of distant blades rang out close to me, smoke catching in my throat as a sharp inhale forced me from sleep and my fingers curled tightly around the shaft of the spear at my side.

Eight days. I had been out here in this jungle for eight days now with nothing but my wits and training to keep me alive as I took part in the Marriage Trial, our empire's great and most esteemed tradition. If I could survive two weeks in this sweltering jungle hell with nothing but my own cunning and skills to sustain me, then I would be rewarded with the Awakening of my magic. Until then, I was little more than a mortal clutching a rudimentary weapon in the dark. A mortal with the gift of The Sight and a lifetime of preparing for this trial, but there were creatures living between these trees born of nightmares beyond the imaginings of any sane Fae.

The leather armour I wore was stifling in the heat of the jungle and a bead of sweat slicked down the hollow between my breasts, though that discomfort wasn't a good enough reason for me to move. The thick brown material covered me from neck to upper thighs, buckled and fastened in such a way to allow free movement while providing me with protection against attacks I may not see coming. It wouldn't stop a spear or sword at close range, but a thrown dagger or arrowhead would be a whole lot less lethal with the protection it offered, and I wasn't fool enough to risk removing it even for some relief from the heat.

I was on my feet in less than a heartbeat, my foot sweeping across the ground to cover the signs of my resting place as best I could with so little time before I would be discovered, a vision flashing through my mind of a savage girl headed my way, a lethal dagger in hand intended for my heart.

Lethia had been hunting me since the trials began. There were no rules to state that the Fae taking part in this tournament had to fight one another, only that we had to survive this place, but in the centuries that had passed since the trials had been instated, it had become the expectation.

Only the highest-ranking members of my father's court took part. Only those of us with enough power in our blood to rattle the stars when it was Awoken. These trials tested our grit, our mettle, our suitability to rule with an iron fist. And they also opened up the possibility to steal ranks beyond those of the Fae taking part.

Lethia was my cousin, though no love was lost between us. We had been raised knowing these trials were headed our way and that this day would come. If she managed to kill me out here in the wilds, she would claim a place closer to the throne for herself and her family. I may have been her princess, but I was her competition too and wiping me from the board before I had even come into my magic would be the perfect way for her to advance her position once she left this place. Assuming she also managed to survive those who were hunting her.

I slipped from the path, damp foliage brushing against my bare arms as I circled the huge tree which I had slept beneath for those few, fleeting hours.

I had spent the last couple of days evading her, but my visions only grew bloodier, the death she intended for me growing more violent every time I slipped from her grasp. Her rage was potent, a thing I could practically taste on the air as she closed in on me, and though I had thought to leave her breathing for the sake of my aunt, I could see now that that path was no longer available to me.

I pushed a stray lock of black hair away from my eyes with dirt-stained, sun-kissed fingers, the dark strands having fallen loose of the braid I had bound them in. This place was a far cry from the beauty of the castle I had grown up in and I was hardly recognisable as the perfectly presented princess known by all in our kingdom. But I had been training for this day since I was old enough to hold a practice sword. We were a warrior people at heart, and I had always been just as at home swinging a sword or firing an arrow as I was when dancing at balls or debating politics. Fae were always fighting someone regardless and I enjoyed the simplicity of a blade just as keenly as the cut of a perfectly phrased remark.

My pulse slowed as I released a slow breath, my gift whispering to me as I closed my eyes and gave in to the call of it.

Bare feet stepping silently on damp soil. A heavy blade clutched in her right hand. A sharp dagger intended for the killing blow in her left. Another step. And another. She was closing in on me. She was-

I whirled from my hiding place, my braid flicking out behind me, my toes pressing into the mud and my spear aimed true just as Lethia broke from the dense foliage exactly where I'd *seen* her coming.

My cousin's razor-sharp eyes flashed with a mixture of fury and triumph at finally finding her quarry, and I gave her a wicked grin as she managed to slip to the right, avoiding the sharpened point of my spear by little more than a breath.

Her short sword swung for my head, but I twisted aside, the shaft of my spear smacking into her left wrist hard enough to knock the dagger she'd been trying to hide from her grasp.

Lethia cursed like an alley cat doused in cold water.

I was behind her before she could get her guard up again, my bare foot colliding with the centre of her spine, making her stumble forward even as she countered the move, spinning my way once more.

But I was already there, had already *seen* what she would do, and with a sound which I was certain would forever stain my memories, the tip of my spear carved straight into the centre of her throat, impaling and ending her with that one, savage strike.

Our eyes met, her death hanging in those endless seconds as she gasped for a breath she could no longer take, her ambitions and plots all come to naught in the face of this single mistake.

"I wanted peace," I breathed, reminding her of the offer I had made her weeks ago in my father's castle. The promise I had made to her to elevate her position at my side if only she would abandon this desire to end me in the trials. I had already *seen* the refusal in her before I even spoke the words, but I had spoken them all the same. I had given her the choice to change this fate for herself, and she had chosen to ignore it. That choice had caused the end of her. She had been running short on time all along and had never even known it.

Her lips mouthed a word even as she choked on her own blood, and I felt the echo of it reverberating through my core. *Coward.*

I jerked my spear back and watched coldly as Lethia slumped to the floor, her hands moving to her throat as she convulsed there, her gaze moving beyond me as she hunted for some gap in the canopy above, any small hint of the stars who watched endlessly on. Did they enjoy it when fate came for someone like this? Did they take pleasure in knowing I had taken steps to avoid this, only to end up in the design they had selected all along?

I supposed it wasn't my place to question that.

I stooped to lift the dagger Lethia had meant to kill me with before hurling it skyward with lethal aim. The blade cut through the leaves above us, carving a small gap which allowed that view of the sky Lethia had been hunting for before disappearing into the jungle out of sight.

"It is not cowardice to hope for a brighter fate," I said in a low tone as she choked and spluttered, her eyes fixed on the stars above while she searched for peace in their embrace. "Sometimes we must look into the darkest of nights to discover the greatest of treasures. I don't balk from that path, Lethia. I just choose to chase a fate greater than my own."

I left her there to die with those words hanging in the silence surrounding her, not looking back as I strode away, my bloodstained spear still tight in my grip and destiny calling my name on every errant breeze.

Three days passed with my Sight guiding me from danger more often than not or helping me to survive the perils of this hell whenever an untold beast crossed my path and forced me to fight for my survival.

The brutality of this ritual was woven into the fabric of my people, the empire I had grown up in. I had never questioned the brutal start to the lives of those blessed to be among the most powerful Fae in our society until coming here myself. It had all sounded somewhat romantic when my father and the Fae of his court described the Marriage Trials. A way to weed out the weakest of our generation and ensure that only the strongest were allowed to continue into magical education, politically arranged marriage, and eventually claim rule over this land. It was right that we should have to face this test of fate. The stars would ensure that only those most worthy emerged from the jungle after all.

Yet living through it was something else entirely. Seeing Fae I had grown up with butchered, hearing screams of pain and death through the trees at all hours, living in a constant state of fear and exhaustion for days on end. Was it truly fate guiding us through this place? Without my gift of The Sight, I wasn't certain I could have survived it. Was I to assume that my clairvoyant abilities had been gifted to me so I could claim the destiny of survival, or was it simply a twist of luck that had me still breathing while others lay dead all around?

I had never questioned the path of the stars before this place. Never once doubted that they knew better than all of us which way the line of fate should be drawn, but now I was beginning to question it. Now I was starting to wonder...

A branch cracking. Dark eyes peering through the trees. Determination, resilience, fear.

"The stars sent me to find you." His rough voice was accompanied by the press of something cold and sharp to my throat, the vision which had found me in sleep coming too late to rouse me in time to avoid this.

My eyes snapped open, a cold flash of dread pouring through my limbs before my mind could catch up to what was happening, who stood over me.

His face had come to me in dreams and visions alike for the last few months, his name whispered upon the wind every time I turned my gaze to the south of the palace walls. We hadn't ever met before this moment, but as I looked up into the hard lines of his features, I *knew* him.

"I recognise you, Marcel," I breathed, surprise lacing my tone even as I realised that this meeting had been inevitable for some time now. I had *seen* him coming. And my life would change from this moment on, irrevocably. That was a terrifying thought, and yet no part of me wished to turn from the fate I felt coming for us.

A breeze stirred the embers of the small fire I had lit for warmth before I fell asleep, lifting them towards the leafy canopy above, and I could have sworn I saw a young boy in the flames as my gaze moved to them. A boy with the same cut jaw of the man who stood over me and a smile which lit me up unlike anything I had ever known.

He would grow to be brave and powerful, his gifts greater than mine and that of the man who held me at the point of his spear in the present moment. The boy's destiny was far greater than I dared to even wish for too, but terrible in ways too. This child of passion and fire, of agony and loss.

My chest heaved as I glimpsed flashes of the life he would lead. The heartache that would come close to destroying him, the despair which I couldn't understand, and which seemed so unavoidable at the same time. And the love. He would love with a passion rivalled by none and felt by all, he would fall hard and fast, painfully and inescapably into a love so great that it would rock the foundations of the world we knew and beyond.

His life was the most important thing I had ever heard called to me on the voice of the stars.

Gabriel.

My dark hearted son, destined for so, so much.

"I'm going to die tomorrow," Marcel said, his voice low and calm with an acceptance and maturity beyond his years. "I'm going to trade my life for yours and the life of our son."

Gabriel.

I swallowed thickly, *seeing* it now so clearly, the visions which had been slipping to me in sleep and wakefulness alike for weeks all coming together. Marcel's fate was set. Death would come for him tomorrow no matter the choices we made here and now. The only thing which could change was the life of that boy who I had *seen* so clearly in the fire.

Gabriel.

I was barely more than a girl myself, eighteen, a princess, destined to marry a man I wouldn't have the luxury of selecting for myself. I had no business taking on the role of motherhood. I had no idea of how to do such a thing, especially as I hadn't even been raised by my own mother, my childhood split between the care of nannies instead. But despite all of that, no part of me wished to deny this fate.

That child, that boy…I loved him already. I loved him so powerfully that it felt like my heart was breaking in two as I looked up at the man who would father him, only to die before ever having the chance to know him in the flesh.

I could *see* so much of the life our son would lead, the visions pressing in on me so thickly that they made tears of pride swim in my eyes before I forced myself to blink them away, push my gifts back and focus on the present.

I didn't have words for this twist of fate. No words I could give which would be any clearer beyond my own actions, but there was a question in Marcel's eyes. This was an offer, not a demand. He had *seen* this possibility too, *seen* the son we could create tonight between us before death came for him with the dawn, and he was asking if I wanted to claim it.

This was my choice and one which seemed all too easy in that moment despite the huge weight of it. I was a princess, destined to marry for politics and power, bound to serve my empire with unwavering loyalty. But this, a child born of fate's whims, was something that would be entirely my own. And as terrifying as that was, as huge as this decision before me seemed, I found myself knowing the answer in my soul. I wanted this, wanted him, and so my answer to the burning question in Marcel's eyes was a resounding *yes* which I knew would make the stars themselves quake when it came to pass.

I sat up and pushed the spear away from my throat, my eyes on Marcel as he let me move it aside before dropping it entirely, the heavy thud of it hitting the ground echoing through my flesh as I reached for him. He was a huge man, impossibly tall and built with muscle, his deftly hewn features captivating me as heat rose through my flesh at the mere thought of his body taking possession of mine. I didn't know him. This was insanity. But as his knees hit the ground at my side and he reached out to cup my jaw in his calloused palm, I knew that I would not back out of this fate.

"Our son will change the world, he'll be the greatest Seer of his generation," Marcel breathed, no fear in his deep brown eyes as he leaned into me, no doubt over his fate even as he knew that his life would be forfeit in payment for it. That he would be dead before the sun set again tomorrow.

He kissed me and I parted for him, a shiver of pleasure racing through my entire being as his tongue teased between the curve of my lips and he tasted me in this slow, decadent greeting as our souls met at last, like they had been longing for this moment all along.

More visions pressed in on me of the life we would create this night, trials and pain stalking our son at every turn.

"His life will be hard," I murmured as I wound my arm around Marcel's neck and drew him down over my body, the weight of him pressing over me so beautifully real. Grief closed in on me then. Grief for this man I knew and yet didn't know. Grief for the boy who would be born of this act and who would never get the chance to know his father.

A tear slipped from my eye and tracked down my cheek as Marcel drew back just enough to gaze at me.

"For a time," he agreed. "But he will know all the best kinds of love in the end. Even if he never knows ours."

His words were laced with a knowledge which seemed to go beyond mine, like he had *seen* more of the fate destined for our child than I had and knew that in the end he would be okay, even if many other things were not.

I took strength from that assurance even as more tears escaped me and I leaned up to claim his mouth once more, wanting to feel that heat again instead of the pain of things that had not yet come to pass.

Marcel's hand moved up the curve of my thigh and I sighed into his mouth as he began to unbuckle the leather armour I wore, his fingers moving in precise actions which had my core heating and a sigh of pleasure leaving me.

His mouth slipped from mine, dragging a line of fire along my jaw and making me gasp at the memory of this. I had *seen* it before, in the dead of night, I had played out this very act while roaming hands sought to release the need those visions had built in me. But it had never been enough. Never quite sated the desire I had felt for this man before I even met him.

Marcel's hands continued to move over the straps and buckles securing my armour in place until it was falling loose between us, a gasp escaping me as he tugged it from my body and laid me bare beneath him.

My spine arched as he ran a hand along my jaw then down my throat, between the valley of my breasts and over my navel, my skin prickling and heating all at once as a moan rolled over my tongue.

I had never been with a man like this before. Never known this touch beyond my own imagination, and yet Marcel seemed to understand exactly what I needed before I could even think of it. I had to wonder if his Sight was showing him my reactions or if this was all him. Either way, I was a slave to his actions, a willing victim to his desire.

A smirk lifted the corner of his mouth as he slowed the progress of that hand, circling it just below my navel as he unbuckled his own armour with his free hand.

I watched with my throat thick as he removed it, revealing cut muscle and the hard planes of a body built for war. And I was the city he was going to lay siege to.

"You're one of the Robarian Tribesmen," I said, not a question, the carefully cut scars across his chest confirming it even if my Sight hadn't already shown me his reply.

"I came from the very heart of the desert to seek you out, Merissa," he confirmed, his hand shifting lower with the low growl of my name falling off of his tongue. "I travelled a long way to claim this fate."

My answer was a cry of pleasure as his fingers found my slick core and rolled over my clit, his brown eyes locked with mine.

"Are you certain you want this?" he asked, his voice rough with desire and a smile tugging at the corner of his lips like he had already *seen* my answer but wanted to make me speak it anyway.

"I want you," I panted in confirmation, a moan building within me as he teased me further, watching me writhe beneath him while he took his time as if he wasn't running out of it.

"You want me to what?" he purred and oh, I wanted to punch him almost as much as I wanted him to make good on the promises which were blazing in his eyes.

I growled at him before grasping his wrist with my own fingers and pushing his hand down precisely where I wanted it.

Marcel gave me a smile which ignited every drop of blood in my body as he gave in and pressed two thick fingers into me, making me gasp as my hips rose to chase the movement of his hand as he moved it in a heady rhythm, playing me like a drum while he watched with hungry eyes.

"Please," I gasped, though I wasn't even sure what I was begging him for, either to end this torment or never let it end. I just wanted more.

"Pretty manners for such a pretty princess," he purred, taking his fingers from me and pushing them between his own lips, a masculine sound of arousal drowning out the crackling of the fire before he drew them free again.

His eyes roamed over my nakedness and my breathing became ragged as he leaned down to kiss me, my own taste on his tongue as it rolled over mine, the press of his solid cock rutting against me through the thick fabric of his pants.

I ground my hips into him, moaning at the friction as I sank into that kiss, his hand teasing my nipple and making me arch against the soft bed of grass at my back.

Marcel sucked my bottom lip between his teeth and bit down hard enough to make me gasp before releasing me and moving that sinful mouth lower, sucking my nipple and flicking the tight bud with his tongue.

I ran my hands up his back, finding the ridges of more carefully cut scars there too, wanting to explore each and every one of them even though I knew we didn't have the time for that. Dawn was coming for us on swift and certain wings, his fate already set in stone.

Tears pricked my eyes at the thought, but before they could fall, he sucked my nipple harder, making me gasp before releasing it and moving lower, running kisses down the deep bronze of my skin while my heart thundered at what he was doing and where he was headed.

A flash of unknown pleasure spilled through my skull before I could make any objections, The Sight making promises I ached to see fulfilled and instead I knotted my hands in his ebony hair as he continued his descent.

Marcel's tongue found my core and the sound which escaped me was more beast than woman, my nails digging into his scalp as he laughed darkly against the heat of me, only licking more firmly, his hand pushing my thighs wider.

My heels dug into the dirt as I bucked against the pressure of his tongue, his name gasping from my parted lips as his tongue moved in this sinful, unknown way which had me burning from the inside out with a heat I had never known before.

"Marcel," I begged as my body began to tighten, pleasure building in every piece of me so fiercely that I feared the release of it, the fall which had to come from such a precipice.

His tongue continued to move, hands grasping my ass as he feasted, refusing me even the slightest respite as he devoured me, and I moaned and panted his name.

My release came so suddenly that it stole my breath, a cascade of pleasure spilling through every inch of my being in an unstoppable wave which had me crying out so loudly that birds were startled from their roosts high above us.

Marcel reared back, my hooded eyes taking in the flex and strain of his muscles as he unbuckled his pants, my throat bobbing as he unsheathed the thick length of his cock and stood to drop the last of his clothes from his flesh.

He was stunning, his body seeming carved from stone in the firelight that flickered across his flesh, a god come to ruin a mortal and I was nothing but an eager sacrifice to his destruction.

He dropped to his knees once more, moving over my body and capturing my mouth with his as I felt the solid press of his cock at my opening.

"Please," I begged again, aching to feel the fullness of him taking me with a desperation that made my entire body tremble with it.

I tipped my head back, kissing him deeply and releasing a low moan which was echoed by his masculine growl as he sank into me, inch by inch, stretching and claiming me. No man had had me before him, he was my first, and I was his last.

For one night I was his creature. One night in his arms before fate came for him. One night to take him and give myself up to him and create a life which was more important than any I had ever *seen* before.

So despite my fear for the dawn and my knowledge of the fate that awaited him, I gave myself up to him entirely. Losing myself in the arms of the man who had found me in this jungle hell, walking the path of destiny, allowing him to wring both pleasure and sorrow from my flesh in equal measures.

And bring about a fate which I knew would change the path of the stars themselves.

HAIL

CHAPTER TWO

ONE YEAR LATER

The throne was as cold as my heart today.

A heaviness was weighing me down since yesterday's battle, the scent of burning Fae still seeming to cling to me despite the scalding shower I'd taken upon my return to the palace.

Blood had washed down my naked body and swirled around my feet before disappearing into the belly of the drain as if it had never been.

The screams rang in my ears even now, and I felt...nothing.

A shadow wrapped around my mind, and I was fairly certain that my heart was turning to stone bit by bit. It hadn't always been like this, though I couldn't quite pinpoint the moment when things had shifted within me. When I had become this monster that struck a chord of fear in the heart of every Fae who heard my name. Hail Vega; the Savage King. That was what they called me now. I had claimed the throne after my mother's death, and I had sworn to protect and serve my kingdom. Those pledges had festered and withered, each battle I fought justified by those vows, but they did not ring true with me anymore. My battles may have been won because I wished to safeguard Solaria, but sometimes it felt like I killed because I *needed* to kill, blackouts where I fell into a ravenous need for death that defied everything I thought I knew of myself.

I'd had such plans once, plans which surfaced in me from time to time and reminded me of the man I had once been. How quickly that had changed. The power had corrupted me, I supposed, though sometimes I woke in a state of dread and terror, a feeling of powerlessness surrounding me and a desperation to know why I was the way I was. As if there were two halves of me, torn down the middle, but it seemed day by day the savage part grew bigger, consuming the other with sharp teeth.

The throne curved up at my back, my fingers curling tightly over the giant Hydra heads which weaved together, hewn from blackest stone. This monster was me, the throne a representation of my Hydra Order form. It had been a gift from a faraway prince who lived in a land divided by factions of Elementals; earth, air, water, fire, all at war with one another. The old throne had been moved to the vault where the treasures of the royals lay deep within the palace, accessible only by Vega blood.

That old, fragmented piece of my soul awoke as I thought of the burning bodies and the city which had been reduced to ash beneath the might of my fire yesterday. My fingers tightened on the stone, biting into it as my muscles bunched and my confusion turned to a bitter, vitriolic hate towards myself.

What have you done?

"Sire?"

My head snapped up at the deep tenor of my friend's familiar voice. Azriel Orion had a frown set into his brow, his handsome features skewed by concern as he approached me. He bowed his head respectfully, causing his dark hair to fall forward into his eyes and he swept a hand through it to push it back, looking like that schoolboy again for a moment, the one I'd studied with at Zodiac Academy.

His gifts in academia and his knowledge of dark magic were invaluable to me, and beyond that, he was one of The Guild members, a protector of the royals and the Imperial Star. Though only I was privy to that information, a secret that ran so deep it would shake the foundations of the kingdom, for the star would be sought by every ruler in the world, and every Fae powerful enough to try and seize it from me if they knew of its existence. The Imperial Star was my most prized possession, passed down from generation to generation through the Vega line, and it remained hidden within the sceptre. It had the power to do almost anything I asked of it, its magic unimaginable, both destructive and capable of doing great things.

"Azriel," I said, my voice an empty, dark thing.

He came to stand before me, that crease between his eyes only deepening. "You're not yourself."

"And who am I?" I bit out, anger sharpening my words to blades, my voice ringing around the expansive hall of the throne room. I could stand in this cavernous space in my fully shifted Order form if I wished it, a beast who ruled with cruelty and no mercy. I was feared to every corner of this earth, but Azriel did not flinch at my booming tone. Instead, he stepped closer, his nearly black eyes like two galaxies staring into the depths of my soul and seeing the truth of me. Though what that truth was, I didn't truly know anymore.

"You are Hail Vega. My friend. A good man."

"Good?" I scoffed at the word. It had no place in this palace anymore. There was no good in me now. What I had done had painted my soul with tar, and the stars would destroy me for it once I passed beyond the Veil. "You are either playing the part of a loyal, simpering servant, or you are blind, Azriel. Which is it? Because you do not seem the simpering type to me."

Azriel's jaw tightened, and a hint of anger crossed his features that I'd had people punished for in the past, dragged into the amphitheatre to be made an example of while a haze of bloody fury took over my flesh. Not Azriel though. Never Azriel.

"I've been gazing into the shadows for guidance," he said quietly. "They whisper of things, awful things…"

"Are you a dark prophet now then?" I growled, leaning deeper into the icy cage of my throne. "The shadows are filled with trickster souls who wish to lure you into their embrace. Is that not what you told me once?"

"True, but there is knowledge in them too," he said. "And I sense something terrible is coming, sire."

I released a short, dismissive breath. "It has arrived. I am the terrible thing. I am the plague which ravages the land. My soul is dipped in blood and there is no knowing what I will do next. But without my efforts, our enemies would have seized Solaria long ago." Those final words were the only thing that kept me sane. That I was doing the right thing. That if I didn't act mercilessly against my adversaries, then Solaria would fall to the hands of a worse power than me.

Azriel's throat rose and fell. "Is this what you wanted for Solaria? For your people to live in fear?"

"When all threats against us are crushed, there will be no need for fear," I said firmly.

"And what if it is *you* they fear?" he whispered, having the gall to accuse me of that, though it was hardly an accusation I could deny. My people may have cheered when I brought another threat to heel, some of them even revered me like a god, but all of them feared me.

"Then let them be afraid," I hissed, but a tug in the back of my mind reminded me that wasn't what I'd wanted for my kingdom.

"Those are not the words of the man I grew up with." Azriel frowned, looking at me like he was trying to find something in my eyes, but they were as hard as slate and would not let him in. "Why not try to change? Why not visit the people and quell this fear in them? Let them know they are safe and that you will keep them so. Bring them bounties and alleviate taxes, remind them who you are beyond bloodshed. You could start by shutting down the palace amphitheatre and be done with public executions that turn killing into sport."

I let myself think on his words, but even as my mind turned to such things, death and fire seemed to spark in my soul. Sometimes the darkness came upon me so rapidly, it was impossible to stop. It was why I kept myself contained within these palace walls as often as possible, only venturing out to hunt my enemies. Deep down, I was terrified of what I might do to innocent people if I lost myself to the monster in me. And as for the amphitheatre, well, it was where the most dangerous of rebels and insurgents were brought to face the price of treason. It was barbaric, yes, perhaps enough so to unsettle the people of Solaria, but it was necessary too, a tool to ensure more enemies didn't stick their heads above the parapet. It was essential, wasn't it?

"Make them pay, let the people watch your enemies die, remind them what will happen if they ever turn against you."

The whispers in my head reminded me why the amphitheatre was important and squashed away my doubts.

"I cannot," I muttered.

"You are in control of your own fate," Azriel pushed.

My teeth ground in my mouth as I found an inch of clarity, holding onto it with all I had, but it fell from my grasp instead, replaced by a violent anger that had me rising from my throne and lifting the sceptre that held the Imperial Star. I pointed it at Azriel and he raised his chin, eyes wide with his impending death. He stared at me, the man he had once known, yet the only thing reflected in that man's eyes now was a murderous stranger.

"There is no control, only chaos," I hissed. "I am tossed to and fro in a tempestuous sea, the sky is dark, the water darker. There is no way out."

"Let me help you find a way," he rasped. "Help me to understand."

A sneer pulled at my mouth, my mind drifting deeper into that pit of black where I could feel little emotion at all except hate.

"Do not insult me. I am your king. I do not need help," I spat, tossing the sceptre onto the ground and raising a hand instead, fire magic crackling ferociously in my palm and proving my power was almighty even without the gifts of the star. I could incinerate him and wipe him from existence in the blink of an eye, and it didn't even look like he was going to fight his fate. Though of course, he no doubt knew that one single finger lifted against his king would see him dead regardless.

"This isn't you," he breathed as my hand began to tremble, like two forces were colliding inside me. One begging me to lower my hand, the other to use the full ferocity of my magic to see Azriel dead. I loved him, but I had to get rid of anyone who opposed me. It was the only way to keep order. That was the role of a strong ruler, was it not?

"My King," Lionel Acrux's rumbling voice echoed through the chamber as he arrived and my eyes lifted, my teeth bared as I met his gaze.

He was dressed in dark green robes with the Councillor's crests embroidered in gold onto the lapel, his blonde hair swept back stylishly and a single eyebrow arched in intrigue as he looked from me to Azriel.

"Has Azriel Orion offended you?" Lionel asked in shock as he moved closer, his gaze roaming over us both.

"Have I?" Azriel pressed of me, and I looked to him again as fire spiralled in my palm.

No…this wasn't right. Azriel was my friend, damn loyal and an honest man.

I dropped my arm, shaking my head before dropping back onto the throne and carving a hand over my face as the fire extinguished within it.

"You should go, Azriel," Lionel murmured. "The king clearly needs rest after yesterday's victory."

"Is that what you call it?" I whispered. "Blood and death. Is that victory, Lionel?"

"Of course, sire. They were your enemies. Set to oppose the throne. Rebels and insurgents. You did well to rid yourself of them before they attacked the palace," Lionel said confidently, and it did something to ease the guilt in my chest. He was right. He had to be right, or else I could not live another day with myself.

Azriel made no comment, and I lifted my head, finding I needed his agreement on this to be sure, to lighten the load of my heart. His eyes were downcast, his posture tight and his hands curled into fists.

"Azriel?" I demanded and he looked up once more. "Do you agree?"

"It is not my place to say," he said.

"Then I am making it your place," I said firmly, a threat in my voice. "Do you or do you not agree that the Fae I burned were rebels?"

Azriel's jaw ticked, and he glanced at Lionel who gave him a prompting look of encouragement. Azriel cleared his throat, turning to me again as he hovered on the verge of speaking, driving me to near insanity.

"Speak!" I barked, the monster in me rising.

"I do not know," he said, his voice ringing out loudly. "I saw no evidence of that, so I do not know."

"You are not privy to such evidence," Lionel said lightly, waving a hand at him. "I was well informed before the decision was made to eradicate the threat. You must not doubt yourself, Your Highness. You have done marvellous things for Solaria; it is becoming as great as it was in the times of old. I for one, admire your decisiveness and your firm hand. It is what the kingdom needs to prosper."

"The people are afraid," Azriel said carefully. "Perhaps it is time for peace."

"Peace?" Lionel tsked. "And what of the Kingdom of Voldrakia who are gearing up for war? They will invade us soon if we do not meet them head on. You are not a Councillor Azriel, it is not your place to speak as one. If you had it your way, we would all be under the rule of some foreign dictator within a week. King Vega is acting dutifully for Solaria, using his fearsome power to protect our nation and squash any threat against us. He is firming up our

Caroline Peckham & Susanne Valenti

borders, squashing any rebellion caused by factions placed here by external forces which could cause harm to his subjects, and making certain that our great kingdom advances. As he should."

Azriel opened his mouth, but I spoke before he could. "Leave us. I wish to speak with my Councillor alone."

Azriel looked as if he wanted to protest, but then he bowed his head, turning and striding out of the throne room.

Lionel smiled, moving closer and clasping his hands at his back. "I can handle Azriel. If you would like, I could have him report to me directly and he will no longer need to bother you."

I frowned, the idea impossible with Azriel's secret position within The Guild, though it was more than that which brought on a protest in me. I loved Azriel as a brother. He was important to me, even when I lost sight of that from time to time.

"No, that won't be necessary," I said, and Lionel bowed his head in submission to my authority. "Tell me what news you have of the movements in Voldrakia."

Lionel's face became grave. "Their army is recruiting in the masses. War is imminent if we do not act soon, sire. Those vile Voldrakians want nothing but hell for us, if they ever got their grip on our land, they would seize our resources and persecute our people. Solaria is frightened of them, my king, horrified at the idea of them pushing into our borders. But I have fine news, as I have acquired the location of their army's training grounds."

"And?" I muttered.

He swept closer, moving to circle the throne before coming to stand at my side, his hand resting on my arm as he leaned down to speak in my ear. But before a word passed his lips, I rose from my seat, an idea coming to me as the veil of blackness in my mind peeled back a little.

"A treaty," I decided. "I will travel to Voldrakia this very week and see what can be done for a treaty. If I can prevent a war, then we can all benefit from peace. Yes…" I latched onto the idea, seeing the good in it.

"But I am to marry next week," Lionel said abruptly, and I turned back to him. "Will you not attend?"

"Ah, yes, forgive me… How about I offer you the palace for the ceremony? You may use it until my return."

Lionel's eyes widened and he nodded quickly, excitement sparkling in his gaze. "That is most generous of you, sire. I will of course greatly miss your presence at the wedding, but I will make sure the press are here to immortalise every moment of it."

"Perfect," I said, my mind turning back to my plans, my heart thumping with the hope that gilded them. *This could make things right again.*

"You should spend some time in Voldrakia," Lionel suggested. "If you are going all that way to strike a treaty, then it would be best to form relationships with the Voldrakian emperor and his family. Take all the time you need. I will hold the fort while you are gone."

"Thank you, Lionel." I smiled a true smile, a rare thing to adorn my face these days. But at last, I had something to hold onto that could change the trajectory of my fate. I would travel light, take only a small host and when I returned to Solaria, I would damn well bring good news with me. I would prevent a war, protect my kingdom, and perhaps become the king I had once longed to be.

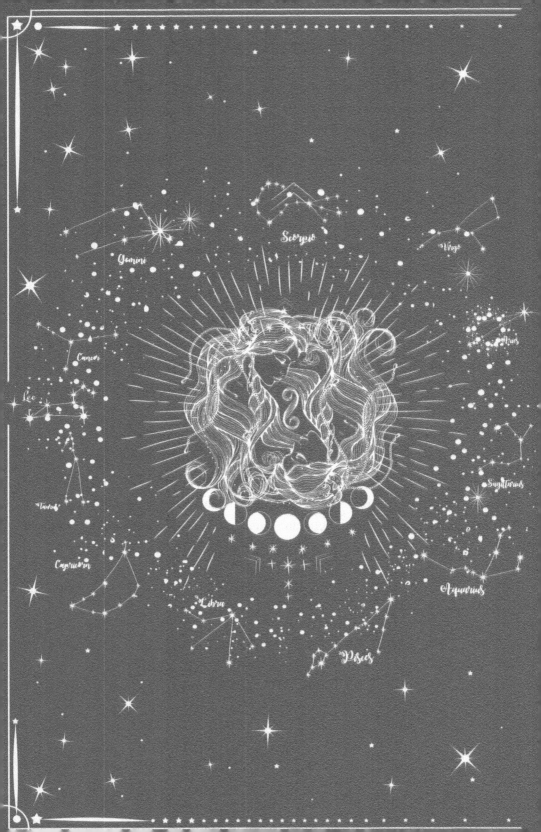

MERISSA

CHAPTER THREE

Pride can often be the cruellest emotion of them all. To change the path of a prideful soul is the most difficult of challenges. But take heart in the light, for all who walk the darkest path will be rewarded with the brightest salvation in the end.

I woke with a gasp, sweat dampened sheets twisted around my ankles and my heart racing to an erratic rhythm as the visions plaguing my dreams burned into me with a ferocity that left me panting in their wake.

I hated when The Sight came to me in sleep that way, leaving my waking moments foggy with confusion. What had been a possibility of the future and what had simply been the work of my imagination?

I rolled over, fingers reaching for the crib which lay beside my bed, the tiny baby boy I had birthed just four moons ago cooing softly in his sleep.

Gabriel. Such a big name for such a little boy. A name for a hero, a warrior, a name I already knew he would grow into and own with such pride and ferocity that all would know it. He would stalk through the halls of the castle here, casting fear into the hearts of his enemies with a single knowing look, while others swooned at the mere thought of catching his atten-

My fingertips brushed against his tiny hand and a vision slammed into me, taking me by surprise in my half sleeping state and I sucked in a breath at what I *saw*.

A diverging path. A future away from the thick, golden walls I knew so well. *A life in a place that saw snow and rain as often as it felt the kiss of sunlight. A girl with bright green eyes and long blonde hair smiling widely up at this boy of mine as a man, his fingers pushing dark hair away from his even darker eyes as he tried to hide what he felt for her. But she knew. Just as I knew while I watched them from a window which overlooked the spot they thought was secret for this rendezvous, the laughter of twin girls drawing my attention back into the room behind me...*

The vision faded away and I blinked as I tried to process it, trying to understand what possible reason my son and I might have for travelling north.

Gabriel's tiny fingers curled tightly around one of my own as he slept soundly on, knowing nothing of the two futures his mother had now seen for him. Or were they one? Was it possible that both might come to pass?

I turned my mind towards the images which had torn me from sleep.

Men and women screaming, burning, a shadow descending upon our kingdom. A man with dark eyes and a darker soul, his hand locked around my wrist as my death flashed violence through his gaze.

I'd *seen* those eyes before. Dreamed of them alongside the brush of a mouth against mine, the crackle of electricity in my veins. Desire and fear mixed in my blood at the thought of the nameless villain who had been tiptoeing through my visions so often this past year. I didn't know if I should feel such an ache to find him, but I couldn't help it.

Not with my wedding so close, not with the life I had had chosen for me rushing in on all sides.

A shiver traced down my spine as I thought on the scent of smoke that still lingered from the vision. War. It wasn't set yet, but it was turning its eyes on my kingdom, I could feel the hand of fate moving and though it was in no way a certainty, I was struggling to see how I could draw it away from bloodshed.

A heavy knock came against the door, and I stiffened, wondering if it had been more than just the visions which had stirred me from sleep.

I withdrew my hand from the crib, standing on bare feet and grabbing a red silk gown from the chair beside the bed as the knock came again.

A tall man with shoulder length dark hair and a rough, unkempt beard smirked to himself as he shifted his belt and raised a fist to knock again.

I blinked away the image of Arturo as it came to me, hesitating for a moment on my way to the door. I glanced back into the room and moved to pull the curtain hanging around my four-poster bed across to conceal the crib on the far side of it.

I flicked my fingers to throw a silencing bubble around Gabriel too in case he woke, wetting my lips as I prepared to face the man I was betrothed to after almost six months of avoiding his presence.

When it had become too difficult for me to hide my pregnancy, I had headed to the southern mountains under the guise of needing to concentrate on my magical studies away from the court. That had been true in part too. I had worked tirelessly to hone and learn all I could about my magic with four tutors my parents had found for me, the academy they ran so exclusive that it only took ten students at any one time, giving us an intensive education over the course of a single year. They were the best in the land, and I was a quick study, working tirelessly to perfect the use of my magical abilities despite my pregnancy. Of course everyone who had been at the academy, student and tutor alike had soon come to realise I was pregnant but they were loyal to my father's crown and had been well rewarded for keeping the secret. Besides, none of them would dare breathe word of the truth now; he would know it had been one of them and likely see all of them dead for the betrayal.

Everyone who had survived the Marriage Trials had been doing some version of the same. Using the time following our emergence from that bloodstained jungle to train in the art of magic for a year, before we would all be required to follow through on our betrothals and take up our places within the court of Voldrakia as fully trained warriors. I had six months left before I would be expected to fulfil my promise to marry Arturo and I felt every passing second like the tightening of a noose around my throat.

I loved my empire, loved my kingdom, but I did not love the man who was destined to become my husband.

I hadn't seen him in months and yet my distaste for him had only grown in that time. He was brutish and brash, a dull weapon with nothing more than strength and arrogance to his name. He was also the reason my baby boy would grow up without a father. The one who had struck the killing blow against Marcel that morning beneath the trees.

If my parents had their way, Gabriel would soon be taken from me, raised as their ward with no acknowledgment of his heritage as a daughter of the princess of Voldrakia. It was a secret that wasn't likely to stay a secret, and yet no one would ever dare question it out loud. A ward of the emperor was bound to be a bastard born royal after all.

In so many ways our court was outdated like that. Power and reputation meaning far too much to the people who should have been able to set the rules for themselves.

I was still working on my plans to evade that fate, my Sight helping me to form a future where I got to keep my son at my side despite him being born in secret. But I was yet to *see* a clear path to a future which would keep me out of this man's marriage bed.

I raised my chin as I stalked to the door, waiting until I *saw* him raise his fist to knock even more forcefully before I yanked it open, making him stumble forward a step, his raised fist hanging uselessly in the air near his temple.

"No need to salute me, Arturo, we aren't in the throne room right now," I said, leaning my shoulder to the door frame and keeping hold of the door so he was under no illusions about me allowing him entrance to my chambers.

"You didn't tell me you were back in the city," he grunted, the scent of stale ale singing under my nose from his breath. It was no difficult guess to tell where he had spent his night. Though he was from one of the most powerful families in Voldrakia, Arturo never quite managed to pull off the pomp and posturing the rest of the court flourished at. His shirt hung messily on his broad frame, the dark hair tucked behind his ears looking lank rather than lustrous like my brother Jorge's whose style he so often tried to imitate.

"I didn't realise I was required to inform you of my whereabouts. And I was more than content with my night of rest. So you'll excuse me if I get back to it."

I took a step away and tried to close the door between us, but his heavy boot thumped into place over my threshold, making the wood bounce back into my grip.

"I didn't come calling just to have you throw the door closed in my face, Merissa," Arturo snarled, pushing forward and stooping so that his face drew close to mine.

Magic coiled in my skin, the power of the earth writhing within me as a slight shift of my fingers started the cast.

"And what was it you wanted?" I asked icily, trying to ignore the sweep his narrowed eyes took of my body in my nightgown. I wasn't afraid of him. I was a warrior with the power of the earth itself brimming in my veins, not to mention his princess.

"A word," he clipped. "With my betrothed. And it might serve you to remember that the crown your family covets so greedily is only yours because of the power of the high families supporting you. You might also want to remember that pleasing me is the surest way to keep that support in place."

"I am well aware of the power my family holds as well as yours. But that is no explanation for you turning up here in the middle of the night."

"I heard a rumour," he said in a low tone, shifting closer. "A rumour about a guest your parents have arriving at the castle today. A rumour I want my beloved fiancée to confirm for me."

Dark eyes and a darker soul. Hungry, angry, hurting.

I blinked the vision away, needing to keep my wits sharp.

I held my ground, raising my chin as I maintained my position before him. He had come here now thinking to intimidate me. The big man forcing his presence on a woman half his size while she was alone and vulnerable. How powerful he must have felt standing over me in the dark, the light of the hall beyond silhouetting his broad frame like a threat as he blocked my only escape from this place. But if that was what he thought true power felt like, he needed to ask himself the real question. If I held the thing he desired then wasn't I the one with the power?

"Speak plainly, Arturo, before I toss you from this room like the lecherous drunk I'm beginning to suspect you are," I replied, my voice hard.

If he thought his marriage to me would be an easy one where I was forced to cower and submit, then he was even more of a fool than I had given him credit for. And if he thought he could use the threat of his size or physical harm against me then he mustn't have been taking my gifts as seriously as he should have.

Arturo's lip curled back, more of that ale scent curling in the air which divided us, and I didn't make any attempt to hide my distaste. In that moment I knew I wouldn't marry him. No matter the customs and arrangements that had been made for the unity of this empire, I would not submit my body to one such as him, no matter the cost.

"Is there a party arriving from Solaria today?" Arturo hissed, his hand moving to snatch my arm, but I *saw* it coming and shifted aside so that he didn't so much as brush a finger against me.

"Solaria?" I asked and a flash of a vision stole through me. *A many headed monster, a ferocious roar, an exquisite banquet with foreigners, though I didn't get a clear enough look at them to recognise any faces.* "I haven't been told of any such visit."

True.

"Don't try and hide your visions from me," Arturo said, his voice taking on a cunning note which told me that was why he had come here, hoping to force an answer from the stars about this via me.

I scoffed. "My visions are many and always changing," I replied evenly, shutting out more of them as a distant roar echoed through my mind. If he cared so much about this, then I certainly wasn't going to give it up to him easily.

"It would make sense for you to wish for your betrothed to have this kind of knowledge. What benefits me will only ever benefit you in the end. Once we are married and the might of our families is united under one roof, you will have to share all of your visions with me regardless."

Have to? Oh, this asshole was kidding himself if he thought he was going to be enforcing any kinds of demands upon me whether we were wed or not.

I let my eyes widen, mouth falling slack as I faked a vision with a sudden gasp that had his eyes lighting.

"What do you *see?*" Arturo demanded.

"A man," I breathed, vines crawling across the floor behind him beneath the power of my magic, creeping closer while his greed for my knowledge left him utterly exposed to my whims. "A man with lank hair and a mindless skull..."

"What is he doing?" Arturo asked greedily, reaching out to grab me again, but I *saw* it and sidestepped once more. I would not let the man who killed my son's father lay so much as a finger on me.

"Flying," I breathed. "Without wings..."

"Flying? Why? Where?"

"Would you like me to show you?" I asked softly, temptingly, as if I was offering up the chance for him *see* what it was that I *saw*.

"Yes," he panted, reaching for my hand as if I really might give it up.

The corner of my lips twitched with a wicked amusement as I met his gaze. "As you wish."

I curled my fingers and the vines shot out, snaring him beneath his armpits and whipping him from his feet before hurling him out into the corridor where he flew a good ten feet before slamming down on his ass and skidding away like a sack of potatoes that had fallen from a runaway donkey.

"I live only to serve you, dear husband," I called after him as he bellowed in rage, the sound turning into a furious moo as he lost control of his Order form and shifted into his Minotaur form.

Arturo got to his feet and lowered his horns, charging furiously, but the noise he was making had already alerted the guards and I could hear them running closer.

I threw the door closed with a wild laugh, my vines binding it shut with fierce strength just before he collided with it and the entire thing rattled on its hinges.

Guards running down the corridor, a call for help, someone else shouting that they'd seen Arturo drinking the night away in The Whale and Whelk and then claims that he must have lost control in a drunken stupor. Four men dragging him away while he mooed furiously.

I laughed louder as the vision faded, listening intently as that exact scene played out in real time beyond the door.

I waited until his moos grew more distant then banished the vines securing my door and tugged it open, gasping in surprise as I took in the few guards who were still there.

"What in the name of the stars is going on?" I asked, the picture of innocence and surprise.

"Looks like a bit of drunken foolery, Princess, sorry for the disturbance," a guard replied, bowing low.

"I assume the culprit will be held accountable?" I replied, trying to look stern while fighting hard against my amusement to banish it from my face.

"We will speak to his father and explain the situation," the guard agreed. "No doubt the punishment will be swift."

I nodded my acceptance of that before bidding them goodnight and closing the door again. Arturo's father would indeed punish him soundly for making such a fool of himself in public, and I had to assume my betrothed would be more than a little hesitant to come knocking on my door without being called for again.

I ran across the room until I slipped inside the silencing bubble I'd left in place around my little sleeping Gabriel before letting my smile show.

As I sank back down onto my bed, the visions from my nightmares pressed in again; *burning, screaming, war. A man with the darkest eyes I'd ever seen, violent and empty and alone.*

I bit down on my lip, wondering what it all meant, hoping I could figure it out in time to make a change that would save those screaming people.

I didn't sleep again, simply lying in bed for the rest of the night with my precious boy in my arms, nursing and fussing over him until the sun rose and spilled through the gauzy white curtains that covered the huge window to the left of my room.

I could feel the heat rising already, the intensity of the sun pressing in and making me kick the covers from my legs.

By the time my handmaid arrived to attend us, Gabriel had long since woken and was babbling and smiling at me as I worked my hardest to entertain him.

"Your parents have asked for your attendance at breakfast," Elena said softly.

I fought the prickle of disappointment that ran down my spine at the summons, understanding what it meant. I was to be seen around the palace today. So Gabriel would be cared for in my absence without me once again.

My instincts balked at the order, but I had no option to argue it. My parents weren't cruel by nature, but they were strict. They ran their court efficiently and without reproach. If I failed to do as requested then they would enforce a punishment, likely take Gabriel away from me for longer than a day or even threaten to have him removed from the palace entirely if his presence meant I wasn't following up with my duties.

I'd already had to fight for the right to have him in my room at all. They'd wished to have him taken straight into the care of a wetnurse when I'd first returned, but I had begged on my knees for the right to care for him myself and they had given in. So long as I kept up with my duties.

I fought away the tears which wished to roll down my cheeks at the thought of being torn from him for hours, hoping he wouldn't miss me too much while I was forced to maintain this ruse.

Elena took him gently and I yielded, though the ache in my heart only grew as I released him to her care.

I focused on him, training my gifts onto his future so that I could *see* all avenues the day might take for him.

"Don't go for a walk in the western gardens," I said in a soft tone. "There's a wasps' nest there and he'll get stung if you venture that way today."

"I'll make sure to avoid it," Elena promised, giving my arm a reassuring squeeze as I dipped my head to kiss Gabriel goodbye.

Aside from the possible wasp sting, I saw no danger in his future and no unhappiness apart from him crying for me, but there was nothing I could do to aid that.

I withdrew, despite my instincts aching for me to stay and I headed into the bathing chamber attached to my room where I found a bath already run for me, wildflowers and goats milk lacing the steaming water.

I disrobed and bathed quickly, dressing in the golden gown which had been laid out for me. It was thin, several sheer layers making up the skirt of it which left a silhouette of my body on show through the fabric while maintaining my modesty and allowing me to keep cool while wearing it. Or at least as cool as it was possible to be in the heat of a Voldrakian summer's day.

Another of my handmaids appeared to brush my ebony hair and I allowed it, though I had always preferred to care for myself. It had taken years to persuade them all to allow me to bathe and dress in privacy. The hair was a compromise.

She left it unbound, placing a thin golden chain around the back of my head adorned with tiny golden lilies over the loose curls which fell down my spine. The back of the dress was open to allow room for my wings to extend if I needed my Harpy, and I liked the freedom of that, the warm air along my spine seeming to urge on the shift in me, but I'd keep my wings contained for now.

She painted my face next, darkening my eyes with kohl and reddening my lips before allowing me to rise.

I stepped into the light slippers which matched the dress then strapped a dagger to my thigh. The thin material didn't fully cover it, but it wasn't intended to be hidden. I was a warrior, my worth proven in that hellish jungle where I had fought for my life and emerged victorious.

By the time I returned to my main chamber, Elena had gone with Gabriel. I forced my mind from worrying about him, knowing that she loved and doted on him almost as warmly as I did. He was in good hands, even if I wished those hands were mine.

I strode out into the castle corridors and headed through the familiar stone building towards the dining hall my parents favoured for breakfast. It wasn't as grand as the one used for banquets but still seated twenty when the long, mahogany table was at capacity.

Guards opened the doors for me as I approached, bowing their heads in deference to my position. I was a princess after all. Though not one anywhere close to taking the throne with four older siblings, three of whom were married and had already born legitimate heirs of their own into the world. But my position was higher than most in the empire.

"Daughter," my father greeted as he noted my arrival, and I dipped my head in respect towards him and my mother where they sat at opposing ends of the long table.

"I am honoured to receive the invitation to dine with you both," I said, allowing a servant to usher me into a centrally located chair.

There was no one else here, but that meant little. Our parents often requested one or all of us to attend them at mealtimes – one of the few points in the days which were set and didn't always include the politics of the court, unlike the rest of their time. One or all of my siblings might yet be summoned, only time would tell, and they certainly wouldn't waste small talk on telling me if they were coming.

"We have some…unexpected guests at the castle today," my father said, a hand smoothing his well-oiled beard from his chin to the golden jewel which clasped it near the base. A tell I had long since realised meant that he was worried. The movement made me sit up straighter.

"They likely mean us no harm," my mother added, drawing my eyes to her as she gave me a soft smile. She was beautiful, her deep brown hair peppered with strands of grey and her mouth lined from countless smiles, but none of them were ever as genuine as they appeared. I supposed I loved my parents, but honestly, they loved their kingdom far more than their children and my own nannies and tutors had been more like parents to me as I grew. I didn't resent it. I was a princess of Voldrakia and knew well that I could live a lot worse, but I had always held out hope for something…more, too.

"We wish for you to find out more about them," my father added, and it didn't escape my notice that I hadn't actually been given anything to eat while their plates lay fully stacked before them.

I nodded in understanding as I rose. "Where are they staying?"

"In the east wing. The starstruck quarters." The rooms reserved for only the most important of guests.

Dark eyes, cruel laughter, the brush of teeth against my neck, fire, screaming, war.

I sucked in a breath as the scraps of vision pressed in on me and my mother cocked her head.

"What did the stars show you?" she asked.

It was her line that had given me these gifts, though she herself only had the barest trace of The Sight, more like good instincts than actual prophesising. But her grandmother had been one of the greatest Seers in the history of our empire, credited for the rise of our family's fortunes. She had always been able to tell when I *saw* something, no matter how briefly the visions appeared.

"Nothing clear," I admitted, knowing my father had no patience for riddles from the stars. "But there is danger."

"All the more reason for you to see what more you can find," my father said with a jerk of his chin to indicate my dismissal. "Return to us this evening with what you glean from your investigations."

I nodded my head, giving that slight bow of respect before turning and leaving the room. I knew why they wished to send me. With my gifts I often *saw* far more than the eyes or ears could interpret and being close to people sometimes gave me insight into their intentions.

I strode away, turning for the east wing before a nudge from my rumbling stomach and possibly the stars too. If I showed up as I was then I would draw more attention, have to announce myself and who I was right away before getting the chance to read much at all from the people who I was supposed to be investigating. But if I came bearing food, they would likely assume I was a servant, at least for a minute or two, keeping their guards down and their intentions easier to read. The future could change on the spin of a coin so easily and something as simple as a visit from one of the royals might shift their plans, so if I wanted the chance to figure out what their current intentions were, then I needed to give myself the time it would take to get a read on them.

No one paid me much attention as I headed from the castle, opting for the use of my own legs over a carriage as the market was so close to the outer walls.

The heat of the ever-rising sun broke over me as I walked, my skin humming with the pleasant sensation of the kiss of it even though I knew I would likely be cursing its intensity come midday.

The market was already busy, merchants calling out to tempt people to their wares beneath the shade of sweeping white canopies erected above their wooden carts and stalls.

Some sand had gathered on the cobbles as it often did, the air wielders who cleaned the streets clearly due to come soon.

I picked out fruits and pastries, paying little attention to the task beyond making certain that everything was fresh and tempting while I tried to turn The Sight towards who I might find in those rooms. But all I received for my efforts was the feeling of phantom lips on my skin, a raising of my pulse and a throbbing ache which I wished to sate beyond all measure of sanity.

I had to shift my mind from those thoughts to keep my head clear, but as I turned back towards the castle with the food I'd purchased, a voice echoed through my head, one I didn't know but sent goosebumps racing over my flesh despite the heat of the sun.

"You think you can tame a creature such as me?"

The taunt was wicked and sinful, a challenge and a promise which made my mouth dry out and anticipation stutter through me. And that voice. It was like a rough scratch of pleasure along my skin, and a warning to run all at once.

Visions started to flash and flicker through my mind as I made it back into the castle, barely evening paying enough attention to my surroundings to lay the food I'd purchased out on a platter in the kitchens before heading towards the east wing.

Those eyes raking over me. Men screaming for mercy. A rough hand around my throat. The scent of burning on the air. A mouth moving down my body, breaking me apart. A many headed monster, the likes of which I'd never known, sewing terror into the world all around us. Words whispered in my ear, promises of worship and torture and a world beyond my knowledge. Blood spilling in the streets I'd grown up in. And the stars whispering secrets like every step I took was echoed by the chiming bells of fate.

I was so lost to the maelstrom of The Sight that I hadn't even given proper thought to my destination until I realised my feet had delivered me to it already.

I stood before the ornate double doors which led into the starstruck suite and blinked at them as a voice reached me from beyond the thick mahogany.

"Are you sure about this, my liege? It could cause a mighty batch of pickle sauce if the stars aren't in agreement." Visions slammed into me. *Fire, screaming, pleading, burning. War. Death. Carnage.*

"Question me again and I'll have your head along with the emperor's," a dark voice growled in response.

My lips parted in shock at the plainness of that revelation, of the threat that had just been made so baldly against my father's life.

I took a step back, my death flashing through my mind, despite no visions rising to agree with such a fate, but the door was flung open before I could escape.

My heart leapt then free fell in my chest as I took in the huge man who stood there. His eyes were a pit of darkness, danger rolling off of him so thickly that I swear it stained the air around us almost as powerfully as the crackle of electricity which made the space between us sing.

He towered over me, his body powerfully built and features breathtaking even set in that cold and unyielding scowl. His strong jaw was lined with stubble and his deep green eyes fell to take me in with a cruelty unlike anything I had ever perceived before.

I should have been running. But I wasn't. I was standing captivated by the sight of those eyes, that mouth, the hands I had felt a thousand times in my sleep and yet never truly experienced the touch of before. This couldn't be real. But the memories I held of the moments I'd *seen* between us promised so much more than the darkness in his eyes.

"Do you know what we do with spies in Solaria?" the man growled, magic crackling between his fingers as he took a step towards me like he intended to flay the skin from my bones.

"It's you," I breathed, fear escaping me as wonder and awe took its place. I had been waiting for him without even accepting it as the truth. I'd *seen* him coming. Though I hadn't expected this...beast of a man.

I stepped closer, closing the distance between us until I was only inches from him, far closer than propriety would allow, especially with a stranger. Close enough to feel the power of all that darkness in him like it was brushing against my skin.

"Lady, step away from his majesty!" another man in the room barked but I didn't look at him, just pressed the plate of fruit into his arms so that I could be free of everything but this creature before me.

The weight of the stars thickened in my throat until I found my tongue bending around words that seemed to spill directly from them.

"On the darkest day and longest night, I'll guide you home with love so bright," I whispered.

I should have been afraid. I knew that. But I wasn't. For some strange, impossible reason, I wasn't.

I reached out a hand and pressed it to his chest like I just needed to feel the thump of the heart which lay within.

He stilled, the magic in his hands blazing, but he made no move to force me back, like he could feel the power between us too, the taste of destiny on the air. I slid my hand up over the fine silk shirt he wore, trailing my fingers over his neck until I held his jaw in my hand, the bite of his stubble a thrill which set my pulse racing.

"I've *seen* the life we're destined to share," I told him in a low voice while he stared at me like I was some captivating creature who had him in my thrall. "Would you like to *see* it too?"

The man's gaze intensified if that was even possible and he parted his lips, seeming to remember himself, looking like he might refuse, but a flash of The Sight told me that he needed to *see* this. A knowing smile drew my lips up.

"The truth will change the world," I promised as I pushed the things I had *seen* of us into his mind, more of our possible future unravelling itself too, as if it had been waiting for this moment to become clear to me as well.

I knew who he was now, not some foreign diplomat or courtier seeking favour, but the man who ruled over the lands beyond our empire. Hail Vega; The Savage King.

Fate called my name and it beckoned me north. To a land I didn't know, and a king feared by all. And I found myself wanting to give in to its call.

HAIL

CHAPTER FOUR

The magic snared my mind before I could stop it, and the brief flash of concern I felt over an attack vanished before my eyes as I fell into a future I had never dreamed I was capable of claiming.

I *saw* myself enraptured with this woman, desiring her more deeply than I had ever desired anything. She looked at me the way no one had ever looked at me, with a love that seemed to defy everything I was and ever could be. In this future, we fell quickly into an obsession with one another, deeper and faster than should have been possible. I *saw* myself taking her back to Solaria, declaring her as my queen and there was a smile on my face that made me look like an entirely different man. She became the centre of my world, the one good thing ever offered to me, and I coveted her like she could turn to dust at any moment.

The visions of this beautiful life surrounded me until I craved it with every furious beat of my heart.

She released me from the power and I was left staring at her, jaw slack and eyes unblinking. She was beauty embodied, from her ebony hair which was in a loose curls down her back to her hourglass curves and radiant bronze skin.

But those eyes, those eyes alone I would have gone to war for. They were deepest brown , glittering with all the golden light of the star-littered sky.

"Your name," I demanded, the bite of my words filling the air and reminding me I was not the man she had perceived in those visions.

If this was a ploy to seduce me, then she was too ignorant to have done her research well to paint me correctly within them. Though the realness of them was hard to deny, the strength of the truth woven into them so certain to me, how could I really refute it?

"Merissa," she said, her eyes still trailing over my features as she lowered her hand from my face, and I instantly missed the contact of her.

We were attracted to one another with the force of magnets, and I could not pull away from her, instead standing there rooted to the floor feeling like my entire life had just been turned on its head.

"Merissa..." I tried out her name and her pupils dilated in a way that set my pulse hammering. Fuck, she was stunning, her features delicate, yet sharp too. She looked exactly like I imagined a star would look if it shifted into Fae form.

"Sire, do forgive the gobbles of my gables-" Hamish started up, inching closer. "But I cannot hold my loyal lollygagger a second longer. The lady has come bearing a bounty, it would be customary of the gentleFae in question – that is, your most magnanimous, majestic self – to offer her a moment of your invaluable time and perhaps a syrupy sup to wet her whimsy, hm?"

"A syrupy what?" I snapped at him, my eyes still on her.

"A sup, my liege," he bowed his head. "A syrupy one at that."

"What are you blathering about?" I demanded, anger splashing in my chest like acid as I rounded on him.

A pang of guilt hit me as he shrank back like I was about to strike him, and I remembered a time when he and I had been close friends. Nowadays, I couldn't seem to get past the way he frustrated me, and even as I worked to wrap my tongue around an apology, it sizzled out and died right there on my lips.

"Perhaps I could give you a tour of the city?" Merissa cut in, reaching out and taking hold of my arm with an overfamiliarity that should have had me teaching her a lesson in respect right here and now. Instead, my blood burned with the touch of her and I moved into the arc of her body, taking hold of her chin to examine her more closely. Her breaths fluttered a little faster past her lips, but she didn't flinch in fear like any other Fae would have.

"You're a Seer?" I guessed and she nodded.

"I've *seen* you coming for a long time, though I didn't know it was you until now," she said, her throat bobbing, and I tracked my thumb down to it to feel it swell and fall.

"Mm," I grunted, desire blazing through me, my gaze falling to her soft lips. "And you know who I am?"

"I do now," she said.

"And yet you remain here while most Fae would run," I commented, my face so close to hers she was all I could see. I was trying to crack her resolve, intimidate her and see that fear in her eyes which I saw everywhere else. But it did not appear.

"Most Fae do not *see* what I *see*," she said with such confidence, it made me ache with curiosity.

I had *seen* a snapshot of a future we shared, and I knew I could not walk away from that fate now that it was presented to me. It had me aware of a reality in which I was profoundly happy, and as unlikely as that seemed, the beast in me wanted to seize it.

"The emperor has offered me use of one of the royal carriages." I snapped my fingers at Hamish. "Prepare it for immediate departure."

"Oh joyous day! Indeed, sire!" He raced off ahead of us down the corridor and I released Merissa, sweeping past her so that she might follow in my wake.

Instead, she moved with speed, taking my arm as she joined my side, chin held high like she had every right to touch me so. I did not scold her or push her away, my chest was expanding and there was a fierce sense of pride in me over having this beautiful creature at my side. It felt impossibly right, and yet defied all nature of logic.

We wound through the castle with its golden walls hung with towering paintings that depicted a land of fortune and prosperity as well as portraits of warriors deep in the belly of a sun-baked jungle, weapons in hand and little else. I had heard of the Marriage Trials Voldrakia was famed for, the barbaric game played to weed out the weak among the nobles and create powerful pairings to ensure the strongest of lineages. It was admirable in ways, proving themselves worthy and wetting their hands in blood before their magic had even been Awakened.

Merissa seemed familiar with the halls, so I supposed she must have been a lady of the court here. She was dressed too finely to be a servant, though probably not important enough to have partaken in the trials, or else she would not be here offering herself to me.

My pulse was pounding with the anticipation of getting her alone, and though this was the definition of madness, I could feel myself already deciding that she was mine.

Outside in the courtyard, white flowers hung from vines across the wooden pergola that stood above us between pillars of gleaming stone. Hamish hurried off to fetch a carriage and Merissa released her hold on me, moving to admire the circular well to our right while I admired her in turn.

"Does our fate not phase you?" she asked me.

"I am phased by little in this life," I said darkly, and she glanced back at me with a frown.

"I have waited so long to meet you, and now I know who you are…" she whispered almost to herself.

"Are you afraid?" I closed the gap between us, the open back of her dress drawing my hand to her skin.

I ran my knuckles up her spine and she shivered, a breath catching in her throat as I passed between her shoulder blades, a sign that her Order possessed wings.

"Should I be?" she breathed as I moved even closer behind her, brushing a lock of hair away from her neck as I leaned down to speak just to her.

"I have slaughtered countless Fae with a cold, vicious brutality in war. I have watched entire cities burn beneath the power of my Hydra's fire and seen the light fade from the eyes of my enemies like candles snuffed in the wind. They say I am soulless, that my heart is made of jet black stone. So you tell me, Merissa, should you be afraid?"

Her eyed widened as she looked back at me, my fingers tiptoeing across the base of her spine, perhaps the softest of touches I had offered anyone in what seemed like a lifetime. These hands had been soaked in blood, they had driven blades into the chests of warriors and cut them clean in two. This poor, beautiful girl must have been cursed by the stars to have been sent to me. But there wasn't enough good in me to let her go. Now she had arrived at my threshold, I was going to do everything I could to draw her into my lair.

She didn't answer my question, turning her gaze from me and looking into the well.

"I wish to know you," I commanded of her.

"You will," she said with a ring of power in her words. "We are inevitable."

Before I could get my mind around that, Hamish returned with a carriage and I placed my hand more firmly against Merissa's back, guiding her towards it.

The carriage was hewn of moonwood, the surface of it silver, gleaming with the light of the sacred celestial being of the moon, which held such influence upon our souls. The Voldrakian royals preferred to travel in more humble, archaic ways than the modern world of Solaria, and the proud white Pegasus shackled in place to pull the carriage was in a position of status far beyond what it might have seemed for such subservient work. It was an honour to serve the royals, and there was fierce competition for all positions working within the Castle of Cassiopeia for the emperor.

While in Solaria we imported and exploited mortal technology, here in Voldrakia, they preferred to keep to the traditional way of things and though I enjoyed the modern comforts of my homeland, I couldn't say I hated the way of it here.

The Pegasus whinnied politely in greeting, her horn glinting with a hint of magic before she bowed her head to us. A porter ran forward to open the door for us, but Hamish slammed into him before he made it, his huge chest knocking the man to the ground before he'd even realised what had happened.

Hamish whipped open the door, bowing so low his nose nearly touched the cobblestones, his fine, blood red jacket straining against the size of him. He was a muscular man, but his fondness for baked goods had seen him soften a little this last year. He may have appeared to be the friendliest Fae on earth, but anyone who underestimated him was a fool. I had seen his wrath in play, his loyalty to the Vega bloodline unfaltering, and with that came a certain defensive fury in him which I rather enjoyed witnessing.

"Thank you," Merissa said, pausing as I encouraged her to enter before me.

My hand was held out in offering to steady her as she climbed up into the carriage, my other held against my back and my gaze riveted on the beauty of her face. She was...unreal. As captivating in her movements as she was her features. I had known beauty before, I'd had it thrown at me, offered by boundless Fae, but never had I looked at someone and felt their beauty right down to the darkest corners of my soul.

There was something different about her, and though I was half aware the visions she had fed me could be some trick, I had spent so many days in darkness recently that I was willing to place my head on the chopping block to discover whether she was a con-artist or not. I was the Savage King after all, the last of the Hydra Order and a man who struck terror into the hearts of children and adults alike. I could handle one Fae if I had to.

"What is your name?" Merissa asked kindly of Hamish and his eyes whipped up to her, his jaw falling slack, his brow breaking out in a sweat.

"H-H-H-H-Hamish Grus, my lady. Oh good gravy nuts, forgive my bumbling and stumbling. It is just - oh! I cannot say. I must not, or my tongue will wrap itself in a bindy knot and then where shall we be? In the ravines of Rabbaganoot, that's where!"

Merissa smiled widely at him like she was charmed by his oddness instead of being unsettled by it. It usually went one way or the other with him.

"Do tell me," Merissa encouraged. "Or you'll leave me forever curious, and as a Seer, that is quite the curse, Hamish."

He stared at her then boomed a laugh, before shooting a look at me and trying to choke it out of existence, literally wrapping a hand around his throat to stop it.

"Come now, Hamish. Do not leave the lady in suspense," I said, my tone sharp as always and he straightened like I'd shoved a rod of iron into his spine.

"Of course, sire. Absotive-alutely. Where are my manners? Lost in the sand like a crab in a cranny, it seems. How dare I jibber and jabber this way in front of you and your elegant companion. You must have me whipped upon our return to the castle. In fact, I shall do it myself with a flogger, your highness. I shall flip and flap and whip my windycoat until I have repented-"

"*Hamish*," I growled and he turned beetroot red, falling into a stream of apologies that made little sense to me. I wasn't sure I'd ever seen him this flustered, and that was saying something for a man who had sobbed like a new-born babe when I'd awarded him a medal of honour for his service to me. I'd had to have two men carry him away because he could not find a way to stop bawling.

"I just meant to say," he composed himself, snatching a handkerchief from his breast pocket and dabbing at his brow, his eyes darting between me and Merissa before settling on her. She was being surprisingly patient with him, and her smile never dropped, giving me time to memorise the shape of it. Her mouth was a playground of sin that I had tasted in the visions she'd shared, and Hamish was taking up far too much of the time I could have been making those visions into a reality.

"I simply meant to say, my lady, that I have not seen his highness stare at a woman this long. He has blinked but seven times in the past minute alone – I have counted every one, and I am yet to count an eighth."

My teeth snapped together as Merissa turned to me as if to confirm Hamish's damn words and I blinked firmly to prove a point, my gaze swivelling onto my servant instead of her and making him double over in an apologetic bow. I had commanded him to speak his thoughts, so I could only blame myself for this, but the sensation of heat climbing my neck left me feeling exposed, and I did not like that one bit.

"Is that true, Hail?" Merissa asked, speaking my name as if I was no king, just a man she could address and demand anything of. It occurred to me that there wasn't much I could think to deny her. "Have you been staring at me?"

My hand was still outstretched, waiting for her to take it so that I might help her into the carriage, whilst also anticipating the enjoyment of feeling how smooth and warm her skin was against mine once more.

"I would not use that word. Studying, maybe. Assessing the threat," I said, using the tone of a powerful man who knew never to show weakness to an enemy. And as I was yet to decide if she was that, I would be sure to assert my position of dominance before she got any ideas of finding my vulnerabilities.

"Threat?" she laughed, and fuck, I felt that laugh everywhere. Cock included.

"What's your Order?" I demanded suddenly, needing to figure out exactly what skills she might possess in an attack.

In answer, she let two beautiful silver wings appear at her back, flexing behind her and gleaming in the sun before she folded them neatly once again.

"A Harpy," I muttered through a lump in my throat as Hamish fell into a spew of compliments I couldn't hear.

She was stunning, every feather like liquid satin, so perfect I ached to run my fingers across them. But then she looked at me in a way that said she had caught me staring again and the insinuation had my fury rising.

"Are you going to continue to leave me standing here like a fool with my hand draining of blood?" I asked roughly, sensing her mocking me with that expression.

I could not remember a time another Fae had not shrunk from me when I used that tone, but this woman did not seem to be like other Fae. She lifted her chin, her smile faltering and power sparking in her eyes, a dominance of her own on display. It got my blood pumping, the challenge in her dark eyes making me believe I had not yet won her over, star-given visions or otherwise. But she was mine, she had declared it as such. So I would lay this claim, because she was the first thing I had seen in a very long time that made me feel like myself again. Like a man with desires that ran deeper than bloodshed and war. I wanted a taste of that, and I had a feeling one taste would not be enough.

"Yes, I think I will," she decided, sweeping past me, her right wing slapping me in the face as she climbed into the carriage without going anywhere near my offered hand.

Feeling the softness of those feathers did little to assuage the anger that exploded within my chest at the insult she had just given me right here in the castle grounds for anyone to see.

"Sire, please, take a breath. Like we practised, one big jiffy jolly breath in, and one huffing Mary of a breath out, remember?" Hamish begged, but I was already climbing into the carriage and snapping the door shut behind us, leaving him to climb on the back or be left in the dust.

Merissa had settled herself in by the window, the white slats across it giving her a view out, but they were enchanted not to let anyone see in. Her wings were gone now, but the insult of the slap she had given me with them still burned against my cheek.

The darkness in me unfolded, waking up like a creature of destruction, and it demanded retribution. I lunged at her, my knee pressing between her thighs into the folds of her dress and my other hand gripping her jaw as I pinned her back against her seat. Her eyes flashed with ire and her hands came up to cast magic, but she had just stepped into one of the enchanted carriages of the Voldrakian emperor. No one could cast magic in here but him, not even me.

She cursed as she remembered she was disarmed and it came down to my physical strength against hers. A match she could not win.

"I am the Savage King," I hissed, a viper of malice coiling within my mind and stealing away every emotion in me. I was a void, but a few cruel, wicked things lived on in me. Hate, rage, bloodlust. Perhaps this woman truly didn't know who she was dealing with here, but I would make it apparent. "That name is not simply propaganda, it is who I am. If you do not know of me yet, then let me warn you now, for it will be your last chance to leave. I will let you run from me, Merissa. I will open this door and cast you back to the life you came from if you wish it. But know this. If you choose to stay after I have told you the truth of me, I will never let you go. You will walk willingly into your captivity, because that is what this will be. The moment I laid eyes on you, an obsession awoke, and it will not die. I know that much of myself. I am possessive, and selfish, and I when I lay eyes on something I want, it is never denied me."

"So who are you, Hail, because my visions show me a man who loves with all his heart," she said. "Is that not who you are?"

I released an empty laugh, leaning close enough to breathe her breath, stealing it from her. "I am hell on earth. I am a plague in Fae form, my veins are gilded with hellfire, and there are times I am not even in control of my own inhumanity."

"You are not who you say you are." She frowned, her eyes glazing like she could *see* some other truth and was deciding it was so. That in itself ignited a pyre of wrath in me. Who was she to say who I was? Perhaps The Sight was lying to her, but I would not lie. I would bare the truth and she would fall upon it like a blade.

"I am the most dangerous creature you have ever met. I am unpredictable, even to myself. Sometimes violence calls my name so loud, I swear the stars have stitched that word into my soul. So if you stay, I cannot promise you will survive me," I whispered, so close to her, my lips grazed hers and she shivered like she wanted more. Like this danger in me didn't scare her, but only drew her closer.

My hand snaked down to her throat, squeezing lightly to test my theory, and her pupils dilated, her thighs parting a little and telling me all I needed to know about the kinds of things she enjoyed. My cock was hardening in my pants and the air between us was starting to feel impossible to breathe, like the only source of oxygen lay within her and I needed to draw it from her mouth into my very lungs to survive.

"So what will it be?" I asked, my voice draped in sin.

Before I was king, I couldn't have claimed to be a perfect man, but something about seizing the crown had sent me spiralling down a path of damnation. I was guilty of heinous crimes, things I still shuddered at when the memories came for me in the dead of night, and between the ruin and regret, I had been twisted into this man. This monster. Now I had finally found something that was pure and so help me, I was going to claim it.

Merissa's eyes slid past me to the carriage door, and I had the most terrible dread that she was going to choose to leave. It would take everything in my power to withdraw from her now and let her go, and I knew I would think of her until the end of time. But this choice was hers, once it was done, it would be final. I made a silent vow on that.

"Choose," I commanded, and her eyes snapped back to me, full of that fire that spoke of the strength in her. She was a powerful Fae, that was clear, but it was more than that. She held the gift of foresight, and she could *see* what paths lay ahead of us. But if all she *saw* was a man who loved her, the stars were surely playing games with her, convincing her to offer herself to a beast who had long forgotten the meaning of love.

"I will stay," she decided, her voice ringing around the carriage.

I lowered my hand to take hers in mine.

"Swear it," I demanded, and though magic couldn't be cast here, the vow would mean enough for now until she could make the deal official. Our palms clasped, her chest rising and falling, determination flaring in her eyes.

So many had left me. My mother and father were with the stars now, and since my ascension to the throne, my friends had grown wary of me, distant. I had pushed them away too for fear of what I was capable of.

In the dead of night, I craved to be wanted in the way any Fae craved such things, and now this beguiling woman had come showing me visions of a life with her, and a love that could transcend time. If it were real, then it was a temptation I was no more able of resisting than a Vampire could resist blood. I was starved of true connection, it had been years since I'd felt anything like this, and nothing truly compared. Now she was here, as wild and impossible as it seemed, I knew she was meant for me. I knew it in the way I knew the sun would rise tomorrow. Like she had said, it was inevitable. *We* were inevitable.

"I swear I am yours. I will not leave you, Hail," she promised, and those words set my heart into a riot. I had no idea what I had done to deserve this, or if I might wake any moment from the dream of it, but I could feel its realness pounding through the centre of my being. She was familiar to me like my own soul was familiar to me. As confoundingly insane as it was, I could not see any other future for myself but her now that we had met.

I released her hand, my mouth coming down on hers and she arched up to meet me like she was as desperate for this kiss as I was. I had tasted her in the visions, but nothing compared to the real thing.

"*Mine*," I spoke into her soft lips and she answered with her tongue tracing my own, taking control of a kiss I should have commanded. I banged my fist against the wall beside me in an order for the Pegasus to get going and the carriage took off away from the castle.

"I'm going to have you piece by piece," I said as I fell down to my knees for a woman I had just fucking met.

I shoved her legs apart and she dragged her dress higher for me, revealing the deep bronze colour of her legs and the white silk panties between her thighs. I gripped her knees, spreading her legs even wider for me and watching her face as I hunted for a blush, a prize for me to claim. But she stared right back at me instead, no shame or fluster there, just a heated lust which burned right through my chest.

The knowing in her eyes left me raw, even my own royal Seer had never made me feel like they were the keeper of my destiny. My life was already intertwined with hers, and she had experienced us through visions before I had even begun to know her. But there was endless time for me to know it all, and I was going to let her guide me into this madness, even if it led me down a doomed path, because whether she was a trickster or not, I was too far under her spell to turn back now.

My cock was throbbing, blood leaving my brain far behind as I fell into the animal within me, and let my basest desires take over.

I released her knees, taking hold of her panties and tearing them clean off of her, but she didn't gasp like I expected, her legs hooking over my shoulders instead and her heels digging into my back in a demand.

"I will find something that makes you blush," I said determinedly.

"I can *see* everything you want to do to me. Try being less predictable, Hail," she taunted, and I growled, nipping her inner thigh which only made her moan for me.

Her legs wrapped tighter around me and I tasted her pussy in one long stroke of my tongue, her hips rising to give me full access to her. The moment my tongue dragged over her clit and she released a moan that coloured the air fucking beautifully, my obsession deepened to something all-consuming. A thing I doubted I would ever return from, and I sure as hell had no mind to.

I slid my hand under her ass, clasping hard and holding her where I wanted her as I drove my tongue against her pretty flesh, lapping at her clit, her hips rocking in time with my mouth to a seductive rhythm. I was so hard, I was dying to be inside her, but I wasn't going to take her yet. No, I would build up to that, enjoy her in every way I could, and have her begging for me to fuck her before I was done playing this game.

She was mine now, and I knew the pleasure that could be had from delayed gratification. The anticipation would nearly kill us before I gave in.

"Say my name when you come," I commanded. "Say it in that entitled tone you keep using every time you speak it. And when you're done, I want you to call me your king and renounce all loyalty to your emperor." I looked up at her as I waited for her to agree, my mouth wet with her arousal as her heels dug harder into my back in a demand for more.

I was asking a hell of a lot here, to release all loyalty to her empire and pledge herself to me. But if her gift of The Sight was as great as she claimed, then she would have *seen* that future already, she would know I would demand this. I had to for Solaria, but it was deeper than that, a trait of my Order, but a simple fact of my very essence too. Like Dragons, Hydras were possessive, but there were differences too. My most coveted treasures were few and far between, but when chosen, they were placed upon a pedestal and nourished with all I had to give. The Palace of Souls was one of them, a home I had poured magic into that came from the root of my being and beyond. The Imperial Star was the second, and Merissa would be my third and final treasure. The most hallowed of all, and the one I would cherish the most. But that did not mean to say she would be safe with me. There was no guarantee of that, because when the darkness came for me again, I could not control what pain I delivered to the world. Her included.

"I will say it," she agreed, and excitement flashed through me. "But only if you call me your queen and vow you will never bed another Fae again but me."

My eyebrows arched at that and I tasted my lips, hungering for more of her, this woman who I had known less than an hour and who already had me on my knees worshipping her.

It was surprisingly easy to agree to her wishes, the thought of claiming any other Fae but her already unappealing. It made me wonder if she would be the making or the end of me. Only time would tell.

"My queen." I bowed my head, hearing her inhale just a little like the stars hadn't been sure of what my answer might be to that. "There will be no one else."

"Have me," she said, and I needed no more encouragement than that.

I reared forward, sucking her clit before driving two fingers into the burning heat of her, her pussy clamping tight around them as she started to come for me. I pumped them in time with the fast strokes of my tongue, bringing her to the edge of ecstasy and groaning as she fell for me. Her hips bucked and her moans grew louder and louder, wrapping around me and setting my soul alight.

"*Hail*," she moaned, making my cock ache for her.

Her thighs clamped tight around my head, and I smiled against her skin, kissing and sucking more gently as I prolonged her pleasure. She finally released me, slumping back in her seat and pushing her dress down as I stood, wiping my mouth with the back of my hand as I grinned savagely.

She panted in her seat, a smile gracing her lips as I rested my hand on the wall above her and arched a brow. "And the rest," I prompted.

Her throat bobbed, but her eyes glinted with smugness like she had won some prize here. It was entirely the other way around though, and I had to fear what she might think when she really got to know me. Would she regret her choice to stay the second she saw my true nature?

"I claim you as my king," she said breathlessly.

"And?" I pushed, leaning right over her as I rested my other hand above her too, gripping the wood to steady myself against the jolts and bumps of the carriage.

"And I will make a wonderful queen," she said, leaning forward and caressing the length of me through my pants, making my thoughts scatter. A villainous look gripped my face, victory sizzling through my veins and feeling far superior to any battle I had ever won. Though I was half aware she had not actually renounced her loyalty to the emperor. I would ensure she did so soon.

Before I could get carried away with how good her hand felt on my cock, I moved to sit opposite her, admiring her as she turned her gaze out the window, my lust for her sharp and demanding. Though that was all part of the enjoyment. I would deny myself of her as long as I could hold out.

I slid my father's ring off my finger and rolled it over in my palm, the Hydra etched into the gold a reminder of the monster in me that had also lived in him. I leaned forward, taking her left hand and moving to slide it onto her ring finger to seal this deal between us, but my way was blocked by a band of silver. The other ring held a surname which curved under a crest, setting off a bell of familiarity in my head.

"What the fuck is this?" I growled and Merissa tugged her hand out of my grip, her features pinching. "Are you married?"

Did she already belong to another man? Was I stealing her away from some poor fucker who had no idea of the miserable fate I was about to secure for him? She was mine regardless, I would find a way to deal with it.

"Betrothed," she said quickly, and I ran my tongue across my teeth.

"I shall have it dissolved."

"It's not that simple," she said, her brow tight. "He won the right to marry me in the Marriage Trials I competed in. Do you not know anything of my kingdom's laws?"

Anger raked through my chest and my skin became as hard as iron as my Order stirred within me. So she had competed in the trials after all. That changed things, but only in terms of making this more complex. I would not relinquish her to anyone, fiancé or otherwise.

Even the mere knowledge that another man already had a claim on her was making murder hum a tune in my veins. Death was my easiest answer, but death of a noble would invoke war, and my entire purpose of this trip was to secure peace and prove I was not always such a merciless king. I had thrown about furious words earlier, threatening to kill the emperor to Hamish, but only because the darkness had slipped in again. I had to remind myself that I was here for peace, not war.

"Who are you?" I boomed, realising I should have asked this far sooner, before I had let my maddening want for her take me to my knees for her.

She sat up straighter in her seat, and I realised even before she said it that she was royal. It was so star damned obvious now. "I am Princess Merissa Adhara, daughter of the Emperor Adhara, and I am betrothed to Arturo Boötes."

I punched the wall of the carriage, the wood exploding around my fist and Hamish yelped somewhere outside. "And you did not think to mention this sooner?" I roared.

Though she remained on her seat and was far smaller than me, she did not appear to be rattled by my outburst, nor in any way submissive to my power. "You did not ask."

I huffed a breath of fury, dark purple smoke spilling from my lips as my Hydra awoke more fully.

"You showed me a future of us together, so you must *see* a way around your betrothal?" I hissed and her lips lifted at me turning to her for advice, an act that seemed so natural despite her being a stranger.

"It will not be easy," she said hesitantly. "Many actions you take could start a war."

"Then there will be a war," I growled, determined to have her even though I was casting away my bid for peace already. The dark always claimed me so easily, and it was getting hungry again.

My suspicions over this entire thing were circling in me now too. Had this all been some plot devised by the emperor? Sending his Seer daughter to me to paint fake visions in my mind and make me vulnerable to her?

Those visions though…they had been so real, how could they be anything but the truth?

"If you go to war with my family, I will not stand by your side," she said in anger. "I will not let you attack my people in some assertion of power to claim me."

"*Your* people are the ones who have been threatening war. I came here for peace."

"Peace?" she scoffed. "I heard you speak of beheading my father when I came to your rooms before."

Fuck.

"I was angry. Sometimes I cannot control myself, what I do or what I say." I scraped a hand through my hair.

"That sounds like an excuse," she accused.

"Excuse?" I snarled. "I wish it was an excuse. I wish I did not have to fight this darkness in me, but it is a part of me, and it only deepens with each day that passes."

I could feel the chaos rising and tried not to fall too deeply into it, knowing when I came back to the light, I would no doubt find myself in a bloody war with Voldrakia and a stolen princess in tow as I made my return to Solaria.

Merissa frowned like she was trying to understand, her anger softening. "You will not go to war. You will make the right decision," she said, her confidence in me clear and I scoffed.

"I do not remember the last good decision I made. Even the well-intended ones tend to rot." I dragged my eyes from her, falling deeper into that twisted place inside me. I could feel it coming upon me, the hunger for war, the need for destruction, to crush all enemies that stood in my way to getting what I wanted.

"Destroy any who oppose you. Seize as much land as you can. Expand the Solarian borders to the edges of the world."

The words echoed through my mind like they were gifted from the stars, though sometimes I feared it was just the darkness talking.

"Hail," Merissa breathed like she could *see* something terrible coming, and I knew it was coming too without the need for The Sight. It always felt like this just before I did something unimaginably terrible, the reins of fate slipping from my grasp and the beast in me taking over.

My hands began to shake, and before I lost complete control, I threw the carriage door open and pointed to the sky. "Spread your wings and fly away from here. I can summon you through the ring. It will burn hot when it is safe to come back." I grabbed her hand, pushing my ring onto that same finger that her fiancé had claimed.

She took hold of my arm but I yanked it free of her, the need for brutality building to a roaring thunder inside me and the stars help anyone close enough to fall at my mercy.

"I'm not leaving you," she said passionately, clasping my cheek in her hand and making me look at her.

The final pieces of sanity slipped from my hold, and I gazed at this precious creature before me, fear crushing my chest as I pictured her bloody and lifeless at my feet.

I fisted her dress in my hand, dragging her to her feet while her eyes flashed with visions of the future, the terror crossing her features showing her exactly what I was capable of. And that fate was coming towards us like a freight train. Was I going to lose her before I had even begun to know her?

I leaned in to speak in her ear, her body bent against mine as I caged her unyieldingly. "You are about learn why they call me the Savage King, Princess. Start praying to the stars, for they are the only ones who can save you now."

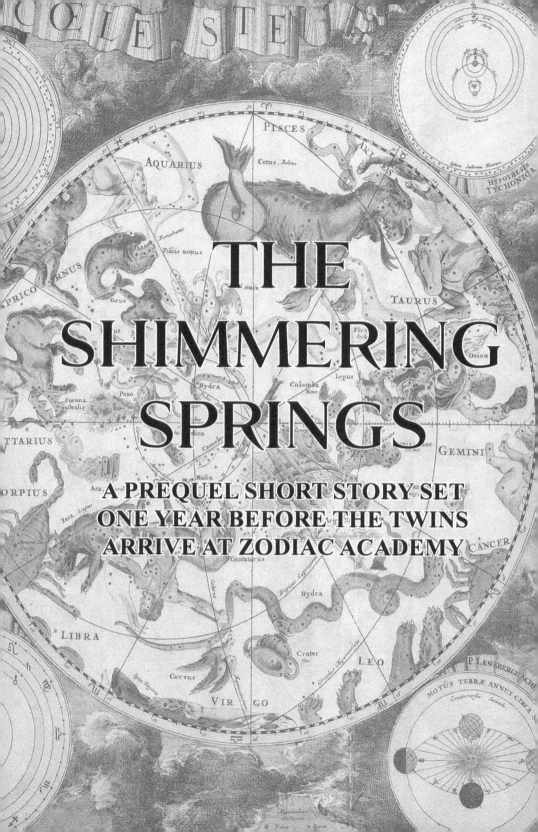

THE SHIMMERING SPRINGS

A PREQUEL SHORT STORY SET ONE YEAR BEFORE THE TWINS ARRIVE AT ZODIAC ACADEMY

LIONEL

FROM THE LAIR OF LIONEL...

And so we move on through the years, bypassing much cunning and brutality on my part, all kept hidden within the shadows as I bided my time and prepared to seize the throne for myself.

Of course, it was not as simple as I'd hoped after I secured the demise of the Vega line – I should have foreseen the need to strike at the Nymphs as savagely as we had to in retaliation for the death of our monarch.

Initially, I needed to maintain my place within the Celestial Council and make certain that no suspicion led back to me. Although I am of course the mightiest of them all, I could not risk them thinking me a traitor. Individually, I had no doubt that I could have taken down Tiberius Rigel, Antonia Capella and Melinda Altair, but if they believed me a traitor they would have struck at me as one to apprehend me and even a Fae so great as I could not stand against the three of them at once.

So alas, I had to unite with them again, joining them in their decimation of Nymph kind and depriving myself of the allies I had so skilfully used to rid myself of the Savage King and his wife.

Lying in wait made the most sense back then. I dedicated years to solidifying my plans and gaining back the trust of the Nymphs who I had been forced to help eradicate – no mean feat indeed. And yes, I had to spend time moulding my Heir into my image too, for what was the point in me claiming a kingdom and having an unworthy Heir to inherit it once my time to rule was done?

That leads us to this tale of debauchery which I have decided to include here for your perusal so that you may see as clearly as I do how utterly unsuitable for rule the following generation of Councillors are. There is very little which those in a position of power such as ours cannot claim in the name of pleasure, but the lines of Capella and Altair uniting is unthinkable. Their union would become of superior nature to the bonds those of my Heir and the Rigel boy held. As such their pairing could never have been allowed to come to pass as well they knew and yet here as you shall witness, they flouted those rules time and again.

Who can blame me for seeing so clearly that a firm hand was needed to take the helm of our fine kingdom? Who can blame me for taking up the position of power before they dared lunge for it themselves? I may not have known about this dalliance at the time, but the existence of it only enforces my own need to claim the power before they had the chance to try and move against Darius themselves.

Of course, the matter of my first-born child is a shame which we will come to later...

SETH

CHAPTER ONE

I raised my wolfy nose towards the full blood moon and howled, the answering call of my pack sending a rush of power slamming through my veins. I'd beaten Maurice down this very morning, the pack politics still a little rocky since I'd arrived at the academy and asserted my dominance. I'd had so many fights this week that if I hadn't been taught healing before I'd come here, I'd have been covered in cuts and bruises just like the rest of the freshmen were.

Most of them were trailing around campus being feasted on by Vampires and Sirens, beat on by Minotaurs and pissed off Dragon shifters too. Well, one pissed off Dragon shifter in particular considering there weren't a lot of those. Darius was taking a sadistic kind of joy in playing predator just like me and the rest of the Heirs were since we'd started at Zodiac. It was a new hunting ground, and the pecking order wasn't fixed yet, so we were having one helluva time establishing it.

The older years were testing us, trying to find out if we really were made from the strongest flesh and blood in the kingdom and fuck did it feel good to unleash the power that had been brimming in my veins ever since our early Awakening.

I'd been pack leader over my siblings for years and no one had posed a challenge to me in so long that it felt incredible to be able to let loose at last. On day one, I'd walked right up to the top of Aer Tower, stormed into the Aer Captain's room and kicked him in the balls. He'd shifted into a Griffin and tried to peck my eyes out with his giant beak, and I'd blasted him with every scrap of air power in my veins, sending him smashing through a window and then I'd beat up his little buddies one at a time too when they'd postured at me.

It was funny how arrogant some of the Fae in this place were, even though I was the Heir of one of the most powerful Fae in the land, they still fancied their chances. But I was an unstoppable force, a hellhound with a thirst for all the souls I desired. My mom always said every goal in life should revolve around power. Every win, every fight, every fuck, it all had to elevate my rank in this world. So I made it my mission in life to succeed in every way possible. I wanted to be the best alongside my friends, the four of us like stars right here on earth, deciding the fates of our kind. We were kings among cattle and I was ready to rule.

That very same day I'd taken my position as Aer Captain, Caleb had fought with the Medusa girl who ruled Terra House. Apparently she'd fallen to her knees and sucked him off right there and then, though maybe that was just my imagination running riot. I mean, that seemed like the natural thing to do after you got beat by a powerful leviathan like Cal. Or me.

It was what my new pack had been doing for me all week. Every time I beat a new challenger, they either fell into line and started begging for my cock, or they came back another day for a second or third beat down. I enjoyed both equally. Sex and fighting were the same kind of thrill, chasing a high while you sweated your way through the match. Someone was always forced to submit. And that someone was never me, because even if I was beat, I'd come back. Time and again. I'd claw my way back from the brink of death just to prove I couldn't be beat. It was in my blood, a fountain of power was bursting through my chest and I wanted everyone to drink from it so they knew the taste of a true winner.

Darius had claimed Ignis House in a ferocious battle with the Cerberus who had been ruling over it which had left the guy in three pieces in the Uranus Infirmary. I'd been there for that one, howling in encouragement as the two beasts collided on the lawn outside their house. I'd even gotten splattered with some of the blood from the hind leg Darius had severed when he'd tossed it aside. It had been epic. Well worth the detention he'd gotten for excessive use of Order skills. Besides, legs could just pop right back on and work right as rain after several days in the infirmary, lengthy magical healing and a whole lot of agony, so what was the problem?

I'd seen Max's fight too when he'd lured the Pegasus girl to the Orb and used the full strength of his Siren gifts to make her give out every dark and dirty secret she kept until she handed him her captaincy with tears running down her face. All of it was as public as we could make it. Our parents had encouraged us to make a splash, to hit the headlines, make the Fae here understand that we hadn't been bluffing when we'd told The Celestial Times of our immense strength.

Sometimes it was cruel, and sometimes I enjoyed it when it was. The darkness in me had grown since I'd gained my power, I knew how easily I could be corrupted by it. But when I was alone with the other Heirs, away from the pressures of the world and the call of ultimate, unending power, I found myself again. The guy who cracked jokes, who loved those boys deeper than I even knew my heart could go, and who wanted nothing more than to stay in that bubble for as long as I could. Ruling this world seemed so damn appealing so long as they were always at my side. It was us against the world, ruling from the top, because anything less was complete failure. It was what I'd been born for, what I was made to do, and I was sure I'd have crumbled under all of the demands upon my soul if it weren't for the fact that my best friends in the whole fucking world shared that burden too. We wore our armour on the outside, so thick and impenetrable that no one could get through it but us. But within it, we had our own circle of safety, comfort, freedom. It was a tiny space built just for us, but so long as it existed, I could face everything else. I could be the monster the world needed me to be, the ruthless creature who was revered and applauded and who everyone placed their faith in.

I barked to my pack in goodbye, veering off the path and darting away from them into the undergrowth to a chorus of mournful howls as I abandoned them, heading towards the three Fae who I needed to be with tonight.

This week had ben exhilarating, but it was exhausting too, and I needed to shed the war paint this evening and just *be*.

I soon made it to King's Hollow, our little sanctuary in The Wailing Wood that we'd claimed for ourselves the very first day we'd arrived here. There hadn't been many Fae attending the academy who were powerful enough to unlock the secret of it since our parents' time, so the place had practically been calling our names to be used for our own secret paradise.

I shifted back into my Fae form and pressed my hand to the trunk, the tree letting me inside as the magic washed over me. It had only ever meant to be for the most powerful of Fae here, and since we'd claimed it for our own, we'd strengthened the wards around it so only we could gain access. Though sometimes Professor Orion showed up here to hang out with Darius, promptly disappearing whenever me or any of the Heirs appeared. I knew Darius had been friends with him for years, but the dude had issues, and since he'd shot a peach into my mouth during sex ed the other day and nearly choked me to death on it for talking too loudly about my sexual experiences, I couldn't say I was much of a fan of him.

I shoved the door open at the top of the stairs, practically panting with how excited I was to see everyone and as I spotted Cal on the couch, I ran at him, diving on top of him and licking his face.

"By the sun, put your fucking cock away," he demanded, though he laughed as I continued to lick his rough cheek and nuzzle him.

I whipped around at the creak of a floorboard behind me, finding Darius trying to tiptoe away from me and I leapt on him next, wrapping my arms and legs around him as he cursed and I howled my joy at seeing him.

"Clothes," Max said firmly, pulling me off of Darius and shoving a pair of sweatpants into my hand, a wave of willingness washing from him into me.

I pulled them on, pouncing on Max next, making sure he got a big lick too. They loved my licks. Even when they grimaced and pushed me off, they never tried that hard to stop me. I guessed I was just irresistibly adorable or something. Magnetic, my mom called me.

"What are we gonna do tonight?" I asked as I released him, throwing myself down on the couch as Caleb flicked a finger and cast a vine to grab me a beer and plant it in my hand. I opened the bottle with my teeth, taking a long swig to quench my thirst from the run I'd been on with my pack. "Shall we watch some more of that Pegasus porn we found online? Two horns, one cup."

"Nah, I wanna party," Caleb downed his beer and I watched his throat work as he swallowed every drop.

"I wanna fuck with some other freshmen later," Darius said darkly, a smirk curling his lips as a little smoke filtered between them. He was a savage bastard, and he always got the wicked in me burning a little hotter. I was pretty sure we were a bad influence on each other, but not even the stars could tear us apart now if they wanted to. We were brothers forged and made, and there wasn't a force in Solaria who could crack the foundations we'd built for ourselves. Our paths were set. The Solarian throne was our fate and there were no roadblocks in our way to stop us from claiming it.

"Have you got anyone in particular in mind?" Max asked, excitement trickling into the room from him and making my own keenness heighten.

"A couple of nutcase royalists have been studying prophecies in the library, trying to find clues to our downfall and the rise of the old bloodlines," Darius said and we all sniggered at that.

Yeah, the chances of the Vegas rising up from the dead and returning for their throne was as likely as the peace sign making a solid comeback.

"Is Grus involved?" Max asked, his voice deepening a bit.

"She's always involved in that shit," Caleb said. "I think she's cracked in the head."

Darius shrugged. "I don't even give a shit about their insane endeavours, but a little birdy told me they're having a party tonight and guess what they called it?"

"What?" I bounced up and down excitedly.

"The Anti-Heir Hoo-Ha," Darius deadpanned. "And according to my source, they're planning some big, *hilarious* stunt to try and humiliate us."

Caleb's finger knotted in my shirt and he yanked me closer, making me look to him and realise his fangs had extended. He was fucking hungry and that made me kinda hungry too.

"Tell me more," he urged of Darius and I was pretty sure he hadn't even realised he had hold of me. Angry little Vampire. I loved when he got murderous. It made me want to howl to the damn moon.

"Alright, sit down." Darius walked away, grabbing another beer and sending a lick of frost out across the glass.

Max smirked as he dropped into his favourite seat.

Darius had an air of danger about him tonight that had my skin prickling all over. I could always sense my friends' moods, whether they wanted my snuggles, needed my snuggles, or if it was simply not snuggle time. But the mood which always got me the most riled up was this one, the animals in us peering from our eyes and the atmosphere crackling with tension. The stars were turning our way, amused by what chaos we were going to cause tonight, and we never disappointed them.

Darius dropped into the wingback by the fireplace and the flames roared behind him, his Element taking charge of them and sending heat blazing through the space. He was left in shadow, silhouetted by the blaze at his back and for a second, he had a look of his father about him, his eyes narrowed and the slant of his mouth twisted by cruelty. A whimper left my throat and I leaned into Caleb, not liking the feel of Lionel Acrux here in our sacred space. Darius was rarely soft with anyone, but if he was, it was with us. And that was the truth of my friend, not the one moulded by his father's hands. I liked to play with power as much as the rest of the Heirs, but I didn't want to be carbon copies of our parents. I wanted to still be *us* when we took our seats on the Council, but sometimes it scared me how easily I could become a fierce and heartless creature. Where did the games stop, and the brutality begin? It all seemed to slip together so easily, especially now that we were in a place where we were encouraged daily to embrace our inner Fae, to crush our lessers, to rise like we were born to.

I shoved my worries down into the place in my chest which I never looked at, locking them away and straightening my spine as I faced the darkness in my friend with the darkness in me. I'd worn it like a cape at first, easily unclasped and folded away whenever I needed, but more and more it felt like a second skin, binding to my flesh never to let go. Between these four walls, I could still peel it off, but it was all too easy not to. The problem with darkness was that it tasted like rapture and freedom. And fuck did I want to be free.

"They'll be down at The Shimmering Springs," Darius explained. "Grus is trying to recruit for some sad little society that'll actively oppose us."

Max barked a laugh, swiping his thumb over his beer and making the liquid sail out of it right into his mouth with a touch of his water magic. "That girl irritates the hell out of me. I can't believe Orion put her on the Pitball team. Do you know what she said to me in Cardinal Magic yesterday? That I couldn't even diddle a dandelion if it bloomed beneath my fiddlestick and told me where to put it. What the fuck does that even mean?" Max scrubbed his knuckles over his chin.

"Yeah, she's nutso, man," I agreed.

"I could diddle a dandelion," Max muttered, clearly still caught up on what Grus had said to him as he frowned moodily at his beer.

"Just ignore her," Cal said, shrugging and slinging his arm over the back of the seat behind me, spreading his legs wide, looking like he gave no shits in the world. His approach was always the chillest road he could take. He was less inclined to be an active prick unless the opportunity was right under his nose, then he couldn't resist. Though I swear he liked watching it more than doing it, his twisty little smile always following me whenever I picked out a freshman to play with.

"Oh, like it's so easy," Max tossed at him. "She's everywhere and she's willing to go against us single handed too. I cast a silencing bubble around her in Water Elemental class so I couldn't hear her speech on the 'Depravity of the Charlatan Council' but she just started miming it to me instead!" Max's right eye was getting twitchy and I could see this girl was really getting to him.

"Don't worry, brother," I said, smiling at him brightly. "We'll crush her tonight and she won't bother you anymore."

Max offered me a half smile in thanks, though I could see his thoughts were still whirling about Grus. Fucking royalists. They were basically a cult at this point, just a few lonely larrys still clinging to the old ideals and pretending things could ever go back to the way they'd been. It was sick if you asked me. The Savage King had bent our kingdom over and fucked it in the ass without consent. Grus had to be cuckoo if she wanted that kind of leadership reinstated, though whenever that argument was tossed at these whackos, they always argued that the king's failings didn't dismiss the good he'd done in his earlier years, or the good the royals had done centuries before him. But what they forgot to take into account was that the Celestial Council were the solution to allowing failings like that to ever happen again. The Savage King had lost his mind and taken it out on Solaria, but if that happened to one member of the Council, then there were three others in place to keep them in check and overthrow them if necessary. It was a balance, a much better way of protecting the people of Solaria than allowing one royal on the throne to decide everything no matter what mood they happened to be in. I may have been a power hungry fuck, but I did take my future seriously. And when I sat on the Council at the sides of my brothers, I knew we'd do the right thing by Solaria because the four of us were bound by duty and had been trained to rule well our entire lives. There was no one better than us to lead our kingdom to greatness, and I believed that from the bottom of my soul. Because if it wasn't true, my entire life was null and void and I might as well just throw myself into the giant volcano in Beruvia and be done with it.

Darius told us some more about the plans he'd heard for Grus's party and I started to relax as we sank a few beers and our conversation turned to light-hearted stories from our childhood instead. I could feel the blackness in my chest giving way to rays of sunlight as I cracked laughs and bounced up and down on the couch.

"Do you remember that time we decided to run away?" Caleb said with a wide ass grin on his face.

"Oh my stars, we were like ten weren't we?" Max said, leaning forward in his seat as his eyes gleamed with the memory.

"It was right after that meeting with our parents where they impressed the 'importance of being an Heir' on us," I said, putting on a deep voice for those words as I mimicked Lionel.

Darius carved a hand down his face. "Fuck, I'd forgotten about that. I took a bunch of Father's gold in my backpack."

"We were gonna hitchhike our way to the Polar Capital," I said, a laugh tumbling from my throat.

"Yeah, only because we couldn't get our hands on any stardust. Even Lionel didn't leave that lying around," Caleb said as he chuckled and sipped more of his beer. "Do you remember that stupid blue flat cap you wore to try and 'blend in'?" Caleb nudged me and I pursed my lips.

"I still stand by that hat. Who's gonna expect an Heir to be wearing a flat cap?" I insisted and Max roared a laugh.

"You looked like such a dickhead," Max said through his laugh.

"You can talk. You turned up in that big trench coat that belonged to your dad," I threw back at him and Max's laugh stuttered out in his throat.

"It had like fifty magical pockets which I could hide shit in," he defended himself as Darius and Caleb shared a look, grinning stupidly.

"It was four times too big for you," Caleb said and I laughed, loving that we were mocking Max now instead of me.

"It trailed along the ground," Darius snorted and smoke poured from his lips as he lost it and Max gave up trying to pretend it had been a good idea, laughing along with us.

"My dad lost his shit when he caught up to us," Darius huffed and a grim memory crossed his eyes, making my stomach knot. "It was still worth it." He sipped his beer, his smile hitching back in place as he swallowed but there was something forced about it now.

"My mom made all of my siblings fight me for dominance again that week," I sighed. "And she wouldn't heal me between any of the fights, but she healed all of them."

"You still won though." Caleb smirked at me and my chest puffed up as I nodded in agreement to that, clinking my beer to his. His mom had just told him to 'take some time to reflect on the future he wanted' which he'd done by sitting himself down beside a window while it was raining before deciding he wanted to be an Heir after all, and that was that.

I leaned against him as peace washed over me, not sure if I even wanted to go out to fuck up Grus's party anymore. I just wanted to stay here, surrounded by my best friends where I didn't have to pretend to be anyone or anything. But if Grus was trying to make some stance against us, I knew the Fae in me wouldn't let it stand. We had to squash it before it gained legs like we did with any opposition we faced.

Another hour slid by and Darius finally got to his feet, the rest of us rising too as the energy between us changed. Our smiles started to slip and I felt a venomous beast awakening from slumber within us, wetting its lips for blood.

I felt the darkness coiling up around me and hugging my skin, and I embraced it, letting it sink within my bones and enjoying the rush it gave me. "It's game time." I bounced from foot to foot and Caleb rolled his shoulders, yawning widely and revealing his fangs.

"That blood moon making you hungry, bro?" I asked and Caleb's eyes flashed onto my throat, the Devil in his gaze. It was a well-known fact that blood moons made Vampires all kinds of hungry and that red beauty in the sky tonight was clearly having an effect on him. The moon really could be a dirty girl when she wanted to be, and I liked her style.

"The hunt is calling," he said, releasing a heavy breath and I realised the restraint he was holding onto tonight. But he wouldn't attack any of us. He could get blood anywhere he wanted and he knew we'd offer out our blood to him too willingly if he needed it. Although...I didn't hate the idea of him trying to claim it from me in a more thrilling way.

"I'll tell you what..." I said, swaggering closer to him as I offered both my wrists out to him, making his eyes dart between each of them like he was trying to decide between two mouth-watering desserts. "You can have a bite of me-"

Cal stepped forward and I danced away, throwing up an air shield to stop him advancing.

"*If,*" I continued, and he licked his lips, staring at me with an intensity that made my heart race. "You beat me to The Shimmering Springs without your Vampire speed." I wiggled my eyebrows temptingly and Caleb smirked.

"Done," he agreed and I shoved my way past Max, flying out the door and throwing up an air shield behind me. Caleb slammed into it with a curse, and I felt him tear through the magic with a flesh of fire at my back as he followed me down the stairs. But I was already out the door, howling to the deep red moon in the sky and racing off into the trees in the direction of The Shimmering Springs.

"Go on Cal!" Max called after us as footfalls pounded close behind me.

"Munch on his neck!"

"Traitor!" I called back and Darius and Max's laughter made me grin as I pushed myself on.

I threw up air shields left and right, hearing Cal colliding with them with growls of anger and my laughter rang through the air as I chanced a look behind me at him. Mistake. I smashed into a wall of earth that Caleb cast and staggered backwards, my ass hitting the ground as I lost my footing and my head spun from the impact.

Caleb tore past me with a whoop and I growled, shoving myself up and taking chase, the two of us breaking out of the woods and hitting the rocky terrain of Ignis Territory. Cal was fast even without his Vampire gifts, but I was one determined motherfucker and I gritted my jaw and sprinted after him. I whipped his legs out from beneath him with air and he went flying up over my head as I took the lead again, trying to hold on to him as he dangled like a fish out of water, but he severed my power with a slash of a vine, the next strike of it slapping right over my ass.

I howled like a new born pup, stumbling to my knees and clutching my ass, finding my sweatpants ripped open across it and my skin stinging from the strike.

Caleb raced past me again, laughing his head off and I healed the sting in my flesh as I shoved myself up and hurried to catch him. He started ripping holes into the earth at my feet and I leapt over them again and again, panting heavily as I used my own earth magic to close some of the bigger ones which I couldn't jump.

"You spank my ass, Cal, I'll spank yours back!" I called after him, casting a paddle in my hand, my eyes locking on my peachy target tucked in his jeans. That ass was *mine*.

The springs came into view up ahead and I cast air beneath my feet, whizzing forward at a tremendous speed as I let the storm gather and propel me toward Cal's back.

I was as fast as a goose racing south for winter, as silent as a gnat caught in an updraft, and I collided with Cal so hard it knocked us both to the ground, our limbs tangling and our heads cracking together as we rolled across the earth.

Caleb softened it with his magic, making us bounce further until finally I was on top of him, him face down and me shoving his head into the mud. I yanked his pants down and spanked his ass with the paddle, victory making me grin ear to ear and Caleb threw an elbow back which smashed into my face and sent me flying onto my back.

I went down like a sack of shit, panting and laughing as I let the paddle dissolve in my hand and Caleb yanked his pants back over his ass.

"Motherfucker," he growled at me, his fangs out and laughter bubbling in his throat.

A massive foot stamped down on his back and he was flattened to the ground as Darius walked casually over him and Max nearly kicked me in the dick as he trampled me too.

"You both lose," Darius said as he and Max stepped officially into the rocky area which sloped down to the springs.

"Na-ar," I growled, getting to my feet. But Caleb was already up, running forward to make it onto the rocks before me then he wheeled around to face me, his eyes alight with his win.

"Blood," he demanded and I rolled my eyes, stalking towards him and shoving my wrist against his lips hard enough to make his head jerk backwards.

"You're a sore loser," he taunted, grabbing my arm and taking his time to decide exactly where his bite was going to go as he examined my veins.

He drove his fangs into me and I growled wolfishly through the pain, the Alpha in me rearing up and demanding I fight him off. But he was the only Vampire in the world I could pull back my instincts for to allow him to feed from me. It didn't feel like he was taking from me, it felt like offering power to an extension of my soul. And the deeper he drank, the more my heart pounded, allowing more blood to pump between his lips as the groan that left him made a smile twitch up the corner of my mouth.

Satisfying my pack members was in my nature, and I pushed my fingers into his hair just before he tugged his fangs free of my skin. My fingers tightened a little and I moved into him, nuzzling his cheek in a way that his kind didn't usually accept from anyone. But everything about me and the Heirs defied all the laws of Fae. Each of our needs were unique and often contradictory to each other's but somehow, we found an equilibrium between us, and so long as all of us were getting our needs met, it worked.

Caleb needed to feed just like I needed to touch. We were polar opposites, but here we were, each balancing one end of a scale like the Libra constellation embodied. That made a lot of sense to me seeing as my rising sign was Libra.

"Better?" I asked him and he nodded, his eyes reflecting that big red moon for a second and making him look more Nymph than Fae.

"And you?" he asked and I nodded, releasing him, though my fingers were always tingling for more. Because every time I spent too long without the warmth of another Fae close, I remembered the Forging my parents had put me through when I was a cub, leaving me on a mountain alone to defend myself for a full week. So now, whenever I was away from my brothers too long, I remembered that chill, I could feel it frosting my bones, fear swelling in me, begging me to find them once more, to reassure myself my kin were near.

"I'm always good when you're close, Cal," I said, giving him a sideways smile as we started walking after Max and Darius, the sound of music reaching us from the springs. My pants were still slit open over my ass, but I was kinda enjoying the breeze dancing across my butt cheeks. "Don't ever disappear on me."

"I won't," Cal swore, and those words gilded my heart in iron, strengthening it until it was an impenetrable thing that no one could get inside. No one but him and my boys.

CALEB

CHAPTER TWO

The thumping of music which sounded almost tribal drew us further into the embrace of The Shimmering Springs, clouds of steam rising up from the pools of heated water and sweeping around us to obscure our vision and hide our approach.

"The royal bloodline must not be forgotten!" Geraldine's voice called out loudly, echoing off of the rocks under the influence of an amplifying spell. "Nor the intended purpose of the Celestial Council – to serve like the underdogs they are!"

A noise followed her which held a few cheers, several drunken whoops and a whole host of booing.

I licked my lips, my heart pumping at the upcoming challenge and the taste of Seth's blood dancing across my tongue.

Since the moment I'd Emerged as a Vampire, I'd been offered up blood from almost every and any Fae I wanted. I had spent the last few years sampling endless varieties of my favourite drink, but nothing compared to the way the other Heirs tasted.

Nothing.

And with the blood moon hanging low, fat and red in the sky overhead, my desire for more and more of it was only growing.

Mom had called me earlier, reminding me that the bloodlust would run hot through my veins all night tonight no matter how often I fed, and I knew I was going to need a whole lot more than that taste to satisfy me before the sun rose, but it was a damn good start.

"Do not fall prey to the allure of those four dazzling dingbats who showboat around our most prestigious of academies as though they were born to sit their unworthy behinds upon the throne of our fallen king and his poor, murdered children! Remember that they are but dogs without a master, running loose among a field of sheep, slathering at the jaws for a taste of power which was never rightfully theirs!"

"And whose should it be then, Grus?" Max cried out as he stepped around a corner between two bubbling pools and the rest of us followed him into the open area where she was conducting her little speech.

Geraldine twirled to face us from her position standing on a tree stump which I had to assume she'd crafted using her earth magic, and the explosion of turquoise taffeta which she had wrapped around her body whipped around from the movement as she raised her chin and looked down on us.

"Oh-ho!" she cried. "Speak of the slanderous salamanders and they shall cometh!"

The crowd of students who were gathered around her all stiffened as they took in our arrival, the thirty or so of them shifting where they stood or sat around the rocky area, most of them in bathing suits and looking like they'd been here enjoying the springs rather than showing up specifically for this gathering of the Geraldine gang.

I looked at the poster which Geraldine had stuck to a rock behind her, the words on it bringing a snort of amusement to my lips.

Join the Maintainers Of Idealist Sovereign Traditions - get your M.O.I.S.T. badge today!

There was a space at the bottom of her poster for people to add their names if they wanted to join her moist club. She had precisely one sign up and that was herself, the big brown M.O.I.S.T. badge pinned proudly over the chest of her impressive dress and a bucket more of them sat waiting beside her in hopes of someone claiming one.

"Who are you calling a salamander, Grus?" Max barked, sauntering towards her and tugging his shirt off to reveal the navy scales which were crawling across his skin.

Seth nudged me with an excited grin and I smiled back, both of us waiting to see which emotion he'd use to bring her to heel first.

"Take a moment to ponder upon your reflection, you great trout," she said dismissively. "Then your question shall answer itself."

Fear crept along my spine as Max flexed his fingers and I gave in to the chill of it for a moment before tightening my mental shields and blocking him out.

The crowd recoiled as they felt the press of his gifts and the four of us stalked forward slowly, the air crackling with tension as everyone waited to see what would happen next, and the feeling of fear grew stronger and stronger.

Darius reached out to shut off the music, taking a bottle from the table of drinks which had been gathered for this little party and knocking the cap off before taking a long drink from it.

His eyes brightened as he swallowed and he grinned widely just as one of the girls from his House stepped forward and touched a hand to his arm.

"Umm, Darius? I just thought you should know that bottle has Footloose Faraday in it," she said, biting her lip in a way which was definitely an attempt at seduction as she twisted a lock of red hair around her finger. She was pretty hot, but either Darius wasn't in the mood to get laid or just wasn't into her because he barely even spared her a glance, his focus on Max who was still facing off against Grus who was scowling at him as she fought off the effects of his Siren gifts.

"Thanks, Marge," Darius said dismissively, shaking her off and offering the bottle to me. "I noticed."

I shrugged as I accepted it, deciding I was up for letting my inhibitions drop and taking a long drink of the magical beverage for myself, the heat of it tingling all the way down to the pit of my stomach as I swallowed.

Seth snatched it from my hand before I was even done, the wolfish look on his face making me laugh even as I cursed him out and the drink sloshed down my chest, soaking through my shirt.

"You're looking a little tense there, Grus," Max growled as he stalked closer to her but I had to say, I couldn't see it. She had her chin raised high, that same haughty look on her face which she always got when she laid her eyes on any of us as she just stared him down and challenged him to do his worst.

"I do not fear the mind games of a petulant patty cake playing at being a ruler," she sneered. "No tricks of your fancy fins will send me a-splutter, you cantankerous crustation."

Max gritted his jaw as he stepped closer to her and the people at the front of the crowd cowered away, one of them shrieking in terror and tearing off between the rock pools as the overflow of Max's gifts got too much for him to handle.

Seth sank the last of the Footloose Faraday, his eyes flashing silver with his inner Wolf as he tossed the bottle aside, smashing it against a rock and making another student scream loudly before the noise turned into a startled whinny as she lost control and shifted into her Pegasus form, her bikini exploding and the elastic snapping out to slap Max in the eye.

He cried out as he lost his hold on his gift and my gut plummeted as unrestrained terror poured from him and slammed into every single person surrounding us without aim.

Seth howled as he was damn near trampled by a fleeing Griffin and Darius barked a laugh as he ducked beneath the claws of a Manticore as it took off into the sky, a half shredded pair of swimming trunks hanging from one of its furry ass cheeks.

I shot away from the carnage and sobbing students, bolstering my mental shields as the wall of terror crashed over everyone and the sight of them all running got the bloodlust in me pumping to new heights.

I sped between the bodies, my fangs snapping out and the desire to take chase consuming me while a little voice in the back of my head purred why not?

The voice was about three parts the magical drink and four parts my own animal instincts, and before I could stop myself I was shooting towards the girl who still stood above the chaos in a swathe of turquoise taffeta while she yelled out for people to grab a M.O.I.S.T. badge before they left.

Geraldine shrieked as I collided with her but before she could do a thing to fight me off, I had her pressed against the rocky side of one of the pools and my fangs were sinking deep into the flesh of her throat.

I groaned at the taste of her blood as it rolled over my tongue, my fists locking in the gauzy fabric which covered her body as I took a deep drink from her and felt the rush of the blood moon's influence pouring down on me.

Damn she was powerful, her blood a mix of flavours which reminded me of that confusing sensation of listening to three different songs while they were all playing at once.

"Remove your fangs from my gizzard you curly haired Lothario or I shall be forced to defend myself!" Geraldine cried, her hands slapping against my shoulders with considerably more vigour than my prey could normally manage once under the influence of my venom.

I snarled at her as I drank deeper, the bloodlust making my muscles tense as I took what I needed, swallowing greedily and ignoring her protests.

There was a rustle of taffeta like a snake striking through the long grass and her knee collided with my dick so suddenly that I jerked back with a curse, releasing her from my bite and wheezing as I cupped my junk.

"By the fucking stars," I hissed a moment before a fist slammed into my jaw and I was knocked on my ass by Max as he bared his teeth at me.

"Back off, asshole, this is my fight," he warned, his eyes flashing with a challenge which I wasn't going to give in to.

I healed my balls with a surge of magic and shot to my feet, a smile cracking across my face as I faced off against my brother and prepared for the fight he was offering.

But before we could get into it, a flash of movement caught my attention from my left and my eyes widened in alarm a second before Geraldine hurled a huge glob of stinking, dripping mud right at us.

I shot away with my Vampire speed half a beat before the strike could land but Max wasn't so lucky, catching the entire heap in the face as he whipped around at the threat and ended up coated from head to foot in it.

"Take that you pumped up pufferfish!" Geraldine cried. "I shall be forever M.O.I.S.T. and you won't ever stop me!"

She ripped her dress off while everyone who still remained stared at her in shock, and I caught sight of her huge tits about two seconds before she shifted into her enormous Cerberus form and took off with a bark of laughter which echoed all around the rocks which surrounded us, the bag of M.O.I.S.T. badges and her dress each clamped in the jaws of one of her three heads.

I fell about laughing, gripping my side as I leaned back against the edge of the rock pool and Max roared a challenge which made the air around us vibrate with his emotions. A mixture of anger, lust and amusement pushed into me and I opened myself to it, enjoying the sensation of his power as it chased away my own feelings for a few minutes and gave me a crazy kind of rush.

We had a whole army of fan girls and guys lurking in on us now, made up of the people who had managed to stay through the terror overflow or had shown up as the news of our appearance spread over campus like it always did. There was a whole host of them batting their eyes, flexing muscles and trying to do everything and anything they could to draw the attention of one of the Heirs who would one day rule this entire kingdom.

I'd been born and bred for this and had had an idea of what it would be like for us when we emerged into the world properly after our Awakening, but the reality of what we had here wasn't something any of us could have prepared ourselves for.

In the years since our early Awakening, the four of us had been privately educated away from everyone else. We'd been given every fundamental lesson that would be taught throughout our freshman year and beyond, and we had been given extra lessons in all things combat to ensure that we would be able to take this place by storm once we arrived. And we'd done that and then some. We just hadn't been fully prepared for what it would be like to be thrust into this place, away from the shielding of our parents and among Fae we didn't know. It was overwhelming, the constant attention, girls and guys throwing themselves at us all the time, wanting to be our friends or more, anything at all really, just wanting to attach themselves to us in any way they could.

And we were making the most of it at every given opportunity.

I couldn't even walk into a room without a line of Fae forming to offer me their blood. And it would have been fucking rude to refuse.

Seth's pack had shown up and were lingering nearby, trying to get close to him as they did most of the time, watching him, waiting for his attention to fall their way. He smirked as his gaze ran over them, giving them a heated look which made me certain that he was thinking with his cock as he considered each of them in turn.

"I'm going to teach that royalist nut job a lesson," Max growled, water magic flooding from his hands as he directed it at himself and scrubbed the mud away in a fit of rage.

There were a bunch of Fae trying their hardest not to laugh but I didn't bother hiding my amusement as I laughed loudly, shooting aside as he sprayed water my way in annoyance and coming to a halt sitting on a ledge beside Seth where I promptly dropped my arm around his shoulders as he laughed too.

"You want help on your hunt, brother?" I asked as Max finished cleaning himself and turned to follow after Geraldine.

"No," he replied in a fierce growl.

"Send us a pic if she manages to cover you in shit again though, yeah?" Seth called after him as he took off and he flipped us off over his shoulder before disappearing down the rocky path Geraldine had taken.

"Well, that was too easy," Darius sighed as he moved to join us, another drink in his hand which the redhead had given him, and she trailed closer to us with a hopeful look on her face as she eye fucked him so graphically that I had to look away from her porno gaze. "I was hoping for a real fight tonight."

"Blood moon got you hungry too?" I teased, grinning at him as I eyed the pulse in his neck.

"When am I not hungry for a fight?" he tossed back, glancing away from us hopefully like he thought a decent opponent might present themselves.

But instead of anyone stepping forward, his challenging look was only met with bent heads and submission all around and he sighed in disappointment.

"I'll kick your ass if you're hungry for a fight?" I offered, flashing my fangs at him as he looked back to me again, his pupils shifting into the reptilian slits of his Dragon form.

"Come run with us, Alpha," a girl pleaded before Darius could accept my challenge and we looked around at Seth as his packmates all started bouncing at the idea of that, howls escaping their lips which echoed all across the springs and set my skin prickling.

Seth tipped his head back to look up at the moon and I watched the way his features lit up at the idea, though he glanced our way hesitantly like he was torn between running with his kind or staying with us.

"How about we all go for a run?" I suggested. "One loop around the grounds then back here for a fight and a party and whatever the hell else takes our fancy."

"Will you actually run with us this time?" Seth asked, narrowing his eyes on me suspiciously. "Because the last time you came running with my pack you just shot off to get laid and left me out there in the dark."

I sniggered because that was an accurate assessment then held my hand out to him. "I swear that I won't sneak off to get laid this time," I promised and Seth smiled widely before slapping his hand into mine and a clap of magic rang between our palms as the deal was struck.

Seth turned to howl at his pack and they all cheered, whooping loudly and stripping their clothes off in a rush as they prepared to shift.

Darius stripped down too, tossing his drink to the redhead who looked like she was in danger of drooling all over the floor. He turned his back on her before dropping his pants and shifting so suddenly that several Fae screamed.

It wasn't every day you got to see a ten ton Dragon appear in front of you after all and Darius was one beautiful golden beastie when he was in his shifted form.

He took off with a beat of his powerful wings and a roar loud enough to make the rocks vibrate all around us. Seth shifted next, leaping forward and landing on four huge, white paws in his Wolf form and he howled loudly as his entire pack shifted at his back, the lot of them taking off down the rocky path which led towards Fire Territory to the east of The Shimmering Springs.

I glanced at the redhead as she gawped after them, her mouth hanging open in awe and I slipped closer to her as my fangs prickled.

"Hey Marge?" I asked, making her snap around to look at me.

"It's err, actually Marguerite," she corrected and I nodded like I gave a fuck about that.

"Right. Yeah. I was thinking you could give me a drink?"

She blinked at me then nodded, whipping around towards the drinks table like I'd been after a fucking waiter and I sighed as I shot after her, snatching her wrist into my grasp and biting down before she'd even managed to look back at me again. The moon was making me damn insatiable tonight and I growled as I drank from her, the bland taste of her blood not even coming close to satisfying what I needed. By the stars, it was boring. It tasted as dull as lukewarm puddle water.

"Oh, sorry," she gasped. "I didn't realise you meant-"

I cut her off by releasing her, shoving her arm back at her and resisting the urge to wipe my mouth clean on the back of my hand. My gaze moved to the path that Seth had taken, the memory of his intoxicating blood sliding down my throat circling in my mind, and I growled as I prepared to go after what I was really hungering for.

"Will you tell Darius about me feeding you?" Marge called as I stalked away from her. "So he knows how willing I am to do whatever I can to support all of the Heirs."

"Right, yeah," I agreed dismissively, forgetting what I'd agreed to before she'd even finished talking and as she started going on about me putting in a good word for her in her mission to suck my best friend's cock, I shot away. She was welcome to pledge her allegiance to Darius's dick if she wanted to. He had a whole gaggle of girls who had already done so though, so I wasn't going to waste my time promising to steer him towards her in particular. Who knew, he might be tempted her way if she put enough effort in, but that shit had nothing to do with me.

I shot away from her boring blood and desperate words, racing after the howling Wolf pack at top speed as the night air tousled my curls and the exhilaration of my pace made my heart riot.

I cupped my hands around my mouth and howled to the blood moon, Seth's answering howl coming from up ahead before setting off the entire pack.

I sped between the furry bodies of the Wolves, laughing as the mixture of booze and adrenaline got my heart pumping to a wild tune, making my way to Seth so that I could run at his side.

Darius roared as he swept back and forth above us and we all howled to him as we raced across campus in a tide of beasts with the entire world at our feet.

Seth nudged his big Wolfy snout against me as we ran together and my heart soared with a pure kind of happiness which I only ever felt in the company of my best friends.

We ran like that for over an hour and when we finally closed in on The Shimmering Springs again, I shot ahead of them, stripping my clothes off as I went and grabbing a bottle of vodka before racing towards the biggest heated pool right in the heart of the springs.

Just before my butt naked self could dive into the water, a blur of motion forced me to skid to a halt and my fangs snapped out as I came face to face with Lance Orion in his professor bullshit suit as he snarled right back at me with his fangs out too.

"Fifty points from Terra for showing your cock to a teacher, Altair," he snapped, his nose wrinkling as he glared at me and I glared right back.

"And what do you lose for *being* a cock to your future ruler?" I replied scathingly as I lifted the bottle of vodka to my lips and drank a big enough dose of it to make my head spin. It was petulant and kinda pointless but the rivalry between us always did bring out the entitled prick in me.

"You and I both know that I have nothing left to lose which is why I'm also considering murdering you for nothing but the pure thrill of it," he deadpanned.

A roar interrupted us and Darius plummeted from the sky, shifting at the last second and landing on two feet in the space between us.

"Lance," he greeted and I noticed that he wasn't docked house points for having his fucking cock out.

"Darius," Orion replied, shooting me a narrow eyed look before going on.

"I have a lead on some of those things you wanted to come and help me deal with."

"Really?" Darius asked, his eyes brightening with a violent look which made my muscles tense.

"What happened to our fight?" I asked him as he moved to find the clothes he'd discarded earlier, clearly planning on ditching us for his special buddy. Orion looked all kinds of smug about that too and I shot him a death glare in reply.

"I just got a better offer," Darius replied, tugging his jeans up and kicking on his shoes, not bothering to hunt down his shirt as he turned to leave with Orion. "I'll kick your ass in the morning."

I opened my mouth to call after them but the sound of my name drew my attention to the water and I turned to find a group of four girls giggling and waving at me, all of them very much naked and the invitation they were offering up clear.

A growl rolled down the back of my throat and I tipped my head back to look up at the moon where it now hung full and fat right in the centre of the sky, the pull of its power the strongest it would be all night and my blood pumping hot and fast in my veins as the need to feed consumed me.

I shot into the water in a blur, making the girls squeal as they found me among them in less than a heartbeat and I grinned at the closest one as she reached for me.

"You look hungry," she said, biting down on her bottom lip, the red colour of the moonlight making her dark skin gleam with its glow, and the need of my kind rising desperately within me.

I nodded once, grabbing her in the next moment and driving my teeth into her throat, making her moan loudly as our naked bodies were crushed together.

Her blood swam over my tongue and I drew it in with an ache in my chest which wasn't in any way satisfied by the low buzz of power she held in her veins.

Her friends moved in to surround me, their bodies pressing against mine from all sides, the skim of hard nipples and roaming fingers dancing across my flesh and awakening other needs in me, but it wasn't enough.

I tugged my fangs free of the girl's neck, turning and grabbing the wrist of the one on her left, sinking my fangs in deep and growling as I tasted even less power in her veins which made my heart pound all the harder with the need for more.

A hand wrapped around my cock which was making some poor effort at getting hard, but the unsatisfying blood was a serious turn off no matter how many girls there were surrounding me. I tugged my fangs free again, even the sight of their blood mixing with the bubbling water nowhere near enough to raise my interest in them.

I swear I could hear the moon whispering in my ears, urging me to take more, find what I ached for. I spun around so fast that the girls shrieked, though the one I found myself facing didn't back away, instead tilting her head in offering and sweeping her brunette curls aside to give me clearer access.

I bit her harder than I meant to, though the loud moan she released said she liked that and her hand found my dick beneath the water once more, pumping it hopefully as I swallowed her blood down in greedy gulps only to be disappointed once more.

"Fuck," I cursed as I tugged my teeth out of her flesh and knocked her hand aside. "I need more than this."

I turned to look at the last girl who was rubbing her hands over her tits and leaning back against the rocky edge of the pool, her thighs parted in offering as she waited for me with a need in her eyes which was kinda tempting.

But before I could give her any more of my attention, a huge splash sounded the Wolf pack arriving, all thirty of them diving into the pool in their Werewolf forms and shifting beneath the surface, causing the rest of the partiers to scream in alarm.

Seth surfaced right in front of me, water washing down his cut abs as he flicked his long brown hair back like he was performing in some kind of fans only video and making me swallow thickly as I looked at him.

His dark eyes met mine as he clawed his fingers through his hair to tame it away from his face, the feral look on his face letting me know that the Wolf in him was still very much present beneath the pull of that beautiful fucking moon.

"Hey, Cal," he said, his voice a rough caress around my name which drew my lips up and revealed my fangs to him. "Are you still thirsty?" he asked in surprise though his eyes lit with the thrill of that fact.

"The beast in me won't be easily tamed tonight," I replied, my heart thumping harder as he closed in on me, and I couldn't help but stare at the pulse points across his exposed body where his blood pumped hot and fast after the excitement of his run.

"Well, I bet I can help with that," he said, shifting towards me and making me lick my lips as my attention fixed on a throbbing vein which tracked through the V at the base of his abs right before the water lapped around his waist to conceal it.

He stopped before me, his eyes running down my body and making me smile as he didn't bother to hide his appreciation.

"Damn, are you sure you aren't at least a little bit gay, Cal?" he teased. "Because you look real good all wet and thirsty."

I took a long drink from my bottle of vodka and shrugged. "Your tits aren't big enough for me," I said as I offered him the bottle for his own drink, though as I looked to his chest to make my point, I couldn't say I hated the sculpted lines of his pecs all the same.

Seth's fingers brushed against mine as he took the bottle from me and I forced myself to hold still even as my gaze zeroed in on his neck and my fangs practically throbbed with the need to bite him. To get what I'd been craving and the moon was demanding.

Seth finished the bottle off then tossed it to one of his packmates as he swam past us, not even reacting as the guy cursed when the bottle smacked him on the head and drew blood.

I didn't spare the blood any attention either, my restraint snapping as I lunged at him, taking hold of his jaw in one hand and driving my teeth towards his throat so fast that Seth sucked in a surprised breath. But the asshole had clearly been expecting it before I struck anyway and I cursed as my fangs slammed against a solid air shield which he'd placed a hairsbreadth from his skin, making me jerk back again with a snarl.

"Woah, calm down big boy," Seth laughed as earth magic flared in my palms and vines curled their way up my arms as I prepared to fight him to claim the drink I needed.

"Give me a taste, Seth," I hissed, my head spinning with the need in my flesh as I felt the gaze of the moon pressing down on me even more forcefully.

"You look like you need to get laid, brother," he laughed, waving a hand at the group of girls who were still trying to win my attention back, but I'd practically forgotten they were even there.

"They can't give me what I need," I snarled, baring my teeth at him in a challenge which I was really fucking close to forcing upon him, and his gaze roamed over me as he seemed to take in how close I was to the edge.

"Yeah…I see that. Come on then, I got you."

Seth took my hand and I frowned at him as he tugged me after him but gave in, my desire for his blood too powerful to resist and my attention fixed on his throat while his grip on my fingers felt akin to the only thing tethering me in place right now.

He barked a command at his pack to move aside for us, tugging me across the pool before striding beneath a waterfall of heated spring water and drawing me into the secluded cavern behind it.

Seth released me as we made it into the dark space, the shimmering pool there making the cave wall glisten with a multitude of tiny rainbows which danced across his wet skin too, making him appear like some kind of ethereal creature brought to me by the moon herself.

He grinned at me as he took a seat in the water, tilting his head to one side and eyeing me with interest.

"You're still shielding," I said in a low voice, my control hanging on a knife's edge as I let my fangs sink into my bottom lip and offered them some small reprieve.

Seth's grin widened at being caught out and he shrugged, not bothering to deny it.

"I kinda like seeing the beast in you, Cal. I'm thinking of riling it up a little more just so that I can find out how dark you get when the worst of you is baited."

His words set a fire in me and I took a step forward, but before I could close the distance between us, a girl stepped through the waterfall at my back and drew my attention to her.

"I thought Alice could help us liven up this party," Seth explained, crooking a finger at her and she offered me a sultry smile as she passed me by, her hand skimming down my arm before she moved to sit in Seth's lap, kissing him passionately while I just stood there and watched them.

Seth opened his eyes as he continued to kiss her, that silver shine to them again as he looked at me, the challenge there clear.

"You want me to play Wolf?" I asked, looking at the beautiful girl in his lap and finding that idea almost as appealing as the thought of his blood caressing my tongue.

"Yeah," Seth agreed, breaking their kiss and giving me his Wolf's grin while she began to move her mouth down his neck, moaning softly.

He beckoned me closer with one finger just like he'd done for Alice and I snorted at the idea of me submitting to him but moved nearer all the same.

"Fine," I agreed, my cock hardening as I closed in on them and moved to take a seat beside him, my leg brushing against his and my skin heating at the contact. "But you'd better know what you're asking for by bringing another

Alpha into your pack."

I held his eye as I reached for Alice, taking hold of her thigh and drawing it over my leg so that she was half straddling both of us and Seth's arm pressed to mine.

She turned her head, capturing my mouth in place of his and sinking her tongue between my lips.

I growled as I deepened the kiss, Seth's hand brushing the back of my neck and his fingers pushing into my curls as he leaned in too.

His jaw brushed against mine and I growled, part in warning, part in lust as Alice turned to meet his kiss once more, leaving me to move my mouth down the side of her neck instead.

My heart pumped harder as the call of her blood drew me in and my fangs grazed against her flesh, making her gasp as her hips rocked with need.

"Tip your head, Alice," Seth growled. "Give him what he wants, and we'll give you what you want in return."

Alice nodded, her head rolling back as she exposed herself for me and I let my gaze roam down to the peaks of her nipples as Seth's large hand moved to tug on one, his heated gaze meeting mine as Alice dropped her hand beneath the water and began to pump his cock in her fist.

I groaned at the sight of his pupils dilating, my pulse thundering and fangs aching, forcing me to lunge forward and bite her with a deep growl.

Alice moaned as I began to feed and I sighed, her blood so much more potent than the others I'd fed from since arriving at this party and getting a whole lot closer to satisfying the need the moon had awoken in me.

I moved my hand between her legs, my fingers scoring a line up Seth's thigh in the process and making him groan as he looked between me and Alice, enjoying the show.

Alice moaned loudly as I sank two fingers inside her, more of her blood rolling down my throat as I began to pump them in and out, loving the way her blood pulsed between my lips the more worked up she got.

Her hand wrapped around my dick and I groaned, fucking her with my hand and drinking more of her blood while the pounding in my head settled just a little.

But the more I drank, the clearer it became that it still wasn't enough, a growl escaping me as frustration filled me and my muscles tightened with a need that wasn't going to be sated.

"Come on, Alice, you can do better than that," Seth snarled, and my heart leapt as his hand moved onto my thigh, the touch of his skin against mine making the animal in me rear its head and my cock jerked in Alice's grip.

Seth's hand joined mine, his fingers caressing the back of my hand before pushing inside her too, making her moan loudly as he found a rhythm with me as she cried out between us, her pussy tightening around us as she began to come.

"Fuck," Alice gasped. "Oh fuck, by the stars, Alpha!"

I drove my fingers into her with a desperate kind of need, her blood pulsing faster as she reached her peak, teasing me with the promise of what I so desperately needed while she cried out and her pussy clamped around mine and Seth's fingers.

Her orgasm sent a rush of blood between my lips and I snarled furiously as the release I needed was denied, knocking her hand away from my cock and pulling my teeth from her throat in frustration.

Seth tugged his fingers out of her, pulling my hand away too and barking a command at her to work harder as his fingers knotted in my hair and he jerked me around to look at him.

"Tell me you want me, Cal and I'm all yours," he said, his eyes flashing with a cocky kind of power and I snarled as I bared my bloodstained fangs at him.

"Fuck you," I snapped, clawing a hand through my curls as I tried to rein in the bloodlust which was threatening to take control of me.

Seth whimpered wolfishly as I closed my eyes and suddenly the water was shifting around me, his body moving towards mine and knocking Alice off of us as I felt him drop the air shield from his skin.

I lunged for him without even opening my eyes, a snarl rolling from my throat as my fangs sank deep into his flesh and I groaned loudly as the rush of his blood finally caressed my tongue.

"By the stars," Seth moaned as I pushed him back against the rock wall, my cock driving against his thigh and the lust ignited by the pure power laced within his blood making me grind my hips against him without thought.

Seth's hand pushed into the back of my hair, fisting tight as he drew me closer and his other hand moved down my arm, digging into my bicep as I gripped his waist and the muscle flexed tight.

I lost myself in the taste of him, the feel of his body bowing to mine and the purity of his power flowing into me through his blood as I swallowed greedily, the power of the moon making my fucking head spin.

I drank until I was intoxicated by him, and his head fell back while he panted through the bloodlust, the rush just as intense for him as it was for me.

His thumb brushed against the side of my cock and I groaned headily, drawing my teeth out of him and turning my head toward his without thought.

Seth's mouth met mine as he turned to me too, my heart leaping with the alien feeling of his stubble raking against mine. The deep sound of the growl which rolled up the back of his throat made a shiver track down my spine.

His lips parted for me and I sank my tongue between them, groaning deeply as he met the stroke of it with one of his own, his thumb tracing up the side of my dick once more and making me lose my fucking head with the mixture of lust and blood drunkenness.

Seth drew me closer, the kiss deepening as my brain slowly caught up to what we were doing, where this was going and how much I found myself wanting to keep it going.

I ground my hips against him, feeling the press of his cock against my leg in reply to the firm thrust of mine against his, and I found myself considering something I'd never once given thought to before.

I drew back a little, looking into his eyes and reading the same lust there that I was sure he could see in mine.

"Seth?" I panted, a question and an offer in that word as his thumb traced a path up the length of my cock once more as I began to shift my hand from his waist towards his.

"Yes," he said, the need in him clear and I bit my lip as I drank it in, wanting this to go further, so much fucking further.

Alice was gone and I had no idea when she'd left but I found myself glad that she wasn't here. I didn't know if this was the moon or his blood, some combination of both or something far more powerful, but I did know that I didn't want to leave this cave until I found out.

I leaned in, my mouth on his and he licked his bottom lip, clearly wanting more too-

"Don't mind me!"

I jerked back in alarm at the sound of Professor Washer's voice behind me, spinning and finding him emerging from the water on the far side of the cave, his Siren scales coating his skin and a smile on his lips which was all kinds of false embarrassment.

"I just need a little gulp of air before I slip back down into the moist depths of this hole. You two know all about that, I'm sure."

He slipped back under the water just as Seth yelled a curse and threw a blast of air magic at his head. I swiped a hand down my face as the madness of the moon's power faded from my limbs and disgust over our gross lurking professor sank into its place.

"Shit," I said, breathing a laugh as I exchanged an awkward look with my best friend. "The moon is all kinds of fucked up tonight."

"Err, yeah," he agreed. "I'm even hornier than usual which is saying something."

I barked a laugh, glancing away. "Me too. And the bloodlust has me all kinds of fucked up. I doubt I'll even remember half of this night come morning."

"What happens beneath the blood moon stays beneath the blood moon," Seth offered with a grin and I nodded.

"Yeah, sounds about right."

An awkward silence hung between us for several seconds and I glanced back over to the place where Washer had disappeared.

"I'm feeling the sudden desire to get the fuck out of here," I said.

"Agreed." Seth followed me as I led the way out of the cave again and we found the pool beyond it empty too, the partiers having moved on or fucked off back to bed for the night.

I glanced up at the moon, finding it lowering in the sky with clouds slipping over it to hide it from view, the most potent of its magic dampened now and letting me think a little clearer.

"See you for breakfast?" I asked, glancing back at Seth and finding him looking up at the moon too.

The corner of his mouth hooked up and he nodded. "Yeah. Breakfast."

I turned away from him and shot across campus towards my House and my bed, leaving the blood moon at my back and shaking my head at the madness it had woken in me tonight. Then again, every night since I'd started at Zodiac Academy had ended in one insane story or another, so I was going to just put it down to another drunken night of insanity and leave it at that. Seth was my best friend and I wasn't attracted to guys anyway.

It was all just a little moon madness, and I knew we'd go right back to normal tomorrow. This wasn't going to change shit between us. We were bros, so screw the moon for fucking with us. Not even she could damage the bond between me and Seth, nothing could. Not the moon, the sun or every star in the heavens. We were the best of fucking friends, and that was how it would always stay.

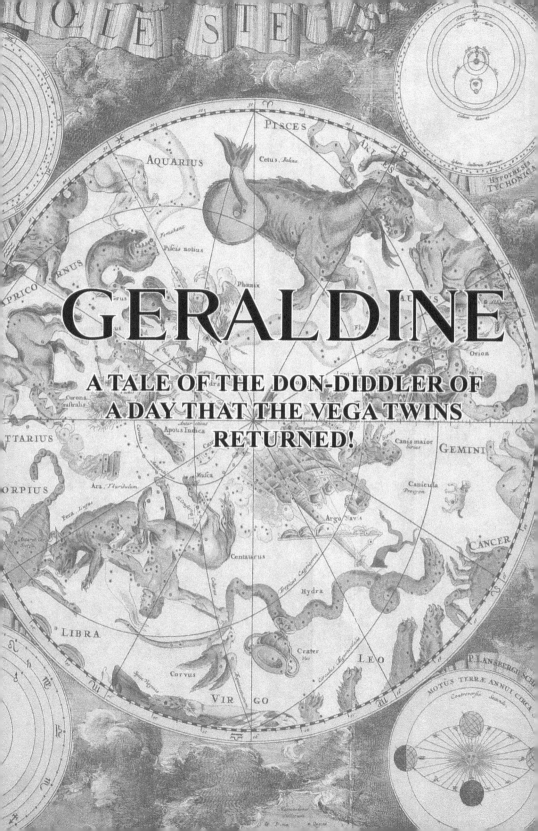

GERALDINE

A TALE OF THE DON-DIDDLER OF A DAY THAT THE VEGA TWINS RETURNED!

LIONEL

FROM THE LAIR OF LIONEL...

At this moment in time, I will admit that I had been feeling rather smug – my allegiance with the Nymphs had once again started to make its way to fruition.

My Heir was excelling at the academy both in magical prowess and cruelty, tales of his dominance over every student in the school reaching my ears on a daily basis.

My work with the other Celestial Councillors was also moving towards the tipping point I had been so eager to reach – Linda Rigel had been recruited into my confidence, her clear preference for her second-born child a little boggling, yet simple to exploit. I only had to breathe a hint of my support for the girl and she was more than willing to whisper titbits about Tiberius's schemes in my ear.

Melinda's family was a closed cavern, but still, I had my eye on her brother for a point of leverage – the man's mind was addled to the point of insanity and I was having quite the jolly old time murmuring nonsense rumours in his presence, then watching him create scandal after scandal to keep his sister occupied and her eyes off of me.

Antonia's pack was of course impenetrable, but the younger members were easy enough to tempt into trouble. While I gathered what little facts I could to undermine her, they kept her eyes from my cunning as I worked to secure my throne.

Yes, it was all going precisely to plan, the power players on the board dancing along to a tune I desired while Stella Orion aided me with dark magic and I prepared to step into the role which had been destined for me for so very long.

But then of course came the news of my oversight – something which I deeply regret and likely will do until the end of my days. Somehow, beyond all comprehension at the time – though of course now their Orders explain it – those squalling Vega brats who I had left to burn in the Mortal Realm had survived.

It was most unfortunate that the discovery of their magical signature was such a public affair, and I was forced to act as if I were thrilled by the discovery that they lived on.

The other Councillors understood the threat which a pair of uneducated and practically unFae children posed to the peace and prosperity of our kingdom, and so we all agreed to have our Heirs test them – ideally driving them to officially abandon all claim to the throne. And I still believe it would have worked had it not been for the rebels I had overlooked within my subjects. The unwavering royalists who insisted on celebrating the return of the Vega twins and giving them ideas of grandeur which were far above the position they deserved. And none were so doggedly determined to see them rise up and challenge me as those damn mutts by the name of Grus…

GERALDINE

CHAPTER ONE

"**G**obbling gargoyles, you malfunctioning gnats, the seconds sweep by and the time is nigh!" I shrilled, my voice bounding off the vaulted roof of The Orb, the gathered clan of rabble all falling over their own feet, unable to get a single thing right.

A rumour. Surely it was a rumour. Such truth could not be so. All summer I had hoped and begged it of the stars, and yet they had not answered my call. I'd heard the whisper of triumph mere moments ago, but I hesitated to believe it, to dare to dream it could be real.

And yet…

My waters. My wet and weeping waters did stir.

"Take your seats, students," Principal Nova called over the clamour of the room. "The Awakened freshmen will be arriving shortly, and we don't want to frighten them off the moment they step into the room."

I grasped Justin's arm, his quaff of dark hair shuddering at the violent tremor I knocked through his flesh as I dragged him nose to nose with me.

Only he and I shared the fullness of this devotion in our blood. Only he and I had been left limp and ruined by the news of the imminent return of our great queens.

"Do you believe it?" I hissed.

All summer I had ached for it to be so, but did I dare? Did I dare allow myself to believe for even a moment that it might be? That *they* might truly be-

"Mother claims it is true," he whispered. "And you know I would never doubt the words of my dear mama. Just this morn, she whispered it in my ear while tucking my nummy pouch into my pocket. She believes-"

"Pah!" I shoved him aside, throwing my arms wide and catching my dear friend Angelica in the eye with a far-flung finger as I cast a web of space around myself and stared at the door with all the longing of a beached whale staring at the retreating waves. "I shall see it for myself before I dare believe it is so."

Justin's mother only dealt in rumours, but I could not dare to give myself to false prophets, lest all my deepest hopes be dashed like the brains of a baboon falling from a tree to a rock.

"Ow," Angelica muttered, setting her fanny on a cushioned chair which I instantly heaved her out of.

"Shuffle, dear Angelica, shuffle," I hissed, taking her seat for my own, its superior view of the door a necessity I couldn't give up.

She didn't feel as strongly as I about who might walk through it. She knew the fullness of the change which may just have been shifting through the air, but her devotion was a mere speck of insignificance beside the radiant glow of mine.

Their power had been felt. *Felt.* And now the entire academy was a jibber-jabber about it. But they weren't worthy. None of us were.

I wriggled on the plump cushion which cradled Lady Petunia, unable to get comfortable while the energy inside me begged to find an outlet. Would the stars let it be so? Might hope at last be restored to our great kingdom?

My lips quivered as I took the welcome home card I had handcrafted from my satchel. I had spent eighteen days working on it, hand-painting seven hundred and thirty-eight daisy petals in thirty-nine different shades and then gluing them in place with tweezers to create the visage of a watercolour painting. It depicted two magnanimous queens sitting on a throne together, whilst I prostrated myself on the floor at their feet like the worthless cretin I knew myself to be in comparison to their greatness.

I had sewn the words I so needed them to read into the velvet of the card itself. The thread I had woven from the fur of forty-three nerbrung rabbits – each hair individually plucked from their fluffy tails at great difficulty while I stalked them through a hawthorn thicket which had almost scratched out my eyes.

It was garbage. Utterly unworthy of the attention of the true queens. And yet I clutched it at the ready all the same, the poem I had sewn inside it rolling through my mind, my lips moving to the shapes of the words as I recited it inside my own head.

Oh glorious queens who were lost for so long,
Where have you been all this time you were gone?
I wished on a star for a miracle to come,
And now you've returned, I know I got one.
I missed you more than words can say,
And I pledge my devotion to you on this day.

I dared a glance at the cluster of codfish who had eyed the royal throne with such eager, unworthy want all these woesome years, and I couldn't help the curdle in my crumble.

Max Rigel laughed like the obnoxious sea urchin I knew him to be, his fancy face lit with a cocksure confidence I hoped to dash like a flan on a flagstone before the night was done.

"It's in my waters," I tossed at Justin as he took a seat at my side. "They tremble at the mere thought. Tell me I am not hopeless in this want."

"The royal line burns with the purity and rightful power of fate itself," he replied like the stalwart centipede he was. "My family never believed it could be wiped out the way it was. We have all been waiting for this day for many moo-"

"Hush!" I roared, slapping a hand over his flapsome jaw, silencing his nilly nagging.

A freshman had appeared. The first. Surely they would be the first.

But this creature was male, his hair coloured with icy tips that made him nothing more than the nincompoop I was certain he must be.

If they were here, then wouldn't they have walked ahead of the rabble? Where was the fanfare? The royal guards? The horses? The pomp? The festivity?

"Oh, sparkling stars in the sky, I have failed so fully," I gasped, unable to draw breath as I realised this deflating donghopper of an evening could have been avoided if only I'd realised I would have to be the one to plan it.

But I hadn't dared believe it to be so. I hadn't prepared. Not a bloom, nor so much as a paper hat in sight. No fanfare, no party, no celebration worthy of the true queens. Just a flop of a card which wasn't worthy to wipe the royal fannies. Had I cursed us all? Was this why hapless face after hapless face wandered through the doors, muttering and mumbling, looking like a bunch of awestruck seals staring at a sparkly rock? Oh, how they gawped at the bronze roof overhead, like they'd never before been inside a building carved from the purest metal and created to embody the shape of the celestial body which deigned to offer us all life.

"Hey, Grus!" that utter cod cuddler, Max called, drawing my attention for a moment, my eyes instantly narrowing on his buxom physique. "Have you been flicking the bean over this moment all week? Because you look about ready to come from excitement alone."

I bristled at the crass comments, pitying him for the inadequate tuna he was, reduced to nothing but nilly nolly insinuations which no doubt reflected his own deflated salmon's antics.

"I very much doubt you have the skills required to know when a lady is about to orgasm, you vulgar ruffian. So kindly take your eyes off of my visage and return to your lollygagging with the other mutts on the reject pile," I replied with a dismissive wave of my arm.

But alas, I should have known that he had not an ounce of dignity about him, for no sooner had I turned my head than he whipped a hand out, using his air magic to snatch the card from my grasp.

I cursed him for the wally whale he was, scowling at him, my own magic rumbling to the surface of my skin as I tottered between the notion to storm over and retrieve my tatty trinket or remain in the prime position to spot my queens upon their arrival.

Max grabbed the card out of the air with a wicked smirk on his salamander chops and the rest of the rabble leaned close to look upon the results of my endless hours of labour.

"Give that back you clam-handed cretin!" I cried, taking a step towards them before pausing and looking back to the door where the new students were continuing to file in.

What a choice. And yet it was no choice at all. They were nothing compared to my ladies. Dirt on the shoe of a flea with rabies. Nothing at all.

I forgot the Heirs and the stolen card. I knew my labours were not worthy of the attention of the true queens anyway, so perhaps it was better they did not have to tarnish their eyes by looking upon it.

A glow of blazing red erupted from the corner of my eye as Caleb Altair set fire to my creation, but I didn't turn to watch, my gaze fixed on the space between the clamouring students, the noise of the room overwhelming, the anticipation driving me to insanity.

And then it all faded away.

The world fell apart, shattered, re-pieced itself and there was a new, brighter sun governing us all.

Not just one either. Two. Two beauteous beings, stepping into the presence of the unworthy without so much as a trumpet tooting their arrival – unless you counted the nervous parp of a nearby Justin, his buttocks clenching to try and stifle the sound, but my ears were not denied it, nor my humble nostrils. It mattered not, for nothing could sway my attention from their arrival.

Their brilliance was clear for all to see, their radiance blinding. I could do nothing but ogle at the deep bronze skin which looked softer than the butteriest drip on the most moist of bagels, hair glossier than the shell of a snagoon, shinier than the brightest of stars. Their eyes were as green as the apple of life, lips two rose petals just bursting with the desire to bloom. They were…majestic.

I couldn't breathe. I couldn't rise.

I had to prostrate myself before them even though they couldn't see me here among the rabble. I needed to lay myself at their feet and declare my unending loyalty to them.

My princesses had been reborn from the ashes of ruin that the death of their father had left laying across this hollow kingdom.

My lips flipped and flapped, my fingernails carving crescent moons into Justin's thigh while he stared on at my side, wonder enrapturing us.

I didn't dare inhale.

I only stared. Even as my lungs burned and ears rang with the need to draw breath, but I wasn't worthy to breathe the air they breathed.

I was nothing, no one. A flea at the feet of two goddesses born of starlight itself.

My lungs cried out with the need to draw breath. But I could not.

I would not.

I. Was. Not. Worthy.

With a sound not unlike a balloon deflating at great speed, darkness consumed my vision, and I lost sight of the fair maidens who now owned all of my heart as I pitched out of my chair and fell to the floor where an unworthy cretin such as I belonged.

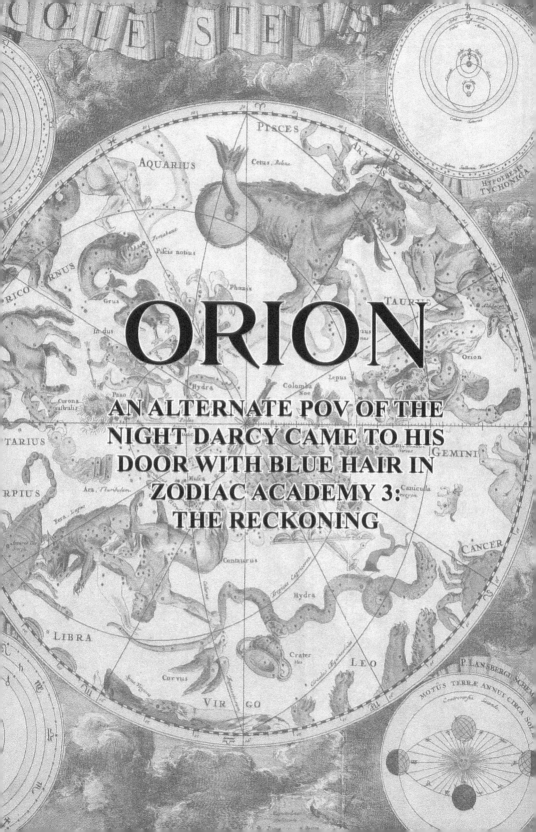

ORION

AN ALTERNATE POV OF THE NIGHT DARCY CAME TO HIS DOOR WITH BLUE HAIR IN ZODIAC ACADEMY 3: THE RECKONING

LIONEL

FROM THE LAIR OF LIONEL...

The Orions. Their family were placed together by my own hand. A victory of mine which I had secured well back in my youth, starting when I had first set eyes on Stella. A well-bred beauty, powerful too. Stella's eye wandered upon my fine exterior more than once, and her obsession with me only deepened over the years. A specimen worthy of my cock's attention, but no more than that in terms of marital efficiencies – she was not of the right bloodline after all. I left her bereft in that department, taking a far more suitable wife in the form of the exquisite Dragon, Catalina. Easily swayed by my prowess at first, though my wife grew more forceful in her own notions as time wore on, and Stella was the key to putting her back in line. Dark Coercion. A fierce power that could only be wielded by the greatest of Fae kind. I put Stella's teachings to use in many apt ways, controlling the Savage King whenever possible and securing my hold over my wife too.

Yes, Stella was a great tool indeed, and she became even more so once I set up her marriage to Azriel Orion. A man who had the ear of the Savage King, and who needed extricating from such a personal relationship. I encouraged Stella to seduce him, and she did so to please me, her interest in him causing

Azriel to become distracted for a time, but even more so when they birthed two successors. His infatuation with his family was so easily manipulated, and a touch of Dark Coercion saw him retreating from the Savage King and his wife, their bond cracking all-too-easily. So in that gap, I placed myself, wielding Azriel and Stella for my own purposes while I noted the prowess of their growing offspring.

Azriel taught his eldest, Lance, the ways of dark magic at such a young age, and it was almost too simple to place the boy in Darius's life. Their bond was keen and his usefulness to my Heir was obvious, his knowledge of dark magic securing him a position as Darius's advisor in such matters in later life. Did I know from the stars that I would Guardian Bond them? Perhaps I had toyed with the thought a time or two. But through all my carefully laid plans, I had somehow never seen Lance Orion's treachery coming. His resentment of me was more potent than I had predicted, and his weaknesses became obvious in the year following the Vega twins' return. A man who is led by the whims of his cock, is no man at all...

ORION

CHAPTER ONE

Orio:

There's a storm hitting Zodiac pretty hard and it wasn't in the weather report. Any chance your friend is involved?

Noxy:

Yes, and it's only going to get worse. Dante's in a foul mood. He's bringing storms down over the whole of Solaria right now, and he hasn't even made it to Celestia yet.

Orio:

Lionel's being a cunt, I presume?

Noxy:

However did you guess?

Orio:

I suppose he had to drop the cuddly act eventually.

Noxy:

laughing emoji

He's summoned his Dragon Guild for a fancy little weekend away in Celestia that he's dressing up as a war council to discuss the Nymphs. But I've had a glimpse of what Dante will endure, and it looks like a lot of schmoozing, cocktails and bullshit to me.

Orio:

Stars help him. The whole weekend?

Noxy:

Awful, isn't it? But I've seen that Dante has a few games in mind to keep himself entertained, and he was allowed to bring a date, so at least he's not alone.

Enjoy your evening, Orio. You're set to have a better one than him, I think.

Orio:

What have you seen?

Noxy:

Nothing specific...

I stepped into Pluto Offices, tucking my Atlas away and disbanding my air shield, leaving me dry from the crashing rain outside. I stalled, finding the one Fae there who could have my heart in my throat in an instant. My teeth clenched as my gaze slide from Darcy Vega to the foul-tasting kid who always followed her around like a stray mutt.

"-come on, chica, I showed you mine, let's see yours." Polaris lunged for Darcy, and she laughed, dancing away from him and holding her satchel behind her back.

"No! It's a surprise," she insisted as he wrapped his arms around her, trying to reach her bag. Darcy's laughter echoed off of the ceiling and she stumbled into the counter as Polaris tugged at the strap.

"Come on! Let me see your package, Darcy," he insisted, sticking his hand into her bag.

"*Diego*," she warned, and that was the moment I saw red. Something in me snapped and I was suddenly moving in a blur of speed, slamming into Polaris and sending him crashing to the floor. He dropped whatever he'd taken from her bag and went skittering across the lobby, and I was left staring at Darcy Vega with my chest heaving and a savagery in my blood that I couldn't name the source of.

"What the hell?" she demanded, hurrying over to help Polaris to his feet. The kid rubbed his head, scowling at me with fury in his eyes, and if he wanted to challenge me to a fight, I'd be more than happy to put him in his place again.

My fingers curled into a fist as I realised I'd just acted like a fucking psycho, and I didn't exactly know why. Only that I'd become defensive the second she had told him no and he hadn't stopped. I moved to pick up Darcy's package, hoping I hadn't broken whatever it was, but as I lifted it, I didn't hear any shattered pieces clinking inside. So perhaps it had survived unscathed.

Darcy stepped forward to take it from me but Polaris caught her hand, pulling her away from me like he was being some fucking knight in a shining hat.

I was the bad guy here. I could see that from the seething looks in their eyes. And yes, maybe I'd overreacted but now that Polaris had his hand firmly wrapped around my – Darcy's – I was starting to think I hadn't gone far enough. My fangs extended and rage built a war tune in my chest.

Get your damn hands off of her.

I wanted to lunge, throw him to the floor and demand he never touch her again. But that crazy notion was held in check by the much more rational voice in my head that told me I had no right to do any such thing. If she wanted him to let go, she would have pulled her hand free already.

"He's not going to hurt me." Darcy looked to Polaris, but he didn't seem convinced. And though she was right in that statement, I reckoned deep down Polaris knew she wasn't the one in danger here.

Damage control. That was what I needed to do. Regain my position over them as their professor.

"Ten points from Aer," I growled, tossing the package at Darcy's feet, giving her the asshole treatment I offered everyone else.

"What for?" Diego balked. "We didn't do anything wrong."

I glared at him coldly, unable to believe he was still going to bat with me. "Are you back-chatting me, Polaris?" I snarled, just hoping he'd give me a reason to punish him again.

Darcy shook her hand free of Diego's, bending down and picking up her package, tucking it into her bag and pursing her lips at me. There we go. Balance restored.

I stalked away, heading to a long row of the staff mailboxes and tugging mine open, grabbing a fistful of letters from inside.

"Come on," Polaris muttered to Darcy, my Vampire hearing picking it up no problem. "Let's leave the sanguijuela to himself."

The heat in my blood rose, my spine straightening. The coward couldn't even insult me to my face; he had to mutter like a frightened little chipmunk.

Their footsteps headed for the door, but there was no chance I was letting Polaris leave without facing the consequences of his actions.

"What did you call me?" I asked in my most calm, most deadly voice.

I could practically scent his fear on the air as I shot over to them and they whirled around. Polaris shifted closer to Darcy as if she might protect him from my wrath.

My letters were crushed in my fist as I glared down at my prey and I could almost hear Polaris's knees trembling.

"I called you a bloodsucker," Polaris said, but his voice cracked with fear.

"It's not an insult, just a fact."

I bared my fangs at that word. Sure, I was a bloodsucker. But the way he'd said it had been tainted with disgust. Like my kind were repellent to him. But you know what I found repellent? Spineless, quivering Fae started fights they didn't have the backbone to finish. But now he was going to have to face the music. Because at Zodiac Academy, you stood up and fought for yourself no matter the fallout. You backed yourself when no one else would, because that was what it meant to be Fae. So he hated me? Fine. I didn't give one rat's ass of a fuck about that. But if he was too afraid to defy me directly, then I'd show him what I thought of his gutless mumblings.

"Professor," Darcy said softly, forcing my attention onto her. "He didn't mean anything by it, did you Diego?"

I looked to the piece of shit and his lips twitched, but no words came out. Not a murmur or a peep. This girl was too mortal for her own good sometimes. Peacekeeping wasn't a trait I usually found in my students, but as my gaze burned into hers, my soul yanked with the urge to fall to her will. She didn't want me to strike at her friend, that was clear. But I could still hurt him without being physical.

I rolled my shoulders back, releasing a slow breath to calm the beast in me. Then I stepped around Darcy, leaning in close to Polaris's ear and he visibly trembled, shrinking beneath me.

"Dear diary," I taunted. "Today I was almost murdered by my asshole Cardinal Magic professor. I won't backchat him ever again because the next time I do I think I'll end up in a body bag for real." I moved to step away then paused, leaning close once more with a calculating grin as I decided on how best to destroy him. "P.S. I have a major crush on Darcy Vega, but she doesn't seem to realise it. I wonder what she'll say when she finds out." I strolled out of the door into the storm, letting the rain beat down on me instead of keeping it away with my air magic.

It chilled the heat in my blood and as I walked back to Asteroid Place, a weight of regret began to build in my chest. Because all I could see in my mind as I arrived outside my chalet and opened the door, were two accusing green eyes that didn't like what they saw before them.

I shoved the door shut, tossing the wad of letters on the kitchen counter before heading into the bathroom. I tore off my soaked clothes, stepping into the large shower unit and sighing as the heated water raced over my skin.

I was tense, my muscles still bunched from the need for a fight I doubted I was going to get this evening. I needed an outlet. Fuck, I needed a drink.

I shut the water off, using air to dry myself and shooting to my bedroom, pulling on a pair of black sweatpants and padding my way to the kitchen where my salvation awaited.

Bourbon. There, perched on the counter ready to steal away the knot in my chest and drown me in oblivion until tomorrow. But as I reached out to grab the bottle, I hesitated, my fingers pressing to the glass.

I'd been better lately. Resisting the urge more often. Because one measure always led to two, and two led to three. And then we were in fuck-it land and nothing good ever happened there. Usually, I wouldn't care. What was the point in resisting? It wouldn't make tomorrow any better. It wouldn't bring Clara back. It wouldn't fix what was broken in me.

Still...

I scored a hand over my face, those bright green eyes of Darcy Vega's still very much present inside my head. It wasn't a sense of judgement I felt from that look, or even disappointment. I just wanted to not be the prick she saw every time she looked at me. The alcoholic loser professor who had no prospects in life and whose only pleasure this world came from tormenting the students he was meant to teach. She was on a path to a far greater life. Regardless of thrones and Councils, even if she never went after those things, she was still one of the most powerful Fae in all Solaria. She could fulfil any dream she desired. She could blaze a trail of glory through her life, and all the while I would still be here. Stuck in no man's land, holding onto my meagre scrap of power through authority, because it was all I was ever going to possess now.

But still... I didn't drink.

Instead, I shoved the bottle in a cupboard and headed to my room, grabbing a numerology book off the shelf on the way and deciding to indulge in a pleasure that wasn't destructive.

I was doing this for her on some level. Being a better man, making the better choice. But why? Because of some inane delusion I had about claiming her? My mind was always ripe with thoughts about her, forbidden thoughts that I knew I could never act on. Not again, anyway. Not unless she wanted it too.

The atmosphere was crackling tonight, the flashes of lightning beyond my bedroom window setting the hairs rising on the back of my neck. This was no normal storm, Dante's power pouring through the sky and signalling his fury at whatever he was being subjected to right now.

But there was something else in the air, some deep, innate feeling that kept distracting me from my book. And nothing usually distracted me from my books.

I glanced at the clock on the wall, glad I wasn't on duty tonight for the Nymph patrols. The ticking of the second hand seemed louder than usual, each one more important, more relevant somehow.

I picked up my Atlas and at that very moment, a message came in which had my pulse rioting.

Darcy:
What are you doing...?

A smirk lifted my lips and I answered her in the form of a photograph, showing me in bed with my shirt off and my book in hand. I knew this was wrong, that we were well over the line again, but she had been in my head all evening, and now she was talking to me, I didn't want it to stop.

Lance:

Reading...

I'm sure I don't need to remind you to delete that picture. What are you doing?

(photographic answers are highly encouraged)

Darcy:

You don't deserve a photo because you were rude to my friend earlier.

I breathed a laugh. The asshole had had it coming.

Lance:

Polaris was asking for trouble. Plus he had his hands all over you so you can blame the Vampire Code. I have to protect my Source.

P.S.

What am I gonna have to do to earn this picture?

Darcy:

You can have a picture if you tell me the real reason you attacked Diego.

I sighed, tapping the edge of my Atlas as I realised I was going to have to come clean. But the truth was an admission she might not like about me.

Lance:

Fine.

Seeing another guy's hands on you makes me want to rip out their eyes so they never get to look at you again.

Darcy:
That is so dark.

You have no fucking idea, beautiful.

Lance:
It's nature, baby ;)
Where's my photo?

I photo came in and my heart lifted before a low chuckle left me, the picture showing a pillowcase over her head.

Lance:
Shit, how did you know about my pillowcase fetish?

Darcy:
I made a decision about my hair.
You're not allowed to see it.

I sat up in bed, needing to know what she'd gone for.

Lance:
Hang on, why am I not allowed?
Is it green or blue?
Or am I way off base?
Please tell me you haven't got a mohawk like Max Rigel. Although, I'd probably still want you just as much. I certainly did when that fuckwit

Capella took your hair.

I waited for my reply, heat raging through my veins at what I'd just said. Shit, it wasn't like she didn't know I was into her but laying it out like that set me on edge. Especially because she still wasn't replying.

I sighed when no message came in, considering sending another one, but I wasn't going to be unFae about this. I had to own my desire for her now, not water it down with bullshit backpedalling.

My mind couldn't settle back to the book though, my eyes continually trailing to my Atlas. She'd probably just fallen asleep, or was still figuring out how to reply to her douchebag professor telling her he wanted her, or maybe she was busy opening the door to her late-night hook-up and now she was beneath him and-

I stalled my thoughts in their tracks, cursing as I gripped my book so hard I bent the spine.

"Dammit." I was acting like a tween loser with his first crush.

I tried to get back to reading for all of two minutes before I tossed the book on the bed and headed into the lounge.

Gabriel would know what to do. But then I remembered that telling a Seer that I was feeling this way over a student meant he'd likely just paint a pretty picture of my future in Darkmore. And I preferred playing ignorant to that reality, assuming it would never come to pass, because entertaining the possibility that it would was too horrifying to acknowledge. Hell, it would be a worse fate than being stuck here teaching for the rest of my days. At least here I was someone, even if that someone was an asshole no one liked. In Darkmore, I'd be forgotten by the outside world, left there to rot with the worst of Fae-kind, and most likely find myself in a bloody body bag before my sentence was up. Nope, I was more than content to pretend that wasn't a fate on my horizon while I paced my living room like a caged animal and scrubbed a hand over my beard.

A light knock came at the door and I paused, frowning, uncertain if I'd really heard it or if the rain was playing tricks on me.

I walked over to check, yanking it open and forgetting to breathe at the sight of the beautiful creature before me. Darcy Vega was soaking wet in her coat, her cheeks flush with colour. Her hair was deepest blue, strands sticking to her cheeks and hanging down her shoulders, the colour of the night sky. My throat thickened as those eyes burned holes into my soul.

"Blue," she said, her breath rising before me in a cloud of vapour, proving to me how cold she was. And I knew that word was meant as an answer to the question I'd asked her. Blue or green. *Blue means you like me.*

This was her declaration, her admission of her want for me, and my head was so messed up by finding her here that I didn't know how to reply to her, rendered mute by her sudden appearance.

"I just...came to tell you that," she said, retreating as she took my silence for rejection.

But fuck if I was letting her go.

I caught her hand before she could escape away into the night, dragging her inside and pushing the door closed. I boxed her in with my arms, keeping her there and pressing one hand to the door as I looked down at her.

"I know this is crazy," she whispered.

Water dripped steadily from her hair and I reached out, brushing my fingers through it, and casting heated air to dry it out, leaving it soft and shining around her shoulders so I could admire the true colour of it. I let the air travel down her body, drying every piece of her and chasing away the cold that clung to her skin, my eyes falling from hers, to her lips, to her blue hair again.

"Come in then." I turned away, moving into the kitchenette, needing a second to breathe, think, process.

"Drink?" I called, buying time. Because I seriously needed to address the hot elephant in the room. Her coming here could lead to more, and by the stars I wanted more. But more was dangerous. More could equal the bloody body bag in Darkmore that I was most-definitely ignoring the possibility of. Then again, at least I might die a happy man.

"Um, just water." I heard her taking off her coat and shoes, keeping my attention fixed on the task at hand. Fill two glasses with water. Simple. So why was it impossible to focus on?

I finally managed it, turning to find Darcy looking flustered, eyes darting in the direction of my bedroom. She wore a revealing pair of pyjamas, her thin white top revealing the peaks of her nipples and making my cock harden at the sight.

I moved to lean against the kitchen counter, watching her as her eyes finally found mine again.

She cleared her throat, taking a step toward the exit. "Actually... I think I'd better go."

Go? That word blasted through my head like a cannon.

Before she could take another step, I shot in front of her in a blur, crowding her in against the back of the couch, offering her one of the waters.

"No," I said. "Stay."

She nodded, taking the glass from me, and her legs brushed against mine, that singular touch making me need more. So much fucking more. She took a sip from her glass, her gaze locked with mine as she swallowed down the water in two gulps while I did the same with mine.

Then I took her empty glass, reaching past her, my shoulder grazing hers as I leaned down and placed them on a table at the end of the couch.

"You're not drinking?" she breathed.

"No." I inched closer, resting my hands on the couch either side of her. *You free my mind more than any drink ever has.*

"And you haven't been drinking?" She raised a brow and a smile finally tugged at my mouth at the accusation in those words.

"No." I took her hand, my fingers intertwining with hers and her breath hitched as I leaned in closer, our bodies almost touching, but I wouldn't take this further until she made it clear that was what she wanted.

"Are you angry that I came here?" she asked, frowning at me, clearly not getting a read on my mood. I was a cagey asshole like that, but I had to drop the act. Had to let her see what this declaration meant to me.

I dipped my head, my mouth grazing the bronze skin of her shoulder, that single taste of her driving me to the brink of ruin. "No."

"Is that all you can say now?" she asked, clearly frustrated as I lifted my head and slid my hand onto her cheek, my fingers tangling in her dark blue hair. She was stunning, too mesmerising for any words to do her justice.

"No," I said with a grin, teasing her as she grew more angry with me.

"Stop it," she demanded, pushing my chest, but I pushed back, closing the distance parting us. My bare chest pressed to the heat of her, and I felt the graze of her nipples and the swell of her breasts against me, making me swallow a growl of want.

"What would you like me to say?" I asked.

"You haven't made any comment on me coming here," she said in annoyance, throwing a glance at the exit again like she was still considering leaving.

I caught her chin, tugging her back to look at me.

"Give a guy a second. One minute I'm messaging you wishing I could have you right here, and the next thing..." I leaned in, kissing the corner of her mouth and taking another forbidden taste of her. She was all my favourite summer delights, sunshine, strawberries and ecstasy. "Here you are."

I painted a line of kisses up to her ear and pushed my fingers into her hair again, taking a small bite of what I desperately wanted until she told me straight that she wanted more.

"I don't want to get you into trouble," she whispered, her hands sliding up my arms to rest lightly on my shoulders.

I trailed my fingers up her spine, sliding under her top and revelling in the feel of her silken skin against mine. I grazed my fangs over the shell of her ear and a shiver raced through her skin, responding to me so well I ached for her to give me full rein over her body.

"*Orion*," she warned, and irritation flashed through me at the use of that name, reminding me of the position of I held over her at the academy.

"Lance," I corrected sharply. "And I know the risks." My hand trailed up her spine, driving her top up at the front too so even more of our bare skin united, making me hard as hell. "But do you?"

I shifted her hair over her shoulder, trailing my lips down to the newly bared flesh in an offering. She tilted her head to one side, giving me more access as a breathy moan left her, that sounded like a prayer to my damn cock.

"I do," she panted, but it wasn't enough.

I hooked my finger under the left strap on her shoulder then paused, lifting my head to look at her with a concerned frown. "If we do this, we can't undo it."

Did she really understand the implications of this? It wasn't just me facing imprisonment if this went to shit, she would likely be expelled. The law was the law. It didn't bend even for Vega princesses.

She slid her hand around the back of my neck, drawing me down to meet her lips in a burning kiss. All my concerns melted away for her, for me, because how could we deny this thing between us? It was a thing of carnal lust, but it was more than that too. Far more. Something I couldn't even put a name to. I just knew it had to be answered.

I pressed my tongue into her mouth, and she kissed me back tentatively at first before giving into this insanity and allowing it to take over. The barriers of our magic suddenly came crashing down and power flooded between us, making me groan at the heady rush of her magic. It was a blaze so furious it outmatched any other I'd felt before, her strength like a tsunami coming crashing in against the shore. She moaned at the sense of my magic too, all of that power nearly too much to take.

I gripped the backs of her legs and hoisted her up to sit on the back of the couch, stepping between her thighs. My fingertips skated up to the edges of her shorts, pausing there as some vague drop of clarity burst through my head.

"If you want me to stop, tell me to stop," I said breathlessly, and she wrapped her legs around my waist.

"Okay, don't stop," she exhaled, and a heady laugh fell from her lungs as I drew her flush against me, needing her more than I needed the sun to rise tomorrow.

"I want you to the point of pain, Blue," I admitted, my desire for her a torture that never ended. I couldn't stop thinking about her smart mouth, her curious mind, and all the beauty of her.

She smiled, sliding her hands over my shoulders and digging her nails into my skin, the bite of pain igniting a wild hunger in me.

"Then have me," she commanded, and the shackles fell from my soul, all restraint lost to that demand.

I scooped her into my arms, my hands tight on the backs of her thighs as I carried her into my bedroom and kicked the door shut. I turned and pressed her against it, my mouth meeting hers hard as I drove her against the wood and kissed her with the kind of passion I had only ever read about it in myths and legends. Stories of lovers who could only be sated by one another, who could never get enough of the most basic of touches from one another.

I pinned her there more firmly with my hips and the hard press of my cock between her thighs made her moan, her hips flexing to grind her pussy against me and driving me fucking crazy.

"Shit, Blue," I growled before kissing her even harder.

I drew back, planting her on her feet, wanting to savour this. Threading my fingers into her hair, I admired it in the light, the dark blue colour glittering a little. It was hard to believe this girl had come here for me of all people. And I wanted to make damn sure she didn't regret it.

I released her hair and cast a silencing bubble, my gaze roaming over Darcy while she gazed at me with equal hunger. I took hold of the drawstring on her shorts, tugging her closer to me with a growl in my throat.

"You can still say no," I reminded her, and she grinned, shaking her head at me.

That look sent my pulse racing and for a second, I didn't feel like her professor, just a man she wanted, and that was a feeling I could get used to.

I gave her a slanted smile and she planted her hand on my chest, pushing me back toward the bed with intention. I let her lead, but I wouldn't for long.

I dropped onto the edge of the mattress, and she pressed down on my shoulders as she knelt over my lap. I gripped her hips, drawing her down on me firmly and she gasped at the sensation of my hard cock driving against her. There was no denying how much I wanted her, this fire she ignited in my flesh burning deep with every second.

I clutched the back of her neck, drawing her into another kiss, this one slower as I took my time to enjoy her.

"I hope you brought your peach," I teased, and a laugh tumbled from her throat as she leaned away from me.

"You're such an asshole." She thumped my shoulder and I chuckled, my hands sliding beneath the waistband at the back of her shorts and gripping her ass.

"I know." I smirked and she moved to kiss me again, but I leaned back to escape her, suddenly realising something.

I stood up, dropping her onto the bed. "Lie that way." I pointed and she frowned at me as she shifted diagonally across the bed. Shit, she looked so good spread across my sheets.

"Why?" she asked with an amused laugh.

I grinned in answer and her eyes drifted down to trace my body while I observed her with a carnal look.

Reaching down, I took hold of her right foot and wrapped my hand around her ankle. She wriggled as I caressed the sensitive skin there and she started to laugh.

"Ticklish, Blue?" I taunted, brushing my fingers over her heel and she yelped, her back arching as she tried to pull free of me.

I laughed darkly, trailing my hand up the back of her calf and she sighed in relief as I left her foot alone. My hand sailed higher, and I crawled up the bed, hovering above her and her laughter fell away as our eyes met. My knees pressed against the insides of her thighs, and I hesitated, knowing I should protect her from the potential outcome of us doing this.

"Don't stop," she said firmly, and I picked up the wild hammering of her heart. "I want this."

Excitement filled me, and I knew there was no turning back now.

"Show me how much," I growled, and her eyes sparked at those words.

She took hold of my hand and drew it to her soft lips, pressing a kiss to my knuckles. Then she guided my palm down to her throat, over the swell of her breasts and stomach, inhaling deeply as she led me beneath her waistband, leaving my hand tingling with the sensation of her skin against mine.

I swore as I slid my fingers over her soaked pussy, finding her so wet for me it had the tip of my cock twitching with need. She tugged her hand free, reaching out to curl it around my neck instead, drawing me ever closer. She parted her thighs wider as I began to tease her, my fingers sliding over her tight hole and making a breathy moan leave her. That sound was my undoing and I leaned down, my mouth crashing against hers as I circled my thumb against her clit, her hips lifting to meet with me.

"Stay still," I commanded thickly as I continued my torment, enjoying having her like this, needing more from me.

She nodded and I cast the contraception spell on her, pressing my hand to her warm skin and letting the magic rush over her. Our eyes locked as she realised what I'd done, the glint in hers telling me she was happy I had.

She dragged me down against her and I gave in to her demand with ease, laying my weight on her and pulling my hand free from her shorts. She tugged her top over her head, and I groaned in delight, palming her left breast and rolling my tongue over her hardened nipple. My fangs grazed her skin and goosebumps fled across my body, my tongue flicking over the firm peak and drawing a curse from her lips.

My thumb skated over her other breast, and she arched into my touch like she couldn't get enough of it, and the feeling was fucking mutual.

She lifted her legs either side of me, her hand riding the flex of my shoulder blades as I moved lower, dragging my mouth over her breasts then down to her bare stomach, the taste of strawberries coating my tongue. I moved lower and lower, sensing Darcy's anticipation as I hooked my hand into her my shorts and dragged them down her glossy legs. When I tossed them aside, I kneeled up and took in her naked body with so much desire that I was felt reduced to nothing but base desires and wicked sins.

I smirked like a heathen, then buried my face between her thighs, rolling the pad of my tongue over her clit in one long stroke that made her cry out in pleasure.

She bucked up to receive every ounce of pleasure I had to give, my tongue lapping and circling, guiding her toward her ruin. I was high on the sound of her moans, my ego growing with every second as I drew her towards the edge of ecstasy, then pulled her back, not letting her fall until I was ready to allow it.

"*Lance*," she begged, and I grinned against her pussy, that plea getting my heart thumping.

I lifted my head, leaving her wanting and taking in the beautiful sheen of her skin beneath me, her eyes shut as she tipped her head back and was left aching for more.

I slipped off the bed, dropping my sweatpants and moving back between her thighs, guiding the head of my cock to her wet pussy and taking possession of her with a powerful thrust of my hips. I slid in deep, the feel of her so much more perfect than I could have imagined.

She reared up with a cry, her nails clawing into my back and her teeth grazing my shoulder as she adjusted to the size of me. I fisted one hand in her hair, yanking to make her look me in the eye, waiting to see if any regret about this surfaced now.

Her legs locked tighter around me, her nails still tearing into my back, and the tightness of her pussy made my head spin.

"For fuck's sake," she gasped. "Move."

I laughed wickedly, my nose brushing hers. "Just checking."

"Stop checking," she panted, rocking her hips, and fuck, that felt so good, I had no problem giving in to her.

I drew my hips back so I was almost all the way out of her again, then slid in slowly once more, relishing the feel of her around me. Darcy writhed beneath me, urging me on with hungry kisses, knowing I was keeping her in suspense.

I drove into her harder and she clung to me, our mouths meeting as I rolled my hips, grinding my cock against that sensitive spot inside her. She moaned loudly, and I did it again, pounding into that place with every strike of my hips, increasing my pace and finding a rhythm that drove her wild. I couldn't get enough of her, the way she fit me, the way her pussy gripped my thick length, growing wetter and wetter for me as I worked to destroy her.

I could feel her drawing closer to coming as she cried out louder and louder, and every pump of my hips had her shivering for me.

I hooked my hand around the back of her left thigh, slowing my pace and luring her closer to climax with the teasing movements of my hips, not letting her fall too quickly. Her inner walls clamped around my cock, and I swore under my breath to hold myself off from finishing, my muscles flexing as I thrust deep inside her again and again.

I shuddered as I struggled to hold myself back. No girl had ever felt like this, none had ever been able to force me over the edge until I wanted to fall.

"I'm gonna lose my mind over you," I gasped, burying myself inside her and demanding her body bow to mine.

She panted, then screamed, lost to her orgasm as her pussy pulsed around my cock and I drove into her one final time, following her into bliss. I spilled myself inside her, the hot rush of my cum making her moan louder as my hands fisted her sheets either side of her, every muscle in my body tensing then relaxing with the release. It was the best fucking orgasm of my life, pleasure tearing through me and leaving me utterly spent.

My body pinned her down and my hips were firmly locked against hers while she moaned and writhed beneath me, as lost to this pleasure as I was.

Then we both fell still, and I stared at her as I brushed my thumb over her lower lip and her eyes fluttered open. Our gazes locked, her green eyes blazing and full of life.

I lifted a hand to her mouth, releasing a gentle flutter of air magic against her lips to help her catch her breath a little easier. Then I drew my hips back, pulling out of her and rolling to lay beside her, staring at the ceiling with one hand on her burning hot stomach.

The quiet settled between us and I came out of my daze and glanced at Darcy, finding a worried look on her face. I wound my hand around hers and reeled her toward me.

"Talk to me, Blue," I urged.

She rolled over, leaning on my chest as I curled my arm around her, holding her close.

"Was this a mistake?" she whispered, and I winced at those words, terrified that that was what she thoughts.

"Not to me," I said quickly. "Was it for you?"

"No," she answered, sliding her hand onto my cheek and grazing her fingers through my beard.

Relief filled me as I trailed my hand down to rest on her lower back, the tension in my body melting away. I slowly circled my fingers, raising goosebumps on her skin and enjoying how well she responded to me.

"If we're going to continue this, we have to be careful," I warned.

"I know." She kissed me gently and I slid my hand into her hair to hold her there a moment longer.

"You can't tell anyone."

She nodded.

"Not even your sister," I impressed, thinking of how all of this could come crashing down on our heads if we made one wrong move. But the thought of not having her like this again was more of an impossible option than risking being together again.

She sighed and nodded, clearly not happy about that but at least for now, I knew she would keep the secret between us.

She groaned, hiding her face in my shoulder.

"If we ever get caught, I'll do everything in my power to ensure you don't get expelled," I said seriously, that truth resounding through me.

"Let's plan never to get caught," she said.

"Plans are the best way to make the stars laugh," I pointed out with a playful grin.

"Well, let them laugh." She smiled and my eyes dropped to her reddened mouth, my cock growing hard for her again already.

"Stay," I breathed, tracking my finger down her arm.

"You know I can't," she said with a frown. "It's too risky."

I sighed, lifting my ass up to tug out the comforter beneath us and drawing it around us to keep her there. My Numerology book tumbled out from somewhere within it and she laughed.

A feral noise rumbled through my throat at that sound. "Five more minutes, then I'll take you back," I offered.

"You drive a hard bargain, Mr Orion."

I grinned. "I can drive an even harder one if you want?"

"Very tempting, but I'm not sure five minutes is long enough for your *hard* bargain."

I laughed as she curled up against me, resting her head on my shoulder while I tried to remember the last time I'd actually cuddled with a girl. Pretty sure it was never. Certainly not like this. In a way that made me want to keep her here for as long as I possibly could.

The storm rattled the windows and though I knew we were risking everything by staying here, something about the wildness of tonight made me sure we wouldn't be found. And as Darcy hooked her leg over me and I caressed the back of her thigh, her gaze meeting mine with the most tempting kind of smile I'd ever seen, I knew five minutes was bullshit. Our desire for one another was too sharp, and as she slid a hand down to grip my cock, I had several ideas of what I wanted to do with her. And I wondered how many I could get through before I had to let her go.

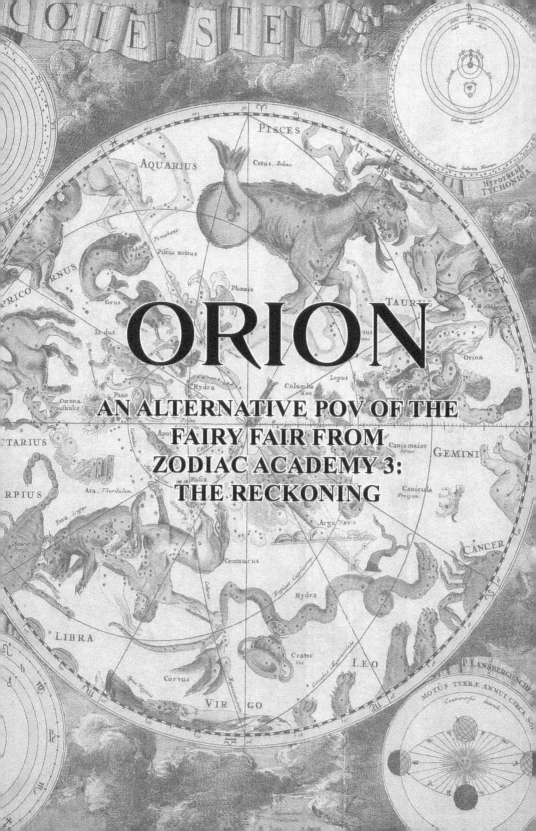

ORION

AN ALTERNATIVE POV OF THE FAIRY FAIR FROM ZODIAC ACADEMY 3: THE RECKONING

LIONEL

FROM THE LAIR OF LIONEL...

At this point, though rattled by the emergence of the Vega twins, I had rallied myself, seeking an advantage in the face of such bad omens and of course, finding one almost at once.

The twins were little more than a thorn in my side, the two of them being watched and challenged by Darius and the other Heirs, their arrival doing little more than stir up the royalists who had been lurking within my kingdom. In fact, the doing of which was something of a boon for me – I had a list of names now. Names of those I knew would never be truly loyal to me.

And so, as any great leader must be well versed in doing, my plans pivoted. I took stock of what was available to me and I used my incredible cunning to come up with the very answer I had been seeking.

The reason I had been forced to languish in the Celestial Council came down to the devastatingly irritating fact that my power levels matched those of my counterparts and so challenging them and taking my place above them by force wasn't something I could easily achieve.

But with the arrival of the Vega brats came the fortunate cosmic coincidence of the stars aligning to offer me another chance at securing that power I needed to enforce my superiority over them.

I had long coveted the shadows, seeing in them the power I desired and so hunting for ways to claim it for my own.

Stella Orion had been a pawn in that regard indeed, and we had come so very close to gaining it all but years before with the use of my dearly devoted Clara.

Alas, Clara had proved too weak to provide me with that power in the end. A weakness I had cursed time and again, the answer to the problem always pointing to a stronger bloodline.

Xavier had been the obvious choice as my next attempt but with the arrival of the Vega twins in my kingdom, I was gifted an even better option. And beyond that – there were two of them so twice the odds of success.

Had I been paying more attention, perhaps I would have noticed the scandal breaking out within the confines of the academy. Perhaps I would have realised that Lance Orion had been bewitched by Gwendalina Vega and was in the process of damning himself for nothing more than the pleasure of wetting his dick with a princess of Solaria. It would have saved me great inconvenience had I realised the truth of their affair sooner and squashed it before the press got hold of it, but I was well occupied in my plans for claiming the shadows.

Plans which did indeed come to fruition after all…

ORION

CHAPTER ONE

I sprinted from one end of the Pitball pitch to the other, holding back on my Vampire speed and pushing myself to the very edges of my limits without the use of those gifts. Every time I reached the end, I dropped to the turf and did as many push-ups as I could until my arms failed me.

Sweat glistened against my skin, my shirt long discarded so just my shorts were in place. When I was exhausted to the point of dizziness, I drained half my water bottle in one go, then grabbed one of the heavy earth balls I'd gotten out of the locker. I threw it as hard as I could into the air, then ran to catch it, turning and bracing for the hard slam of the metal against my chest, digging my heels in to keep my balance. Then I did it again, and again, until there was a reddened bruise rising across my pecs and I had to stop for more water.

Since I'd thrown the bottle of bourbon out of my office window, I hadn't indulged in a single drop. And thanks to my ragingly fun need to escape my head most of the time, especially since things still felt so fucked between Darcy and I, I'd resorted to this shit.

I moved into drills at the edge of the pit, making a fireball hover above me on a gust of air while I did sit-ups beneath it. Every time my back hit the floor, I released the power of air which held the ball skyward so it came flying down towards me in a fiery blaze, and I only let myself cast air again to stop it if I made it upright in time. I called these death-ups, and often had the Pitball team do them while relying on the air elementals to keep the fireballs from hitting them. Suffice to say, a lot of people ended up burned in those warm-ups, especially since Seth Capella and Max Rigel focused on keeping them and their little foursome safe from harm and often casually forgot to help out anyone else. It was carnage, but that was Pitball. And if you couldn't hack it in training, you sure as shit weren't gonna hack it on the field.

"Trying to kill yourself, Orio?" Gabriel's voice called to me from somewhere above, and a flash of dark wings crossed the sky.

He landed with a thud beside me, grabbing the ball out of the air, using his water Element to freeze it and douse the flames. They'd burn through that ice though, the balls all enchanted with powerful magic that couldn't easily be tampered with.

He tossed it from hand to hand, and I slumped against the grass with my breaths falling furiously from my lungs. "What are you doing here?"

"Me and the family are in town for the Fairy Fair," he said, and I noted the nice white shirt stuffed into the back of his jeans.

"Oh, is that today?" I muttered, although I already knew it was because I'd asked Darius to go Nymph hunting with me and he'd said he was busy with his Heir buddies heading to the fair. And as every asshole and their owl on campus would be going there too, I was giving it a firm miss. Although, there was one little owl I wouldn't have minded attending with...

She was probably getting ready for it now with her friends, looking ten shades of tempting.

Gabriel picked up the bag for the fireball, slipping it inside and tossing it to the ground.

"Why don't you join us?" he suggested, and I shook my head as he offered me his hand, tugging me to my feet.

"Nah, I'm just gonna stay home and…"

"Lay on the couch alone and watch old re-runs of your favourite Starfire games?" Gabriel finished for me with a pitying look. "Yeah, that sounds real pathetic, Orio."

"That's not what I was gonna say." I folded my arms, and he gave me that all-knowing, all-*seeing* look that made a growl of annoyance rise in my throat. "Fine. But it's not pathetic, it's a perfectly reasonable evening."

"Wow, you're right. I can only strive to have a 'perfectly reasonable evening', that sounds like the peak of existence." He smirked.

"Fuck you." I cracked a grin, but it fell fast away as my dark mood settled over me again, barely tempered by the intense workout I'd been subjecting myself to for the past couple of hours.

"Look, I've got to go, everyone's waiting for me. I just came by to give you this." He pushed a hand into his pocket, taking out a small scroll and passing it to me.

It was held closed by two delicate golden clasps, and as I unrolled the parchment, I realised what I was looking at.

"This is one of the original Fable Curses," I breathed in disbelief, the mark of the Fable family stamped at the top of it, a cursive G decorated with ivy. They were a family steeped in a history of dark magic and were famous for their creation of many twisted curses, all of which were now illegal.

"How did you get this?" I asked in awe. "Weren't these all locked up tight in the Museum of Fae Antiquities?"

He opened his mouth to answer, but it dawned on me who had retrieved this before he even said his name.

"Leon," he said with half a shrug.

"That Lion is one hell of a thief," I said, then snapped my head up from the scroll to look at Gabriel. "Don't tell him I said that. He'll send me a fucking gift basket full of dildos or some shit."

"That was one time," Gabriel said with a snort.

"What in the actual hell did he think I needed fifteen dildos for?" I said, shaking my head, confounded all over again by the bizarre gift Leon had sent me after I'd helped him out with some dodgy shit they'd all gotten caught up in back in their days at Aurora Academy.

"I'll tell him one would have sufficed," Gabriel chuckled, and I gave him a hollow look.

"Don't you laugh. You wanna know what happened to those dildos? Fucking Washer happened to them. Found them in the trash and made a dream catcher out of them that he hung in his window."

"By the stars." Gabriel grimaced, and I turned my attention back to the scroll. "Do you think that could be what you're looking for?"

I frowned at the curse laid out on the scroll and the sketch of the moon and sun crossing over at the top of it. This dark magic could only be performed on a Lunar Eclipse, and I knew for a fact that Lionel possessed a very rare, very outlawed collection of the Fables' works because my own mother had gifted them to him. The curse was all kinds of messed up and sounded just like the sketchy sort of shit Lionel would be interested in.

"Could be," I said with a nod. "I'll show this to Darius and see if he can find any sign of his father gathering these items." A lot of it was rare as hell, and some of it didn't even exist anymore, so far as I knew. The curse required the use of a Blentle feather, but those birds had died out a long time ago. "Thanks, Noxy."

"No worries." He flexed his wings, then hesitated, grey eyes glazing over before he returned to the present moment, a knowing smile playing around his mouth. "You should get home for your night of fun."

He clapped me on the shoulder and took off into the sky, leaving me there with the sense that he knew something I didn't. But that was kind of inescapable when it came to being friends with him.

I watched his dark-winged form disappear beyond the open roof of the stadium, then sighed and shot forward with a blur of speed. It took me exactly one second to tidy up all the Pitballs, then I was in the shower in the changing room, butt naked and lathering body wash against my skin. In the fifth second, I was by my locker, fully dry from the combined use of my air and water magic, and by the sixth, I was dressed in my suit pants and shirt. I kicked on my shoes, the soles of them made with toughened Minogum, just like all of my shoes were. The Vamporium was a designer store specialising in footwear for my Order, and they were made to withstand grinding against any surface right up to our top speed.

I grabbed my bag, tossed my locker shut, and raced out of the stadium again, finding the pathways busy with students all dressed up for a night out at the Fairy Fair. *Fucking upbeat, smiley little shits.*

I weaved between them, tearing across Earth Territory in the direction of Asteroid Place, but slowed to a normal pace as I spotted a glimmer of blue hair ahead, my heart colliding with my ribcage full force.

I paused at a kink in the path that passed through a small cluster of trees, listening to every word she spoke to the prick accompanying her. Diego motherfucking Polaris. He was hatless. And had he cut his hair? Asshole. He was all dressed up like a fancy little fuckwit too. What was his aim, was he trying to impress my girl? Shit, was she going to the fair with him?

Her hair was half pulled up with a silver clip and a knitted black dress hugged tightly to her figure, drawing my gaze along her curves. Curves which I had dragged my tongue over and tasted the perfection of not so long ago.

My fangs prickled in my mouth, and I started walking again instead of lurking here like a creep.

I trailed behind them, watching their every move as my jaw began to grind. Their arms were hooked together, and they both looked all too fucking comfortable with each other for my liking. It struck me like a truck at what this shitstorm of a reality was. They were going to the fair together, just the two of them, no whiff of another freshman in sight. And that sounded an awful lot like a fucking date.

Darcy suddenly glanced back over her shoulder like she'd sensed me there, and her bright green gaze slammed into me like a tsunami. I stepped smoothly down the path to my right which led toward Asteroid Place, proving I was just coincidentally right behind her instead of following her like a stalker, keeping my expression void of the blazing hellfire rising in my chest.

My gaze tracked over the place their arms were locked together, and my heart hammered out a painful beat. Violence coated my tongue and possessiveness sent my mind into a furious mania. So that was it, was it? We were done and now she was dating fucking Polaris?

It hurt, like a knife driving under my ribs and finding the beating muscle that lay beneath, carving it up real good.

Darcy pressed her lips together, her persisting anger with me clear as she turned away just like that, returning her focus to *him*.

No one even knew about Darcy and me, so if she didn't speak to me again from this moment forward, that was it. We were done, and no one would ever even know we'd been something. Like a flash of fire in a too-hot pan, burned out before we'd found enough fuel to sustain us.

I had the tormenting feeling that I'd fucked up, that this was entirely my fault and I had played my cards all wrong.

I scored a hand over my face as I continued walking, and the moment I was out of her sight, I took out my Atlas and scrolled my way to Francesca's name, hitting call. She answered on the second ring, and I hoped she was up for a night out as surely as I suddenly was.

"Hey," I clipped. "You wanna go to the Fairy Fair?"

"That is so crazy. I just got a call from my friend saying she can't go with me, so I've got a spare ticket."

"You ready to leave soon then?"

"I can be there in five."

"Perfect."

I hung up, then ran forward with a burst of energy, speeding my way back to the Asteroid Place and leaving the gate swinging shut behind me as I made it to my front door. My fist slammed into the wall beside it before I could stop myself, a crack splintering out across the masonry that was going to serve me a scalding from Elaine.

I shoved the door open and prowled inside, a roaring noise going off in my head. I needed to get to that fair. I could use the fresh air and time with Francesca. It'd do me good. And in no way was I going there to keep an eye on Darcy and her little date.

If he touches her, I'll slice him open and bake all his innards into a pie. I don't even bake, but for him, I'll don a little pink apron, make the pastry from scratch, and cook up a pie so damn good that I win first prize in a local baking contest.

The door swung open, and I turned, finding Francesca there in a fitted red dress and a long jacket, frowning at me in concern. "I fixed your wall. Why was it cracked?"

"You were quick," I said, glancing down at my knuckles which I realised were shredded and dripping blood onto the floor.

"Lance," she gasped, grabbing my hand and healing it in an instant, looking up at me in concern with dark, familiar eyes.

"That wall's had it coming for a while," I muttered dryly, pulling away from her and heading to the kitchen, tossing cupboards open in search of a bottle. What was I staying sober for anyway? Bourbon had always been my answer, so why would I change that?

"What are you looking for?" Francesca asked, but I didn't answer, continuing to hunt the backs of understocked cupboards and cursing every time I came up short. I'd cleared out every bottle and now I was paying the price of that idiocy.

"Lance." Francesca caught my arm, turning me to her. "Talk to me."

I sighed, my hair falling forward into my eyes as I dropped my head. "It's nothing." *Or everything, depending on which way you look at it.*

"Do you ever feel like the stars are against you?" I asked her, and her eyes widened at my sharp tone. "Because I'm starting to think they have my name on the top of their shit list, Francesca, because they take away every good thing I set my sights on."

She reached up, cupping my cheek, and I took a breath to centre to myself, feeling myself slipping into that dark place I was so accustomed to. At least, I had been before Darcy had cast a few drops of sunlight into the pool of desolation I'd been lost at the bottom of. I'd finally found a direction to swim, and no matter how wrong it had been to follow her light, I'd let myself chase it, knowing I might eventually find myself in an even deeper abyss when I lost her. Because of course, I'd always been going to lose her, I just hadn't expected the light to fade so fast.

"Not everything," Francesca said gently. "What's happened?"

My gaze fell from hers and I shook my head marginally, this secret too deep to share. She may have been my Nebula Ally, but she worked for the Fae Investigation Bureau, and she was the last person in the world I could share this with. I didn't think she'd rat me out, but I could put her job in jeopardy if this secret was ever exposed by other means and I was put under interrogation. I couldn't do that to her.

"I just had a rough day," I said, hating having to avoid the truth when it came to her. We used to tell each other everything, but really, I'd been a pretty shitty friend since Clara had died. Losing her had made me cold, distant. Smiles weren't easy anymore, not like they used to be for the man I'd been when we'd known each other at the academy. I'd changed, and for some reason she'd stuck by me, even though I forgot to call or cancelled plans with little notice. And when she tried to talk to me about it, I just shut down, because the last thing I wanted to do was bring up Clara and feel the loss of her all over again. So instead, I just sort of drifted along, fulfilling my duties here at Zodiac with the minimum effort I could get away with and finding meaning in pretty much nothing except helping Darius train to take on his father.

It was the only thing that kept me getting up in the morning, the knowledge that one day soon, I would see Lionel fall, and maybe then I would gain some peace in retribution. At least, that had been the only thing getting me up in the morning until Darcy. She had no fucking idea how much I looked forward to seeing her in Cardinal Magic, watching the way her eyes lit up with the knowledge I gave her about this world or the way she got that little crease between her brows when she was contemplating the vastness of her capabilities. And it had become so much more than that, each look we shared holding a secret that set my heart pounding and my fangs prickling with want. I craved her in a way that held all of my attention, made me forget all the dark shit that plagued me until there was just the hopeless possibility of us.

I felt Francesca's eyes on me, sure she wanted to press me further on my vague reply, but when she spoke, thankfully, she let it go. "Well then, you're in luck." She waved something under my nose, and I took in the silver tickets to the Fairy Fair with a sparkly Faerris wheel embossed on it. "Because we're going out. And we're going to forget all about the shit eating at us."

"What's eating you?" I frowned.

She sighed heavily. "My boss is riding my ass for the latest Nymph report, and he wants me to discount the nest we raided last week because it was half a mile beyond the border of our hunting parameters. He's trying to play down the threat in the area so the public don't lose their minds. But shouldn't we be out there exposing the truth? People need to be prepared."

"That's bullshit," I agreed, and she nodded.

"Anyway, forget work. Forget everything, in fact. Let's just have a good time where you don't have a fight with any more walls that have pissed you off. Pretty please." She fluttered her eyelashes at me.

"Alright, let me get changed," I said, then shot away from her into the bedroom, putting on jeans and a black shirt before tossing on my leather jacket.

I returned to the lounge, and Francesca's eyes dipped down to take in my outfit before she moved forward and grabbed my arm. "Ready?"

"Uhuh," I said, letting her tow me towards the exit.

"I've got stardust," she suggested, but I hadn't driven my car in a week, and I was really in the mood for it. Maybe a drive might release some of this potent energy in me too.

"Let's take the Faerarri." I grabbed my keys and whipped her off her feet, shooting out of Asteroid Place with her laughter rising around me. I ran as fast as I could, the air whirling madly around us and my heart thumping furiously, almost powerfully enough that I couldn't feel the knife Darcy had slid into it earlier. Ha, who was I kidding?

I only stopped when we were standing right beside my beautiful red car in the parking lot, swiftly opening the passenger door for Francesca as I placed her down. She combed her fingers through her windswept hair as she dropped into the car, a bright smile lighting her features.

I shot around and slid into the driver's seat, pressing the button to start up the engine, and the car purred deeply. I backed up and drove us out of the lot and away across campus, soon sailing through the gates onto the open road and turning down a lane to take the more interesting route to the fair.

I pressed my foot to the gas and used my heightened hearing to sense if anything was ahead of us on the road, but it was all clear.

I let her fly, driving with wild abandon around horseshoe bends, carving through the woodland and climbing over the hillside.

"What's got into you?" Francesca called, her laughter turning to a whoop as I took another hairpin turn at high speed, my knuckles turning white around the wheel.

"Nothing." *Just a blue-haired princess who's an heir to the throne of our entire kingdom, and my student, who I am entirely forbidden from laying a hand on.*

I was guessing having her pinned beneath me, moaning my name while I lost myself to the tightness of her body and the heat of her bare skin against mine wasn't okay. Yeah, that wasn't going to land me hundreds of feet underground in Darkmore Penitentiary at all if anyone ever found out about it, was it? And as she currently held no loyalty to me and was off turning those enchanting green eyes on someone else already, I couldn't say for sure whether she was going to keep our secret either. Fuck.

I took another turn at speed, descending downhill as the sunlight died all around us and the stars came out to play, glittering up there in their bed of darkness.

I had to get a grip. Darcy wasn't spiteful. She wasn't going to give me up to the authorities unless she had a damn good reason to, and what we'd had had been real, hadn't it? It sure as hell had been for me, but the way she seemed to be moving swiftly on already made me wonder if I was a complete idiot to have believed she had actual feelings for me.

I made it to the Fairy Fair, turning into the field where rows of cars were parked up in front of the carnival, picking a place at the far end next to a flashy white car which belonged to Seth Capella.

I got out and Francesca joined me as we walked towards the entrance beneath a glittering arch. Beyond it, a Faerris wheel rose up from the dark along with several rollercoasters, standing high above the avenues of stalls, games, and vendors. Francesca offered the tickets to an attendant, and we were let into the fair where neon lights blazed at me from every direction. My eyes instinctively hunted the crowd for blue hair before I forced myself to stop and led Francesca toward the first row of stalls.

We wandered along, pausing at a van shaped like a giant beer bottle to grab some drinks, but despite my hunt for Bourbon earlier, the want had subsided. I ordered myself a coffee and got Francesca a beer, then we wandered deeper into the fair, catching up on general shit going on in our lives.

"Oh hey, there's Anika." Francesca pointed to her friend. "I'll be back in a sec." She jogged over to greet her friend, and I drained the last of my coffee, the crowd moving around me, people smiling and chatting, having the time of their star-damned lives. Couldn't relate.

"Cooweee!" Washer's voice set my nerves on edge, and I didn't turn my head in the direction it had come from, praying it wasn't my attention he was after. But apparently, I wasn't so fortunate. Go fucking figure. "Lancey boy! Look behind you!"

I turned reluctantly, finding him waist deep in purple Jello in a wide rubber ring on the ground. There was a sign beside it naming this game 'Fight a Fellow in the Jello'.

"Hello, Brian." I nodded to him curtly, hoping that would be enough to avoid more of his attention, but of course it wasn't.

"Come have a little rompy-pompy in the Jello with me. Elaine is just stripping down in the changing tent to prepare for getting wet and wild, but you could go next. What do you say?"

"Nah, I'm good," I said with a false smile. "I'd rather pluck my eyes out with a fork."

"What was that?" he called, cupping a hand around his ear. "So loud in this place, isn't it? Now, come on, strip off and I'll wrestle you into submission, big boy."

He started sloshing up and down in the Jello so it made a gross noise, the purple sludge slapping him wetly against his tanned chest and dripping down it. He rolled onto his hands and knees, his speedo-bound ass jerking up in the air as he started arching his spine, tossing his head back so Jello flew from his hair and showered over him.

"By the stars," I cursed, backing up a step.

Elaine Nova stepped out of the changing tent in a black bikini, leaping straight into the Jello and slamming down on top of Washer, knocking him flat on his front.

"Ha!" she cried, and Washer flipped backwards to knock her off of him with a whoop of excitement, rolling over onto his back and half sitting up in the Jello. Elaine threw a leg over his waist, straddling him, and the two of them started see-sawing in the sludge, shoving and slapping each other before they started kissing with way too much tongue.

Francesca caught my hand, and I turned to look at her in horror over what I'd just witnessed.

"Run," she whispered, tugging me away, and I broke out into a sprint, letting her guide me along through the crowd in desperation to escape the sight I could never unsee.

We turned down another row of stands, coming to a halt beside one of the game stalls, and the two of us broke a laugh, sharing a look of relief.

"Thanks," I said, tossing my coffee cup away into a nearby trash can.

"Any time," she said through a grin, throwing her beer bottle away too. "Seriously, *any* time. No one deserves to be subjected to Washer as often as you are."

"It's like his fate is entwined with mine," I said with a grimace.

She patted my arm with mock pity. "Yup. Maybe you're Elysian Mates."

I barked a laugh. "By the stars, if there was ever a reason to turn down a perfect match, that would be it. I'd wear my black rings with pride and never love again."

She grinned at me. "Guess what? Anika's new boyfriend has this cabin up in Lucena by the coast, she was saying we could all head up there in the spring and-"

She went on but the sound of a girl cooing excitedly made my eyes snap away from her through the crowd, right to where Darcy was standing beside Diego in front of a game where a large Pegasus toy was up for grabs.

"I'll win you it," Diego said, puffing out his chest like a peacocking asshole and placing his drink down on the counter. A long-barrelled red gun sat at the centre of it, and a single magical target was suspended in the air at the back of the stand.

The guy behind the counter sidled closer. "Are you going to have a go, missy?" he asked Darcy.

"Sure," she said brightly, stepping forward to pick up the gun.

"I'll do it," Diego insisted, passing over the money before Darcy could get there, and my jaw ticked. *She said* she *wanted a go, you little cock.*

Darcy sighed, folding her arms in disappointment as Diego picked up the gun, and my teeth ground together in my mouth.

"I just have to hit that target?" he asked the man.

"You have to hit it three times. You get thirty seconds and unlimited shots," the vendor confirmed with a look that said it wouldn't be so simple, and I hoped Diego was about to make an ass of himself. "Ready?"

Diego nodded and the man grinned, stepping aside to let him shoot, and he lifted the gun to fire at the wide target. An explosion of red light burst from it with a powerful kickback that made him stumble away from the counter, and I smirked at his failure. The target sped sideways, and the blast exploded into a shower of sparks as the shot missed. Diego cursed, raising the gun and firing again, but this time, the target shrank to the size of a pea and Diego missed once more.

Well, if this was his attempt to impress Darcy, then maybe I didn't have so much to worry about after all.

"That's impossible," Darcy said with a laugh, but Diego looked furious as he lined up the gun again. He took shot after shot, the target darting left, right, up, down, moving all over the place and not letting him hit it a single time.

I was moving before I'd realised I'd walked straight away from Francesca, fuelled by the primal need to show him up.

Diego slammed the gun down in frustration, and I stepped in beside him.

"Move over," I commanded, pushing Diego aside as Francesca joined me.

I refused to look at Darcy at all, knowing she was going to throw off my concentration, and I really, really wanted to make a point here.

Francesca tilted her head, resting her hand on my arm. "For me?" she asked.

I curled an arm around her waist and tugged her against my hip, wanting Darcy to see, wanting her to hurt the way I hurt when I looked at her with another guy. "Do you want the blue Pegasus or the silver?"

In my periphery, Diego caught Darcy's sleeve to draw her away, but she dug her heels in and satisfaction poured through me. *Good girl, now watch what a real Fae can do.*

Francesca caressed my arm. "Blue," she decided, which was just perfect.

"My favourite colour." I kissed the tip of her nose, knowing it was overkill and half expecting Francesca to knock me away for going all PDA on her, but for some reason, she didn't.

I moved to face the target, pressing the end of the gun to my shoulder, aiming down the sight. The man behind the counter restarted the game and the target flew sideways, my gaze speeding after it and locking tight. I pulled the trigger and it exploded into a shower of multi-coloured sparks as I hit it dead on. *Easy.*

The target reappeared in a tiny form, whizzing about like a bee, and I shifted the gun with a flash of my Order speed. I pulled the trigger and a display of sparks followed as I hit it, following up with the final shot so quickly that I managed to shoot the target even before it had settled into its next form. It was child's play.

The guy unhooked one of the huge blue Pegasus toys from where it hung on a rack, handing it over to me, and I passed it straight to Francesca. I slung my arm over her shoulders and led her away, not looking back but not focusing on where I was going either as my hearing remained trained on the girl behind me.

"Let's go on all the rides until we puke," Darcy said in a bright tone, and bitterness threaded through me. Was she not at all affected by any of that? Was she not going to make a single comment about it?

"Er...okay," Diego said, and I glanced back, catching sight of her grabbing Diego's hand, and leading him away into the crowd. My heart was butchered, sliced up and laid out for the crows to pick at.

"Do you want a drink?" Francesca offered, and I blinked back to my own reality, finding we'd stopped in front of a coffee stand.

I shook my head, letting her get one while craning my neck to try and spot a flash of blue hair moving away through the crowd, but she was lost to it now. Off on her little date, clearly not caring that Diego had the aim of a blind, legless pigeon.

I moved forward, plucking the large Pegasus toy out from under Francesca's arm as an idea came to me. "I'll drop this back in the car, if you want?"

Her brows raised and she nodded her agreement, opening her mouth to reply, but I was already gone, speeding away through the fair back to the parking lot. I tossed the toy in the trunk of my car and returned to the fair, doing a circuit of the whole carnival and tracking Darcy down. My fangs tingled with the adrenaline surging through me, and I tried not to lean too deeply into the call of the hunt, though it was damn tempting.

I found Darcy queuing for a rollercoaster and returned to Francesca with a direction in mind, capturing her hand and leading her that way.

I pulled her to one side by a couple of stalls, and as Francesca turned to browse them, my gaze fell firmly on my target.

Darcy was facing Diego, the two of them standing far too close, and the moment I thought that, his arm slid around her waist and drew her even closer. She gazed up at him and I saw the exact moment when he decided to kiss her, his head tilting, his eyes going all blank and dreamy.

Venom spewed so hotly through my veins that it made me take a step forward, but it was already too late. His mouth came down on hers and I froze, my muscles becoming rigid as pain and jealousy ripped a black hole through the centre of my chest, sucking everything into it until all that remained was a madness that urged me towards violence.

Darcy stepped back suddenly, and the crowd shifted so I lost sight of her expression, and by the time they moved the fuck out of the way again, she was turning out of the queue, abandoning Diego and the ride. Her eyes found mine like she felt the intensity of my glare, and her face paled as I worked to keep every single emotion from my face, not letting her know how much she'd just obliterated me. She started pushing through the line of Fae, making a beeline for me as if she had something she desperately wanted to say, but I didn't want to hear a single word of it.

I was fuelled with spite, my mind clouded by it, and as Francesca turned to me with bright eyes, my mind locked onto an answer to this feverish agony. One that was purely selfish and full of malice.

I caught hold of my friend, pulling her close, and her eyes widened as she realised what I wanted, her hand gripping my leather jacket and yanking me nearer in encouragement. Our mouths met, and I tasted the wickedness in this act, the intention of the wound I wanted to deliver.

"Darcy!" Diego called, telling me she'd left him behind and was headed this way.

I twisted us around, pushing Francesca firmly up against the side of the stand, fisting a hand in her hair while locking the other one tight around her waist. Her tongue met mine in hungry strokes, and I willed my body to react to her touch like it used to, but it was as if a flip had been switched in me the moment Darcy Vega had come parading into this world to consume every one of my thoughts.

Francesca clung to my jacket while her free hand gripped my jaw, her fingers grazing through my beard, and I let it all happen, happily throwing fuel on the fire which was burning mine and Darcy's world down. But *she* was the one who'd lit the match.

I felt Darcy's eyes scalding the flesh from my bones and was relieved to finally be getting some reaction from her, to know that this hurt her just like she'd hurt me. It was petty, immature, and cruel, but I was so full of jealousy that I knew if I didn't do this, I'd do something far worse to Polaris. I'd rip his head clean from his shoulders and earn myself a stretch in Darkmore for a far less tempting sin than the one I had already committed with Darcy.

I thought of nothing but her as I kissed a woman I could kiss without consequence, wishing I could claim the one I was forbidden from touching instead. My mind was so full of Darcy Vega that she became part of this kiss, twisting a knife in my chest and glaring into the darkest recesses of my soul.

What Darcy witnessed on the outside of this kiss was a lie. She saw my rejection of her, she saw my declaration of my desire for another woman over her. But it was a fucking mirage painted by my hand because *she* was what I truly wanted. She was the girl I could never have, never keep, and never carve from my thoughts.

This would surely put an end to the madness for good, because she was here with Diego, not me. She wanted him now. Not. Me.

She would put up her walls, shut me out, and there'd be no more stolen looks, no more unlawful messages, nothing more to give me any hope that she still wanted me to cross those lines.

Francesca clawed at my shirt and moaned into my mouth, her back arching as I shoved her carelessly against the stall. The kiss tasted like acid, and I swear I felt the stars reaching down from the sky and grasping me by the fucking throat to force me off of her. Why they were so intent on messing with me lately, I had no idea. Maybe someone had put a dark curse on me, because sometimes it felt like there wasn't a thing that went right in my life anymore.

I stepped back, but Francesca stepped forward, sucking her lower lip into her mouth seductively and reaching for me once more. I moved back again, pushing my fingers through my hair and praying for the clarity I'd hoped that kiss would give me. A feeling that the doors were closed for good now between Darcy and I, bolted and impenetrable, but instead, I found my head turning and my eyes roaming the crowd, hunting for her already. Maybe if I could see the hurt in her expression, the shutters snapping into place against me, I'd feel this bond sever between us. Maybe then I could move on. But I couldn't find her among the crowd, and that was somehow worse, because I'd hoped to find her watching me with anger and betrayal in her eyes, showing me she still cared.

Francesca said something to me, but I couldn't hear it, still looking for the blue-haired girl who had my attention always trapped so tightly in her fist. I was a wasp, and she was a honey pot. Every taste of sweetness I stole only lured me closer to my end, but I was a slave to my own desires, walking too willingly into my demise.

"Lance." Francesca snapped her fingers in front of my face and the drone in my ears lifted, the sound of the world coming sharply back into focus at last. "What's gotten into you tonight? One minute, you're all over me and the next, you don't even seem to see me."

I pinched the bridge of my nose, realising my fangs were out, hungering for a bite of a girl I craved like an addiction.

"Sorry, I..." I shook my head, having no truthful end to that sentence that I could voice aloud. I was a prick, using her like this. She was my friend, my Nebula Ally, for fuck's sake. I should have been confiding in her instead of using her as some sort of Vega bait.

Yeah, Lance, tell the FIB agent all about how you took a student to your bed, let's see how well that goes.

"It's been a long week," I muttered, thankful that was the truth at least.

Francesca moved into the arc of my body, caressing my bicep, and I folded my arms, placing something of a barrier between us.

"Why don't we head back to mine? You're clearly not enjoying this. We can just have a quiet evening, put a movie on and share a bottle of wine. I'll help you forget all about it." She gave me a flirtatious look, and my cock sent an email to my brain written in all caps.

DEAR BRAIN,

FUCK NO.

SINCERELY,

COCK

I sighed, about to pull the Vampire card - again- because like a fucking asshole, I'd been using that excuse a lot lately. I needed alone time, sure, that was understandable as an Order need. But Francesca wasn't going to buy it forever. I wasn't a star-damned hermit.

"I think I just need some alone time," I sighed. "Think I'll head home."

"No, come on," she insisted. "Stay. I'll cheer you up." She gripped my arm, pulling me along. "Let's go on the rollercoaster."

"I'm really not in the mood."

"You used to love the rollercoaster." She glanced back at me with a frown, continuing to tug me along.

"Francesca," I growled.

"I'm not taking no for an answer. My horoscope said to be there for a Libra today, and now I know it means you, that's what I'm going to do. Wherever you go tonight, I'm coming with you."

I knew she was trying to be a good friend, but I seriously needed to be alone right now, and I felt like a dick for coming here at all. Francesca clearly wasn't going to be letting me go anytime soon though, and I really didn't want her to come with me back to campus.

I spotted a row of porta-pottys and pulled away from her. "Be back in a sec."

I jogged away, slipping into one of the toilets and shutting the door firmly. It was a miniature luxury bathroom inside with marble flooring and a gilded mirror on the back of the door, soft classical music playing around me and the scent of vanilla in the air.

I took out my Atlas, quickly downloading an app which would keep my number anonymous, then making a call to the FIB. I ran a hand over my throat, casting a spell on my voice to make it sound different as the call connected.

"I've just seen a Nymph in east Tucana," I said frantically. "On the corner of Majesty Street. Hurry, please."

"We'll dispatch a unit immediately," the officer said, and I hung up, pushing my Atlas into my pocket and meeting my gaze in the mirror as I released the magic on my voice.

"Asshole," I muttered at myself, then shoved the door open and returned to Francesca.

"Rollercoaster. Now," she demanded, grabbing my hand.

Her Atlas started ringing and she pulled it out of her bag, a frown forming on her brow before a professional mask slipped over her features.

"Dammit, it's work," she said, then wandered away as she answered the call, and I wondered if I should just have been more straight with her rather than sending her off on a wild goose chase. But here we were.

I stood there alone, watching Fae hurl coconuts at a magical box that kept vanishing within the nearest stall, lifting a hand to my mouth and wiping my lips on the back of my hand, trying to get any lasting feel of Francesca off of me. It wasn't her fault. Everything just felt wrong with her lately. Maybe I needed a vacation, but with Lionel always keeping tabs on my attendance at Zodiac so I could be close to Darius, I wouldn't get a chance for one of those for a long time. No, I was fucked. A damned man possessed with the need to dig his own grave.

Put down the shovel, dammit. You can still get out of this.

"Hey, Professor!" someone called, and my gaze slid reluctantly in that direction, finding Seth Capella strolling along with a large polar bear plushie tucked under his arm. Max and Darius walked on either side of him, and the crowd parted for them like a repellent enchantment was radiating from their bodies. But I knew better. It was their fame, drawing attention from all around, people gasping and pointing them out while they acted like they hadn't noticed. Or maybe they were so used to it that they really hadn't.

"Did you come here all alone?" Seth asked as they approached me.

"Hey, man," Darius said, and I took a step forward the same time he did, the two of us drawn to embrace as the Guardian Bond hummed keenly between us. But we both realised it at the same moment and pulled up short instead.

"Woah, you taste like heartbreak and jealousy, man," Max commented, smoothing a hand over his red mohawk, and I slammed my mental shields up hard, forcing him out. "Who gutted you and left you here like an unwanted fish?"

"No one," I growled.

"So you did come here with someone?" Seth pushed, taking a lollipop out of his pocket, unwrapping it and stuffing it into his mouth. "But then they dumped you?"

"I didn't get dumped," I sniped, trying to keep a level head while Max prodded at me with his Siren powers.

"Who are you here with?" Darius asked, the tight lines on his brow telling me he wasn't in the best of moods himself tonight. I wished Tweedle Dee and Tweedle Dipshit would piss off so we could have a moment alone to talk about it.

"Francesca," I said. "She's just taking a call."

"Riiiiiiight," Seth said sarcastically, swirling the lollipop between his teeth. "*Sure* she is, sir. Hey, why don't we all go on the log ride together? Darius can't wait to go on it, can you, bro?" He looked over at Darius, who seemed about as excited to go on a log ride as he would be to take a shit in public.

"He's a barrel of laughs today, I can feel how much he's dying to get on the teacup ride too," Max said with a chuckle, and Darius casually flicked a hand, setting fire to the grass around his friend's feet. Max doused it with a blast of water, laughing harder.

"So where's the fourth Ninja Turtle?" I looked around for Caleb, and Darius spewed smoke between his lips, making me arch a brow at him. "You haven't had a fight with Michelangelo, have you?"

"Pfft," Seth cut in. "Excuse me, but *I'd* be Michelangelo. Caleb's Leonardo. Darius is Raphael, and Max is Donatello. Oh, and I guess that makes you the mutant rat, sir. Master Splinter." He and Max started laughing, and I gave them a dry look before stepping closer to Darius and pressing a hand to his shoulder, casting a silencing bubble around us and cutting out the two assholes who had hijacked my TMNT analogy.

"You good?" I asked seriously.

"No, you?" he tossed back, and I frowned.

"No," I admitted.

"Wanna talk about it?" he asked.

"Nope. You?"

"Not even a little bit," he said, shoving his hands into his pockets, and I nodded, figuring this was just some Heir drama he didn't need me for. I wished I could be honest about what was really killing me inside, but Darius would feel so damn betrayed by me if he knew I'd been seeing a Vega. It was all just so...fucked.

I thought about mentioning the Fable Curse scroll that Gabriel had brought me but figured it could wait until we were alone to discuss it properly.

I released the silencing bubble, and Seth sauntered closer. "What are you two whispering about?" The scent of blueberries carried from his lollipop as he rolled it between his teeth again.

"I was just telling Darius how well your mom took it last night," I said, goading Seth, and he snarled, tossing his polar bear plushie into Max's arms.

"You motherfucker," he hissed, lunging at me, and I shot out of his way so he went crashing into the stall behind me.

"Yeah, that's me," I said, and he spun around in fury.

I thought he was going to launch himself at me again, but instead he recomposed himself and a vicious little smile pulled at his mouth. "You know, it's kind of pathetic how you trail around after Darius everywhere. Just because no one wanted to go to the Fairy Fair with you, doesn't mean you have the right to creepily follow us around, *Professor*."

"Shut your mouth, Capella," I warned.

"Or what?" He opened his arms wide. "Are you gonna attack an Heir in public?" He strode up to me, butting his chest to mine, and I bared my fangs in a threat. "You sure you wanna get your ass handed to you like that? I can see the headlines now, 'Seth Capella forces washed-up Pitball star to put his head up his own ass'."

I stepped forward with the challenge, more than happy to engage in this fight.

"That's enough, Seth," Darius warned, the deep rumble of his Dragon lacing his voice.

Seth glanced his way with his jaw pulsing, like he was deciding whether he was going to listen to his friend.

"Come on, man," Max encouraged, sending calming vibes into the air. "Leave it."

Seth's gaze slid back to me as he took his polar bear plushie from Max and slowly draped it around his shoulders, like that was supposed to be sinister.

"Watch your back, *sir*." He shouldered past me, and magic burned against my fingers with the need to destroy that asshole and put him back in his place, but Darius moved toward me, giving me a look that urged me to drop it.

I released a heavy breath, backing down and nodding to him in goodbye, but as they headed away from me towards the rollercoaster, I couldn't resist weaving some subtle air magic that sent Seth's lollipop rocketing to the back of his throat.

I pushed a hand into my hair, casual as fuck as he began choking on it, a smirk tugging at the corner of my mouth.

Francesca reappeared, walking over to me with a frown on her brow. "Sorry, Lance. I've got to go into work," she said as she reached me. "There's been a Nymph sighting in Tucana."

"No worries, I'll head home," I said, relief spilling through my chest. "This night is a shitshow anyway."

"It is?" she asked, a touch of surprise in her voice and maybe a fleck of hurt too.

"Not with you, I just mean… it's too crowded here," I backtracked. Sure,

I hated people, and being this close to so many people at once wasn't exactly my favourite way to spend an evening, but it wasn't the real reason I was having a shit night.

She cracked a smile. "You're such an introvert."

I shrugged. "Guilty."

She moved in close, tiptoeing up with the clear intention to kiss me, and I moved my head fast enough that she just brushed the corner of my lips. "Goodnight."

"Night," I said, and she pulled away, leaving me there alone.

I started walking, winding my way back toward the parking lot, feeling the weight of the night hanging over me. It didn't feel right, all of this shit between Darcy and I. Everything had been so perfect for a heartbeat, how had it all crumbled to dust so easily?

As if the stars had guided my feet to her, I spotted her at the front of the line to the Faerris Wheel with Diego at her side. I found myself slowing to a halt, watching her with blood thundering through my veins.

My head said it was time to walk away, but my heart was begging me to do something. And I got the sudden ominous feeling that if I walked away from her now, things would fracture irreparably between us.

Maybe I had to make a stand, one last attempt at fixing us before it was too late. If I didn't, I might just regret it forever.

She climbed into the carriage as a couple vacated it, and as Diego moved to follow, I shot forward with a burst of speed that brought me to his back in a flash. I knocked him onto his ass and climbed smoothly into the carriage beside Darcy.

"I need my Source," I barked at Diego as he scrambled upright, needing an excuse that everyone around me would swallow.

"Hey – no!" Darcy shouted, fury lining her tone, but it was too late.

She jumped forward to get out of the carriage, but I snatched the back of her dress, tugging her firmly down into her seat and locking her in place with one arm. I knocked her head to one side with my chin, inhaling the strawberry scent of her and driving my fangs into her throat. I didn't mind sticking to my story for being here as I tasted the perfection of her, stealing away her power and connecting the two of us through this instinctual act of my kind.

A short scream ripped from her chest, the sound piercing and travelling right across the fair, but no one was coming to save her from me. She struggled in my hold, but she was in my trap now, her magic locked down and the sweet taste of her blood riding over my tongue.

The guy attending the wheel whistled to himself as he casually locked the gate, and we moved upwards at an ever-climbing pace, securing me some time alone with her.

"Get off of me!" She shoved me in a rage, and I grunted, reluctantly tugging my fangs free of her skin but keeping my arm firmly locked around her waist.

I moved my face close to hers, teeth bared, my thirst for this girl so sharp it made my head spin. And it went far beyond blood.

Her lips parted at my expression, her pupils dilating and the sound of her heartbeat thrashing like a caged bird in my ears. I waved a hand to cast a silencing bubble around us, and her expression filled with wrath.

"This has gone far enough," I snarled, cutting to the chase. "You brought him here to piss me off."

Her mouth opened in disbelief, her eyes hard with the rejection of my words. "You *asked* me to talk to him. And you're not exactly here on your own, Professor," she snapped.

"Lance," I demanded, hating her calling me that after all we'd shared together. We weren't student and teacher here, we were something so much more, and I was certain she felt it too. I wasn't going to let her cower away from it now.

"No," she hissed, trying to unknot my fingers from her dress, but my grip was iron. "I'm not calling you that because we're not a thing anymore. I do not screw taken guys. If *Fran* doesn't give you what you need in the bedroom, then

I'm certainly not going to."

Satisfaction resounded through me as I saw the jealousy in her, and a dark smile pulled at my mouth. "She isn't my girlfriend."

"Right. Is that why you rammed your tongue down her throat earlier? Because she's *not* your girlfriend?" Her eyes glinted with the hurt I'd cast upon her, but she wasn't the only one hurting here.

"You're a hypocrite," I accused, my smile falling as I pictured Diego's mouth on hers again, laying a claim to something he had no right to claim. I lifted my hand and dragged my thumb across her lips, wiping them hard. She wriggled and fought, trying to stop me, but I had her completely cornered.

"What the hell are you doing?" She shoved my arms, but I ignored her, keeping her in place by pushing my knee against her thigh.

"I'm trying to get Diego Polaris's saliva off of my girl," I growled, and there it was. My hidden desires pouring out of me like a raincloud breaking at long last. I'd called her my girl, proving that was what I wanted her to be. And now I was this close to her again, it felt like the truth, not just some idle declaration.

She pressed a hand to my chest as confusion crossed her face, trying to get some space between us, and the doubts began to creep in again.

"Diego kissed *me*. I was caught off guard. But you kissed her because you wanted to," she hissed, emotion burning through her eyes and letting me know how much it had killed her to see me kiss another woman. It was a relief, honestly. Even if I was a total asshole.

My lips pressed into a tight line. "You know why I did it."

"Don't do that. You always turn it back on me, expecting me to read your damn mind," she snarled, still trying to push me back, but I pressed back against her and laid my hand on her thigh, trying to cross this chasm between us.

She grabbed my hand, throwing it back at me. "And don't do *that*."

"Why?"

"Because we're done," she said breathlessly, carving up my heart oh so prettily. "It was a one-night thing, let's move on with our lives."

"Do we *feel* done to you?" I asked, convinced she could sense this raw energy humming between us in the air. I wasn't completely insane, was I? This was real, and she felt it too.

My gaze shifted to the bloody pinprick marks on her neck, and I lifted a hand to heal them, grazing my thumb over her silken skin and feeling her shiver for me.

Come on, Blue, admit you feel this too.

I waited for her answer, her pulse warring in my ears as the seconds ticked by.

"I can't believe you kissed her," she hissed, eyes sparking with fire and the power in her brimming at the edges of her skin. She was bottled chaos, strength brewing in her like lava in the belly of a volcano, and I doubted she even realised it. But one day, she was going to blow her top, and the whole world was going to realise the danger that had been lying in wait beneath the surface all this time.

We were nearly at the top of the Faerris Wheel and Darcy remained silent, turning to look across the fair while my gaze remained on her. The sea of lights flickered and danced in her eyes, and I fell under her enchantment all over again. She was a goddess who had so easily plucked my heart from my chest, deciding whether or not she wanted to take a bite out of it.

"You brought Diego here on a date to hurt me," I growled, drawing her gaze back to me.

"You asked me to talk to him," she said, shaking her head in anger.

"You know I didn't mean take him on a fucking date," I snarled.

She turned away, but I caught her chin so she couldn't escape this fight, drawing her back to look me in the eye. "When I saw you leaving campus with him, I called Francesca."

Her throat bobbed as she absorbed my words. "To get even?"

I nodded, regret washing over me. "Biggest fucking mistake of my life. I'd rather bleed than feel what I did when I saw his mouth on yours."

"So you kissed her to get back at me?" she bit at me.

"Yes," I said, drawing away a little, guilt hitting me over using Francesca like that, but I just wasn't myself tonight. I'd descended into a madness I didn't know how to control.

"I'll ask you again. Are we done, Blue?" I gripped her arm tighter, needing the answer to that question, whatever way the axe might fall. If she was done with me, I had to know it here and now. Then I'd find a way to move on, but living in the unknown was torture.

Slowly, she shook her head, and the tension ran out of my body, relief cast into every corner of my bones.

"But maybe we should be," she said quickly, seeing my reaction. "Part of me doesn't want this to be done, but you hurt me."

"You hurt me first." My jaw locked tight in stubbornness, and she shook her head at me.

"What I did was *not* on the same level." She glanced away, jaw set and anger blazing across her features.

I sighed, reaching out to cup her cheek, but she pushed my hand away, and my pulse rioted. "I'm sorry, okay? I shouldn't have kissed her."

She nodded stiffly, clearly not accepting that apology.

"If you want to hurt me in future, use your hands," I said with a dark look. "I think physical pain would be preferable."

"Well, I won't stop wanting to hurt you until you apologise for what happened with Darius and Tory," she said sharply, revealing the real crux of the matter. "You never said sorry, and that's what breaks me the most. You don't care about what you did."

Her eyes glistened wetly, and my heart splintered at the sight of her pain. I knew she was mad about that, but it was the way of our kind. Fae on Fae.

I frowned, remembering she hadn't been raised like I had with parents who actively encouraged me to fight with my sister and settle our issues with combat. I had been getting into fights at school since I could swing my fists, and so had every other Fae in this realm.

It was how we dealt with things; and no one was allowed to step in. It was shameful to do so, and most Fae would rather end up beaten bloody, defeated in the dirt, than have someone swoop in and rescue them. But Darcy and Tory had only ever had each other in the mortal realm, and their rules were different to ours, their culture entirely alien to me. They'd probably fought side by side in fights and never thought anything of it. They'd come to each other's aid the moment their other half was in danger, and I'd stopped Darcy from doing that when her sister had been in trouble.

This clearly went deeper than I'd realised and wasn't something that could be resolved by explaining the ways of our kind. She'd figure that out after she'd been here a year or two, then she'd get it. Because she was as Fae as I was, she just had to shake off the final shackles of the mortal realm.

"You need an apology, Blue? Fine. I'll give you the best one I can think up." I kissed the corner of her mouth, then stood up and climbed over the gate holding us in the carriage.

I jumped, hearing Darcy gasp behind me as I fell towards the ground, using air magic to guide me smoothly onto my feet.

It took me a surprisingly short amount of time to come up with a completely unhinged idea to get Darcy to forgive me, but as soon as I found the circus tent where they were holding an electrocution challenge, the plan simply slotted together.

There was a show finishing up in the tent, which a few of the professors from Zodiac were watching, so I waited until the coast was clear before messaging Darcy.

Lance:
I'm ready to make my apology.
Come to the circus tent in five minutes.

I arranged everything with a guy called Rusty Star who was running the game I'd be partaking in, and he guided me backstage to wait to play 'The Numb Man'. A big guy stood there with his shirt off, eating a burrito with all the savagery of a wild goat, and I was left with him to await my fate.

A beautiful woman in a gemstone-encrusted bikini with a huge pink feather pluming up at her back came prancing over, smiling at me. "Hey sweetie, take your shirt off. We need to strap you in. It proves you're not cheating, 'kay?"

"Kay," I echoed dryly.

She walked over to me on her high heels, eyebrows lifting. "Oh my stars, I've just realised who you are. Lance Orion, right? You were tipped off to be the next big Pitball star once."

"Key word 'once'," I said, and she breathed a laugh.

"I was supposed to be a dancer on the stage of the Sunshine Theatre, but here I am, a shitty apprentice to a shittier act," she sighed. "Guess some people get starlight sprinkled on 'em at birth, huh? We're not the lucky ones. I'm Zena, by the way." She glanced at the big guy, then back to me. "Don't kill yourself out there, sweetie. It's worth tapping out before you start wetting yourself publicly."

"Great," I muttered.

"Welcome to the Cirque de Sol-Fae! I am your host, Rusty Star. Gather around, we have a daring contestant backstage who wishes to take on The Numb Man!" Rusty called from the stage and a cheer went up from the crowd.

Zena headed out, and I pulled my shirt off, tossing it onto a plastic seat.

"Got any tips?" I asked as the big guy finished his burrito.

"Don't die." He chuckled as Rusty summoned him, heading out to get on stage.

"Thanks, asshole," I muttered.

"Please give a warm welcome to our fearless contestant, Lance Orion!" Rusty cried.

I walked out onto the stage, hitching a smirk onto my face, knowing exactly how far I planned on taking this.

I took a seat in the metal chair that was waiting for me, glancing at the big guy who was already shackled tightly to his own seat. Zena locked me in place with a wicked smile brushing her lips, the metal cuffs icily cold against my skin.

I searched the crowd, and relief hit me when I found Darcy there, clearly willing to give me a chance so long as I proved myself to her. She gave me a questioning look that said she hadn't worked out what the game was yet, and I smiled wider as Zena stepped away and walked over to a huge red lever that jutted out of the stage.

"If our contestant can outlast The Numb Man in this dangerous game, he will win our incredible prize. The crown of glory!" Rusty pointed to a glass box suspended above us and it lit up in a shower of golden sparks. "The Numb Man has a pain threshold higher than anyone who has ever stepped on this stage. No one has *ever* won the crown, so will our latest contestant be any different?"

Darcy looked to me with a flash of concern in her eyes.

"Are you ready, Diamond?" Rusty asked Zena – so I guessed that was her stage name. She nodded, taking hold of the lever, while Rusty gazed at the crowd with a manic gleam in his gaze. "Each chair is hooked up to an increasing flow of electricity. Whoever taps out first will lose the game."

Darcy's eyes widened, and I relaxed back into my seat, my gaze set on the beautiful creature before me.

"All you need to do is raise your hand and the electrocution will stop," Rusty said, and laughter filled the air.

I flexed my muscles against the restraints holding me down, and they didn't bend from my strength, telling me they weren't going to bust easily.

Rusty tittered. "Alright, you can just say the words, Mr Orion."

"You're assuming I'll tap out first," I said with a dark grin.

An *oooh* went up from the crowd and Darcy mouthed, "Don't," at me, but I ignored her plea, waiting for the electricity to start flowing. She needed an apology, and I intended on giving her the best one I could.

"We have a very confident competitor, ladies and gentlemen. Let's see how long his confidence lasts," Rusty said with a vicious smile, gesturing to Zena. "Pull the lever!"

She yanked it back and electricity shot into my veins, making me tense up, my hands curling into fists to stop myself from using magic against it. The sound of zapping and crackling energy filled the air alongside thundering music, building the atmosphere in the room and drawing even more of a crowd.

The Numb Man smiled broadly, having no reaction to the electricity at all.

"Higher!" Rusty commanded and Zena drew the lever back further.

My teeth ground together as the electricity coursed deeper and sharper through my body, setting my nerve endings on fire, but it was bearable.

"Higher!" Rusty called again.

A whole lightning bolt seemed to slam through me, and I released a gasp of pain. I wasn't tapping out though, no damn chance. All I had to do was look right at my reason for being here and I could withstand it, even with my shoulders shuddering and my brain rattling in my head.

"You've proved your point!" Darcy yelled, but I wasn't done. I'd take this as far as I could, because surely that asshole beside me had to break at some point. One glance his way told me he didn't look remotely affected though, and I had to wonder if this entire game was rigged.

"Higher!" Rusty commanded.

I roared in pain, the electricity blinding me as I was subjected to fuck knew how many volts, and before I could even adjust to the new level of hell, Rusty shouted, "Higher!"

"No!" Darcy shouted, but her voice was like an echo in my head, dancing between the flashes of electricity that were tearing through my skull.

A bellow of pain sounded from The Numb Man, and a glimmer of hope cascaded through my head.

"STOP, STOP!" he cried, and Rusty looked around at him in alarm while I fought to stay conscious.

"Diamond!" Rusty snapped, and she pushed the lever to turn off the electricity. All at once, it was over, and I heaved in a lungful of air, slumping forward in my seat, my hands still balled up into tight fists as the lasting waves of electricity subsided.

Zena hurried to untether The Numb Man, and I heard him running off stage with a whimper. She moved to help me next, unlocking my shackles and leaning low to whisper in my ear. "Well, you didn't piss yourself. Maybe you're luckier than I thought."

I released a breath of amusement, managing to sit upright and smiling in victory at her.

"Our first ever winner, ladies and gentlemen!" Rusty stuttered in obvious shock, and applause rang through the air.

I staggered to my feet, lifting a hand to heal myself, and the pain fell away just like that.

Rusty cast magic at the glass box to bring it down to the stage, opening it with a reluctant expression and holding the crown out to me.

"Congratulations," he said through a false smile, apparently not a fan of people winning his little game.

I grinned as I took my prize. "And here I was thinking this thing was rigged."

"Never," Rusty said, clearing his throat.

I headed backstage to grab my shirt, pulling it on before heading back out to hunt down my girl and find out if she'd forgiven me at last. A line of teachers walked into the tent, and I spotted Darcy turning away from them, glancing around in search of me.

I slipped my Atlas from my pocket, tapping out a message to her, figuring I couldn't be seen with her right now.

Lance:

Do you want a ride home?

I watched as she read the message, biting on her lower lip and making me think about doing that very same thing. My Atlas pinged, and I read her message with a smile hooking up my mouth.

Darcy:

Are you freaking crazy???

Lance:

Yes. For you ;)
Come with me.

She didn't answer straight away, and I glanced over at her, finding her frowning with indecision, but in the next second, she answered.

Darcy:

Okay, where should I go?

Lance:

Behind the tent is a fence that borders the road.
Wait on the other side of it.

I shot out of the tent, unleashing my Vampire speed and racing away across the fair, making it to the parking lot in under five seconds. I slid smoothly into my Faerarri, tossing the crown I'd won into the backseat and heading for the road.

I circled the fair, getting stuck in the jam of traffic that was heading to and from the carnival before finally making it around to the quiet road that ran behind the circus tent.

Darcy was waiting beside the tall wooden fence, her breath fogging in the cold night air, and anticipation rolled through me at finally having her to myself at last. I pulled up beside her, dropping the passenger window and leaning across to look out at her.

She slapped the side of the door in a rage, and my eyebrows arched. "How could you do that? You nearly gave me a heart attack."

"To be fair, I nearly gave myself a heart attack, Blue, so can we call it even?"

She shook her head, blinking hard before kicking the front wheel.

My brows pulled together. "Can you stop attacking my car? She doesn't like it."

Darcy sniffed, turning her back on me and looking up at the sky.

Fuck, was she crying?

I shoved my door open, shooting around to her with a burst of speed, my expression taut.

"I didn't mean to upset you," I said seriously. "I don't apologise very often. It's not a very Fae thing to do. Did I not do it right?"

She smacked my chest as a tear spilled down her cheek, and I caught it on the edge of her chin, wiping it away with my thumb, feeling like a complete prick for causing this.

"You could have just said the words," she whispered, and I gave her a hopeful grin, inching closer into her personal space.

"I'm sorry." I pressed my hands either side of her on the car and her breathing hitched.

"You smell like her," she murmured, and I hated the whole mess I'd caused with Francesca tonight. I didn't want her, I hadn't wanted that kiss, and it could have cost me everything.

"Then make me smell like you," I commanded, and she grabbed hold of my jacket, dragging me down to meet her mouth.

I tasted her tears, her pain, and I kissed her harder to chase it all away, trying to fix what had shattered between us. I felt it all fading away to insignificance, because this close, there was nothing else but us and the hungering of our souls for one another.

"Come on," I said, stepping back. "This evening is still salvageable."

"I wish we could stay at the funfair together." She frowned, and it was a stark reminder of how few places we could actually go right now.

"Well...I hear another funfair has popped up in my bedroom for the night," I teased to lighten the mood.

A laugh broke free of her throat, and I grinned at the sound, pushing a lock of hair behind her ear.

"If you want to go back and find your friends, I get it." I squeezed her hand, and she interlaced her fingers with mine.

"Hm, well I quite like the sound of this other funfair. Is there a rollercoaster?"

"No, but there's a slip and slide?" I offered.

She laughed again, and I tugged the door open so she could get in. She dropped into my car, and she put the window up as she shut the door. I took a breath, glancing at the stars and asking them to stretch this night into the longest one they could forge, then I shot around and dropped into the driver's seat.

Silence fell, and I listened to the heavy thumping of Darcy's heart before starting the engine and pressing my foot to the gas.

"Where's Fran?" she asked lightly.

I released a laugh at the iciness she was trying to hide beneath those words. "You know, she'd really kill you if she heard you calling her that."

She shrugged.

"She got called into work. Apparently, there was a Nymph sighting in east Tucana. The anonymous caller was very insistent," I said, tilting my head innocently, and her mouth fell open.

"You didn't?"

"I did." I barked a laugh. "Where's Polaris?" I asked darkly.

"We had an argument," she said tersely.

"About?" I inquired, reaching over and placing a hand on her knee, despising that kid ever more.

"You," she admitted, and my heart juddered over what she might have told him.

I shot her a concerned look. "He doesn't know anything, does he?"

"Of course not, he just thinks I have a crush on you and that I'm pathetic for doing so. And a whore, apparently."

That word sent my mind into a frenzy, awakening the more primitive instincts of my Order and urging me to do one thing and one thing only. Hunt.

My grip tightened on her knee as I warred with the feeling.

"Fuck that kid, I'll tear him a new one the next time I see him," I snarled.

"I might join you in that." She rested her hand on mine and her touch was icily cold.

I wrapped her fingers in my hold with a frown.

"You're freezing." I cast a wave of warm air that rushed over her, and she shivered appreciatively.

I turned us down a dark road where the trees leaned overhead, creating a long tunnel that panned away into the shadows. It seemed endless, yet I knew it wasn't. All roads had an end. Even ours. Especially ours. But in this fracture of a moment, we were still moving forward, and I could at least enjoy the journey while it lasted.

"So have you forgiven me now?" I asked.

"Technically, you owed the apology to my sister," she pointed out, and I gave her an incredulous look.

"By the stars, am I going to have to electrocute myself again for Tory Vega?"

She laughed. "You know that numb guy wasn't hooked up to the mains, right? Well, he wasn't until I hooked him up myself."

"What?" I gasped, searching her expression for a lie.

"Yep." She squeezed my fingers, a look of defiance crossing her eyes that had my cock hardening for her.

I pulled over to the side of the road and dragged her in for a kiss, crushing my lips to hers. Then I noticed the seatbelt was half choking her and quickly released it, pulling her closer and sinking my tongue between her soft lips.

She climbed into my lap, straddling me and clawing her hands into my hair as our kiss became more frantic. Fuck, I'd missed her. She tasted of sunlight, igniting my world in colour again at last, and I never wanted to return to the grey.

My hands slid under her dress, and she urged me on by lifting her hips, her fingers digging hard into my shoulders. A deep growl emanated from my throat as I found my way barred by her pantyhose, and I ripped a hole in them between her thighs, making her gasp.

"Orion!" she laughed, but her laughter turned to a moan as I found my way into her panties and pushed two fingers into her soaking heat. Between that sound and the feel of her tight, wet pussy around my fingers, I was already rock hard for her, aching to be inside her.

"You owe me a new pair," she said breathlessly, leaning against me for support as I slowly pumped my fingers in and out of her, loving how ready she was for me.

"I'll get you a whole new wardrobe if you make that noise again."

"What noise?" she panted, and I pumped my fingers harder, drawing another greedy moan from her lips. It was full of a need I intended on sating again and again.

"That one," I grunted, shifting my free hand between us to undo my jeans.

She arched upwards to give me room and her head banged against the roof. My laughter tangled with hers, and I removed my hand from her pantyhose, tugging her dress over her head, wanting to see her properly.

"Let's get rid of these." I tore her pantyhose in half, and she gasped as I peeled them off her legs, baring all that beautiful bronze skin and skating my fingers over it with a burning want.

"Hey, how about we tear some of *your* clothes?" She tugged at my shirt, and I caught her wrists with a wild grin. *I'm in control here, Blue.*

My gaze travelled down her near naked body to the lacy red underwear she was wearing, her breasts straining against the thin fabric and giving me a glimpse of her tight nipples beneath.

I tasted my lower lip, taking my time to enjoy the sight from the tight nip of her waist to that sultry look on her face.

"I've missed this." I leaned in to kiss her collarbone and goosebumps raised beneath my lips, showing me exactly how much of an affect I had on her. "And this." I curled a lock of blue hair around my finger and brought that to my lips too. "And these." I squeezed her breasts and she laughed. "Hm... you're missing something though."

"What?" She frowned.

I reached behind my seat and produced the crown I'd won at the fair, placing it on my girl's head. A smile split across her cheeks that lit up her green eyes, looking like the royalty she was as she pressed me down beneath her.

"Better," I said, resting my hands on her silken thighs and drawing her closer.

"If you go around placing crowns on my head, you're going to be in trouble," she teased, and my mouth skewed as the weight of politics fell on me, but I wasn't going to let it ruin this moment.

"Well let's not tell anyone then," I said, leaning in to kiss her neck, tasting the fire in her.

She started unbuttoning my shirt, and our movements grew more desperate, my kisses turning to bites, while she clawed at my chest to get the buttons open and finally pushed my shirt over my shoulders so I could shrug out of it.

I tugged her bra down to free her right breast, my mouth encasing her hardened nipple and my tongue rolling over it, making her shudder deeply with pleasure. She arched her back, grinding down on my hard cock, and I groaned, sucking her nipple harder and gripping her waist to keep her right there.

She lifted up on her knees to free me from my pants, and her ass bashed into the steering wheel, setting the horn off.

She snorted a laugh as I tugged her forward by the hips to stop the noise.

"This is way more difficult than I expected," she joked, and I grinned devilishly at her.

"Definitely worth it, though."

I freed my cock, pushing her panties aside, and all amusement fell away between us as I guided her hips down, hungering for the feel of her.

She rested her forehead to mine, inhaling as I lined up the head of my cock with her slick entrance and pushed slowly inside her. I hissed between my teeth as she lowered onto me, and she moaned as I filled her up inch by inch, eyes locked and magic humming against my skin. It was pleasure in its purest form, and I needed more. Always more.

She started riding me, and I chased her mouth for kisses as she rocked on my lap and I held her hips, pushing her down onto me and thrusting my hips up to meet her. My cock ground deep inside her, and she took every inch of me so damn well, her body made for mine.

She rolled her neck, bracing her hands on my shoulders, her lips parted and her breaths falling softly against me. She was a creature designed to ruin me, and in that moment, I would have let any fate befall me just to keep her.

"Don't fight with me again," I demanded, my teeth raking against her ear.

"Don't give me a reason to." She sank her nails into my shoulders, the bite of pain making me groan, and I thrust harder into her, driven mad by the way her pussy clamped around the length of me.

One of her knees banged against the parking brake and the other slammed into the door, but she didn't seem to care, needing this as much as I did as we came together in this desperate act of passion and infatuation.

Her hips quickened to meet the movements of mine, and we fell into a cadence of lust, our bodies in perfect synchronisation. But as I watched her pant for me, I remembered Diego's mouth on hers, and I wrapped one hand in her hair, tugging hard enough to make her yelp.

"That's for Polaris," I growled, my rage over that rising once more.

She scraped her nails down my chest so hard she drew blood, her gaze sparking with anger of her own. "That's for Fran."

I looked down in surprise, then released a breathless laugh. "I like you angry."

"Let's not make a habit of it though," she panted.

"Deal," I groaned as I pushed deep into her again, ecstasy hounding our movements.

Darcy pressed one hand to the window, her spine straightening and her pussy tightening around me in a way that told me she was close to the edge. My hand rode the curve of her spine before forcing her onto me, grinding my cock against that sensitive spot inside her and sending her into that chasm of ecstasy she was teetering on. She moaned through her climax, falling against me for support, and I fucked her harder and faster, finding my own release inside her pulsing pussy, grunting her name in the back of my throat as I came with an explosion of pleasure.

Her legs trembled as she slumped against me, resting her head against my shoulder, our breaths blazingly hot, leaving a fog on the windows around us.

It was pure bliss, having her this close, and I trailed my fingers up and down her bare thighs, memorising each waning second of our time alone together. I caught her chin, tilting her head up so I could touch my lips to hers, and I felt her smiling against my mouth.

She climbed back into her seat and we both dressed in silence, but we kept catching each other's eye and sharing grins.

As soon as she was done, I restarted the engine and headed on down the road.

"So did you get any information from Polaris during your *date*?" I asked a little bitterly.

"You're never going to let that go, are you?" she mocked.

"It just fucks me off that you can go out in public with *him* and not me."

"Well, that's how it is," she sighed, turning to gaze out of the steamy window beside her. She painted a grumpy face on it and wrote Orion above it, and I glanced over at it with my mouth tugging up at the corner.

"Is that what I look like to you?"

"Not quite." She added angry eyebrows and fangs, turning to goad me with a grin.

I laughed, somehow feeling as far from being that grumpy prick as possible right now.

"Diego didn't say much about his uncle, just that he's an asshole. And that his mother and father go off with him sometimes to help him with his 'work'." She shrugged. "Is that useful?"

I thought on that, not having realised his parents might be involved with Lionel too. "Yes, it gives me a couple more Fae to look into. Much as it pains me to say it, I'd appreciate if you keep spending time with him. See what else he'll say about them. But no dates."

"Well, that's gonna be pretty difficult as I'm majorly pissed at him and I'm guessing he is at me too."

"What's he pissed at you for?"

"I slapped him," she revealed.

"Good," I said. "But he deserves more than that for calling you a whore."

"Actually...I slapped him *before* he said that." She twisted her fingers into her skirt, her brow lowering in anger.

"Why?" I asked curiously.

"He said he wished you'd died when the Nymphs attacked," she said with a bite of fury to her voice.

My grip tightened on the wheel. "I'm going to kill him."

"You can't. He'll know I told you. And I didn't exactly deny that I have a thing for you, if you go after him, he might figure out there's something between us."

"What kind of thing do you have for me?" I shot her a mischievous glance.

"It will sound crazy," she said slowly.

"I like crazy. Did you not get the memo when I tried to cook myself earlier?"

"Promise you won't laugh?" she asked, her cheeks colouring a little.

"On the stars."

She nodded, looking out of the window so I couldn't see her expression. "When we were in the battle and you were about to die, I felt compelled to save you. Like...if I didn't, a part of me would die too. And ever since then, that part of me is getting stronger, like it's become this tangible thing that lives in me. I've never been a jealous person before, but when I see you with Francesca, it's like I turn into an animal with nothing but basic instincts."

I didn't immediately answer, floored by that admission and unsure if I was really lucky enough to have this girl feel that way about me. Plus, she'd just put into words exactly how I'd been feeling, like we were on this runaway train and there was no way to escape our destination now. Even if the tracks led us right over a cliff and into a ravine.

"I told you it was crazy," she muttered.

I took her hand, winding my fingers between hers and pressing my mouth to the back of her knuckles. She glanced my way, and I realised we were so far down the rabbit hole, not even Alice herself could get us out.

"Good, because I feel it too."

PLANISPHÆRI

STUS MARIS PER MOTUM LUNÆ

AQUARIUS

PISCES

ARIES

Triangulum

TAURUS

Caput Meduse

Andromeda

Cassiopea

Cepheus

Cygnus

Perseus

Lira

Pegasus

Equuleus

Delphinus

CAPRICORNUS

Antinous

Aquila

SAGITTARIUS

Auriga
Erichtonius

Capella

Ursa
minor

Draco

Polus Arct.

Dragonatli
Hercules

Serpens
Ophiuchi

GEMINI

Castor

Pollux

Ursa maior
Celesto

Corona
Bor.

Booteta

CANCER

Coma Berenices

Serpens

SCORPIUS

LEO

VIRGO

LIBRA

TMINATIO LUNÆ
PER SOLEM

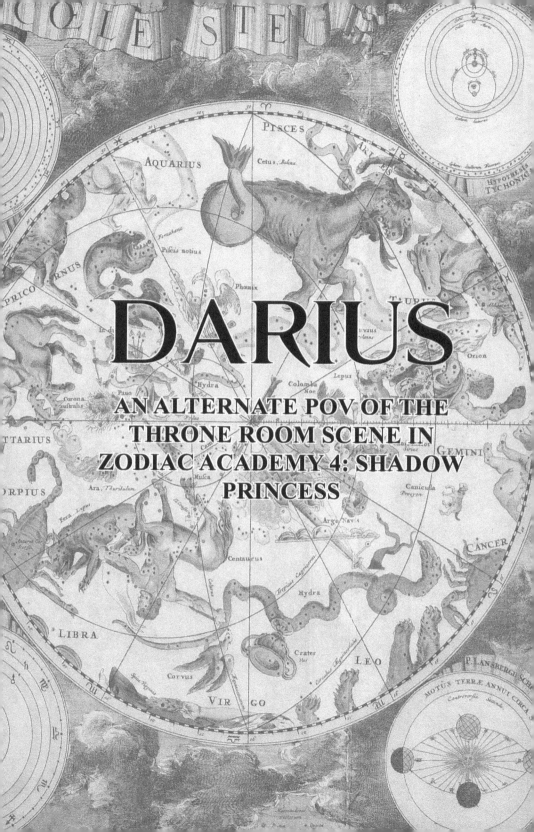

DARIUS

AN ALTERNATE POV OF THE THRONE ROOM SCENE IN ZODIAC ACADEMY 4: SHADOW PRINCESS

LIONEL

FROM THE LAIR OF LIONEL...

I will admit that, for a time, my focus was captured by the overwhelming brilliance of my plan to trap the shadows. I had done it – I had become far greater and more powerful than the other Celestial Councillors and I stood upon the cusp of claiming my throne at last.

There were complications, yes. Clara's return was not something I had foreseen, much less the fact that she would not be entirely herself when she came back to me.

It took me quite some time to pick apart the threads of truth which explained away her survival in the Shadow Realm, and I was more than a little surprised to find that her body was in fact shared with the Shadow Princess herself.

I had to be cautious, yet the Guardian Bond which linked me to Clara seemed to affect Lavinia too and it was with no great difficulty that I guided them into the proper place for such useful servants — beneath me at all times.

It took a lot of my focus to bring the Shadow Princess to heel, and though there were countless opportunities to be found in not only the power of the shadows I now possessed but in her command over them too, I had not come so far without being cautious.

So, I suppose I can excuse myself for allowing my gaze to shift, for not seeing sooner the spell which Roxanya Vega was weaving over my Heir.

The clues were all there. The way he spoke of the twins to me was the first of them – always with greater ire and a deeper anger when speaking of Roxanya than Gwendalina. Foolishly, I put that down to her being the more contentious of the two. And of course, Roxanya was housed in Ignis, right under his nose, able to rile him so much more often. But that meant she was able to tempt him so much more often too.

I wonder at which point I could have squashed his infatuation sooner. But in hindsight, I do not think it was a thing I could have achieved. She was clearly set on seducing him, no doubt just as desperate for power as her mother and just as willing to spread her legs to get a feel of it. And that was without the involvement of the stars in the matter.

I had it on great authority that she was even sucking his best friend's cock and yet still he found himself utterly embroiled with her.

I saw it at Christmas. I saw the way his eyes trailed her just as I had seen it in my own home before that.

Foolishly, I'd thought that him fucking her would rid him of the want. I'd thought it just another of his ploys to destroy her – the ultimate degradation, to use her for his pleasure and abandon her while she was still cleaning the evidence of him claiming her from her flesh.

I never had liked to admit that Darius was his mother's son. Catalina was a beautiful, powerful woman, well suited for breeding my Heirs, but she was soft of heart. Enamoured with the idea of love. And even after I had ensured that she couldn't coddle my boys into a similar fashion of weakness, the flaw had still appeared.

Perhaps I should have stepped in sooner. Perhaps I should have stopped things before they progressed so far as they did, but I will admit that in this, I made a mistake...

DARIUS

CHAPTER ONE

The usual Christmas bullshit parade consumed the majority of our afternoon, the endless photoshoot only made mildly more tolerable than usual because we had the Vega twins for company during it.

I watched Roxy throughout every moment, though I knew how to hide the object of my attention from the cameras and scandal-hungry press. But my focus stayed hitched on her, sometimes slipping to Caleb as he threw her flirtatious smiles and flashed heated looks her way between shots.

Roxy rolled her eyes at him or simply looked to her sister in some silent form of communication which often made Darcy smirk to herself or hide a snort of laughter. I wasn't sure what to make of it, whether Roxy was still interested in what Cal was clearly offering her or if she was utterly unimpressed by him. Though I hoped it was the latter.

The twins played their parts, posing by a huge Christmas tree, handing beautifully wrapped empty boxes to each of us while they smiled prettily for the cameras. There were no real gifts, not even the pretence that there might be when I looked into their eyes.

Seth cracked endless jokes and Max pumped the air full of Siren magic to help us all get into the festive spirit. Some of Darcy's smiles even seemed genuine, but not Roxy's. She flashed her perfect teeth at all the right moments, following the instructions of the photographers to the dot, but it didn't take me long to figure out that she was only doing so to make this sham pass faster.

It bothered me. I knew it shouldn't have. Knew I should have been pleased, if anything, to know that we were fucking up her day, but I wasn't pleased. And every time she was forced to look my way with a fake-ass smile on her face or pass me an empty box in some pretence of liking me enough to hand out a gift, the knot in my chest only tightened.

"Relax," Max murmured as the photographers backed off for a few moments, heading away to view the shots they'd taken while discussing how to change things up, shift the light or whatever else they required for this well-staged vision of bullshit.

I glanced to the far side of the enormous ballroom where our parents were being photographed around the blazing fireplace, glasses of mulled wine in hand, raucous laughter breaking out between shots. It looked like Tiberius was using his Siren gifts to work them all up into a frenzy of mirth, and even my father was smirking like the cat who'd gotten the cream while he let the power take root in him. I'd watched them do this very thing during endless photoshoots throughout my life, using the Siren magic to conceal any truth which might have been captured on camera. To the outside world, they were an unbreakable unit of four, their spouses just as devoted to their relationships with one another too. Their strength, unity, and love for each other as unending as the passage of time. At least so far as the world beyond these walls was concerned.

"Darius?" Max drew my attention back to him, and I gave him an easy smile, knowing that even between shots, the cameras were never fully off of us during a shoot.

"I'm good, man," I said, clapping him on the arm and letting him feel the still pool of nothing which was my emotional standard.

"I'm so full from that meal that I'm in danger of popping a fucking button," he said, a hand touching his stomach briefly. "You didn't eat all that much though, weren't you hungry?"

"Ravenous," I replied, my gaze back on Roxy as Caleb caught her attention by shooting all the way around the Christmas tree, grabbing every perfectly wrapped fake gift and piling them up around the twins in a flash of movement until they were hidden from view entirely.

She laughed from beyond the wall of empty boxes, and that sound made something twist in my gut. It might have been the first moment of actual happiness she'd experienced since we'd shown up here to ambush their day.

"Why didn't you eat more then?" Max asked while Seth dove headfirst into the pile of gifts and sent them flying in every direction before diving on Darcy and licking her cheek.

She shoved him off, and I let myself grin as the cameras began flashing, picking up one of the boxes and hurling it at the back of Caleb's head like I was part of the game too.

It may have hit him harder than necessary, but I was still pissed about what had happened at the dinner table when he'd had his fucking hand on Roxy's thigh at the same time as me. I still didn't know what to make of that fucked-up little nugget of my day, but as he shot towards Roxy and flung her over his shoulder, her laughter-filled yells of not-entirely-believable protest were a clear enough answer as to why she had consistently chosen him.

Not that I was an option or had ever presented myself as one aside from that single time. That single fucking time when I had given up the charade over what I wanted from her and what I needed, and I'd felt the intensity of our connection when it was unleashed to its fullest in the Shimmering Springs.

She'd made it clear enough then that it hadn't meant anything though, so I had no idea why I was even surprised to see her laughing with the pretty boy, falling for his charm and smiles. I'd pick him too. As much as it pissed me off to admit it, Caleb was easily the better choice. He was laidback, fun, simple.

I was… well I was a head-fuck all on my own, and she clearly had no desire to get any closer to me than we'd already done.

My mind moved to the way her skin had felt beneath the rough pads of my fingers as my hand had skimmed up the inside of her thigh just a few hours ago, and I frowned. Maybe she'd been fucking with me, drawing me in just so she could reject me and offer a little payback for all the shit I'd gifted her.

I tapped my fingers against the small box sitting in my pocket. I hadn't wrapped it. I wasn't even sure what I'd been thinking when I'd bought it. Maybe I'd just known that us showing up here today was going to fuck up her plans and I'd wanted to give her something to apologise for that. Then again, I probably should have bought something for her sister too, if that were the case.

It didn't matter anyway. Whatever madness had possessed me to buy the stupid thing had faded, and I had no intention of actually giving it to her. She didn't want a gift from me. And I didn't really want to experience her laughing in my face as she rejected it either.

Caleb finally set Roxy on her feet, and my gaze fixed on the two of them as his hands lingered on her waist in that green dress, pretending to make sure she had her balance in her heels. He released her before the press could get a shot of them in the compromising position, shooting away to tackle Seth just as the first flash of a camera went off, leaving them with nothing.

Not that that would stop the stories. I'd had the distinct displeasure of reading more than a few speculative pieces about their possible relationship. The wider press, which was controlled by our parents, wouldn't print anything of the kind, but there were online forums and fan sites which had documented more than enough of their not-so-secret hook ups for it to be a fairly public theory that they were in some way involved.

The twins were ushered away to take some shots on an elaborately decorated sleigh which had been set up just outside in the snow, and I chewed on the inside of my cheek as Roxy finally offered up a real smile. Just for

Darcy, something her sister had said lightening that darkness in her expression.

I couldn't stop thinking about what they'd told us earlier, about the two of them always being unwanted additions to their foster families' festivities. It bothered me. I didn't know why it bothered me so much, but I guessed that if I ever gave thought about the lives they'd had in the mortal realm, I'd simply assumed it had been bland and unremarkable. Not plain miserable.

I mean, my life wasn't exactly a bag of kittens, but I had the other Heirs, Xavier, Orion…

"So where is it?" Seth demanded suddenly, his lips so close to my motherfucking ear that I flinched away from him.

"Where's what?" I asked innocently, Max chuckling beside me while Seth narrowed his eyes.

"Come on, man, it's been all day already. I can't wait any longer." Seth dropped down onto my lap, throwing an arm over his eyes like some fainting fan girl, and I laughed as I shoved him off of me to land in a heap on the floor.

"You're being ungrateful as fuck," I told him, ignoring the puppy dog eyes he was trying on me as I rearranged myself in my seat.

"It's not funny anymore," he pouted, and I had to work to flatten the smile which was trying to force its way onto my lips.

"No. It's not," I agreed. "I went out of my way to buy gifts I knew each of you would really enjoy. I put my heart and soul into selecting that car for Cal and the speedboat for Max, and you don't see them complaining, do you?"

"You gave me a bag of freaking Snausages," Seth whined, looking to the others for help.

Caleb only grinned at him as he dropped into his seat, while Max shrugged like he couldn't understand the problem.

"Did you, or did you not, eat all of them?" I asked slowly.

"Well, yeah, but-"

"And did I or did I not, call you a good boy when you balanced that one on your nose for five seconds before scoffing it?" I added, and Seth growled.

"You can't just casually abuse my praise kink by going all Alpha Daddy on me with a pack of Snausages and get away with not giving me a proper gift," Seth growled, pushing to his feet.

"Since when have you had a praise kink?" Caleb asked with interest, and Seth shot him a dark look.

"Only when Darius does it," he shrugged. "He has that whole dominant, 'shove me around the bedroom' vibe going, and sometimes I think he might even be able to do it to me if the mood took him."

"*I* could shove you around the bedroom if the mood took me," Caleb said, and Seth barked a laugh, his attention stolen by the turn in the conversation.

"Nah, Cal. You're pretty and all, but you don't scream 'dominant daddy' to me the same way that Dari-" Caleb shot towards Seth so fast that I lost the movement in a blink, the two of them crashing back against the table where several of the fake gifts were sent flying. Cal pushed Seth down beneath him, one hand locked around his throat and his fangs bared as he leaned over him, their bodies flush with one another.

"Call me pretty again," Caleb growled while Seth blinked up at him in surprise.

"So fucking pretty," Seth breathed, his chest rising heavily as Caleb pinned him down on the table.

Max released a low whistle of amusement, and I arched a brow at the two of them, their gazes locked with an intensity that made the air surrounding us crackle.

Caleb leaned in slowly, and Seth blinked rapidly as the space between their mouths was reduced to almost nothing.

"Good pup," Caleb said roughly before shooting away again so fast that I didn't even see his ass hit the chair beside me and he simply appeared to have been sitting there lounging in it like he owned the world the entire time.

Seth whimpered in frustration as he pushed himself upright once more, the camera flashes going off too late to catch Caleb up to anything that could even be half considered scandalous. I couldn't help but grin at him as he sat there looking smug as fuck with himself, and he inclined his head to me in reply, our issues over Roxanya Vega put aside for the indisputable reality that our bond was utterly impenetrable at its core.

"Is that my gift then?" Seth asked as he not-so-subtly rearranged his cock. "The four of us are finally going to give in to this raging masculine sexuality that burns so hot between us and fuck like the beasts we are all night long in a four-way to end all four-ways?"

"Well, that was going to be my choice of gift before I spotted the Snausages and knew you'd much prefer-"

Seth tackled me before I could finish that sentence, his weight slamming into me so solidly that my chair was knocked over and we went crashing to the ground with the thing splintering beneath our combined weight.

I cursed him as he managed to get a few decent punches into my ribs, a solid crack echoing through my chest from the impact, then swung my forehead into the bridge of his nose to force him back.

Seth barked a raucous laugh as his blood splattered my shirt, and we rolled across the floor as we continued to scrap like a pair of drunk mortals in a back alley.

Max and Caleb began taking bets while Seth's mom called out at him to go for the jugular from across the room.

One glance towards our parents let me know that Father was watching with quiet interest, and my amusement plummeted as I realised this would be another thing he'd judge me on. A simple game with my best friend becoming a pass or fail situation which would see me having a private discussion with him later.

Father arched a single brow, and I knew what he wanted. He could tell I was holding back, knew there was a line I wouldn't cross with the other Heirs, and he wanted me to step right over it to prove what I could do. No doubt that would be the best Christmas gift I could give him – a headline stating my victory in a scrap with my friend, an insinuation that I might be the strongest of the four Heirs.

It was petty, and I knew I'd suffer for it, but as I gave my focus back to the brawl with Seth, I ended up on my back beneath him and failed to block a blow from his fist straight to my jaw. My head cracked back against the floor, momentarily dazing me, and Seth howled his victory before thrusting his hand into my pocket and snatching the small box straight out of it.

I cursed as I shoved to my feet, swiping a hand over my face and using my water magic to take all the blood from my skin and clothes before depositing it in a glass I crafted out of ice beside Caleb.

"I knew it!" Seth crowed as he held the little grey box up above his head, and my stomach dropped as he waved it around victoriously.

I could feel my father's eyes on my back, his fury burning through my spine, but I ignored him. I didn't give a fuck about winning or losing some nothing scrap with Seth, and I wasn't going to beat the shit out of him in front of the press just to save my own ass from Father's disappointment. Besides, I had bigger concerns as my gaze fixed on that fucking box Seth had snatched from me.

"That's not for you," I called out firmly, but Seth, being Seth, totally ignored me and sprinted for the door instead of giving the damn thing back.

I cursed him as I took chase, Caleb and Max hooting and catcalling us as they followed, the press snapping endless photos the entire time.

We ran out into the vaulted hallway, and I snarled a warning at Seth as he started tugging at the box, trying to rip it open despite my continued insistence that it wasn't for him.

I chased after him as fast as I could, and he howled at the game, sprinting away from me with the box held high in his fist.

I put on a burst of speed and slammed into him at last, throwing him back against a heavy wooden door and pinning him with my forearm against his throat as I reached for the box in his fist.

But before I could snatch it, Caleb shot past us and stole it for himself.

"Give it to me," I demanded, smoke rolling between my teeth as I whirled on him instead, my eyes flashing into reptilian slits as my temper built and the Dragon in me stirred. "I'm not fucking around. That isn't for any of you assholes, and I want it back."

"By the stars, Darius, who shit in your cornflakes this morning? It's Christmas day – the one day of the year when we steal a little bit of mortal madness and celebrate the winter solstice with gross consumerism, coupled with an indecent amount of pressure, to show love to people who we may or may not secretly think are pieces of shit just because we share blood with them. It's special," Caleb teased, always the least likely to back down to me, but I wasn't in the mood for his crap right now, and as my gaze darted to the little box he now held, I could see he knew it too. "Well, now I really am curious."

"In here, Cal, you can help me open it!" Seth called, throwing open the door behind him and running into the dark space.

Caleb shot in after him, and a snarl erupted from my throat as I moved to take chase.

Max's hand landed on my arm, his Siren gifts pushing against my mental barriers as he offered to calm me, and I gritted my teeth, allowing it purely because I knew that losing my shit would only equal what I was trying to prevent. If I went head-to-head with Caleb and tried to force him to do what I wanted, he'd open the fucking box just to prove he didn't bow to me. *Asshole.*

"You really care that much about some trinket in a box?" Max asked me curiously, and I knew I was letting my emotions slip past my defences if he could tell how much it was bothering me.

"No," I grunted. "It's not...it doesn't mean anything. I just don't want anyone thinking it does."

"What the fuck is that supposed to mean?" Max asked, but I'd already slammed my mental walls back up like a fortress around my mind, and I strode away from him as I stalked after Seth and Caleb into the dark.

Lights blazed to life, and I paused as I realised where we were, the throne sitting right in the heart of the enormous room, the black stone Hydra heads which adorned it seeming to stare at the four of us indignantly, like Hail Vega himself had seen who had just set foot in his throne room.

"Well, fuck me, she's a pretty chair," Seth sighed, the box momentarily forgotten as he and Caleb looked up at the imposing throne like a pair of naughty school kids caught where they shouldn't be.

I strode up to them, ignoring the throne in favour of claiming my prize. I tugged the envelope which held Seth's real present from my back pocket before slapping it against his chest and snatching the box from Caleb.

Caleb bared his fangs, slamming into me so fast that I dropped the cursed box, the damn thing skittering away across the floor while I was distracted by having to fight off a Vampire who seemed inclined to bite me for nothing more than wanting a bit of fucking privacy.

"What's the big deal about some Christmas present?" Caleb asked, his palms slamming into my chest with the force of his gifts so that I was knocked back a step.

"It's for your mom," I lied, shoving him in return. "I just didn't want you crying about me one-upping whatever flashy bullshit thing you bought her with your pocket money."

"Fuck you. My mom loves flashy bullshit," Caleb laughed, and I snorted.

"Ohmastars!" Seth cooed loudly as he finally opened his gift from me and read the information on the tickets. "Two nights in a luxury mountain cabin and a moonlight hot air balloon trip for four! How will I ever choose who to bring with me??"

"What the fuck is that supposed to mean?" Caleb demanded, whirling on him and forgetting about me. "You're taking the three of us, asshole."

"Right, yeah, probably," Seth began. "But I do have other friends, you know. Some of whom like the moon waaaay more than you guys. And if I took my pack, we could have a balloon orgy right up by the moon-"

"Someone is going to be piloting the thing, are you planning on them joining in with your orgy or just making them watch?" Caleb asked.

"That depends," Seth mused.

"On?"

"Are they hot?"

I left them to their ridiculous argument and turned to hunt the floor for that fucking gift, cursing myself for ever even getting the thing in the first place. I wasn't going to give it to her. She fucking hated me, and I…was not a fan of her. At least, I wasn't a fan of *what* she was.

Fuck. Was I really this screwed up over a Vega?

I frowned as I turned around, looking everywhere for the little box before finally spotting it right by the foot of the steps which led up to the throne. I moved to pick it up but paused as I realised the box had come open, the lid fallen off and the contents gone.

"Looking for this?" Max asked quietly, and I whirled towards him, finding him leaning against the wall, the small crystal ball rotating slowly in his hand as he inspected it.

My spine prickled as I stalked towards him, reaching for the glass sphere and glancing into the heart of it as he released his hold on it without protest.

It was about the size of a plum, the thing itself fairly unremarkable so far as crystal balls went. The magic I had added to it was what I had been attempting to hide from the three assholes I called brothers.

I watched as a little motorcycle ridden by a tiny girl all made of flame sped across the centre of the crystal ball, a fiery Dragon chasing after her as they weaved back and forth in a hunt which was almost a dance. The echoes of the memory clung to the magic, pulsing against my skin as I held the crystal ball in my hand, watching as the bike veered away, then raced over a cliff formed out of ice crystals. It fell out of sight, turning to smoke while a Phoenix leapt from it, facing off against the Dragon, then tearing away through the sky. The chase went on and on, the fury, excitement, and heat I had felt during those moments rattling through the crystal ball with enough force to make my heart race like it had that day.

I didn't know what the hell I'd been thinking when I'd poured my power into the thing to capture that moment for her. Maybe I'd wanted her to know how fucking furious I'd been while I'd chased her, but the heat, the desire, the boundless energy which crackled through the crystal ball into my skin was all too clear as well.

Max flicked a silencing bubble around us, and I shoved the stupid thing back into my pocket, sighing in anticipation of what he was going to say.

"You got something you wanna tell me about that?" Max asked, his dark eyes serious as he studied me, and I kept every grain of emotion locked up inside me as I gave a nonchalant shrug.

"Just another way to fuck with her," I said dismissively. "I wanted to remind her how close I came to destroying her that day."

"Uh huh."

Max stared at me expectantly, and I just stared right back, waiting for the reprimand, the reminder of what we all had to do, the endless reasons for why it all mattered so fucking much and why me having any kind of feelings beyond hatred and the full desire to get rid of the Vegas would be utter insanity.

Instead, he just sighed, clapping me on the arm and turning for the exit, releasing the silencing bubble. "We should get back before our parents lose their shit about us not doing our part for the press. A few family shots and we'll be free to get ready for the ball."

"Oh, I can't wait for the ball," Seth cried excitedly. "I'm gonna get so wasted, and I'm gonna hook up with someone so hot they burn me."

"Like who?" Caleb asked as we all turned our backs on the throne which had caused so much turmoil in our lives, returning to the sham Christmas we were putting on for the press.

"That is yet to be decided, young Caleb. But don't you worry, I'll be balls deep in someone ultra, magma-level hot before the night is done. Mark my words."

A knock at my door jolted me from the reverie my mind had drifted into, and I called out for Lance to enter without needing to ask who was there.

Father had just left, and I was sitting on the edge of the bed I'd been given to sleep in while we stayed here, bloodstains still splattered over the front of my shirt and my broken arm screaming in agony.

"One of these fucking days," Lance snarled as he dropped onto the bed beside me, snatching my arm into his grip a little rougher than he probably meant to as his anger burned through into his actions, and I sat quietly while he healed me. "I swear, Darius, the time will be upon us soon, and you'll be the one left standing over him when it does."

I made a vague noise of affirmation, letting my friend fuss over me as he drew the bloodstains from my clothes with his water magic and started straightening out my shirt, brushing imaginary dirt from the shoulders and cursing my father the entire time.

Sometimes I joined him in his verbal annihilation of the man who had sired me in these situations. Other times, I felt like this, absent from the world, from my own flesh, unable to really feel any of it or even care about what punishment I'd endured at Lionel Acrux's hands.

It was nothing new. Just a part of my day to day which I might have preferred not to endure but was well beyond used to by now.

"Darius," Lance growled, and I forced myself from the view through the window to meet his steely gaze.

"I'm good," I told him, my voice a touch robotic but it was the truth, nonetheless. "How late are we for the ball?"

Lance pursed his lips, glancing at the ornate clock which hung on the wall beside the door. "A little. Wanna blow it off and get shit faced on cheap bourbon with me?"

I weighed his offer for a moment, but as he glanced at the clock again, I got the impression he didn't actually want to do that. For some reason, he was looking forward to this fucking thing.

"Nah," I said, brushing him off as he began to fuss with my bow tie and getting to my feet. "I'd say it would be better if I didn't piss my father off again quite so soon."

"Right," Lance bit out, and I knew he was holding back on saying a shitload more, but what was the point? This wasn't our first trip around the bullshit reality of my life, and it wouldn't be the last. Better to just suck it up and move on than sit here crying about it.

I strode up to the long mirror standing beside the window and carefully retied the black silk bow tie, eyeing myself critically and pushing my hair back away from my face before working some product into it to keep it there. I needed a shave, but I never bothered entirely removing the stubble from my jaw, so it wasn't that noticeable really.

"Darius," Lance began behind me, but I didn't reply, my gaze catching on my own eyes in the mirror and fixing there.

Did I always look like that? So empty and fucking hollow inside? Like I didn't care about a single thing in this world and nothing could touch me. No wonder it was so easy for Roxanya Vega to see the worst in me at all times.

"Darius?" Lance repeated, and I blew out a breath lined with a hint of smoke.

"Let's go," I said, moving to grab my jacket from the hook by the door where Father had ordered me to hang it to save it getting rumpled during his lesson on the importance of never backing down.

I slid my arms into the sleeves and took a step towards the door, but Lance was suddenly between me and it, his brow lowered over a dark expression, his hand on my shoulder to stop me.

"Tell me he's a piece of shit," he demanded, and I arched a brow. "Tell me he's a fucking bully and a coward and one day soon, you're going to show him the monster he created over all the years of treating you this way."

"I dunno what you want from me, Lance," I sighed. "Yeah, he's an absolute cunt. And yeah, I still plan on beating his ass in front of as many witnesses as possible and taking his place on the Celestial Council just as soon as I can. Is that what you wanna hear?"

"Mostly, I just want something from you, Darius. Some sign that you're in there and not..."

"Not what?" I asked. "Broken? You think he fucked me up so good this time that it was the final straw and something snapped beyond repair in me? He gave me a kicking and a broken arm. I was hardly close to death, so I dunno why-"

"It's fucked up that you dismiss it like that."

"Well, my entire life has been fucked up by that man every damn day, so what do you want me to say about it? You don't need to worry that I'm losing faith in our plan or backing out or anything like that. I can have shit on my mind and it not be about Lionel fucking Acrux, you know?"

Lance sighed, shaking his head as he released me, backing up a step to give me some space.

"You wanna tell me what that shit might be?" he asked, and I pushed my tongue into my cheek, unsure where to even begin or how to say it, especially after the argument we'd had on this subject the last time it had come up.

I turned away from him and strode towards the windows once more, looking out of them over the darkened landscape of the palace grounds. It was peaceful here in a way that I hadn't experienced in many places in my lifetime. Everything felt expectant, like the walls themselves were waiting for something big to take place to wake them all up again.

"I can't get her out of my head," I muttered, my eyes on fat snowflakes as they tumbled from the sky. "Every cutting word, every taunting look, even all the shit she does which isn't aimed my way. I'm always watching her, my eyes finding her in every room, and if I can't look directly at her, I'm stalking social media for any and every glimpse I can get. Grus posts so much that I can pretty much track her entire day if I want to. I see what she has for breakfast, who she hangs out with, how often that fucking hat kid sidles in too close, who she faces off against, who she smiles for, where she disappears to when it's just her and her closest friends, and I can't stop looking."

"Tory?" Lance guessed, and I looked over my shoulder at him with a scowl.

"Who else would I mean?"

"No one, apparently. But the last time you mentioned this obsession with her, you also made it abundantly clear that you hate her for it and that she hates you right back…"

"Yeah," I muttered, looking to the falling snow again.

"Unless you were lying to yourself and to me…"

"Stop with the leading sentences," I bit out, and he snorted a laugh.

"I've never seen you this flustered by a girl."

"Fucking flustered," I grumbled. "You make me sound like a thirteen-year-old girl without a date to prom."

"If you like her, you should just-"

"I don't *like* her," I ground out. "I'm infatuated with her; that's not the same thing."

"So what is it you want from her then? Because you already slept with her, and that clearly did nothing to rid you of this so-called obsession. You said you were set on getting rid of her. Has that changed or-"

"By the stars, how should I know? It's not that simple, and I don't have an answer, or I would have done something about it myself. All I know is that every time she lets her mask slip around me, every time she's even the slightest bit civil or offers me the hint of a smile or I think she's flirting with me, I lose my goddamn head and want nothing more than to pull her into my arms and make her beg to be mine."

"Well, at least you're not getting all weird and intense about it," he joked, and I groaned.

"This is a nightmare. Her entire existence is a nightmare sent to torment me for all the shit I've done in my life and will likely do before my death."

"My vote would be for some honesty between the two of you. Tell her how you feel, tell her you're sorry for being a stars-awful prick and explain it's in your DNA and hope for the best. She watches you at least half as much as you watch her, so I'd guess you have a semi decent shot at her hearing you out."

"And what about the whole throne issue? Or the fact that even if by some miracle she wanted me in any way too, I'm already engaged and have a responsibility to ensure the stability of the Celestial Council with my Heirs, so-"

"That all seems like more of an issue for *after* she agrees to give you a shot, wouldn't you say?" Lance nudged me, and I turned to look at him, the barest hint of hope breaking through the bleak stream of my thoughts.

"Let's go get drunk," I suggested, done with this conversation and unlikely to take his advice, regardless. Roxy Vega was the worst idea I'd ever had, and no matter how much I fixated on it, I knew I would do better to steer well clear.

"Last one there has to sink three shots," Orion challenged.

The asshole sped out of the room so fast that he was little more than a blur on the edges of my vision, and I called a curse after him as he raced away ahead of me, leaving me to walk my ass down to the ballroom alone.

I hesitated as I started towards the door, my gaze moving to the nightstand briefly before I gave in to madness and headed over to it, taking the box containing the crystal ball from the drawer and dropping it into my pocket.

I'd made the damn thing for her, after all, so I might as well give it to her.

The sound of music and polite conversation led me to the ballroom, and I rolled my shoulders back as a pair of servants swept a set of double doors open before me, bowing as I walked through.

There were familiar faces everywhere; Fae with positions running the kingdom beneath my father and the other Celestial Councillors, people with money and power, always eager to claim some more of it.

I sought out Lance by the makeshift bar, weaving my way between the crowd, greeting people as I went while making sure I moved fast enough to keep them from snaring me into conversation.

He'd already laid out my shots on the bar, and I didn't make any objections as I sank them one after another, letting the burn of the potent liquor roll down my throat and pool in my stomach.

I turned to look across the dance floor, my gaze skimming between every dark-haired girl in the room and failing to find her.

"The Vegas are running even later than we are," Lance commented, clearly realising who I was looking for. "The whole room is in unending suspense over what they might be wearing and whether they might be accompanied by anyone when they arrive."

I chose not to comment on the possibility of Roxy turning up here with a date. She hadn't even expected to be ambushed with all of this today, so I doubted she'd have had time to get one for herself. Unless...

I found Caleb within moments of searching the crowd for him, standing with Seth and Max to the side of the room near the glass doors which stood open to the grounds beyond.

"You coming?" I asked Lance as I started towards them, but he shook his head.

"I need to have a word with my dear mother, stars save me," he replied. "She's been calling me all day, and if I don't at least pretend to wish her a happy Christmas, she'll never stop harping on about it."

I followed his gaze to see Stella slipping through the crowd in a sparkly green dress which was so tightly fitted to her frame that I could see the outline of her nipples through it. I tipped Lance a farewell salute and left him to that particular brand of torture before making my way over to join the other Heirs.

"Did you get lost somewhere?" Seth asked as I made it to them.

"Just had to have a word with my father," I replied, looking away from Max as the touch of his Siren magic danced around me. I didn't let him feel anything though, and he withdrew once he realised I wasn't going to.

"We have a bet going," Seth began dramatically, and the corner of my lips twitched in anticipation of whatever this was going to be.

"Before you launch into that, I was wondering if you might be in the mood to talk to me yet?" Caleb cut him off, his navy-blue eyes bright with a challenge as I looked to him.

"About?" I asked.

"What happened at the dinner table earlier."

Irritation spilled through me at the reminder of that head-fuck as the dual reality of Roxy encouraging me to slide my hand up the inside of her skirt and me finding Caleb's fucking hand there too clashed within my brain.

"I thought you and her were done?" I asked, Seth's gaze whipping from Caleb to me while he tried to glean the unspoken details as if he were watching the back and forth of a tennis match.

"What can I say? I'm hard to get over. I think the bigger question is what the hell you were-"

"They're here," Max interrupted just as my anger spiked.

I looked around to see Roxanya and Gwendalina stepping out of a door at the top of the spiral staircase on the far side of the room.

My breath stalled as I looked up at her, the black halter dress she wore like a second skin on her body, her hair loose and green eyes darkened with makeup which made her look somehow above this place and these people, like she didn't even see any of them aside from the girl she was walking with.

Hamish Grus and his band of insufferable sycophants started a round of applause, and my lips twitched in amusement as I noticed her cringing at the attention.

She hated this.

She was born for it and yet she was like a fish out of water every time she was forced to endure it, and there was something about that which just drew me to her. I didn't know anyone else who was so unaffected by the concept of fame and adoration as she was. She didn't want it. Didn't like it. Didn't care about it at all. And that was like a breath of the freshest air I'd ever inhaled.

My fingers dropped into my pocket, and I toyed with the little box I'd hidden there, wondering if I might actually give it to her or if I was just as deluded as every other no-hope loser in this place who was staring at her with desire in their gaze. It wasn't like she wanted a gift from me anyway. It was beyond clear to me that the only thing she wanted right now was to escape this place and the unwelcome attention from all of these strangers, but it would be a whole lot more difficult to offer her that.

She was swallowed by the crowd as she reached the dance floor, and I drew my attention back to the others, trying to ignore the frantic beating of my heart over the nearness of her. It was ridiculous. I likely only cared at all because of the impossibility of her, enjoying the challenge of obtaining her more than I could possibly want *her*. But even as I tried to convince myself of that for the hundredth time, I knew I wasn't fooling myself. This thing, this tangible thread of need I felt between me and her wasn't going anywhere. I'd tried everything I could to banish it, from hating her to hurting her to giving in and claiming her that one, endlessly unforgettable time. Yet here I was, unable to think of anything other than her nearness while surrounded by hundreds of people who faded to irrelevance just because she was close.

"I think I might see if Roxy wants to-" I blinked at Seth and Max in confusion, finding Caleb missing between them and Seth pointed through the press of bodies as the music picked up again, pointing him out.

Caleb caught her in his arms before she even saw him coming, shooting straight into the middle of the floor and bringing her into a fluid twirl as he pulled her into his arms and began to lead her in a waltz to Have Yourself a

Merry Little Christmas by Bing Crosby.

I fell utterly still as I looked between the two of them, the smug grin on his face making me want to stride straight through the press of bodies and smack it clean off again. But it wasn't the look on his face that had my gut tightening to the point of pain or my chest twisting so hard that I felt momentarily unable to draw breath.

She didn't push him away, didn't snarl or bite at him. She smiled. It wasn't radiant or joyful, but it was real, plain as day, pure happiness in his company, amusement unlike I had ever earned from her. And I knew then that some muttered exchange over crappy Christmases and one arguably pathetic gift were never going to make a difference to her. Because she had never looked at me like that, her gaze unguarded, her smile easily won.

I couldn't hear the words they exchanged, but she wasn't pushing him back and her lips stayed curved into that note of amusement, some secret being shared between them which I held no part in.

Max was saying something about Geraldine Grus, but the Dragon was stirring inside me, and I couldn't fucking breathe.

I said nothing as I turned from them, putting my back to the dance floor and striding away through the crowd fast enough to draw more than a few mutters of complaint as I knocked Fae aside in my haste to leave.

Cold air swept over me as I made it outside and I drew in a sharp breath of the icy air, enjoying the sting of it as I started walking along the outer wall of the palace.

I dropped my hand into my pocket as I went, my footsteps marking my path through the snow as I ripped the little gift box open.

I was such a fucking fool.

I didn't know if it was because it was Christmas or maybe I'd just lost my stars-damned mind, but had I seriously thought she'd want some dumbass crystal memento of the time she'd fucked me and ditched me even though she had never so much as mentioned it since?

I pulled the crystal ball from my pocket, my spine prickling with the thought of what she might have said if I'd actually tried to give it to her. I must have been a glutton for punishment. Perhaps I'd been hoping her second rejection would be the exact toxin I needed to help break the spell she'd cast on me, because there was no sane reason for me having spent the time I had in creating this piece of shit.

My fist tightened on the crystal ball, the Dragon in me snarling softly as I exerted my strength over it until I was finally rewarded with it shattering.

The glass sliced into my skin, and the little flames I'd trapped within it burned my fingertips, but I welcomed that pain over the twisting, jagged feeling that was slicing through my insides as the vision of her in Caleb's arms on that dance floor branded itself on the inside of my skull.

There was a decorative pond at the foot of the lawn, and I heaved my arm back before launching the shattered debris that remained of the crystal ball towards it.

I turned away before I even heard it hit the water, blood dripping from my cut hand to mark the snow.

I healed the wounds with half a thought, stalking away from the pathetic reality of that moment, hoping to all the stars and back that there hadn't been a single witness to Roxanya Vega's silent annihilation of my heart.

A window stood open, leading back into the palace, and I climbed through it before crossing a dimly lit sitting room and making my way into the palace hallway again.

I turned towards the room I'd been given to sleep in for this stay, knowing that Father would be pissed at me for ditching the ball and wasting the opportunity to garner some extra political support with the powerful Fae in that room, but I just couldn't spend my evening watching her dance with Caleb, knowing at some point or another the two of them would slip away and I'd be left there, less than half a thought on her radar.

It was fucking pathetic, really, but if I wasn't allowed to indulge in self-pity and wallowing at Christmas, then when could I?

A glimmer of light caught my attention as I walked down the pristine corridor, and I paused, turning my head at the prospect of treasure and finding a shimmering footprint fading away on the tiled floor instead.

I cocked my head, moving closer and spying a second silvery footprint, then a third. The heavy wooden door to the throne room swung open and they disappeared through it.

My skin was prickling with the heat of my Dragon, the urge to shift so potent that I almost turned and strode back to that window, ready to take off into the sky and fly until dawn rose over the world and this hell of a day was done with.

But even as I considered that, I dismissed the idea. My father had made it clear on several occasions that he wished the Vegas no end of harm, and I couldn't just take off into the night while they were all beneath this roof together. It wasn't like I really expected him to attack them right in the middle of the Palace of Souls, but I couldn't bring myself to stray too far from any of them until he had left this place, and them, far behind.

Smoke slid between my teeth, and I headed into the dark throne room, pushing the door closed at my back as I did so to drown out the distant sound of music and people partying at the ball.

There it stood; the black stone monstrosity carved with fifty ferocious Hydra heads illuminated by a single beam of pale blue light.

I shrugged out of my jacket as I prowled around the enormous chair which had caused so much anguish, scowling at the many heads of the Hydra which decorated it.

"So much fuss over a place to rest your fucking ass," I muttered, tossing the jacket to the floor and placing my foot onto the first of the three steps which led up to the imposing throne.

Maybe if I just sat on it, claimed my place like we had all been promising to do for so long, then I'd feel...something. Clarity would be nice, or even just a little bit of nothing.

I snorted at myself, tugging my bow tie loose as I ascended the final steps and undoing several of my shirt buttons too. I just needed to breathe.

My skin prickled as I stood before the throne, its dark aura wrapping around me like a silken fist, purring in my ear, warning me away, daring me to come closer.

I wetted my lips. So far as I knew, even the Councillors had never sat on this thing, leaving it empty in memory of the Savage King who had perished so many years ago. They served it, and it ruled them.

I turned my back on the throne and exhaled slowly as I sank onto it, the cold stone pressing against my heated skin through my clothes.

A breath of laughter escaped me as I pushed my fingers into the dark strands of my hair, breaking it free of the product that had held it before clasping the back of my head and looking up towards the roof, that blue light falling down over me.

It was utterly…anticlimactic. It wasn't even all that comfortable. Just a stone chair in a cold room set up to be something so much more than it really was.

I dropped my free arm over the armrest and spread my legs as I relaxed into it, looking out over the room and wondering what the hell I was even doing. It was Christmas day, and here I was, having a pity party for one on the throne which had dominated every single moment of my life from the second of my conception.

I probably should have just left, gone to find some booze and drowned my sorrows at the bottom of a bottle, or on Orion's shoulder, but I didn't make any move to rise. It wasn't like I had anywhere else to be. And if anyone was missing me, they'd no doubt find me soon enough.

The sound of the door opening behind the throne made my heart thump out of rhythm, and I tensed before the slow click of a pair of high heels sounded on the cool floor at my back.

I stilled, something in the air itself charging around me, and without her so much as saying a word, I knew who had just entered my space. It was like I was aware of her on a primal level, the beast in me always knowing when she drew close. I'd known it for a while now, even if I had never admitted it aloud. My head turned her way whenever she entered a room, my muscles tensed, my pulse picked up. I was an apex predator, and she was the only prey I desired.

I didn't move as her footsteps drew closer, waiting there in the shadows for her to either leave or discover me. No doubt she would have a few choice words to hurl my way once she spotted me lounging on her father's throne, but I welcomed the sharpness of her tongue. I welcomed her ire and wrath and hatred, because if it was all I could get, then I'd take it, no matter what that said about me. Ever her villain.

Roxanya Vega rounded the foot of the dais which held the throne, her breath catching as she found sitting me there in the shadows, a monster lying in wait.

Her gaze roamed over me for several seconds, my pulse thumping harder as I studied her in turn. That dress shouldn't have been legal, the way the fabric hugged her form, nothing more than a temptation designed to drive me insane with want.

Her lips parted as I met her gaze and for a moment, she seemed to be lost for words. I saw the thoughts and memories all working their way through the darkness in her eyes, the things I'd said and done to hurt her clashing violently with the desperate ache I felt when I looked at her like this. Like she wasn't a princess born to unseat everything I had worked my entire life to achieve, but instead, she was a star beyond the reach of a desperate man.

"What are you doing here?" Roxy breathed, her low voice echoing in the stone room.

"I couldn't watch you dancing with Caleb," I admitted, holding her eye and simply owning how I felt. This didn't seem like a time for lies to fall between us anyway.

"Why?" she asked, staying right where she was even though we were alone, even though she knew better.

I shifted in my position on the throne, leaning closer to her and resting my elbows on my knees as I gazed down at her, studying every inch and simply answering her question again, uncertain if I was mad to do so or if I would go mad if I didn't. These words had been choking me for too long, this truth burning its way up my throat every time I was in her presence, and the need for them to break free was too powerful to deny now.

"Because you're in my head all the time. You pulse through my blood with each beat of my heart. I live for every scrap of attention you offer me and suffer through every moment you spend ignoring me," I admitted darkly, holding her eye as I tried to gauge how those words landed.

"I thought you hated me?" she asked, like it could possibly be so simple.

"I do," I agreed. "Because you represent everything I want and everything I can't have."

"You want me?" she asked slowly, taking a step closer, and I fell utterly still as I found her approaching instead of recoiling. I'd expected her to scoff, or laugh, or call me any number of things, but this...

"You know I do," I replied roughly, sick of her pretending this wasn't real between us.

"No, I don't. I know you like to hurt me and tear me down," she said, her green eyes still locked on mine, while I remained entirely still and my heart rioted in my chest. "I know you want to control me and take from me and make me bow at your feet."

"I do," I admitted, not denying it because I did like doing those things to her, I liked doing anything and everything I could simply to make her see me, and when she was hurting, she always looked. When she was suffering at my hands, she came alive for me, for better or worse. "And I think a fucked-up part of you likes it when I do those things."

"Fuck you," she hissed, but she didn't leave because she knew I spoke the truth. The twisted, ugly truth of the rotten creatures we were at our cores, the ones who revelled in the hurt we doled out to one another because we didn't know how to offer anything better.

"I think you like it when I hurt you because on some level, you believe you deserve it," I said, my voice laced in grit and her eyes flashing with that rage which turned me on so fucking much.

"Why would I feel something that fucked up?" she snarled, still standing right there, not backing down, never running from a fight. She was Fae right down to the bones of her, built in the image of her father, whether she wanted to admit it or not.

"Because we're the same. Every time my father hits me or hurts me or chains me, a little piece of me relishes the pain. Because I know I deserve it. For not getting Xavier away from him. For not stopping him from claiming the shadows. For letting him hurt you and your sister." I frowned, hating those things about myself but knowing it was the truth, just like she could see it was too.

"I was the reason no one ever kept us," she said in a low voice. "I was the loud one. The rude one. The one that no one liked, let alone loved. I actually overheard one of our foster carers asking social services to find me a new placement while they offered to adopt Darcy alone. I could have told our social worker that I'd agree to that. I could have let her be happy instead of dragging her down with me. But that's what I do. I'm the one who stopped her from having Christmas traditions or friends who lasted more than a semester. I'm the one no one has ever wanted long term..."

A frown tugged at my brow as I took in that admission, the vulnerability she was sharing with me as if I might be someone she could trust with it...or someone who could understand. It was her truth, but that didn't make it any less tragic. She'd been Fae, that was all. A Fae child was pre-programmed to push boundaries, to ignore danger, to find the hard limits, then break through them. That might have been too much for the mortals who had been tasked with caring for her, but it was exactly what drew me to her in turn. She wouldn't be caged, wouldn't be told no, wouldn't let the world push her around. She simply refused to conform to anything less than the fullness of her desires.

"That's why you push me even when you don't have to," I said. "You want me to punish you, and you want to hurt me in return." Her scowl deepened at my words, her hands curling into fists at her sides, but it was true. She thrived on the tension between us, it brought out the very worst in both of us and it lit us up too, awakening that feral piece of us which we had been told to contain all too often. But together, we were free to unleash it, free to see what power it might really hold and what hurt it might be capable of causing. "And I think you get off on seeing me in pain."

"How have I ever hurt you?" she snapped, but she knew, she had to fucking know what she did to me with every moment of her disregard and every word of disrespect.

"You hurt me every time you ignore me. You hurt me every time you spend time with Milton or that douchebag with the hat or Cal or any other fucker who catches your eye," I accused.

She pursed her lips at me, but she didn't deny it. Not outright. "Maybe you've been believing your own bullshit. I'm not the one who told the world I was a sex addict."

"You did, actually," I pointed out, my rage intensifying as my thoughts fell on that interview she'd done for The Daily Solaria, those pictures of her which had stuck in my mind ever since, the taunting words, the unnecessary addition of those male models.

"Only because you gave me no choice," she shot back.

I stared at her for a long moment, wondering if she truly believed that. Did she think I'd forced her to take those photos? Or had she secretly loved every moment of that shoot, knowing what it would do to me when I saw it, knowing how it would rile me up and lash back at me far more effectively than any other form of response could have.

"I had that model fired," I admitted, more than a little smug over that knowledge even if it did make me an even bigger piece of shit.

"What?" she asked with a frown, like she had no idea, like she couldn't even remember him.

"The one in that photo shoot with you," I growled. "The one it looked like you really did screw."

I wondered if she'd admit it, and I wondered what I'd do if she did, if she'd fucked him and screamed his name and let him taste the sins on her lips. I'd hunt him down if she had. I didn't care what that made me, I didn't care if I had no right to feel that level of possession over her. I'd hunt him down and-

"Wow. You're insane," she said harshly, realisation dawning in her green eyes. "That poor guy probably really needed that job."

"He didn't need to take his work so fucking seriously," I snarled, thinking of his hands on her body, his gaze roaming, the lust he hadn't even tried to hide.

"What the hell is this, Darius?" Roxy asked angrily, and my heart leapt as she took that damn tone with me, scolding me like I was hers to do so to. "What is it you want from me? Because you're acting a hell of a lot like some scorned lover, but we never even made it off the starting line, so I don't understand why-"

"Neither do I," I growled, knowing she was right on some level, even if I rejected that with my entire being. She was mine. And yet she wasn't at all. "But when I see you, all I want is to lay claim to you. I want you to be mine and I know you never will be, and it's making me even more fucked up than I was to begin with. That's why I hate you. Not because I'm supposed to or because my father wants me to, but because you represent every freedom I've never been given. It's like you were designed entirely to taunt me and toy with me and crack me open, and I won't let it stand."

"So what do you want from me?" she demanded. "Do you want to sit up on that throne with me on my knees before you. Would that end this feud between us?"

Silence. A single beat of it which left me with a terrifyingly clarifying notion.

"I don't know."

She stared at me as the seconds ticked past, and I swear something in the air itself shifted, like she heard that admission for what it was. I'd told her plainly how I ached for her, how I wanted her and burned for her and even though I didn't dare move, I was utterly consumed by the desire to reach for her.

This want was a need which was destroying me in every moment that I denied it. I hadn't been able to remove the taste of her from my tongue since that day in the Shimmering Springs. I hadn't slept a single night without dreaming of her, hadn't gone a single day without seeking her out. No other girls even registered with me. That single photo she'd sent me so fucking long ago had spent so much time on my Atlas screen that it might as well have been my screensaver. But no matter how hard I fought it, no matter how often I gave in and fucked my hand to the thought of her flesh against mine, thinking I could banish the need myself, it didn't change, it didn't ease. She was under my skin, and I was starting to think there could be no cure to it.

I blinked at her as she placed her foot on the first step of the raised platform beneath the throne. There were three stairs which raised me up above her. Just three. Though that distance seemed endless as my breath caught and held and I was left staring at this creature who had taken full possession of my thoughts.

She made it to the second step, and I sat up straighter, staring at her expectantly, like she might be about to tell me what I needed to rid myself of her, like she held the answer which had evaded me so eternally. But I didn't want that. As much as I hated to admit it, the closer she got, the harder my cock grew, the desperate need in me pounding through my blood and begging her to come just a little closer, though I knew it was a fool's hope.

She held my gaze, and I sucked in a sharp breath as she slowly lowered herself to her knees in front of me, my mind racing with confusion as she dropped down before me, almost as if she were about to-

"I'll never bow to you," Roxy breathed, the sight of her on her knees before me freezing me in place as I tried to understand, refusing to hope for what it was too unbelievable to be. "But if you like me on my knees, then there are better things that I can do down here than kiss your feet."

The taunting, sultry tone had me sitting up straighter, words escaping me entirely as she placed her hands on my knees and slowly pushed them up the insides of my thighs. Her touch was a brand on my soul, my dick already throbbing with need while she toyed with me, and I fell prey to her oh so easily. She may have been the one kneeling before me, but it was clear which one of us held all of the power as I simply stared at her, afraid of doing anything which might break this fragile spell.

Roxy slid her hand up over my solid cock, smiling darkly as she felt the rock-hard ridge of my arousal, knowing exactly what she was doing to me.

"Is this what you want from me?" she taunted as she slid my fly down and pushed her fingers into my boxers, my chest heaving as she touched me, my heart racing and my tongue stuck to the roof of my mouth as the shock of what she was doing froze me in place.

I was a mouse in the paws of a cat, and I had the feeling that she would snap her jaws shut around me the moment I admitted the depth of my need for her. She had me utterly and entirely, and I had to think she was about to shove me away at any moment, to laugh and sneer at the idea of the two of us, but I couldn't hold my tongue. The truth rose to my lips and wouldn't be denied.

"I want everything from you," I said fiercely, and as her gaze met with mine again, I got the feeling that she might just let me have it.

Roxy tugged my cock free of my boxers, her hands wrapping around my girth, and a breathy moan escaping her as she took in the full, hard length of me. Her gaze filled with desire, and my pulse raced with the need for her to do whatever filthy things she wanted to me.

She pushed up further onto her knees, and I watched in a haze of pure lust as she slowly took the length of me into her mouth, her tongue lapping my tip before swirling around it and making me groan as she drove her lips down my shaft. It was bliss unlike anything I had ever known. I'd dreamed of this, imagined it, and fantasised over it so many times, but nothing came close to the ecstasy of her tongue riding the length of my dick as she slowly withdrew again.

"*Fuck*, Roxy," I hissed through my teeth as she took me in again, my cock growing even harder, swelling with desire as she took me right down her throat and her fingernails bit into my thighs.

I lost all hint of restraint as I watched her, my hand fisting in the silken strands of her hair, and she moaned as I pushed her down harder, driving my cock into her mouth possessively. I wanted to come down her pretty throat so badly that I was practically trembling with the need to watch her swallowing every drop.

Roxy moaned in excitement as I fucked her mouth harder, and I damn near lost my mind at the sight of her on her knees for me, taking my cock so fucking perfectly, the sight nothing short of euphoric.

Every time she moaned around my length, my grip on her tightened, my cock thrusting deeper, my claim on her building. I was still reeling at this sudden turn of events, but I refused to blink at it, to let this moment pass like I had the last. She'd come to me like I'd been aching for her to for too long, and I needed to mark every inch of her flesh with the scent of me before this was done, making her understand how good it might feel if she would just let herself be mine.

The sight of her sucking my dick was enough to bring me to my own knees, the thrill of her doing so here while I sat on this throne making the entire thing seem unreal, like an impossible fantasy. How many times had I thought about getting her on her knees for me? How often had I demanded that she bow? But this wasn't her bowing. This was her showing me that she could own me even from the floor at my feet, and I was suddenly struck with the desire to worship her like the princess she'd been born to be.

"Stand up," I commanded roughly, tightening my grip on her hair and drawing her off me. She blinked up at me in surprise as I tipped her chin back and studied the beauty of her face, the desire in her green eyes, her pupils blown wide and her gaze full of want.

I reached for her, catching her arm with my free hand, and drawing her up into my lap so that she was straddling me, her dress hitching up over her thighs.

I kissed her then. Kissed her the way I'd been aching to kiss her every single day for weeks on end, tasting the fullness of her lips as my tongue pushed into her mouth. She opened for me like she'd been just as hungry for it too. Roxy wound her arms around my neck, drawing me closer until we were sharing every breath, our bodies pressed together in as many places as possible and that kiss devouring what little space was left.

She rolled her hips over me, my cock riding the seam of her clit, and she moaned softly into my mouth, her nails digging into the back of my neck as she kissed me harder.

I yanked her back by her hair so that I could look into those beautiful eyes, my heart racing with need and my mind swarming with the desire to capture this moment and keep it close always. I swiped a thumb across her mouth where her red lipstick had been smudged either by my cock or my lips, and whichever it was, the sight of it had every muscle in my core tightening, desire devouring me. But she needed to know this, needed to understand what she did to me with every waking second, how she was under my skin and caught on a loop in my mind, sending everything I had thought I knew so certainly spiralling off course.

"I don't want you on your knees. I want you fighting me and hating me and fucking me like you mean it. You're Roxanya Vega, and you weren't built to bow to anyone," I growled passionately.

"You want me to hate you?" she asked in surprise, her gaze roaming over my features like she wanted to study me too.

"I want you to feel for me. And I'll take hate if that's all you're offering."

I kissed her again, unable to hold back a moment longer, and this time, there was a shift in her as she kissed me in return, like any reservations she'd been clinging to had fallen by the wayside and she was ready to prove to me that I had met my match in every way that counted.

Her hands moved to my chest, releasing my shirt buttons with hurried, needy movements, like she was just as desperate for me to be inside her as I was.

She yanked on the buttons to force them open, and I caught the hem of her dress, tugging it up, wanting to see every piece of her body, to study and worship it for as long as she would let me. The back of her dress was laced with a bunch of knotted ribbons, and it caught on her waist as the knots pulled tighter, refusing to move another inch.

I grunted as I yanked harder, needing the fucking thing gone, and Roxy broke our kiss with a curse as the material simply dug into her soft skin.

"Ow," she snapped, her eyes blazing with the desire to smack me, and the Dragon in me rose at that challenge, a growl building in my throat.

"Why are you wearing something that's so hard to take off?" I demanded.

"Because I don't actually plan on hooking up with assholes all the time, it's just something that keeps happening to me," she growled.

I blinked at her in surprise, my frustration shifting to amusement, followed by a much simpler idea on how to remove the damn dress. The corner of my lips hooked up as fire magic rushed to my fingertips and Roxy's eyes widened in alarm.

"Wait," she warned, like I might stop just because she'd be angry over it. But I loved it when she was angry with me. Anger meant I was getting under her skin just like she'd driven herself beneath mine. "This dress belonged to-"

Roxy yelped as flames burst to life across her back, destroying the ribbons which had been keeping her in the dress, and I tore what was left of the fabric off of her before tossing it aside.

"What the fuck?" she snapped as my gaze dropped to take in the matching set of deep red underwear she was left in, all the blood in my body heading straight to my cock as the need to be inside her just about obliterated me.

"Did that piss you off?" I asked, her anger so potent I could taste it.

"Yes," she snarled, tensing in my lap, but she wasn't making any attempt to leave.

"Then show me how much," I dared.

Roxy shoved me back against the throne so hard that my shoulders hit the back of it solidly and a dull thud echoed around the stone room to match the sting of the blow. She'd already unbuttoned half my shirt, but she wrapped the material in her fists and ripped the rest off with a snarl of anger that sent buttons flying and had my cock throbbing with desire. Fuck, she was so sexy when she was angry, this spitting little tom cat, looking to fight the world and everyone in it, no matter how much bigger they might be than her.

I laughed, and she bit my lip so fucking hard that she drew blood, the metallic taste rolling between our tongues.

She pushed the torn shirt off of me and I helped tug it free of my arms before throwing it aside. Roxy broke our kiss to press her mouth to the tattoo which curved around my collarbone, her lips hot against my skin as she kissed her way across the ink that decorated it, moaning like she'd been wanting to do that for a while.

I gave up on trying to hold myself back and moved my hand between us, pushing my fingers into her panties and groaning as I found her soaked core. She was fucking drenched for me, her pussy so wet that it was practically begging me to sink my cock deep inside and fill every dark place within her.

I circled my fingers around her opening, teasing her with what she was so clearly aching for, while her fingernails bit into my shoulders and she panted needily against my skin.

Roxy's thighs tightened over mine, the heels of her stilettos cutting into my legs and drawing a grunt of pain from my lips which she clearly enjoyed all too much. But I wouldn't give in so easily. I wanted to hear her begging for it, I wanted her moaning my name and saying 'please' before I'd sink my fingers into her tightness and make her come all over them.

My fingers circled within her panties again as I forced myself to hold back, wanting to hear my name on those pretty lips of hers, but of course she wouldn't just give in to me like that.

Roxy pushed herself upright, leaning back as her hands moved behind her spine and she unclasped her bra, drawing it off and making my throat tighten as I took in the perfection of her tits. I lost all focus on whatever game I'd been trying to play, groaning as I took my hand out of her panties and pushed her back so that I could gain access to that newly revealed flesh.

I sucked her nipple into my mouth, making her spine arch to give me more room and dragging it between my teeth just roughly enough to make her cry out. Her voice echoed off the stone walls of the throne room, and a fucked-up piece of me wondered if someone might hear us and find us here. The press was crawling all over this place, and the sight of me with my cock deep inside a Vega on the throne we were supposed to be warring over would most certainly make the headlines. But despite knowing that this was insanity of the purest kind, I couldn't even imagine stopping now. She was right here, in my arms at last, and I needed to be inside her more than I needed anything else in this world.

Roxy gripped my hair in her fist, kissing me again as I shoved my pants down, done with waiting, just needing to feel her around me. She stared down at me with such heat in her eyes that it scorched my skin, and I drank in every perfect inch of her body in return. She was unreal, this creature of myth whose beauty had enraptured me beyond the point of all reason, and my need to lay claim to her was a burning, desperate thing which could only be put down to some spell she'd laid upon me. But whatever it was, I didn't care. The need

I felt for Roxanya Vega defied all logic, and I wasn't fool enough to question it now.

I lifted her up, and her nails bit into my biceps hard enough to draw blood as she held herself there, letting me drag her panties down her thighs, baring herself to me and making my mouth dry out with desire.

I leaned in and kissed her again, worshiping her mouth and marvelling at the fact that she was here in my arms, wanting this just as much as I did, laying claim to me despite all I had done and how little I deserved her.

She drew back, her gaze locking with mine as she lowered herself down onto my cock, and I gripped her ass as I pulled her down harder, inch after inch of me filling that soaking tightness, knowing she could take it all.

Her breath caught as I drove in deeper, a groan burning up my throat as she took me, and I pressed her down, needing to be as deep in her as physically possible, stretching her and filling her until she moaned for me.

"You're so fucking beautiful, Roxy," I breathed, my eyes roaming over her features, and her green eyes flashed with anger at that name. But it *was* her name. She was Roxanya Vega, daughter of the Savage King and heir to the throne which we were currently fucking on. It was the reason for all the animosity between us, and it was the reason for this being such a terrible fucking idea, and yet the feeling of being inside her was so undeniably perfect that I wasn't ever going to be able to look on it as a regret.

She rocked her hips, beginning to fuck me, and I watched as she rode me, thrusting deep to meet her every move, the sharp points of her stilettos cutting into my thighs only making this high better. I deserved the pain, deserved whatever punishment she might offer me in payment for this pleasure, and I'd take everything she was offering so long as it meant I got to be here with her like this.

My hands roamed over her body as I thrust up into her, my mouth on hers or sucking on her nipples, biting at her neck, anything and everything while we fucked so fast and brutally that my mind spun with it. Roxy cried out for me with every thrust as the rage between us collided, her spine arching beautifully and the sounds of pleasure echoing all around us. Someone would hear. I half thought to cast a silencing bubble, but I was so lost in her that I couldn't focus to do it. I just needed more and more, harder and deeper, her screams making my pulse pound as she took my cock so beautifully.

Her hands fisted in my hair, her nails cutting into me as she punished me for all I was and all I'd done, using me and challenging me with every roll of our bodies against one another. I met her brutality with my own, relishing the way she moaned for me as I did.

Our kisses were bruising, my grip tight enough to mark her perfect flesh. I pulled her long hair and bit her skin, every touch of pain met with more moans of pleasure as she simply challenged me for more and more.

I drew water magic to my fingertips, coating them in ice, then running my hand down her stomach, steam rising as they met with the burning of her flesh which was alight with the power of her Phoenix.

Goosebumps rose wherever I touched her, and she groaned as I dropped my chilled fingers to her clit. She swore at me for it, and I kissed that filthy mouth, tasting her anger as I found a rhythm for my fingers in time with each powerful thrust of my cock deep inside her pussy.

Her body tensed where I held her, her climax coming, and I knew she was fighting it, making me work for it as I fisted my free hand in her hair once more, holding her in the perfect position as I fucked her deep and hard.

Her spine arched as oblivion captured her, and I growled with satisfaction as she finally lost all sense of control and came with a cry of utter bliss laced with the perfection of her calling my name.

Her pussy gripped my cock as her orgasm tore through her, and I thrust deep into her as she drew me after her into euphoria. My grip on her tightened to the point of bruising as I came so hard my vision darkened and a growl of utter pleasure tore from me. I came deep inside her, filling her, marking her, making her mine, at least for that moment.

She sagged against me, our heavy breathing filling the space as she pressed her forehead to mine and trembled in the wake of that explosion.

Without thinking, I dropped the shields surrounding my magic and she let hers fall away too, the intensity of our power uniting making every buzzing piece of flesh between us light up once more. Her pussy pulsed around my shaft, and she cursed me as release found her again, the aftershocks of what we'd just done consuming us both.

I folded my arms around her as I drew her to me, not wanting to let go, and I coaxed her lips to mine as my need for her to see me made any trace of sense fall away. My tongue pushed into her mouth slowly, and she kissed me back with the same devout worship I was offering her as my hands slid up her spine in a gentle caress, soothing any small hurts the brutality of our fucking had left behind.

That kiss was something different, something far beyond lust or desire, my heart thundering to the tune of it as I offered myself to her with it, every scrap of myself, every flaw and truth of me.

Her fingers trailed up my chest until she was cupping my jaw between her hands, and the depth of that kiss made my chest ache with all the unspoken words that hung between us.

We finally broke apart, pulling our magic back into ourselves as we tried to catch our breaths, and I frowned as I tried to make sense of what was happening between us. Of what had been happening for a long time now.

"You're going to be the ruin of me," I growled in her ear, and she pushed herself back just enough to look down at me, her gaze open and unguarded for once as she studied me.

"Not if you destroy me first," she breathed, painting the lines of my jaw with her fingertips, the caress so unexpected that I could only stare at her as she did it.

I gently swept her hair away from her face and inched her back so that I could look deep into those endless eyes. "Is that what you think I'm trying to do?"

She gazed back at me for a long moment, and I could see the walls slowly building themselves up again as she thought over all that had passed between us, my heart thundering with the desire to tell her whatever it would take to keep us in that moment, even as I felt it slipping away already.

"I don't know," she replied.

"Maybe that's a good thing," I muttered, unsure how else to respond, what I was supposed to say. It wasn't like I could undo all I'd done. Wasn't like I could change who we were or what stood between us, but some foolish part of me wished I could.

I leaned forward to kiss her again, wanting to just linger in this moment with her, spend the night worshipping her over and over again, just make it last that long. But she drew back, gripping one of the Hydra heads as she climbed out of my lap and moved to retrieve her clothes.

My lips parted on some protest or admission or maybe just a plea for this not to end, but the words caught in my throat. I didn't know what I could possibly say to her to change the way this was going, and I honestly didn't even think she wanted me to. The set of her shoulders told me what I needed to know. This was just another mistake to her, a lapse of judgement which she wanted to forget, just like she had the last time we'd lost ourselves to this madness between us.

I watched as she drew her underwear back on, then she took my shirt from the floor and put it on too. That made sense as her dress was currently little more than a few burned scraps of fabric, but I didn't hate the way she looked in my clothes.

I followed her lead and pulled my pants back on, feeling her eyes on me as I refastened my fly.

We looked at each other for a moment where a thousand words rose to my tongue and none of them made it past my lips. I could see that wall in her eyes once more, and I knew that nothing I could say would bring it back down again. And it wasn't like I could remove the objects which would always stand between us anyway, no matter how much I may have wanted to.

Roxy blew out a breath as my gaze roamed down to her exposed thighs, the sight of her in my shirt enough to make me ache, the possessive beast I was liking it far too much. Should I tell her that? Should I tell her that despite everything, I wanted her to be mine? That I had no idea how that would work, no way of promising her anything at all other than the fact that I wanted her to be mine and I would be hers if only she said the word…

Roxy snatched her ruined dress from the floor, then turned and walked out of the room, without so much as a word.

My heart twisted as I watched her go, the need to call out to her and say… fucking any of the things which were consuming me. But as she strode up the staircase which led out of the throne room and into the Queen's wing of the Palace of Souls, she didn't so much as glance back at me.

And I didn't figure out what to say before she was gone.

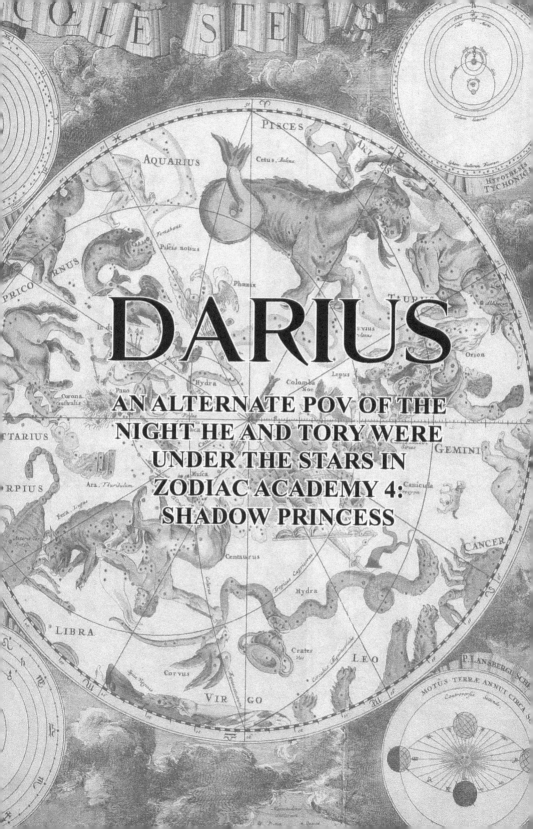

DARIUS

AN ALTERNATE POV OF THE NIGHT HE AND TORY WERE UNDER THE STARS IN ZODIAC ACADEMY 4: SHADOW PRINCESS

LIONEL

FROM THE LAIR OF LIONEL...

By this point, no doubt my folly was clear. My son, my promising, brutal, powerful son had been bewitched by a Vega whore. Just as his Guardian – the man selected to keep him alive - had been bewitched by her whore sister.

At this point, when I saw it oh so clearly, when I looked at my boy and saw longing mixed in with the hatred he felt for Roxanya, I knew I had no choice but to act.

My gut told me to kill her then and perhaps I should have done so. But I have never been a rash man and the bloodline of the Vegas wasn't something I wished to squander. Yes, I had her twin, but two tools were better than one.

So I devised a cunning plan, as so often I did, and instead used my power to compel Roxanya through Dark Coercion to break my foolish son's weeping heart. It was – and I do say so myself – a stroke of masterful brilliance.

Even I could not have predicted the foul fate the stars had planned. Even I could not have realised they meant to bond my legacy to that mixed-blooded girl with her Harpy mother. I can only imagine the horror of that bond having been accepted. I would have had no choice but to publicly endorse it — for even I know that standing against the choice of the stars would be a political disaster – but as ever, my cunning won out.

I made Roxanya break his heart just as I had planned. She said no. And though I was riled by the knowledge that Darius had so pathetically wanted to accept the bond, I slept deep and well for many nights after her rejection of him in the knowledge that I had finally realigned his head.

No more would he pine for that whore. And in a matter of time his sole desire would be to make her pay for his suffering.

It was perfect. Utterly perfect...

DARIUS

CHAPTER ONE

Snow swirled all around us and I watched Roxy as she looked about in confusion, the frown furrowing her brow letting me know that she had no idea what was happening – no idea what fate had chosen for us.

We were in this eerily perfect bubble of calm, the snow storm buffeting all around us but unable to penetrate the area reserved specifically for the two of us. A thousand things clicked for me at once, my obsession with this girl, my utter infatuation, the reason why I hadn't been able to keep my mind away from her. It all made sense now, why I couldn't convince myself to forget her, why I found myself baiting and harassing her if that was what it took to claim her attention. I'd been on the hook the moment my eyes had first fallen on her because it had all been leading to this. And like a fucking fool I'd tried to convince myself it was hatred instead of destiny. I was so, so, stupid. It was clear now. Of course she'd been meant for me. She was…everything. Every single thing about her that infuriated me was precisely what I had found so desirable, precisely what had me coming back for more no matter how deeply she cut me whenever I did.

"Roxy?" I breathed, needing her to look at me instead of the magic which had us captured here.

She looked up at me with accusation and mistrust in her eyes, no doubt thinking this was some game or trap instead of realising that it was our destiny come to tell us to wake the fuck up.

"Why am I here?" she asked, tipping her head back to peer up at the stars which shone in the open circle of space above us.

I followed her gaze, swallowing against a lump in my throat as I found her constellation and mine hanging in that impossible opening in the clouds, the heavens themselves realigning so that Gemini and Leo could come together just for us.

I looked back at her, unable to pretend that I wanted to look at anything else. She should have been shivering out here in this cold wearing nothing but a pair of blue leggings and a crop top, her bare feet pressing into the snow, but she didn't look cold. Then again, I didn't feel the bite of the cold either and I was no better dressed for a blizzard than her in a black T-shirt and jeans. Perhaps that didn't matter anyway; we were both creatures born of fire after all.

Her gaze finally fell back to meet mine and my heart lurched as I looked into her green eyes, the erratic pulse telling me what should have been so clear to me before this moment and suddenly made sense of it all.

Those eyes demanded answers and my lips parted on the one she needed most, but hesitation stuck my tongue to the roof of my mouth. How was I supposed to simply tell her that all of the anger and hatred she felt for me was really misguided want? How was I supposed to excuse away all I'd done to her in the name of this greater purpose which we'd both been too blind to see. With anyone else I might have guessed at what the connection between us meant, but the two of us had been pitted against each other from the moment of her arrival back in this realm. And I'd been consumed by the pressure put on me to win a conflict that had seemed so utterly unavoidable anyway.

"We...this..." I glanced up at the stars again, wondering if they might give me the words I needed, but they simple watched on, leaving this to me. No doubt a final test on their behalf. I swallowed again, hoping the raw magic of this place might make her see the truth of my words even through her scepticism. "I think that this is our... Divine Moment," I said slowly, watching her closely, waiting for her reaction and doubting it would include her hurling herself into my arms.

Roxy scoffed lightly, her eyes raking over me like she was waiting for me to bark a laugh or reveal the rest of the Heirs, all lying in wait to ambush her. I released a slow breath, needing her to listen to me, to take in what I was saying and realise what this meant for us. I took a step closer to her, wanting to reach out and take her hand in mine but not knowing if she'd let me or simply try to bolt.

"You mean you actually think the two of us could be Elysian Mates?" Roxy asked incredulously, everything in her expression telling me how ridiculous she thought that idea was. The look she was giving me felt like a dagger puncturing my gut, the raw outrage and horror at the mere suggestion of us being anything more than what we were clear in every line of her face.

"We're more likely to be Astral Adversaries," she spat.

Ouch. But shit maybe I deserved that. Maybe I deserved the look of pure hatred she was giving me and the contempt with which she was taking this suggestion, but she had to see the truth in it. The fucking stars had realigned for us. This wasn't some joke and the time for arguing and rivalry was long past. We were becoming something else now and she would have to see that.

"This isn't a joke, Roxy," I breathed, inching closer to her, waiting for that moment when she realised the full truth of this situation and understood what we would be to one another after this. She just had to see and then... my heart beat faster as my eyes moved over her face, the want I had tried to deny to myself bleeding from me as I just fucking looked at her and let myself admit that I wanted nothing more than for her to be mine. "It's not something either of us can choose. The stars picked us for each other. They've been challenging us and driving us together at the same time. That's why we keep colliding the way we do, why you're all I think about… Don't you think about me too?"

"You mean when I fantasise about ways to hurt you for all the things you've done to me?" she asked darkly, though something deep within her eyes flickered like she couldn't quite pretend that that was all it was. She felt this. I knew she did because it had been devouring me night after night, every spare moment dedicated to my obsession with her and when I peeled away the forced hatred, it was just so undeniably clear to me that it was something so much more powerful than hate. She needed to admit that too and if it meant cutting myself open and letting her see me bleed for her then it was the least I could do in light of everything else I'd put her through.

"I mean, like the way I lie awake at night, remembering what it felt like to hold you in my arms. How still the world felt, how pure that moment was between us. How I imagine I can still smell your perfume as my eyes fall closed and how I reach across my bed in the night wishing you were really there. Or like the way my heart beats harder when you walk into a room and my throat thickens when I try to think of the right things to say to you. How I fight to get your attention in any way I can because I can't bear it when you ignore me."

Her lips parted but she didn't seem to have any words for that declaration, the weight of them falling over her and making her look at me in a way she never had before. Like maybe she was finally seeing me beneath the layers of brutality and expectation.

"You've hurt me more than anyone I've ever known," she breathed, and I wished I could deny the ragged truth of that statement, wished I could pretend I was a better man than I was, one more worthy of her than I could hope to be.

I swallowed hard, moving a step closer and taking her hostage in my gaze. She was so small really. So fucking small in stature compared to how big her presence was in my life. So fragile to look upon compared to the strength which burned so brightly within her that it was all I could see. And she was worthy of so much better than me.

"I'm sorry," I breathed, my voice cracking with how much I meant those words. They didn't come close to making up for it, for any of the vile and heinous things I'd done to her. They didn't come fucking close, but they were the truth of me. They were the secret I had been choking on for months, burning in the back of my throat with the want to escape. But it had taken this moment for me to feel brave enough to utter them. If you could even call this quiet desperation brave. But I needed her to see the truth of that declaration, to feel the truth of it and understand that it would never be like that between us again. That I would be everything she needed of me now and forever fight to make up for all that had come before this.

For a moment it seemed like she did see that, like she understood how deeply I meant it. But then her gaze shuttered, some thought occurring to her which made her whole body go rigid in a way that made my pulse thunder with panic.

"Why now?" she demanded. "If we weren't standing here tonight, if we were somewhere else, would you have apologised to me?"

I was so thrown by the question that I knew the truth had danced across my expression before I could even gather my thoughts on the answer. My brow furrowed, the reality of my own stubbornness, of my inability to see this for what it was until this fucking moment pressed in on me. No. I wouldn't have apologised to her tonight without the stars having pushed us to this place. I wouldn't have had the guts to do it and honestly, I knew she wouldn't have wanted to hear it even if I'd tried. Besides, there was a reason for the animosity between us, the truth of who we were, what we were both destined to claim, my father... but had I wished I could fix it? Had I secretly ached for her in the darkest hours of the night and wondered what else we might have been if neither of us had any claim on a crown?

"You don't know how many times I wished I could fix what I'd broken between us," I rasped, needing her to understand the why of it because everything I had done hadn't been about me and her. It had been about what we were not *who*. And in so many ways, what I was was the only thing that had ever really mattered in my life. Before this moment when I was finally looking at the one thing I had never even dared to wish for myself. I had always known I would be given a bride not of my choosing and had never allowed myself to dream of the kind of love an Elysian Mate might offer – but even my father could not deny the wishes of the stars themselves. She had to see that. She had to understand. "But I had to do those things…I had to make sure you and your sister didn't rise up and claim our throne. It wasn't about you and me, it was about the Council and the Royals. About Solaria and what's best for all of its people. Darius and Roxy weren't a factor in any of it."

"Roxy?" she echoed scathingly, arching a brow at me and the glimmer of understanding I had imagined in her expression vanished like a candle being doused with cold water.

Panic bore into me as I realised she was withdrawing, her walls slamming up between us and that fucking name having ruined it all. She saw it as a barb when all it had ever been to me was a reminder. Darius Acrux might have been able to steal some semblance of something with Tory Gomez, a girl brought up by mortals and uninterested in any crown. But an Acrux and Roxanya Vega were a wholly different beast. She was the epitome of what I could never allow myself to even dream of and using that name served to remind me of who she was whenever the temptation to forget it grew too much.

But how was I supposed to explain all of that to her? Especially now, here, when beyond all the odds, none of it fucking mattered. The stars were letting it be so. Hell, they wanted it to be so and all she had to do was kiss me and then she would see, she would understand, I'd make it right, I'd fix it, all of it.

I shook my head as I stepped closer, begging her to forget everything that came before this moment and accept me as I was right here and now. Because I was hers if only she could admit to wanting me. I was hers whether she liked it or not.

"Tory, please," I choked, reaching for her, desperation clinging to me as her walls only grew thicker.

"You don't get to call me that," she snarled. "You call me Roxy, remember? You do it because that was what my mother called me. And you want to remind me that she's dead every time you talk to me. Because that's who you are. That's what you are. And I don't want anything to do with you."

"No," I growled, the realisation of what she heard when I used that name crashing against the reality of it and forcing me to scramble for the explanation she needed. "I don't call you Roxy because I'm trying to hurt you. I use that name so that I don't forget who you are or what you are. You're a Vega Princess. You could shatter everything I've worked for my whole life. And if I didn't force myself to remember that fact, then I knew it would be too easy for me to forget about. Forget about challenging you and knocking you down and just...let myself imagine you could be something else. Something that I've wished you could be in the darkest corners of my heart for so long that I can't deny it anymore. I want *you*. And I don't care if you're a Vega or not. I don't care if your name is Roxy or Tory or anything else. I just want *you.*"

My pulse was thundering erratically as she looked up into my eyes and hope speared through me as her expression softened just a little. She had heard me, she understood. I was getting through to her and she had to see that everything would be different once we accepted this bond, everything would be just the way it always should have been.

"If I'm right about this, we won't get another chance," I begged, desperation burning in my eyes as I looked at her, seeing the doubt that warred through her, wondering if she fully grasped what this was, the finality of it all. "Don't you understand? We'll be Star Crossed. Bound to be alone forever. We'll never find love with another. We're meant to be together - it's fate."

But instead of the acceptance I had expected to dawn in her eyes, I realised I'd said the wrong thing again as her jaw tightened at my words.

"Fuck fate," she snapped, spearing me straight through the chest with the brutality of that declaration. "I don't want it. If it's bound me to you then it's a cruel and twisted thing. I don't need destiny to choose my life for me. I'll make my own fate and it won't be with you!"

Panic roared through every inch of me at the weight of those words, at the dark and empty fate which awaited us beyond them if she really meant them.

"Please," I pleaded, wanting to grab her and make her listen to me, but I was too afraid to move an inch in case I fucked it up again. "Think about what you're saying. If I'm right then this is the moment that our stars have aligned. This is the moment when our souls are due to meet and connect with each other. I know you feel the same pull to me that I feel to you. You're all I think about. All I dream about. You're under my skin and in every thought and I know that I've done a thousand unforgivable things, but I swear I'll never hurt you again. You're meant for me. I'll protect you with my life-"

"It's too late," she said, her voice low and unmovable, those walls within her eyes impenetrable.

A decision rang in the air which would steal this one, fragile chance of happiness right out from under us and with a horrifying clarity, I knew that it was my fault. All my fucking fault.

"This isn't the moment when our fate is decided," she hissed. "This isn't the reason we will never be able to be together. The moment that decision was made was the moment you first laid eyes on me. The moment I walked into this academy with the chance to find my place in this world for the first time in my life, when I should have been able to make this place my home but you decided to make it my hell instead. So instead of looking at me like I'm the one who is denying fate and stealing your one true chance at happiness from you, then why don't you look at yourself? Look at every vile thing you've said and done to me. Remember burning my clothes off and humiliating me. Remember finding out my fears and bringing them to life. Remember how your magic felt when you used it to trap me beneath the ice in that pool and you left me in there to die."

Each word she threw at me was like a whip lashing across my soul, forever scarring it in the regret of my actions. How many times had I wanted to stay my hand? How many times had I gritted my teeth and forced myself to show her nothing but the worst of me in the name of what was expected of me? How many tests had the stars thrown our way only for me to fail time and again. I'd had so many opportunities to do things differently, but every time I had let anger rule over the desperate want of my heart because I was too afraid of the alternative. Afraid of my father, yes, but more than that I had been afraid of her. Afraid of wanting her and letting her see it only to find my heart crushed in her fist. And now here I stood, looking into those green eyes and watching as the blood from that furiously beating organ in my chest dripped between her fingers to stain the snow. Every single drop a testament to my failure and a mockery of what I had been so afraid of because that fear had been the very thing to cost me it in the end.

"I know," I said, my voice breaking on that word because I couldn't fix it, I couldn't take any of it back, I could only offer her the pathetic truth of me and swear to do all I could to make it right. "All the awful things I've done to you will haunt me forever. But please, *please* just give me forever to fix them. Let this bond form between us and I'll prove to you how good our lives could be together. I won't force you to do anything or be with me if you don't want to, but at least give us a chance. Kiss me again with the stars overhead and let our story begin anew here."

Silence rang in the wake of my words and the smallest ray of hope kindled in my chest as she simply looked at me, really looked and weighed me in the fullness of her stare.

I mustered what little courage I had left and drew closer to her, reaching out tentatively and taking her hands into mine. Her skin was so soft and so warm, the zap of electricity which pulsed between us present as always, my body reacting so keenly to hers.

I held my breath as she remained in place, looking up at me while the snow swirled all around us.

I watched her as she assessed me and I let myself see everything about her which I had wasted so long trying to convince myself I hated. She was a pillar of strength, this unbreakable force of energy who had survived the odds time and again, refusing to back down or bow in the face of any of the challenges which had arisen before her. She was hard and likely as savage as her father had ever been, but she was soft too, the love she felt for those few she did let close like this blazing force of nature that only a fool would dare to rile. And of course she was beautiful, so fucking beautiful that I hadn't thought of a single woman besides her from that very first moment I'd laid eyes on her. I had wanted her then. For a few blissful moments I had looked at her and laid a claim on her, meaning to make her mine through any means necessary. If only I'd remembered that instead of letting myself forget it the moment I found out her name.

She was faltering. I could see it. There was a want in her eyes which called to me, a need which I felt in the depths of my soul for a love like the one we were being offered.

I slowly trailed my right hand up her arm, giving her every opportunity to tell me to stop but that hope in me blazed a little brighter as her lips remained still and she allowed me to touch her like that.

I wanted her so fucking much. I wanted her mouth on mine and every piece of our skin connected. I wanted her pinned beneath me and hell, I even wanted her to pin me down too. I wanted her heart to beat only for mine. And I wanted to know every secret which she kept locked up so tightly within her sharp mind. I wanted it all and as I stared at her, I knew she wanted me too.

My fingertips brushed the length of her neck before reaching her jaw, her skin so soft against mine, my gaze fixing on that fucking mouth which had filled so many of my fantasies and riled so much of my temper.

The stars leaned closer to look as the space dividing us disappeared inch by inch, the weight of their presence building around us as the magic of this moment led to this final act.

My fingers scored a line along her jaw, my thumb tracing her bottom lip, stroking, caressing. I wanted to kiss her so bad that I wasn't even sure my heart was beating anymore. I wanted to taste her soul against my lips and promise her the world with the pressure of my mouth against hers, and still she wasn't pushing me away. She knew what we were. She was accepting it. She wanted this too.

Relief infused me as I stared down at this perfect creature and dared to move closer. The stars glimmered in the sky overhead, expectant energy coiling about us, and I leaned in.

Her breath danced with mine, my desire for her so overwhelming that I was trembling with the force of it. How had I gotten this lucky? How had I been chosen for a woman like this? There was no part of me which could claim to be worthy of her love, but I vowed on all the stars watching and on every scrap of my wretched soul that I would become everything she deserved and more. From this moment on, I would be her creature and I would do everything it took to make up for all of my mistakes which came before this. Before *us* - how we were meant to be.

My hand slid to cup her cheek, our gazes locked, my soul held out in offering to her as her lips parted for the promise of this kiss and I leaned in further, so desperate to claim it that it fucking hurt.

"No," she breathed, the word shattering through me and forcing me to fall utterly still.

I blinked at her, that simple word failing to penetrate my mind because I couldn't have heard her right. She couldn't feel the truth of all we were destined to be for one another and have spoken that word in place of taking that kiss.

But all I found in her green eyes was refusal, anger, hatred.

I shook my head, my grip on her face tightening as I tried to deny what I'd just heard her say, tried to find the words I needed to make her take them back.

"You don't understand," I said desperately. "We're meant for each other. We're destined to be together."

She felt the truth of that, I knew she did, but the solid wall in her gaze told me that the truth, no matter how blindingly, earth-shatteringly powerful it was, simply wasn't enough.

"So you've realised that all the time you spent torturing me, you should have been falling in love with me?" Roxy asked bitterly. "Well it's too late, you can't undo what you've done-"

"I *was* falling in love with you," I replied, my voice cracking because of course I had been. Couldn't she see that? Couldn't she feel it? "Everything else wasn't real. That's not who I really am! I-"

"Yes it is," she said fiercely. "It *is* who you are. You can tell me you hated doing it or felt obligated for whatever reason you want, but *you* are still the one who did all of those things to me. You're the one who put us on this path. I never wanted a war with you. But you didn't give me a choice in that. And now I'm not giving you a choice in this." Her voice rang with a clarity which cleaved me apart and I couldn't find the words to change her mind, couldn't find the excuses or apologies for any of it.

"Please," I begged again. "I'm giving you my heart. If you give me yours in return I'll spend every moment of our lives proving to you that I can be worthy of it."

"It's too late," she growled fiercely, ripping my heart clean from my chest with every single word. "If fate is so cruel as to only offer me true love with a man who could hurt me as much as you have, then I'll go without love," she swore. "You want my heart? I'd sooner cut it out than give it to you."

I shook my head, denying the words she'd thrown at me, drawing her closer in some desperate bid to make her see what was so blindingly obvious to me now. I was hers. I was all fucking hers and she had to accept me. She had to or I was going to shatter into a million pieces which would never be the same again.

That traitorous glimmer of hope reared its head again as she let me draw her closer, let me pull her to me even though that wall in her eyes remained as thick as ever.

"*Please,* just be mine, Tory," I begged but I could already see that it wasn't enough.

"I'd rather be alone," she whispered, destroying what little was left of me with those words as she pulled her hand out of mine, stepping back as I just shook my fucking head, refusing to believe her, refusing to accept that she meant it.

Tears spilled down her cheeks, the clarity of her own pain cutting into me because I knew I was the cause of it, that I'd been the cause of it ever since we'd met.

"Tory, I-" I followed as she stepped away, but she backed up again and again until I fell still, any false pretence of hope whipped away on the frigid wind.

The clouds drew closed overhead, the stars hidden once more as our constellations fell out of alignment and I felt the shadow of them fall over every piece of me, all the way down to my soul.

Roxy's gaze locked with mine just as a black ring formed around her pupils and the horror of it froze me in place. We were Star Crossed. The impossible truth of it closed in on me like a veil of darkness which I knew I would never escape.

The bubble of peace we'd been standing in suddenly shattered and the blizzard howled in around us to claim this place like it had never existed at all.

She turned and ran from me, leaving me standing in the snow, feeling like every step she took from me was marked with the bloody remnants of my heart.

The pain tore through me like nothing I'd ever felt before, the reality of what we could have been, of what I'd fucking done weighing so heavily on me that I couldn't even breathe.

Something was cracking apart in me which I knew would never be reforged and as the agony of it all became too much, my Dragon tore from the confines of my flesh.

I leapt into the sky, racing away from that place and the awful words which would never stop ringing in my ears as she rejected me. A roar filled with potent agony ripped its way out of my throat, echoing away across the sky and I simply flew and flew and flew, like maybe I could escape the rotten truth of my life if only I could move fast enough.

Roxanya Vega should have been mine, but in the end, she had seen the pathetic truth of all I was and had destroyed me rather than bind herself to me, and I had no one to blame but myself.

.

LEON
THE NIGHT HE AND THE
RUTHLESS BOYS MET THE VEGA
TWINS – BEWARE OF SPOILERS
FOR THE RUTHLESS BOYS OF
THE ZODIAC SERIES IN THIS
CHAPTER!

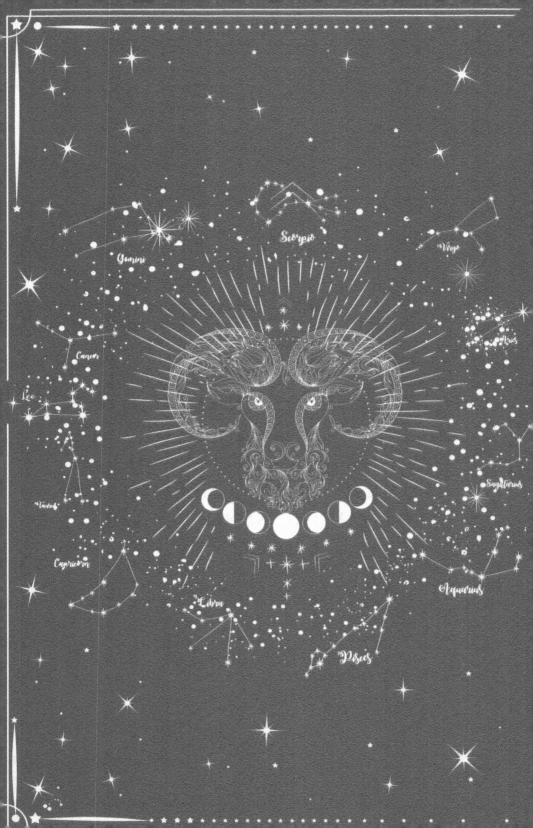

LIONEL

FROM THE LAIR OF LIONEL...

I have long been troubled by the errant Fae who lurk in the gutters of Alestria. Their uncouth ways leave me uneasy, and their lack of propriety causes me great unrest. There are many powerful Fae who live in that wasteland of a city who have been of use to me, but many others who have been of great irritation.

The Nights, for one, their family well-known for their thievery, even if there has never been evidence enough to put them in their rightful place in Darkmore and secure me the access to the trove of treasures they guard so well.

At least not until one such Night broke into my property and gave me the opportunity I had long sought to lay him in the depths of the infamous horrors of incarceration in Darkmore. Though I sadly could not lay claim to his family's treasures, this action lent me the sway I needed to lock down my relationship with the Storm Dragon, Dante Oscura. A stubborn, boorish Fae who would not bow to the power of the Dragon Guild for far too many years.

Despite his questionable ancestry from a vulgar pack of Werewolves, his kind is of such rarity, I could not leave him to his felonious endeavours in

Alestria without keeping tabs on him myself. My hope was to extract him from his crude family by offering him mounts of gold and a position of grandeur in the kingdom. Alas, his lewd and unrefined nature led him to taking another path. Defying me along with his associate Leon Night and his relationship with the despicable Altair girl who sought to disobey me at every turn.

No matter, for the war comes to a head, and once every Night, Oscura and Altair lay dead, I will claim all the riches of their families as my own. It is only a matter of time…

LEON

CHAPTER ONE

"**D**o you think the gift basket is too much?" I asked, planting my hands on my hips as I gazed at the huge hamper which was bigger than the couch and overflowing with so many gifts that I'd had to place half of them outside it.

I'd had the Mindys get some specially designed wrapping paper with little Basilisks, Lions, Dragons, Harpies and Vampires all over a lilac spread. They'd worked through the night to get all of these presents wrapped. I'd helped too. I'd wrapped up the biggest one which had been really hard, so I'd taken a nap afterwards and when I woke up it was nine am and the rest of it was done. It was exhausting all this party planning shit.

"Yes," Ryder growled from his seat by the window. He hadn't moved from there at all while I'd been hanging the final decorations that the Mindys had left for me - no wait, he had moved once when he'd knocked off the Lion King themed party hat I'd balanced on his head an hour ago with Scar's face on it. I'd cast a levitation spell on it now so it hovered a few inches above him and I was planning on him not noticing it, especially as he was currently occupied by The Lion King Two playing on the TV.

"Nah, they'll love it." I dismissed my moment of doubt and Ryder's dark green eyes slid across the room, taking in all of my decorations.

"You're overdoing it, Mufasa. Why would you theme a party based on The Lion King?

They aren't gonna get the significance of that to us."

"Not with that attitude they aren't," I said, plumping up a pillow with Zazu's face on it.

"Leon!" Gabriel roared from the kitchen, and I rolled my eyes at the rage in his tone. "What?" I called back innocently.

"You know what," he snarled. "Get in here."

I groaned, eyeing the giant stack of presents as I considered diving in there to hide among them.

"Don't bother," Gabriel warned and I huffed. Damn him and his Sight. I was off my game, I needed to make my decisions more randomly, do something unpredictable to get his attention off of me.

I dragged my feet into the kitchen with a pout on my face, finding him arching a brow at me, his chest bare and his wings folded behind him from the recent flight he'd just taken.

"What the fuck is that?" He pointed at the banner hanging over the arch I'd just walked through that I'd had specially made for tonight, and I looked up at it innocently, reading the words that were written in blue and silver letters across it.

We don't care you fucked a teacher and got him sent to prison, Darcy!

"And that?" Gabriel pointed to the red and gold banner hanging over the window to my right.

Starcrossing yourself with an Acrux is a power move, Tory!

"I'm failing to see the problem, Gabe?" I questioned with a shrug.

"Don't call me Gabe." He whipped out a finger, casting vines which yanked the banners down to the floor. "Look, I know you're excited." I nodded several times.

"But let's not freak them out by pointing out two of the most painful moments in their lives, yeah?"

I started purring, bobbing up and down on my toes. "Okay, scrap the banners. I just wanted them to know we're totally cool with who they are. I could put an illusion on my irises to make them black like Tory's?" I suggested.

"No," he said with a head shake.

"I could tell Darcy about the time Ryder fucked a teacher and she ended up getting arrested, power shamed and her whole life was destroyed?"

"Don't do that," he warned.

"Right, right, Orion's not like that *obviously*, but she could bond with Ryder over their common ground. Oh, that reminds me, I wrote out some talking point cue cards." I took the stack from my pocket. "Well, technically my Mindys wrote them out. They've been researching all of Tory and Darcy's favourite things and compiling a file for me."

"It's really not necessary to-" he started but I cut over him, reading out one of my amazing talking points.

"So Tory, you said no to the stars and refused to bind yourself to the son of the most psychotic man in Solaria. Discuss."

"*Leon*," Gabriel growled, stalking toward me with intent like he was going to snatch away my cue cards. But I'd *die* for my cue cards.

"The baby kicked!" Elise shot into the room in a blur, her lilac dress spinning up around her legs before fluttering down again, hanging from the small bump of her belly.

Dante came sprinting into the room soaking wet and butt naked from a shower.

Fuck the cue cards. I threw them in Dante's face to blind him, diving into his way as I dropped to my knees and pressed my ear to Elise's stomach along with my hand, purring even harder.

"Stronzo," he snapped, using his air magic to blast them away from him as he dropped to his knees beside me, placing his head next to mine so that we were looking at each other.

"Leon, that tickles," Elise laughed, her fingers pushing into my hair and making my eyes hood with how good that felt.

Gabriel moved behind her, kissing her temple before laying a hand on the top of her bump.

Ryder appeared with the Scar hat still levitating above his head, spinning slowly as he hurried to join us, pushing his hand between Dante and my faces before kissing Elise firmly on the lips.

"How hard did it kick, carina?" Dante asked. "As hard as a Storm Dragon?"

"Does it feel fuzzy like a little cub?" I demanded.

"Or coldblooded like me?" Ryder asked, smiling darkly.

"Shh, it's going to do it again," Gabriel said excitedly and we all held our breath. Gabriel's fingers moved at the last second, right onto the spot where the baby kicked and I shifted my hand up fast to feel it too, like tiny butterfly wings against my palm.

"Woah," Elise breathed, her eyes alight with pure magic.

Dante moved his hand there too just as it moved again and we all laughed, except Ryder who grunted at missing out on it, moving his hand beside mine as he tried to feel it.

"Here." Gabriel took hold of Ryder's wrist, moving his hand a little lower and Ryder's eyes widened as he felt it kick again. We all looked to Elise and my heart thrashed with a potent energy that made it feel like it was going to burst.

Something soft and warm pressed against my leg, making me look down and I realised Dante's bare cock and balls were right on my knee.

"Um, dude…" I muttered as he gazed up at Elise, transfixed by her as his mouth parted and he was lost to a moment of utter fascination. I didn't wanna ruin it, but also, like, I was in a cock and ball crises. I mean, it wasn't like I hadn't been in close proximity with his Dragon dong before, but I hadn't been used to prop up the dong before. It was weighty all that dong, and even when I tried to ignore it and stay in the moment we were all sharing, my eyes kept sliding back to it.

I'll just pretend it's not there. Keep it classy.

Or maybe I can shift back enough to get it to slide off my knee...

I tried that, my back immediately hitting Ryder's leg which was blocking me in and I tried to focus on the debate they were all having about what to name our baby – Leon Junior duh – and focused on my dilemma.

Maybe if I just lift it gently, I can slide it off without him noticing. But do I lift it by the balls or the cock?

Both. Definitely both.

Okay, lil guy, let's get you back home.

I went for a wrap-around-ball-scoop move with both hands, cupping his junk in a gentle hold but he instantly zapped me with a bolt of lightning that threw me into Ryder and knocked us both onto our asses.

"Fuck," Ryder groaned as he fed on both of our pain and my skin sizzled with the crackle of Dante's storm powers.

"Dalle stelle," Dante cursed, getting to his feet. "What the hell were you doing?"

"You could've warned me he was gonna do that." I narrowed my eyes at Gabriel who was now the only one with Elise in his arms, kissing her neck like he had no clue what was going on. But when he glanced up, there was a knowing smirk on his lips as he shrugged.

"I was distracted," he said.

"Bullshit," I accused then Elise started laughing as she pointed at me.

"Leon, your hair," she laughed harder as Ryder pushed me off of him and we scrambled to our feet. I patted my hair with a frown, realising the static was making it stick out in every direction and a roar of anger left me as I ran to the mirror on the wall.

"No! I spent hours doing my hair!" I cried, trying to comb it back into place with my fingers, but it was no use. I needed serums, an afro comb, my defrizzing spray – no, there wasn't time. There was no star damned time. The spray would have to be enough on its own.

"Don't be dramatic," Ryder said with an eye roll, his shortly cropped hair just as boringly unmoving as ever, then the doorbell rang and I wailed, clutching my hair with both hands.

"They can't see me like this!"

"At least you're fucking dressed," Dante said, hurrying from the room and I ran after him, nearly knocking his naked ass down as I sprinted up the stairs, panic shredding my insides.

"They won't care about your hair," Gabriel called after me but even if that was true, it was a matter of pride. My hair showed my status as a Lion, and I wanted his sisters to think the best of his husband-in-law.

I ran into the bathroom, rummaging through the products by the sink as I searched for my defrizzing spray.

"Little monster, where's the Marvelion spray?!" I yelled to her.

"I used the last of it on your hair this morning," she called back.

"No," I gasped, shaking my head in horror as I spotted the empty bottle in the trash. I fell to my knees, grabbing it from the can and ripping the lid off of it, trying to conjure up something from inside it, but nothing came out.

I grabbed my comb from the sink, staying on the floor as I teased it through my hair, working to flatten the frizz, but there wasn't enough time to make it perfect.

Footsteps carried this way and I panicked, scooching backwards on my ass before my back hit the bathtub and I grabbed a towel, throwing it over my head half a second before the door opened.

"By the stars, Mufasa," Ryder sighed. "Get up and stop being ridiculous.

The twins are here and they want to meet you."

"No," I said. "Not like this. I'm hideous."

His footfalls pounded closer and he whipped the towel off of my head, scowling down at me as he folded his arms. His dark green shirt brought out his eyes. He looked perfect. Like a Basilisk should look with his face all angry, hiding away the cute little viper inside that just wanted to snuggle. It wasn't fair. I needed to look perfect too.

I lunged up at him, knotting my fingers in his shirt as I half climbed my way up his body, hanging from his shoulders. "Help me," I begged.

"Argh, get off of me." He tried to untangle my hands from him, but I wouldn't let go.

"You're acting like a cub, get your shit together."

I drooped against him, burying my face in his neck as I let out a mournful mewl. "Pity me, Ryder. Pity meee." My Charisma washed from my flesh and he sighed, patting my back and giving me a little of the attention I needed to calm down.

"Follow me, asshole." He pulled away from me and I padded after him out the door and into the room across the hall which he used as his potions lab. There were vents on the walls and a large round table where a cauldron sat in the middle of the room, a bunch of books laid out on it alongside some ingredients. On the back wall was a huge rack full of all kinds of elixirs, herbs and tonics in endless colours.

He moved over to them, plucking three different ones from the rack and moving to the cauldron as he started to mix them. I peered over his shoulder, watching him work closely and he jerked his shoulder every time I rested my chin on it.

"Here," he announced after a couple of minutes, offering me a dob of the creamy paste he'd made on the tip of his finger.

I tilted my head toward him in an offering and he pursed his lips for a second before giving in and rubbing the paste into my hair, teasing his fingers through it to make sure it was spread evenly. It felt so good, him stroking his fingers all the way through my locks and I purred loudly, making him mutter swear words under his breath.

When he was done, I raised a hand to it, feeling the silken smoothness of it with my lips parting in surprise. "Oh my stars, how does it look?"

He shrugged. "Like hair."

"Ryder," I tutted at his lack of style then turned and ran to the bathroom to check it.

It. Was. Puurrrrfect.

"Holy shit!" I whooped, running back to find him walking toward the stairs, a smirk playing around his lips as I fell in to step with him. "Thank you, Rydikins."

I nuzzled the side of his face and he batted a hand at me, but his smirk only grew as we made it downstairs.

"I can't believe we're heirs to the throne of Solaria," I said excitedly.

"We're not," Ryder balked.

"Pfft, yes we are," I insisted.

'How'd you figure that?" he asked in confusion.

"Because we're heirs-in-*law*. If the twins died and Gabriel died, and Dante died, and stars fucking forbid Elise died, then we'd be next in line."

"That's not at all true," Ryder said with a head shake.

"It is. You and me would have to fight for the throne, and when I won-"

"*I'd* win," Ryder cut over me, entirely confident of that.

"No chance," I scoffed. "You'd have to come and kill me eventually though after I took the throne, because with Elise dead, all that power would go to my head and I'd become a supervillain who made it the law for everyone to dye their hair lilac. I'd have Mindys serving my Mindys and I'd make them all dress like you, Gabe and Dante so I could remember the good old times, but then sometimes I'd get so sad seeing you all that I'd go on a Mindy murdering spree and-"

We stepped into the kitchen and my words died in my throat as my gaze fell on them. The two Vega twins. The girls I'd heard so much about, had followed in the news, had gotten Gabriel to tell me every detail about their existence, and now they were here, in my kitchen, drinking my lemonade from my Lion King themed cups, breathing my air.

"Take a breath, Leon," Gabriel encouraged, his arm around Elise as he stood beside his sisters. Sisters from another mister, but still, I could see the resemblance. They looked like him even more than I'd realised from the photos.

"Hi," Darcy said, her blue hair a dead giveaway, waving a hand in hello to me and Ryder.

"We've heard a lot about you guys," Tory said with an encouraging smile.

"Gabriel doesn't shut up about you two," Ryder said, moving forward to shake their hands like an awkward celery.

Dante moved forward to cheers them with his golden chalice, smiling brightly. "Alla nuova famiglia – to new family."

They drank to that while I continued to gawp, unable to make my legs move and Tory glanced at Gabriel, jerking her head subtly at me in a question. She was feisty that one, I bet she'd like to see my stolen sword collection. Maybe she'd even play stabfest with me – though Gabe had banned me from playing that again after I nearly cut Dante's leg off. He was such a killjoy. I'd bet Darcy would love my bounce house, but Gabe didn't like me playing on that either without supervision since I'd gotten a friend of a friend of a friend to cast an air enchantment on it that sent me flying three hundred feet up into the sky when I bounced. But Darcy had air magic. She could be my safety net.

Oh my stars, this is going to be the best day of my life. If only I could make myself move, or talk, or do anything at all but just stare.

"It's alright Leon," Elise encouraged.

"Just don't – oh shit," Gabriel cursed, moving to intercept me, but it was too late as I broke free of my trance, bounding toward the twins with my arms outstretched. Their eyes widened before I dragged them into the fiercest bear hug known to man, better than any bear shifter could give.

"I'm Leon," I said around an intense purr. "Leon Night of the Nights, the best thieves in Solaria and your new brother."

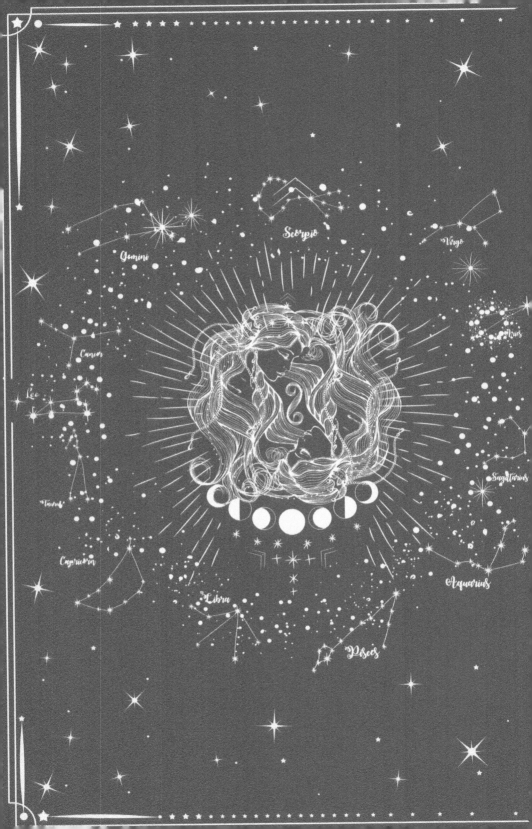

DANTE

CHAPTER TWO

"Let me take your things upstairs," Elise said with a bright smile, whizzing over to the twins and grabbing their bags.

"Stop," Ryder growled, catching hold of her. "Don't do that."

"What?" she asked in confusion, and I bit back a laugh, knowing exactly what he was thinking. Gabriel threw me a knowing look, seeming on the verge of cracking up too. Falco was in on this joke even though he'd never breathed a word to tell me that, he just had that all-*seeing* look on his face.

"You could outrun the baby," Ryder said seriously, and Darcy and Tory exchanged a concerned glance, while Leon not-so-subtly peered into one of the twins' bags in Elise's hand like he was hoping to find treats.

"What are you talking about?" Elise frowned.

"I've been reading about it this morning," Ryder muttered. "Vampires can outrun their own babies and leave them outside the womb."

It took everything I had not to snigger. *Stupido serpente.*

Ryder had been trying to out-read me on every baby book we bought. He had even taken one from my hand while I was sleeping so that he could finish it first, so I'd had one of my cousins print a new book for me full of ridiculous, untrue facts about Fae pregnancy. When I'd brought it home last night and announced that it was a brand new, bestselling pregnancy book, Ryder had predictably stolen it from me. Now, the fun would begin.

"Pfft, *my* baby book doesn't say that, stronzo," I said, goading him.

"Well I've got the most up to date book in Solaria, Inferno," Ryder said with a smug smirk, thinking he'd gotten one over on me. But oh how the serpente was going to fall.

"Come and open your presents!" Leon cried, grabbing Darcy and Tory's hands, tugging them away into the lounge.

Elise gave me a look that said she knew exactly what I was up to then sped out of the room with their bags, heading upstairs.

"Elise!" Ryder shouted after her, looking worried and I clapped a hand down on his shoulder to keep him from running after her.

"Maybe you misread that fact, eh serpente?" I suggested and he turned a narrow-eyed look on me as Gabriel swallowed a laugh and headed after Leon and the twins.

"I didn't misread shit," he hissed. "That book is far better than any old dusty tome you're reading. I bet you don't even know about the Verme Credulone."

I nearly choked on another laugh, keeping my expression neutral instead. Because Verme Credulone meant gullible worm, which was exactly what he was.

"What's that?" I gasped, pretending to be worried that I'd missed something vital.

"It's a condition where the baby becomes long, skinny and its arms and legs fall off while it's in the womb."

Dalle stelle.

"And it can be caused by too much sex," he said seriously.

"Is that why you didn't join us in the hot tub last night?" I asked.

"Yeah, and maybe if you assholes had listened to what I was saying, you wouldn't have put our baby in fucking jeopardy," he snarled.

"Oh mie stelle," I said worriedly and he nodded.

"Wow this really is...a lot," Tory's voice carried to us, and we headed into the lounge, finding Leon opening all of the presents meant for the twins, offering up cuddly toys of Lions, Harpies, Basilisks, blue Dragons, lilac-haired Vampire dolls, a little plushie of a blue Ghost Hound, endless memorabilia for our fucking famiglia. There were Phoenixes too, branded on all kinds of shit. It was sweet in a psychotic kind of way, I supposed.

Gabriel looked from Leon to his sisters, smirking at their expressions as Leon laid mountains of stuff at their feet.

"And look! These ones talk." Leon pressed the belly of a large plastic Storm Dragon made in my image and it cried, "A morte e ritorno!"

I barked a laugh and the twins did too.

"That's pretty cute actually." Darcy took it from him and Leon offered up the black Basilisk toy next which had a cowboy hat fixed to its head. He pressed the button on its stomach and it growled, "I love pain and dry oatmeal."

Ryder scoffed at it and I roared a laugh as Tory took it keenly, grinning over at Ryder.

"Dry oatmeal? That's rough dude," she said, and Ryder folded his arms.

"It was an old habit," he grunted.

"Could you not add some milk?" Darcy asked in confusion.

"No," Ryder clipped.

"Or sugar?" Tory offered, but he just shrugged.

Leon stood, tossing an arm around Ryder's shoulders and squeezing. "Our little Rydikins used to punish himself for fun. He's like a sad little stray snake we took in."

Ryder shoved him away with a deadly hiss. "You know what they say about people who keep snakes in their house. They're the snake's next meal." His eyes flashed to slits and Leon shoved his arm playfully, not taking the threat seriously at all.

Elise shot back into the room, hugging me and I slid an arm around her waist, placing a kiss on her temple. She smelled like cherries, and my skin sparked with electricity as I drew her closer, running my hand over her stomach and seeing if the baby responded to the power of its dad. There was no chance the little bambino wasn't mine. My swimmers had the storm in them and would have destroyed any other competitors easily.

"What does the Lion one say?" Darcy asked and Leon pressed the button on the toy.

"I'm about to rain down fire on your star damned souls!" it cried, then a powerful Lion roar sounded from its belly.

"What the fuck is that, fratello?" I balked. "You don't say that."

"What are you talking about? That's my catchphrase, I'm always saying that," Leon insisted.

"You've literally never said that in your life, Leo," Elise sniggered.

"I'm alwaaaays saying that," he insisted, waving his hand dismissively and the twins shared a grin.

"What does Gabriel's do?" Tory asked and Gabriel pursed his lips as Leon pressed the button on the black-winged Harpy doll like he had already *seen* what was coming.

"Don't call me Gabe," it said irritably.

"What's wrong with being called Gabe, Gabe?" Darcy teased him.

"Don't you start that," Gabriel warned her, and Leon began bouncing on his toes as he looked between them chanting 'Gabe, Gabe, Gabe' under his breath.

"Nah we'd never call you, Gabe, would we Darcy?" Tory smirked and Gabriel sighed, *seeing* his future painted out before his eyes.

"Of *course* not," Darcy said, the two of them sharing a look that said they absolutely would.

"My fate is sealed," Gabriel said heavily.

"Come eat, nuove sorelle," I called to the twins, moving to drop an arm around each of their shoulders and steering them away from the crazy Leone who was rummaging through the present mountain again.

We ate in the dining room, the huge table carved by my cousin Bendito with intricate images of my famiglia's Orders. Light streamed in from tall windows that ran along one wall and I spotted Periwinkle sitting out there with her head cocked to one side. Ryder moved to let her in, and the moment the door was open, she stepped through the window beside it instead, flicking her tails and prancing through the room.

"What is that?" Darcy gasped, her eyes widening with a glint of adoration in her eyes.

"She's a Ghost Hound," Ryder said, picking her up and the little creature nuzzled his neck.

"I swear I heard a senior talking about how one of those poisoned them," Tory said, seeming less inclined to move closer as Darcy dropped to her knees in front of Periwinkle and offered out a hand to pet our little Ghost Hound.

"This one's pretty tame," Gabriel said. "Thanks to Ryder."

"I didn't do anything." Ryder shrugged.

Periwinkle circled Darcy like she was assessing her, round and round until she finally pressed her head into Darcy's hand.

"Tor, come here and stroke her," Darcy insisted, and Tory moved to kneel beside her, smiling at her sister like she was glad to see some happiness in her. I guessed after the scandal of Lance Orion being dragged off to prison and her heart left shattered in his wake, she was putting on a brave face for us today.

I wished I could twist fate and free him from that place, but if I was capable of that, I would have saved Leon's brother Roary a long time ago too. Not that he could walk out of there anyway thanks to Lionel Acrux. *Cazzo di stronzo.*

We worked our way through endless food while we told the story of how we'd all ended up with Elise and Leon dramatically acted out various moments of our family's forging. I drew the line when he started acting out the first time we'd all claimed Elise though, playing the role of each guy while accosting a pillow he'd cast an illusion on to have lilac hair.

"Ryder didn't smile ever, did he Gabe?" Leon elbowed the Harpy beside him as he dropped back into his seat, abandoning the pillow as Periwinkle took a seat on it. "But he started giving Elise little smiles and *that* was when I knew." He bashed his hand down on the table. "That he had a happy little snake inside just waiting to come out and play."

"That's deeply inaccurate," Ryder hissed, placing his hand on Elise's knee beside him, his fingers brushing mine where they sat on her other leg.

"We had to teach Ryder how to be a person again," Leon barrelled on as if he hadn't spoken. "I remember one time, our old professor locked me and him in a shed on campus for detention and cast a spell that meant we had to power share to get out. That was the first time Ryder admitted he loved me."

"What?" Ryder snapped. "I did no such fucking thing, Mufasa. You kept trying to power fuck me."

"To what?" Tory snorted and Elise cracked up.

"You kept telling me to put the tip of my power in you." Ryder scowled at Leon.

"Which you did. And you loved it," Leon said, grabbing a bread roll and taking a savage bite out of it, sending crumbs flying everywhere.

"It's just as weird as it sounds," Elise whispered to the twins across the table.

"Did you see this coming? All of you together?" Tory asked curiously.

"No fucking way," Elise laughed. "But...I never saw myself picking either. I didn't look much beyond the next day anyway back then. It was a strange time. So much pain, yet...so much joy came out of it in the end."

"Life's like that, amore mio," I said, lifting my hand to grip her chin, turning her head to me and placing a kiss upon her lips. "I brutti momenti generano i bei tempi."

"The bad times sire the good times," Elise translated, her grasp on my language almost perfect these days.

"To the bad times." Gabriel raised a glass of Arucso wine and we all lifted ours in kind. "May they sire the good ones as soon as possible."

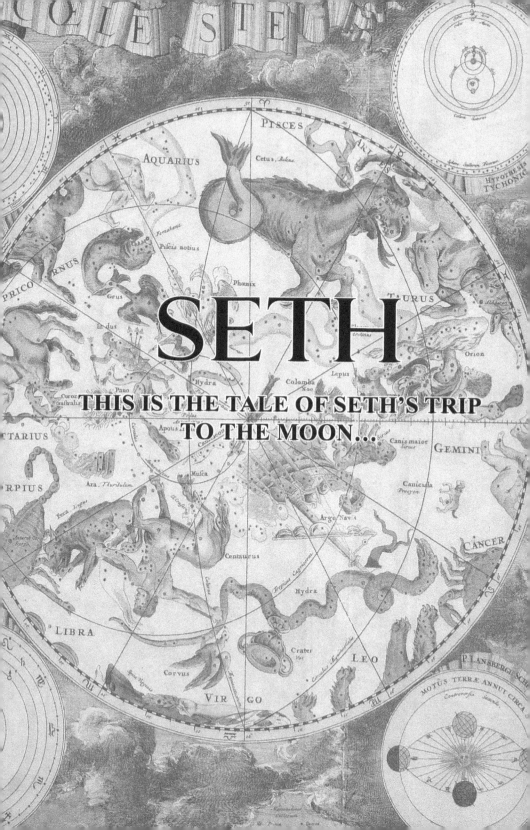

SETH

THIS IS THE TALE OF SETH'S TRIP
TO THE MOON…

LIONEL

FROM THE LAIR OF LIONEL...

The Capellas. Malleable, easily distracted, and mercurial. Or so I thought. Of the four Heirs, Seth Capella seemed to be the most easily controlled. His wants were basic, his ruthless nature keen. Werewolves are like hunting dogs, loyal and easily tempted into the hunt by a meagre scent of blood. Scraps of meat keep them content, even when their bellies stay only half full. I had few concerns about Darius's ability to control him given time, but the unpredictable nature of this particular Capella took me by surprise, especially when he took a pivot towards making friends out of Gwendalina Vega. The vile, candid shots of them arm in arm across the summer in magazines was enough to set my blood boiling.

In the end, his mutt nature was easily swayed to the loyalty of the Vegas, perhaps their scraps were fatter. Perhaps if I had foreseen this change in the wind, I might have lured that doggish Heir to my side if I had offered him a fuller meal than they.

In hindsight, I can see the way the wind was blowing, how Caleb Altair and he were embroiled in a secret affair, and the two of them were united in their betrayal as they sided with the Vega twins. It is hard to pinpoint exactly what lured them over initially. Roxanya, of course, was spreading her legs for the Earth Heir long before she got her hooks into Darius, and maybe she extended that courtesy to all four of them.

Gwendalina was clearly not shy of such things, and when Lance Orion had been sent to Darkmore Penitentiary, taking the fall for her like the mindless fool he was, perhaps she had turned her attentions to more powerful lovers.

Yes, I had likely surmised the truth of it, but the bitterness of their betrayal still irked me some...

SETH

CHAPTER ONE

B eeeep, beeeep, fucking beeep.

Who was beeping that horn at four in the star damned morning?

I rolled over in my bed with a growl of anger, my brothers and sisters shifting around me with grunts and barks of annoyance. Someone hit the floor with a yelp as I rolled onto my back and I huffed, stuffing my large fluffy head under my pillow. All of my siblings had wanted to sleep in with me tonight, and it was elbows and hip bones galore. Athena's paw was pressed right to my face and I swatted it away with my own as the loud beeping continued.

The light suddenly turned on and my mother appeared in the doorway like a wraith emerging from the shadows.

"Seth Capella, get up this instant and tell me why Caleb Altair is outside our house blaring his horn in the middle of the night?" she snapped furiously.

I shifted back into my Fae form immediately, grabbing a pair of pale blue sweatpants and tugging them on. Caleb? Why was he here?

"I dunno, Mom," I said through a yawn.

"Well find out!" she commanded.

I snatched my Atlas from the nightstand as the fluffy bodies of my siblings all rolled and adjusted, taking up the space I'd vacated at the centre of them. Grayson's tongue was hanging out of his mouth near Nick's butthole and the consequences of that didn't look good.

I checked my messages, but there was nothing from my friends apart from a goodnight message from Darcy in response to mine. She was staying with Gabriel and her family tonight, so I knew she was okay. Well not okay, okay. The girl's heart had been ripped out, stomped on, shoved through a blender, eaten by a Griffin and shat back out again. Everything sucked lately and I felt fucking helpless to it all. Especially when it came to her. I'd been the cause of her pain for so long and now I just wanted to soothe away the pain in her and see her smile again. I just didn't see how that was gonna happen though.

I grabbed a shirt and ducked past my growling mother, jogging down the large stairway, across the shaggy grey carpet in the entrance hall and tearing the huge oak front door open. I stepped onto the porch as Caleb's headlights lit me up, his black sports car glinting in the moonlight.

The balmy air twisted around me and my heart beat harder as I ran down the porch steps and onto the brick driveway up to his car window. He lowered it, smirking like an asshole and I arched a brow as I eyed that perfectly hot mouth of his which I wasn't allowed to have filthy thoughts about. But I did. Regularly.

"And you woke my entire family up in the middle of the night becauuuuse…?" I asked curiously.

"Get in," he insisted and my arched brow sailed higher.

"What's up? Has something happened?" I asked, a bubble of concern rising in me.

"Nope. But if you don't get in, we're gonna be late," he said then did up the window to end our conversation.

It was blacked out so I couldn't see his face as I pressed my middle finger to the glass. Then I parkoured my way over his bonnet and did a fancy little backflip with my air magic on the other side of it, landing beside the passenger door which opened like a wing.

I dropped into the low seat and the door slid smoothly closed beside me. There was a bag of snacks in the footwell which I immediately grabbed, snatching out some chips and tearing into them.

Caleb backed out of the driveway at high speed, using his Vampire senses to drive like a nutter and spin the car around onto the road. He tore away from my house, giving my mother some much needed peace and I whooped as he raced into the dark, the road flanked by a thick forest.

"So what's the occasion?" I asked, eyeing him while he couldn't look at me, taking in the strong set of his jaw and the way he sucked his lip for a moment before he spoke. It did forbidden things to me, so I looked back out at the road and shifted in my seat. *Don't you dare get a boner over your best friend.*

"Well, remember how I got you that ticket to visit the moon?" he said, throwing me a grin and my jaw dropped as I realised what day it was.

"No, Cal. I said I'd go next year when this shit show blows over. I can't leave you guys right now."

"It's only for a few days," Cal said in a growl. "And you can't put your life on hold just because the world's in danger. Fuck the world. You deserve to have some fun."

"Since when do I deserve to have some fun?" I balked. "I've been a royal asshole for a solid year. No, two years. And I can't say I'm really planning on giving up the trend."

"Yeah well, you're good to your inner circle," he said with a laugh.

"Guess that's true," I said thoughtfully and he punched me in the shoulder playfully.

"You're going. It's my gift and I say you're using it."

Mmm, bossy Cal. Holy fuck, yes please.

"Alright," I gave in, because by the stars, it was the moon. The moon! Not

Mercury or Venus or boring old Neptune. This was the honest to shit moon we were talking about. The bright, glowy thing that gave me my magic. "Oh my stars I'm going to the moon. Cal I'm going to the moon!" I threw myself at him, wrestling him in his seat as he fought to keep control of the car. I licked his face and my hand slid onto his chest as I braced myself and he tried to bat me off. He tasted like pure man, his stubble rough against my tongue, and my dick liked it all way too much.

I dropped back into my seat before I could get overexcited, but to be fair I was pretty sure I could partly blame the moon for my hard on anyway. I shoved the bag of chips between my legs as the perfect boner shield and grinned from ear to ear. *I'm going to be the first Werewolf on the moon. I'll probably come back with moon powers.*

"We've gotta be there before dawn. I figured the drive would be more fun than stardusting," Cal said, stuffing his hand into the bag of chips between my thighs and I twisted awkwardly in my seat with a strangled noise as I tried to stop him from hitting my hard dick.

Cal tossed me a look as I half lifted my ass off the seat and pretended to be looking for something in the door pocket.

"You alright, bro?" he asked.

"Yeah totally." He stuffed a handful of chips in his mouth and I settled back in my seat, shoved the chips further towards my knees.

"I did a playlist for the journey," Cal said keenly, tapping his Atlas in the dock on the dash and The Killing Moon by Echo and The Bunnymen started up, making my heart race excitedly.

"You're the best, dude. I'm gonna get you a whole swimming pool of blood for your next birthday."

"You know that's illegal," he snorted.

"Not if no one dies to supply it," I said insistently. I'd definitely looked into it already and there'd be Fae lining up to offer their blood when they knew which Celestial Heir would be drinking it.

He growled low in his throat and I shot him a look. "Someone's hungry."

"Nah." He waved me off.

"You are. Drink, go on." I offered him my wrist under his nose and his throat bobbed as he sensed the closeness of my blood. "That's premium quality blood. Tuck in, brother."

He resisted a moment longer, then his fangs snapped out and he drove them into my wrist, his eyes hooded as he kept them on the road and fed from me at the same time. His mouth on my skin was like a match striking against my flesh. My breaths came unevenly and I couldn't drag my gaze from the point of contact as he fed. It was too good. And I wondered if he had to suck extra hard to get hold of my blood because it was currently all rushing to my cock like an unstoppable train.

The car swerved violently and Caleb yanked his fangs free and spun the wheel to avoid crashing, making my pulse pound wildly.

We both laughed nervously as I tugged my hand away, running my thumb over the bite mark to heal it.

We drove on for a couple of hours and Cal finally took a turning up a long, winding drive which led onto Mr Nakatuki's property. I'd been here a couple of times before when I'd stalked him down and begged him to take me to the moon. The answer had been a forceful no the first time. The second time, he'd just let the security deal with me and my name had been splashed through the press. Thankfully, my PR team had spun that story beautifully to make me look like I was so in love with the moon that I just wanted to go there on behalf of all Werewolves in Solaria to thank it for its gifts. Yup, the team were damn miracle workers. I'd been caught climbing out of a famous singer's hotel room once, butt naked and covered in glitter after making her come so hard she'd shifted into her Pegasus form. Thankfully my dick had been out of her at that point, I wasn't into Order fucking, though I was also a try everything once kinda guy. Anyways, her boyfriend was her co-artist who would have wanted my balls for the photos splashed all over the newspapers of me post screwing his girl, but the PR team had twisted the whole story to make it look like I'd heard her choking from the room next door, bounded in to save her life whilst shifting out of my Order form, then climbed down the fire escape to fetch help. Her boyfriend had sent me all of their albums signed by the two of them as thanks. I did him so dirty, man.

Caleb pulled up the car in front of a huge wooden house with a long porch and large glass windows that gave me Twilight vibes. I could have eaten Edward Cullen for breakfast. Literally and sexually. He could have it anyway he liked. Jacob too. The way mortals conjured up Vampires and Werewolves was pretty funny. Cal and I had watched the movies together while pissing ourselves laughing and acting out scenes between Edward and Jacob. We'd even visited the mortal realm and pranked a couple of mortal girls who thought we were gonna Twilight them. Not strictly legal, but strictly fucking hilarious. Especially when I'd cast that light spell on Cal's face to make it look like he was sparkling.

"I packed you a bag." Cal reached over into the back seat, grabbing it and dropping it onto my lap.

A doggish whine left me as I looked at him, clutching the bag to my stomach. "I wish you could come too."

"Nah." He shook his head. "The lack of gravity would fuck with my Vampire speed, I don't think I'd be into it. Take lots of photos though."

"I will. And videos." I grinned, my gaze locked with his eternally as I hesitated to leave. Fuck it. I leaned in and hugged him tight. "Thanks, man," I said in his ear and his fingers fisted in the back of my shirt for a moment, holding me there as my heart thundered against his chest and his pounded hard back against mine. He smelled like my downfall, and I really hoped I was smart enough not to fuck up our friendship forever one day.

"I'll pick you up on Monday." He let me go and I gave him a sideways smirk as I stepped out of the flashy car and jogged up the porch, waving goodbye before knocking on the door.

Cal turned around and drove back off down the road and the door opened in front me. An old guy with a long grey beard frowned at me. His clothes were long, baggy with colourful patterns on them. He raised a stern eyebrow as he took me in.

"So you finally got a ticket," he said with a tut.

"Yes, sir," I said brightly. "Sorry for the er, stalking, and attempted break ins. And when I held your cat hostage...and the damage I did to your doorframe when I tried to hold onto it and you got those four security guards to pull me off. Oh and the dent I left in your car when I punched it. And the death threats-"

"Yes, let us not rehash it all, shall we?" he interrupted sharply, stepping aside. "In you go. You're late, the others are already waiting to leave."

I bounded inside and he strode after me, directing me through a door at the end of the hall. I swore beneath my breath as I stepped into a moon themed room with grey walls and floor, photos of the moon all over the place, the lightning low and a video of the stars playing above us on the ceiling. The nine other lottery winners were standing at the end of the room, chatting together, wearing shiny grey suits. They all looked over at me, falling quiet as they realised who had just joined them. Sometimes being famous rocked, other times it sucked. Like this time. I hated being looked at like that. Like I was an alien who'd just crawled out of Mr Nakatuki's butt.

"You'll need to put this on," Mr Nakatuki handed me a metallic grey jumpsuit while he started pulling on his own. "As I just finished explaining to the others, it has a tracker in the lining in case you get lost and the suit is imbued with spells of my own design to keep you safe in the atmosphere up there. As an air Elemental, you may use your own magic to supply your oxygen, or you can use the spelled helmets. Once we arrive at the moon base-"

"Ooh, moon base," I cooed and he cleared his throat as I zipped up the suit right to my neck. I looked *so* cool.

"Yes, the moon base," he reiterated. "You will have access to all the helmets you require, however, as you are a Werewolf, your magic reserves will likely remain full the entire trip anyway so the helmets are optional." He stepped closer to me and held an Atlas under my nose that he produced from the stars only knew where. "I need you to sign this waiver."

I took it from him, skimming my eyes over the text. "Blah, blah, blah, if I die you're not responsible, blah, blah, blah." I scribbled my signature at the bottom and handed it back to him with a grin. He didn't smile back. Oh well, I'd make him my good old pal by the time this trip was over. No one could resist me when I turned on the charm, and it was the guy's lucky day.

"Dying is not your only concern, Mr Capella," he said seriously. "I have not tested the affects the moon could have on a Werewolf. Your magic could become so overwhelming that it damages the channels in your body that connect it to your hands, or it could cause trauma to your fingers when your magic is used or-"

"Yada risk yada. Let's go!" I sprang across the room to my new friends, clapping them on the shoulders and they all went fame shy on me. Not even one of them looked me in the eyes. *Gah. Really?*

Fine. I don't need moon friends. The moon will be my friend. And Mr Nakatuki.

He walked past us to what I'd first thought was a shiny black door at the end of the room, but now realised it was a swirling dark space of nothingness.

"What's that?" I asked, bouncing on the balls of my feet.

"This is a stardust portal," he announced with a smug grin. "It has been made with the permission of the Councillors and tempered with moondust. As you will have all read in the documentation you received in the mail-"

I glanced away from him very unsuspiciously as he gave me a look like he knew I hadn't read that documentation. I'd just looked at the pictures and slapped my siblings with the magazines when I'd rubbed it in that I was going to the moon and they weren't.

"- you will know that you cannot discuss any magical technology viewed upon this trip. Failure to comply with this rule will result in prosecution. Keeping my technology secret ensures that the moon is not overrun by companies looking to make a cash cow out of our beloved celestial body. We must protect this most sacred of places and treat her with the upmost respect. Do you understand?"

We all nodded and the blonde girl in front of me looked back over her shoulder at me, fluttering her lashes before turning away again. I didn't have eyes for her though, I had a date with the moon and she was probably dying to meet me.

"Single file," Nakatuki called and I shoved my way to the front of the group, barking excitedly. He gave me a grouchy look, but didn't stop me as I approached the stardust portal.

Holy shit, I'm going to the moon.

Nakatuki beckoned me forward and I lifted my chin, striding into the portal confidently and the stars ripped me away into their grasp. I tumbled through them and my head spun as the air seemed to thin and I felt like I was hurtling forward at a thousand miles an hour. This wasn't like normal stardust, it was incredible, like I was being catapulted right into the stars themselves.

I was suddenly thrown out and my feet slowly descended onto a soft, chalky grey ground beneath me. I stared at it with my jaw dropping. The moon. I was on the moon. Magic swelled inside me so forcefully that it made me gasp for air that wasn't there. *Oh shit.*

I lifted my hand to my lips, adjusting to the strange sensation of less gravity as I cast a bubble of air around my mouth and nose, inhaling deeply.

I gazed out across the dark surface to a huge white domed building which must have been the moon base Nakatuki had mentioned. It kinda looked like a polytunnel, except it had clear windows that gave a view inside to a glitzy interior.

The stars twinkled above and the earth glinted faraway in the distance, just a tiny ball of blue and green, my whole world left behind.

I tipped my head back and howled, bounding forward and laughing at the way I could jump so high and sort of float back down to the ground.

"Mr Capella, we need to have an orientation before you run off!" Mr Nakatuki's voice sailed after me but I kept prancing along, too exhilarated as I ran across her beautiful surface. If she was a pretty little tease from afar, she was one dirty slut of rock up close.

"Mr Capella!" Nakatuki roared as I bounced up and over a small hill, floating out of sight beyond it and waving a vague goodbye to him. I didn't need an orientation. Me and the moon had an affinity, an understanding. The way she was filling my body up with magic was all I needed to know about how much she loved having me here. I was her bitch, her little Wolf boy come from earth to pay his respects. And I'd pay them alright.

I got down on my knees, kissing the rocks, grinding into them. I left snow angels in the dirt, painted *I heart Cal* in the dust then rolled across the ground, needing to feel her all on me. What could really happen if I took the suit off anyway?

I started stripping out of it, kicking off my boots until I was naked and standing with my hands on my hips as I looked out at the dark and rolling landscape of my moon mistress.

My cock was hard and as my eyes hooked on a little crater a couple of feet away, a hungry grin pulled at my lips. Far be it from me to come all this way and not show the moon a good time.

I soon had my dick deep in the hole, thrusting away into her as I clawed my hands in the dirt and showed the sexy bitch what she'd been missing her whole life. I dominated her, topping her good and she loved every second of it.

"Mr Capella!" Nakatuki suddenly shrieked like a woman just as I finished with a long groan and I lifted my head as I panted, finding him with his mouth agape and the whole group of lottery winners at his back in their suits and helmets. Utter shock was written across all of their faces and some of them looked away with red cheeks and wide eyes.

"You have defiled the moon!" Nakatuki wailed, looking faint as I got up, covered in moon dust which I could taste on my lips.

"She wanted it!" I called back and he tried to usher the others away, trying to cover some of their eyes when a few of them remained in place.

"You've desecrated this holy being," Nakatuki half sobbed.

"She liked it," I insisted. I wasn't a star damned moon rapist. I could feel her calling my name, drawing me in.

The magic in my veins and the power of the ground beneath my feet was making my head buzz. I felt purely animal. Just a wolf with cravings in the wilderness. I turned away with a howl, bouncing across the ground as I made my escape and laughed like a madman.

"She loves me and I love her, you can't keep us apart Nakatuki!" I cried with another manic laugh and his sobs followed me into the dark, where it was just me and the moon whose giggles I was almost sure I could hear. Either that or I was pumping a little too much oxygen into my brain.

I had to wonder if Cal had known he was setting me up on a date with the moon all along. He always did go above and beyond for me. And I was gonna make sure I had more than a few stories to bring home just for him. Deep down, I knew why I liked this place so much. Even more than because I was a Werewolf and I worshipped her every night. It was because Cal had been the one to buy the moon for me. And somehow, I would find a way to buy him the whole world in return.

SETH

AN ALTERNATE POV OF THE END OF ZODIAC ACADEMY 8: SORROW AND STARLIGHT

LIONEL

FROM THE LAIR OF LIONEL...

The Vegas defeat of so many of Vard's creations left me reeling, and when their subsequent crowning reached my ears, I was most displeased. They dared to call themselves queens in *my* land, *my* kingdom. It was the greatest insult they could offer me, and I vowed to crush them so completely that there would be nothing left of them or a single Fae who had supported them in their rally against me.

I would not stand for it.

I was the Dragon King. The Fae born to rule. I had worked too hard, the stars had given witness to my efforts, and they had named me king as surely as the crown upon my brow did.

The final stand is coming, my army ten times the size of theirs and the might of my Bonded Dragons along with so many other unspeakable weapons will see them eradicated once and for all.

I had taken down the Savage King, and his daughters would follow swiftly in his path. If those snivelling brats of his really thought themselves worthy of this fight, then they would soon be proven deathly wrong. I would strike their names from existence, and no one would remember any royal within this land but *me*...

SETH

CHAPTER ONE

"Where's Tory?" Darcy looked around the dorm corridor in Aer House in desperation and my Wolfy heart squeezed. Damn, it was good to see her again. Her face. Her hair. Ha, remember the time I cut all that off? Good times. We'd probably have a hearty laugh about it later, but right now...well, I guess we had to save the world and shit. Or maybe just the academy, but same difference.

"She's not here," Caleb answered, and Darcy looked crestfallen, like a little bird who'd tumbled out of its nest and realised it couldn't fly yet. Poor, sad little baby bird Darcy, missing her sister... "She left a few days ago and didn't tell anyone where she was going."

I felt Orion stepping closer at my back with Gabriel and a dangerous aura seeped from them, like two of my pack were ready for the hunt.

"She'll come back. She always comes back," I said encouragingly, needing to fix the ache in my friend's eyes. "Sometimes she's frownier when she returns, and sometimes she does crazy shit like sending her soul out of her body but-"

"What?" Darcy gasped in horror and Geraldine bristled beyond her.

Oops. Better get Caleb to explain this. He'd do that thing where he said stuff in a calm and reasonable way, and Darcy would learn that Tory liked to let her soul go off on moonlit strolls without her body these days, and that she had it *all* under control.

I elbowed him. "Tell her, Cal. Tell her how Tory does weird, dark magic stuff now, but it's okay because her soul did come back that time. And if she's off soul-walking again it's probably completely fine, because…because…" Oh fuck, I really thought I had something there.

I whined, nudging Caleb in an anxious bid for him to take over and dig me out of the hole I was six feet deep in already, shovel still in hand.

"Yeah, she'll be fine," Caleb reassured her.

My room cracked open at the far end of the corridor and my spine straightened, a wave of fierce protectiveness shooting through me as Frank's eyes met mine.

"Is it safe now, Alpha?" he asked.

"Just stay there and lock the door tight until it's over. I'll make sure the tower is clear," I said firmly, and Frank nodded in submission, his eyes darting onto Darcy.

"Oh my stars, it's you," he gasped then snapped the door shut, and my pack broke out into hushed chatter beyond it.

"We should move," Max said, wincing as screams carried across campus.

Xavier pressed his shoulders back, looking ready for the fight as Tyler and Sofia closed in on either side of him.

Darcy drew a gleaming white sword from her hip, and a thrill rushed through to my core at the thought of fighting alongside my friends again. That was a real fancy sword she had there. White like my Wolf form. It would look really good in my hand now I came to think of it. Maybe she'd lend me it later for a photoshoot. Maybe I could borrow it after the fight and leave a note that says *BRB white Wolf photoshoot in progress*. Yeah, she wouldn't mind. I could even give her the photos as a thank you. Not the naked ones, of course. I'd save them for Caleb. I'd just *accidentally* leave them lying around my room, then invite him over for a few beers and-

"What's happening here?" Darcy asked in confusion. "What are those monsters and why are they here?"

"It would seem that the false king has sent them, my lady. Here on some gruesome mission to hunt down the rebels who had been working against him from within these fine walls," Geraldine explained.

"They're killing people who stood up to him?" she gasped in disgust, and we all nodded in confirmation. "Then we have to help them."

"Yes - it is time to unite as a legion of justice!" Geraldine bellowed, wiping her damp cheeks, moving closer to Darcy. "Point me at your enemies, my lady. For I am your weapon forged of havoc and punishment. We shall carve the heads of a thousand monsters from their bodies this very night, and the whole world will shudder with the knowledge of their queen's return. For the night is deep and the dawn is yonder. And between the now and the rising sun, blood waits to be spilled and enemies wait to be slain. We are the knights of the Vega Court, and we are at your service." She spun around on her heel, facing us with a flare of fire in her eyes that sparked an inferno in me. Hell, she was good at this pep talk shit. I'd seen her pull a few fancy speeches or two in the Pitball changing room, but this was something else. "Listen close and listen well. The stars have returned our queen to us, and it is our duty to fight like the soldiers of the Perrypot and slay the ganderghouls who have come to spread peril across the precious lands of our academy. It is time to take up arms and sing our song of slaughter and misery into the flapping ears of our assailants! There shall not be a single soul in Solaria who does not know of our victory by dawn! Long live the true Queens!"

I howled a long note full of my need for bloodshed, and it went on so long that by the time I looked down again, everyone had already moved into the stairwell heading for the fight. Caleb was waiting for me though, eyes bluest of blue and looking like a twilight sky in summer.

"Coming?" He asked, tone hard. The tension between us since the night Venus and the moon had played together in the sky hadn't dissipated even a little. If anything, I'd say it was growing with every passing day we didn't acknowledge it. So obviously I was going to continue pretending there was no issue.

"Aw, did you wait for me, Cally baby?" I taunted, stepping after him and bashing my shoulder against his.

I moved down the stairs, breaking into a jog to catch the others. Caleb shot to my side, keeping pace with me with ease and his gaze flickered dangerously.

"Just making sure you didn't lose your footing on the stairs. I know how clumsy you can be." His foot whipped out, tripping me, and I went flying forward with a snarl, throwing out my hands to catch myself with magic.

Air rushed around me, keeping me upright, but I stumbled a good bit first, my feet skidding stupidly on the stairs and my hand slapping loudly against the wall. When I looked up, Caleb was gone, his Vampire speed carrying him down to the others with ease.

I cursed, picking up my pace and almost colliding with Orion and Xavier as I made it around the next turn in the spiralling stairway.

We ran out of Aer Tower in a tight unit and Darcy took off into the sky, fire blazing across her wings and her blue hair bursting into flames too. She raised her white sword and led the way onward in the direction of The Howling Meadow while I bayed to the sky in excitement, the sound of monsters roaring across campus spurring me on into battle.

It was almost like old times, except we were missing two of our gang, and one of them was irretrievable. As my mind turned to Darius, I stuffed the pain down into the box in my chest, locking it tight and burying it deep. I couldn't face that hurt right now, I needed to focus, to fight.

We made it to the meadow where a group of students were fleeing from two more monsters, and I vaguely recognised them as Ass Club members.

"Yonder into the trees, good fellows!" Geraldine called to them, casting a barrier of earth between them and the monsters to give them a chance to escape. "One of the true queens has come to your aid – look skyward and see her flames roaring aloft!"

Darcy flew forward at speed, hands raised and upper lip peeled back as she released a torrent of hellfire down on one of the monsters. It was a horrid beast, the thing resembling a giant slug with jagged legs which jutted out of its body to drag it along the ground. It was bigger than the other one, which was more ant-like with bony limbs that were starkly white, but it was slower too.

I ran to intercept it as it shrieked and burned in Darcy's fire, igniting the gauntlets on my hands and slashing the metal claws across the monster's side, ripping into its gunky flesh. Green blood splashed the ground, and I dove aside before Darcy released another wave of deadly fire down upon it, while Caleb, Orion, Gabriel and Xavier ran to fight the other one.

Max, Geraldine, Tyler and Sofia joined me, stabbing at the beast between Darcy's blaze, the gunge coating its body seeming to give it some protection from the fire.

Darcy switched to water, releasing a torrent down upon the monster that blasted holes in its skin, and I staggered back to take in the immensity of her power, the aftershocks of her strike rocking the earth beneath me.

"Great gandergooks in a hollywock," Geraldine breathed, tears in her eyes as she stared up at the Phoen Dream. "She is power embodied, a crocksack filled with migbombs."

Suddenly another blazing creature joined Darcy in the sky, racing this way at high speed and my lips parted at the sight of the only two Phoenixes in existence, lighting up the heavens in trails of blue and red. Tory Vega looked beyond relieved to see her twin, but I couldn't watch their reunion for long. Max leapt forward with Tyler and Sofia, taking on the monster Darcy had wounded, working to bring it to ruin and I shot a blast of air its way that tore through its body like a bullet.

"The true Queens herald the coming morn!" Geraldine cried, amplifying her voice with magic so it echoed all across campus.

The sound of Caleb gasping in pain had my head snapping in his direction, and I was running before I even had a location. I spotted him down pinned between the pincers of the other monster while Orion ripped one of its hind legs off with his bare hands and Xavier and Gabriel blasted it with vines, trying to rip it away from Caleb.

I body slammed the monster without thought, the claws of my fiery Phoenix gauntlets slashing at every bony limb and body part I could find, snarls tearing from my mouth. I dragged the beast off of Caleb and he shot to his feet, healing himself in a flash and lunging forward to make the kill.

But the monster reared up, throwing me backwards so hard that I slammed into Xavier and knocked him to the ground, the two of us rolling for several beats before we managed to stop. I was left with my head spinning and a healthy dose of bruising, but I wasn't done yet.

Orion was thrown aside by the beast next, but he cast air at his back to propel himself straight back into the fight, speeding forward with his Vampire gifts. Gabriel had been tossed into the trees, but as he came running back out, his eyes glazed with a vision and he stopped in his tracks.

Tory and Darcy still hovered in the air above us, their eyes set on something in the distance that I couldn't see, but as I shoved to my feet, I heard it. The buzzing and droning of more creatures coming this way, the noise so loud there had to be hundreds of them.

Max stopped mid-fight, his gaze snapping up to the twins and his features twisting with a sense of what they were feeling.

Orion cast a chain of ice and Caleb grabbed one end of it, the two of them speeding in opposite directions around the ant-like monster, binding it with the chain then yanking it so tight that the thing was cut in two with a shriek of death.

Tory sent a wave of air magic down from the sky, ripping a bone right from its twitching corpse and I let out a gasp, looking up at her in horror.

"Cal, she's doing creepy shit again," I said urgently, and Caleb sped to my side.

I couldn't hear what they were saying, but it looked like Tory was chanting now, and Caleb and I shared a look of concern as the roaring and baying of monsters carried to us in the distance. Darcy looked concerned about that dead beast's bone in her twin's hand, but power was building around her so potently that she turned her attention to the droning noise once more.

"How many?" I asked Caleb and he focused on listening for the oncoming monsters, his brows drawing together.

His throat bobbed and his gaze met mine with a look of certain death that made my throat tighten. "Too many."

I caught his shirt in my fist, pulling him close and thinking of all the things I needed to say to him, trying to narrow it down to a single few that would make him understand the depths of my feelings. I was still angry at him, still *everything* at him actually, but maybe it wouldn't matter if I could just get the words out.

"Holy shit," Caleb breathed, his eyes glittering with fire as his gaze was drawn to the twins again.

I looked up, finding the two of them blazing with power, magic shimmering against their skin as they trembled with the magnitude of it. It merged between them, the two of them seeming to become one divine entity which radiated power, the hum of it buzzing in my ears and making the air ring.

They held hands, but raised their free ones, and all at once, they let that impossible power tear from them, blasting out in every direction through the sky. A quake ripped through the ground and Caleb gripped my arm to steady me. Phoenix fire blasted out across campus, twisting together with all their Elemental magic, the power so bright it rivalled the stars.

Screams carried up from students across campus, and I realised more and more people were arriving in the meadow, drawn here by the beacon of light the two of them created in the sky. The first touch of their power killed the slug-like monster that Max, Geraldine, Tyler and Sofia were still fighting, and it fell between them, sizzling to nothing within the flames.

Shrieks lit up the air as their fire found more and more of the beasts, devouring them one by one within their deadly power. All of us banded closer together, Orion staring up at the twins with reverence in his gaze that almost matched the look on Geraldine's face. One glance at the others told me they were feeling that same admiration, and my own jaw had fallen slack with it too.

A boom resounded out towards forever as the twins' magic impacted with our foes. The entire academy had come to witness the immense power of the savage twins and honestly, I felt proud to be their friend in that moment. Remorseful over how difficult we had made it for them to reach this point, yet not entirely regretful. Because we had been the fire in their forge.

"They're all dead," Max exhaled, feeling it down to his core. "Every last star-damned monster."

Silent tears sailed down Geraldine's cheeks and I felt the world shifting, sensed it in my bones like the very fabric of our realm had just been altered forever. Gabriel moved closer to us, a hum of prophecy about him as his eyes danced with a thousand things I couldn't see, half here and half not at all.

Tory and Darcy came down to land and everyone backed up, creating a wide circle around them at the centre of The Howling Meadow, their eyes still glimmering with unshed power.

Awe was written into everyone's faces, the students, the teachers, and us. Us most of all. Gabriel had a knowing look in his gaze that said he might have *seen* this coming, but he was no less proud of his sisters. I could practically feel his wonderment emitting from him, and fuck, I felt it too.

The silence weighed down like the sun itself had come to land between us, but suddenly that silence was broken as heavy boots strode this way.

Gasps of fear, disbelief and confusion rippled through the crowd to my right, and I craned my neck to try and see who was causing the stir.

"All hail the true Queens," Darius's deep voice cleaved the air in two, and I jerked sideways into Caleb, shaking my head in disbelief, only to find the fourth one of us, my best friend, my missing piece stepping out of the crowd to stand before the twins.

Geraldine screamed, her voice sailing out among the masses and pitching through the centre of my soul.

"Darius!" Orion cried in desperation, shooting forward, but Gabriel slammed a hand to his shoulder to hold him back, giving him a look that said it wasn't time.

I wanted to move too, but my legs had turned to stone and my heart was beating out an all too fast rhythm. He was there, really fucking there, defying death itself and standing among us.

My friends shouted to him, but I couldn't find the words, my hands beginning to shake and pain slicing through my chest at the possibility that this was some lie cast here to destroy me. I couldn't entertain the idea of him returning to us if it was going to be snatched from our grasp again, and I wouldn't let my heart fall for it until I was sure it was true.

A cacophony of people cried out around me, and Xavier fought his way through the bodies at my back. "Let me see," he demanded. "Get out of my way – move aside!"

The ground rocked from an explosion of power and the people were forced to part, allowing him a view of his brother. He fell still, lips parted in denial of what he was witnessing and silent, sparkling tears spilled over to trail down his cheeks.

Darius dropped to one knee before the twins, placing the head of his axe against the ground and bowing his head low in submission.

"I pledge my life to your service," he spoke low but the words carried across the masses, everyone falling quiet once more.

"Cal," I whispered. "It's not real."

"It is," he growled, like he needed it to be, but I couldn't face it if it wasn't.

"It's him," Max said, moving in on my other side, and I turned to my Siren friend, seeing the truth blazing in his eyes.

"It's time," Caleb said, not needing to explain what he meant as he strode forward and fell down to kneel at Darius's side, bowing to the Vegas.

"I pledge my life in your service," Caleb said loudly, and the stars grew brighter in the sky, every single one of them turning their gaze this way to witness this moment. The air was thick with the power of it all, and I had to wonder if the twins had the power over death itself, because there he was. My friend, firmly present in this world despite death having had other plans.

Max strode forward, falling to his knees on Darius's other side, his head lowering and a rush of love and respect flooded out from him to touch against everyone in the crowd, including me.

"I pledge my life in your service," he echoed.

Darcy and Tory remained hand in hand, staring at the Heirs beneath them in stunned silence. Something shifted inside me, like a flower that had been waiting to blossom. I felt the petals unfurl and the sweet scent of the pollen rising in my chest. It was the start of a new spring, an era I couldn't have comprehended the first time I met them, but now it was all so blindingly obvious that I had no idea how it had taken us so long to end up here. They had proven their power time and again, but tonight, they had gone beyond all bounds of any Fae in this world, and we were left with no choice. For their magic outshone mine, and their hearts were gilded in starlight. I was no match for them, never had been, but I could be their warrior, a Wolf who would wield the shadows of the moon for them.

My legs moved at last, and I strode up behind the other Heirs, my gaze set on Darius as my throat thickened and my heart accepted the truth of his return. But one glance back at Gabriel told me it wasn't time for selfish reunions, now was the time to bind us all as one. To shift the hand of fate and show the world where our allegiance lay so that they might follow in our footsteps. This was the path of golden futures, and it was time we started walking it.

I lowered to my knees beside Caleb, feeling like I was slotting into my rightful place in this world at long last. A home I had ached for at the sides of my friends, all four of us united once again. We had moved through this life as one, like our souls made up a river that flowed together in one direction, and it ended here, in this sea of kismet.

"I pledge my life in your service," I breathed with reverence in my voice, looking up at the two women who had strolled into our lives and shaken the foundations of everything we had ever known. But I had no doubt now, that this had always been our destiny, to kneel before them and lay our lives in service to the Phoenix queens.

The stars flared overhead as Geraldine ran forward, dropping to her knees with a wail of her devotion, and I looked back to find Orion following in her stead, smirking like the asshole had known we'd end up here eventually. Gabriel followed suit, then the shellshocked Xavier who was still gazing at Darius in incredulity, then Tyler, Sofia, and the entire school beyond them, every one of them falling to their knees before their new regents.

"Long live the True Queens!" Geraldine bayed.

And I lifted my head to howl those words to the rising dawn, everyone around us crying them too as the sweet orange rays of sunlight poured across the sky. The first bright dawn of a brand new age.

LIONEL

FROM THE LAIR OF LIONEL...

And so you see, in great and painstakingly tedious detail, the torturous trials which I have suffered at the hands of such insipid Fae. I am merely a man seeking to rightfully set the balance of our kingdom.

Do our laws not state that power is claimed by those most worthy to hold it? Does our own governing system not demand that I do as I have, that I take my position above all those who are lesser than me?

If only this kingdom followed the line of reasonable thinking and was not so easily swayed by the theatrics of a pair of orphaned twins and their despicable hangers-on, I would not even be forced to engage in this war.

But of course, I cannot allow their challenge to stand. I cannot allow the possibility of such lowly creatures to rise up.

If their questionable heritage and lack of understanding of our world wasn't enough, then their moral standing speaks clearly for itself.

I have no need to beg or plead with you for your loyalty. I can command it as the true and rightful king of Solaria.

As such, you are hereby summoned to join me in my fight against these rebel half-breeds to take up arms in the coming war on the right side of history.

All those who fight for what it is to be Fae in the army of the Dragon King will be rewarded with the knowledge of their own supremacy and the satisfaction of ridding our kingdom of those so much less deserving of residence within it.

I look forward to seeing you on the battlefield and accepting your oath of allegiance.

Forever your true and humble monarch,

King Lionel Acrux the First.

AUTHOR NOTE

Ah, the end is nigh. Writing these characters and this world has been an epic undertaking which has, in all honesty, changed our lives beyond recognition. And none of that would have been possible without our wonderful readers falling in love with them just as we did.

So thank you so much for not only coming on this journey with us but for diving in deep and wanting every bit of extra content we can rustle up – hopefully this little collection has put a smile on your face just as it did ours.

Lionel is eager to greet you on the battlefield just as soon as you can get yourself across Solaria to join with his army and we hope you are as excited to conclude his story along with all the other characters in the final book of the Zodiac Academy series Restless Stars which should be winging its way to your grabby hands very soon. (Or if you are a person of the future and are reading this after its release and after reading it already then hello, future reading warrior, I salute you and your mysterious ways of the mystical days beyond this one).

As always, we can never fully express how much we love you as our reader and how grateful we are to find you here devouring our words – may your ravenous appetite for books never fade and your consumption of them guide you through life like a series of dear friends cheering you on in all you achieve and live through.

Love, Susanne and Caroline xxx

Caroline Peckham & Susanne Valenti

DISCOVER MORE FROM CAROLINE PECKHAM & SUSANNE VALENTI

To find out more, grab yourself some freebies, merchandise, and special signed editions or to join their reader group, scan the QR code below.